Marine Scouts

Marine Scouts

CHUCK JOHNSTON

CASEMATE

Philadelphia & Oxford

Published in the United States of America and Great Britain in 2021 by
CASEMATE PUBLISHERS
1950 Lawrence Road, Havertown, PA 19083, US
and
The Old Music Hall, 106–108 Cowley Road, Oxford OX4 1JE, UK

Copyright 2021 © Chuck Johnston

Paperback Edition: ISBN 978-1-63624-058-9
Digital Edition: ISBN 978-1-63624-059-6

A CIP record for this book is available from the British Library

Printed and bound in the United States by Integrated Books International

Typeset in India by Lapiz Digital Services.

For a complete list of Casemate titles, please contact:

CASEMATE PUBLISHERS (US)
Telephone (610) 853-9131
Fax (610) 853-9146
Email: casemate@casematepublishers.com
www.casematepublishers.com

CASEMATE PUBLISHERS (UK)
Telephone (01865) 241249
Email: casemate-uk@casematepublishers.co.uk
www.casematepublishers.co.uk

The Department of Defense's Office of Security Review (DoD/OSR) has reviewed *Marine Scouts* and cleared it for open publication, under case number 11-S-3448; and DIA case number is 11-422.

Author's Note

This is a work of fiction. While based on and inspired by true events, the names, characters and incidents are products of the author's imagination or are used fictitiously and are not to be construed as real. Any resemblance to actual events, locations, organizations or persons, living or dead, is entirely coincidental.

I would like to acknowledge and thank Colonel Cesar Cardi, USMC (retired), for giving me command Scout Platoon, Second Tank Battalion, Second Marine Division during Operation *Desert Storm*.

Semper Fidelis
Chuck Johnston
Lieutenant Colonel USMC (retired)

Scout Platoon, 2nd Tank Battalion

Scout Platoon Table of Organization

Scout Platoon

Platoon Commander: Captain Joseph "Quarry" Samuels
 Radio call sign: "Six"
Driver: Lance Corporal Dole
 Call sign: "Six Delta" (Delta indicating Driver)
Platoon Sergeant: Staff Sergeant Grier
 Radio call sign: "Five"
Driver: Lance Corporal Slayer
 Call sign: "Five Delta"

1st Squad

Squad Leader: Corporal Marion
 Call sign: "One." When acting as a Team Leader of 1st Squad, 1st Section, call sign is "One One," as is his vehicle when acting within the platoon
Driver of vehicle One One: Lance Corporal Davis
 Call sign: "One One Delta"
TOW gunner and spotter for Corporal Marion: Lance Corporal "Bots" Botsford
 Call sign: "One One Golf" (Golf indicating the Gunner of the TOW missile system)

Team Leader 1st Squad, 2nd Section: Lance Corporal Marek
 Call sign: "One Two"
Driver of vehicle One Two: Lance Corporal "Cat" Kantner
 Call sign: "One Two Delta"
50-caliber machine-gun gunner and spotter for Lance Corporal Marek: Private First Class (PFC) Stone
 Call sign: "One Two Golf"

2nd Squad
Squad Leader: Sergeant Caine
> Call sign: "Two" or "Two One"

Driver of vehicle Two One: Private First Class Orsini
> Call sign: "Two One Delta"

TOW gunner and spotter for Sergeant Caine: Lance Corporal Guy
> Call sign: "Two One Golf"

Team Leader 2nd Squad, 2nd Section: Corporal "Specter" Speckman
> Call sign: "Two Two"

Driver of vehicle Two Two: Lance Corporal Throop
> Call sign: "Two Two Delta"

50-caliber gunner: Lance Corporal Peterson
> Call sign: "Two Two Golf"

Scout: Private First Class Surkein
> Call sign: "Two Two Sierra"

3rd Squad
Squad Leader: Sergeant Ogdon
> Call sign: "Three" or "Three One"

Driver and spotter for Sergeant Ogdon: Lance Corporal Mathews
> Call sign: "Three One Delta"

TOW gunner: Lance Corporal Tellado
> Call sign: "Three One Golf"

Scout: Private First Class Laumeyer
> Call sign: "Three One Sierra"

Team Leader 3rd Squad, 2nd Section: Corporal Hauser
> Call sign: "Three Two"

Driver of vehicle Three Two: Lance Corporal Carleton
> Call sign: "Three Two Delta"

50-caliber gunner: Lance Corporal Ferrado
> Call sign: "Three Two Golf"

Snipers and spotters
While all snipers are Scouts, not all Scouts are snipers. The primary duty of a sniper is to be able to hit a man-sized target consistently from 800 meters (or more), using the M-40A1 or current 7.62mm sniper rifle, regardless of weather and wind conditions.

A spotter is the second half of a sniper team. Spotters observe down range, watch the entire target area, look for and help prioritize threats, and confirm the distance to targets. A spotter's duty in life is to protect and support their sniper. This allows the sniper to select, focus on and neutralize specific targets.

While exceptionally lethal, a Scout's primary mission is to collect intelligence through observation of the enemy. They are trained to call in supporting arms and artillery, and may be trained as Forward Air Controllers.

Prologue

0138, 1 August 1990

When you take away the mobility, speed and shock effect of a tank, it is nothing more than what World War II veterans called a "pill box." That which does not move, can be killed.

The enemy tank platoon protecting the shore from an amphibious assault had chosen their battle position well: close to roads and improved trails for increased mobility, with open ground giving clear fields of fire to the shore. As night fell after a long day of waiting and watching for an attack that never materialized, what they didn't know was that their B.P. had already been enveloped by a Marine Corps Scout squad.

Corporal Marion took off his night-vision goggles, and let his eyes adjust to the moon and starlight from the green bleach-out. Eventually, depth perception returned. Moving so slowly that the sounds of nature continued without disruption, he neither snapped a twig nor disturbed a branch. Frogs croaked and crickets sang as four Scouts passed among them. They crossed the road without contact or incident as Marion led the dismounted teams further east. He angled his approach slightly to the right so that he might inspect the hard-packed dirt trail that the tanks would have driven in on. At a low spot in the ground, he bent and examined a slight depression in the moonlight. A slight sheen of discoloration caused by mosquito larvae glistened in the moisture of the half-inch-deep tank track. *The tanks haven't moved in at least three days*, the squad leader thought. Imitating the sound of a Texas bullfrog, Marion beckoned his second team forward. He had expected to encounter an observation post by now, but the lack of human voices or hiss of a radio indicated an observation post, or O.P., was not emplaced. As "Death Before Dismount" is a commonly known tanker axiom, no movement meant no roving guards. The Scouts entered the enemy battle position undetected. The next task: find which tank was awake and on duty.

Using a bastardized version of American Sign Language, Marion ordered the flankers to take a knee and focus in opposite compass directions. Marion and his second team leader, Lance Corporal Marek, concentrated on the enemy. Both came to the same conclusion. Marek made a motion with an open palm toward the ground, then pointed east. Marion nodded in approval. Marek started a trek that would take Team Two deeper into the tank's battle position. With faces darkened with alternating bands of green, brown and black camouflage paint, sleeves rolled down and gloved hands, the Scouts were essentially invisible from all but the tank's infrared sights. Moving behind but slightly to one side of his team leader, Lance Corporal Stone provided security. Looking beyond his team leader to the objective, Stone periodically scanned downrange with the monocular night vision sight attached to his M-16 rifle. Lightly armed, Scouts depend on stealth, not firepower, for survival.

Twenty-five meters further into the enemy B.P., Marek signaled Stone to take a covering position: one finger touching an open palm. He then pointed towards himself, then the tanks. Stone took an additional few steps to a natural low spot in the ground where he would blend into the earth.

Marek continued his approach cautiously, using hearing, smell, and his own intuition, until he was five feet behind the north-most tank. No heat radiating from the vehicle indicated this tank had not run its engines that night. Snoring came from the turret. The lack of voices or movement from inside confirmed this tank wasn't a threat, providing of course, one of the sleeping beauties didn't wake up to relieve his bladder.

A light came on from inside the tank closest to the trail. That tank, most likely on duty, would be the last tank Marek would check. If the tank on radio watch had a roving guard, the troops in the two tanks in the middle should be asleep. He'd check them first.

After three minutes of standing motionless behind the next tank in the line, Marek confirmed his suspicions. The enemy was at its lowest readiness. Ready Condition Four meant that only 25 percent of the tanks were awake at any given time. He'd head towards the trail to see what was happening on the south end of the B.P.

The biggest threat was the changing of the guard. If the tank on duty woke up another tank to go on watch, Marek would have to start the process of waiting and observing all over again. As he approached, he saw the light of a red-lens flashlight dancing inside the turret through the vision blocks of the cupola. Someone inside was awake. Moving so slowly that even his spotter lost him in the shadows, Marek came to the last and most dangerous tank.

Once again, coming up from behind, a direction even the most seasoned tankers seldom check at night, Marek continued the familiar ritual. Stopping five feet behind his target, he listened, smelled, felt and sensed. Marek stretched out his hand until it was 18 inches away from the engine exhaust vents. The slight amount of heat that still lingered indicated the engine hadn't run in hours. Since all the other engines were cold, that meant this crew was the only tank on duty. If that was true, it also meant that this tank was rotating personnel on and off duty to allow the others to sleep throughout the night. Of the four, one tanker would be on radio watch, one had just come off and should be asleep, and one would be coming on watch soon and should also be asleep. That meant only one person might be restless enough to wake up. Contented wheezing came from sleeping bags on the engine's armor deck and from on top of the turret. *Two down, one on watch, one to go,* Marek thought.

A tank's track wraps around the sprocket at the rear-most end of the tank. The final drive connects the sprocket to the transmission, thus bearing the entire weight of engine and rear armor deck. An additional 180 pounds would not be noticed. Marek placed one foot in the track as he reached up, one gloved hand grasping a deck hinge while the other grabbed the storage compartment handle. Breathtakingly slowly, Marek simultaneously and equally transferred his bodyweight from the earthbound foot to his other limbs. His free foot moved to the middle of the sprocket and once again took its share of body weight. Repeating the process, Marek inched his way onto the armored engine deck. Gradually he made his way past four feet of open space and two sleeping tankers, to the storage rack on the back of the turret. Taking time to allow his heart rate to return to a close proximity of normal, he welcomed the newest sound to his ears, the rhythm of a third set of inhalations and exhalations. Marek stuck his nose into the air and rotated his head forward to avoid exposing the top of his head before he could see above the turret. He moved until he saw the most welcome sight of the morning, a third sleeping bag, fully zipped, with the head cover pulled up and drawn closed. Adjusting his feet directly under him, Marek squatted, stopped moving and breathed shallowly.

After a few minutes, Marek continued up and over the tank's cupola until he could see inside the turret. *Pay-off!* With his face about 14 inches from the top of the enemy's communications helmet, Marek looked at the map in the tanker's lap. Each goose egg represented an enemy B.P. Each hash mark represented the size of the unit. A flag represented the command post. Triangles showed the locations of the enemy outposts.

At 0330, the tanker inside the turret answered a radio check. Then, speaking to no one in particular, he continued, "Yeah, we're still here. Where the hell else would we be at this time of the god-damned morning." Feeling he had overstayed his welcome, Marek started the process of getting back to mother earth. Waiting a few minutes to ensure his last moves hadn't been felt or heard, Marek started moving back to Stone's position. With each step towards his spotter, his stride picked up and his crouched stance rose slightly.

By the time he was 20 meters from the enemy tanks, he was almost walking upright and at a normal stride.

Without needing to be told, Stone fell in behind and to the enemy side of Marek, checking their rear and flanks as they went. In what seemed no time at all, compared to the time it took to get into the enemy position, the team neared their rally point. The bullfrog croaked from in front of them. The sound of a scurrying squirrel was the countersign.

Corporal Marion and his spotter, Lance Corporal Botsford, stood from the shadows and took the lead, on an indirect path that would take them back to their vehicles and First Squad's base of operations. Long before they were close enough to give the next challenge and password, Marion heard the ticking of the thermal sights of the TOW missile launcher, but not before Lance Corporal Davis detected his squad leader's heat signature and approach in the thermal sights. Lance Corporal Kantner, the driver of the Team One Hummer, was behind the squad's 50-caliber machine gun and recognized the outline of his squad leader in his night-vision goggles. Approaching the vehicles, Marion gave a rapid succession of orders.

"Davis, Cat, fire 'em up. Let's get out of here. Marek, with me." Davis dropped down out of the turret and into the driver's seat as Botsford took his position behind the TOW system. Within the minute, the squad was heading out.

"What ya got, Marek?" Marion asked.

"The entire enemy order of battle running through my head, Corporal."

"Won't do me any good there. Take a map, rough me up grids and unit strengths. And hurry up, I don't want you to bump your head and forget everything before I send it higher."

"Yes, Corporal," Marek replied, earning him a grin from his squad leader.

When Marek's task was completed, Marion spoke into the radio's handset.

"Scout Six, this is Scout One," he said, calling his platoon leader.

"One, Six," the radio hissed without hesitation.

"Enemy platoon, dug in, facing east, conducting deliberate defense, break. Grid 327, 861, Charlie Three, time minus 20, four M-60A1s, over."

"Roger, One." The scout platoon commander acknowledged the transmission thinking the report was over.

"Six, One."

"Send it." Over the next four minutes, broken up in 15-second intervals, Marion relayed the disposition of the entire enemy battalion.

"Corporal Marion?" Marek asked when the transmission was finally complete.

"Yeah," Marion answered without moving.

"Why just one team tonight, why not the whole squad?"

"What's the normal and extended frontage of a tank platoon in dense woods?" Marion answered Marek's question with a question.

"Normal is 300 with extended up to 500 meters depending on terrain, cover and concealment," Marek said as if he were reading directly from a field manual.

"Correct. And what was the entire area of the enemy's battle position tonight?"

"Less than 100 meters total."

"Exactly, so why put two teams in, when all they would have done is bumped heads?" That made sense to Marek. He fell silent, wondering if he would ever put his skills to use in combat and not just another training exercise.

Part I

Desert Storm: The Air War

The Al Wafrah oil fields. Located in the southeast portion of the country, the Al Wafrah oil fields are four miles north of the San Arabia border and 20 miles west of the Persian Gulf. The southern approach of the oil fields were guarded by the 29th Iraqi Infantry Division. Hill 224 is west of the fields, just to the east (right) of the "S" in Dhulai at Al Fawarais.

One

December 1990, Kuwait, North of the Saudi border

They had lost all track of time. No one had any idea what day it was.

"*Naqeeb! Naqeeb* Aziz!" 1st Sergeant Zamir ran up, out of breath. "We will be moving soon," the *raqiib awwal* said excitedly. "Brigade maintenance was ordered to send bulldozers to pull us from our fighting positions and to provide maintenance necessary to get all tanks started and running." Captain Abd ul-Aziz looked over his command, the 1st Company, 1st Battalion, 1st Brigade of the 108th Iraqi Armored Division, and thought back on the events that had got them this far.

It was 1 August when it began. The Republican Guard, with its three divisions of armor, one division of mechanized infantry and one battalion of commandos, spearheaded the offensive. From the border near Safwan, the Guard drove south using one armor division to secure Al-Jahra, while the remaining three divisions continued east and seized Kuwait City. The commandos, already in the city, disrupted communications and secured key road intersections. The 1st Armored Corps, and thus Aziz's division, had been on the western flank of the Guard spearhead. But Kuwait was a brother Arabic nation, so who was the enemy?

At Al-Jahra, his battalion commander's tank turned southwest onto Highway 70. There were silhouettes of buildings on the horizon: the Ali Al Salem Air Base. The commander aligned the battalion with the long axis of the runway. It wouldn't be long before the tanks were within the 1,000-meter maximum effective range of the T-55's 100mm main guns. The squelch on the radio broke: "Destroy the enemy, save the buildings if possible," and the commander fired his main gun at a sandbagged bunker producing machine-gun fire. Small-arms fire was intense but didn't damage tanks. The tank round overshot the target. As if finally realizing they were in combat, other Iraqi tanks

3

also fired main-gun rounds, one of which finally silenced the machine-gun team. As targets presented themselves, other tanks started firing.

Aziz realized his tank was not in the fight yet and gave a fire command: "Gunner, machine gun, troops next to the building." Seconds later, his gunner acquired the target and laid a long burst of machine-gun fire into the middle of the troops. From behind his ten-powered sights, Aziz watched as the 7.62mm rounds ripped into the unprotected flesh of aviation mechanics and crewmen.

"Cease fire, new target. Plane next to the far hangar. High explosive. Fire when ready."

Both the gunner and the loader acknowledged the tank commander's order. Seconds later, the plane and the soldiers around it were engulfed in flames. Aziz fired into a group of soldiers with his turret-mounted 14.5mm machine gun as the tank's main gun continued to find new targets. Using the 50-caliber against people is not a violation of the Geneva Convention, it's simply not an effective use of the ammunition's capability. Aziz didn't care; the fight would soon be over and he wanted his share.

The battalion continued, in line formation, until it came to the far end of the runway. In its wake, organized resistance was shattered; not a single piece of equipment was intact. Lone Kuwaitis who threw down their weapons simply made easier machine-gun targets.

The 108th Division, and therefore Aziz's brigade, was task organized, meaning it was a combination of tanks and infantry units. Behind his battalion of tanks, the B.M.P.s of 2nd Battalion discharged their infantry. Soldiers herded prisoners, looted offices or started to dig defensive positions around the airfield. 3rd Battalion tanks were integrated into the defensive perimeter at the entrance to the airfield. After dawn the next day, for their actions, 1st Battalion were allowed to pull their tanks into the shade of the hangars. For his part, Aziz was given one of the spare tanks from the maintenance battalion. Aziz now had nine tanks under his command, the single strongest company in the brigade.

They stayed at the airfield for a week before moving south to a defensive position near Al-Jahra, following Highway 6. As they approached Doha road, from the north side of the cloverleaf a lightly armored four-wheeled reconnaissance vehicle raced from the intersection. The B.R.D.M. turned directly into the path of the T55 tanks and trained its 14.5mm and 7.62mm machine guns on the lead tank, stopping it dead in its tracks. Two Republican Guard *jundi awwals* wearing their distinctive black berets came running from the back. One leveled his A.K.47 machine gun at the driver of the tank while the other pointed his rifle directly at the brigade executive officer. Aziz couldn't hear what was being said but noticed that the X.O. didn't talk back to the two young privates. He simply handed over a piece of paper without making any rapid or sudden movements. The private who received the paper ran back to the B.R.D.M., handing it to the vehicle commander, who in turn, looked at the paper and made a radio transmission. After several tense minutes, the vehicle commander jumped to the ground, approached the lead tank and pointed to the cloverleaf. After a one-sided exchange of information, the soldier waved the tank driver on as if he were allowed to continue. The soldier turned his back to the tank and went back to his vehicle. The two privates returned to the rear of the B.R.D.M. without saluting the *muqaddam*. More importantly, the lieutenant colonel didn't attempt to correct the blatant lack of disrespect.

The B.R.D.M. drove southeast; the brigade executive officer followed obediently. The hiss of Aziz's radio broke with a transmission.

"This is the executive officer. Inform your men that the burning rubble they see to the left is all that remains of the Kuwaiti military barracks of Bahra Umm-Ghar."

The column continued southeast toward another cloverleaf. At a ramp that led south into the desert or north into the city of Firdous, another gun-wielding enlisted man demanded and received the written orders from the executive officer. The process of being stopped and interrogated became more frequent the closer they got to Kuwait City. At one intersection, a bent and bullet-laden sign read "Al-Tuwari Police Station." Here, a full-strength company of ten T-72 main battle tanks controlled the exit to the north.

Aziz spat on the ground. *The elite Republican Guard. Just because they swear allegiance to Hussein and not to Iraq itself, they get the newest weapons, the freshest food and three times the pay of regular soldiers. That does not make them elite, it makes them mercenaries. If I had a tenth of their operational budget, I would show them an elite unit.* But tactical proficiency did not get a soldier into the Republican Guard, political alignment did. *Maybe if I distinguish myself in combat again, I will consider the matter further, if just for the chance to command a T-72 tank company. What an honor it would be to command a full company of ten well-maintained main battle tanks, manned by volunteers.* Aziz dreamed of riding into battle at the front of an assault instead of a supporting operation. *Would swearing political allegiance be such a great price to pay?*

The next morning, after prayers, Aziz and the other company commanders met the battalion commander.

"We will travel south on Highway 40 until we come to the Saudi Arabian border. There we will reinforce an infantry division who guards the road." The company commanders looked at each other but said nothing. "We will leave after the tanks are fueled. That is all." The company commanders departed without asking questions. The three combat veterans of the Great Patriotic War knew this campaign was not a "rescue" of suppressed Muslim brothers.

None were happy with the course of events; none were proud of the actions taking place around them.

It was dark when 1st Battalion passed the Kuwaiti customs inspection center. The number and types of radio antennas suggested this was now a military division headquarters. A hundred meters past the towers, the battalion turned west and continued in column until one end anchored Highway 40 and the other end extended into the desert. Once they obtained their spacing, they turned their tanks 90 degrees to the left, forming a single continuous line, facing south. The radio informed them that the infantry in front of them was the 1st Brigade of the 8th Infantry Division.

"If enemy vehicles attempt to overrun the infantry," the battalion commander transmitted, "destroy them." Aziz thought about what was just ordered. *If we are facing south into Saudi Arabia, what enemy vehicles would there be?*

The next morning, 2nd Battalion of Aziz's brigade arrived and took position on the east side of the road. 3rd Battalion set up straddling the road, 500 meters behind both 1st and 2nd. A hundred meters in front of his position, Aziz saw infantry soldiers in trenches. A hundred meters in front of them, more soldiers were already busy stringing barbed wire. Another 100 meters in front of the barbed wire, bulldozers and other combat engineer vehicles were digging yet another trench line. A tower, similar to the Kuwait customs building, stood a kilometer further south. *It is one thing to help liberate brothers of a nation that was poisoned by western ideas and culture, but it is quite another to be aiming guns at a nation that believes in the one true faith. This is not right.*

Days later, the trench works were complete in front of them. Barbed wire thickened and grew in height. Truckloads of mines arrived daily and were emplaced, with accidental detonations killing only five men.

In places, the original trenches were filled in and offshoots were dug to create a series of interlocking trenches that resembled south-facing triangles. Each small triangle was the home of a single infantry platoon consisting of an officer and 25 enlisted men. Larger triangles with two platoons forward and one back created company positions. Companies' positions formed battalions, battalion formed brigades, until the 8th Infantry Division formed one huge triangle, thousands of meters wide and 2,000 in depth. Anti-air assets and anti-tank weapons were emplaced in the gaps. By identifying the 120mm mortar platoon behind the rear center company of each battalion, one could determine the number of battalions. While not all the defenses were complete, the two battalions of the 8th Infantry Division to the immediate right and left of Aziz were tactically ready.

And now the bulldozers were on their way. It seemed the 108th would be moving again, soon.

Two

11 December 1990, Al-Jubayl, Saudi Arabia

It was mid-day when the Boeing 747 landed at the Jubayl Naval Airport. The facility received aircraft from the military, military airlift command, U.S. civil air fleet reserves, and chartered commercial aircraft at a rate of about one per hour. The result was a thousand troops per day joining coalition forces already in country. As the door to the plane opened, cool, dry 40-degree air greeted the Scouts of 2nd Tank Battalion, 2nd Marine Division. Captain Joseph "Quarry" Samuels' first introduction to Saudi Arabia was noticing that from horizon to horizon, it was perfectly flat. Quarry's gaze turned to where many were pointing. Across the taxi area, a Soviet Aeroflot Airlines airplane was discharging passengers: a Soviet plane, disembarking British troops, on an American-run naval base, in a Muslim country. What a way to start a war.

"You'll be going down to 1st SRIG," a corporal at the Marine Expeditionary Forces reception center told Quarry. A ten-minute drive later, they arrived at Camp Five. The driver dropped them off in front of a set of trailers and told the Scouts they were home. The office was a flurry of activity. As soon as Quarry and his platoon sergeant, Staff Sergeant Grier, were noticed, a lance corporal walked over to help. Quarry handed the Marine a copy of their orders. The Marine motioned to a sergeant who came over and tore off a copy of the MEF's endorsement. The sergeant asked Quarry to follow him.

The sergeant knocked on the commanding officer's door and waited for him to look up. Colonel Brodrick, a mountain of a man, motioned Quarry in. After a quick look at Quarry's orders, the colonel asked, "What do you know about our Group, skipper?"

Quarry was being tested. His heart thumped. The next few minutes would determine the fate of the Scouts.

"I'm aware sir, that SRIG, or Surveillance, Reconnaissance and Intelligence Group, is a composite of several individual units that were once part of

MEF Headquarters. Your subordinate units will most likely consist of Radio Battalion, Communications Battalion, Remotely Piloted Vehicle Company, Naval Gunfire Company, Intelligence Company and Force Reconnaissance Company, sir." Quarry waited for a response.

Eventually, the colonel spoke.

"Actually, we have 8th, 9th and 6th Comm Battalions; 1st, 2nd and 3rd Remotely Piloted Vehicle Companies; 1st and 3rd ANGLICO; 1st, 2nd, 3rd and 4th Force Recon. Once everyone comes aboard, we'll have over three thousand Marines." Quarry subconsciously let out a whistle. "I agree," the colonel said, smiling. Apparently Quarry passed the test. "So with all those assets, Captain Samuels, what am I supposed to do with you?" Quarry's heart skipped a beat.

"Sir, I have 23 Scouts with me. We are organized into three squads of two Humvees, each armed with a TOW and 50-cal respectively. Headquarters consists of a logistics and a command vehicle, both with an upgraded comm suite. I have five school-trained Scout Snipers with five M-40A1 sniper rifles, many of us are Tactical Air Control Party and Forward-Observer qualified."

The colonel thought for a few moments before replying.

"The question arises again, what do I do with you?" he said, this time talking more to himself than to Quarry. He turned and saw Quarry's unease. "Don't worry, skipper, you'll be gainfully employed. It's where to place you for the greatest use of what you bring to the table." For the first time since walking in, Quarry's pulse rate returned to normal.

"I'm going to send you down to Lieutenant Colonel Dillion. He runs Intel Company for me. You'll be doing the shitty little jobs that require trigger pullers. Just as MEF has Force Recon and ANGLICO, and Division has Recon Battalion and LAVs, Dillion will have you." Quarry had no idea of what they had just gotten into, but the way the colonel put it didn't make it sound so bad. "Sergeant Edwards will get you some transportation and a place to bunk down. If you have any other questions come back and we'll get you fixed up." Realizing he was dismissed, Quarry came to attention. "Good luck son," the colonel said, offering Quarry his hand.

Quarry walked out of the office wondering what the immediate future had in store for his Scouts. His question was partially answered when Grier met him in the central area.

"I talked with the Four rep," Grier informed his boss. "Our vehicles and gear are on the pier, north side. I have a row and column number."

"And I have our assignment."

Intel Company didn't get many visitors. Everybody looked up when Quarry and Grier walked in. A staff sergeant came around the counter that separated the office area from the entrance.

"Good evening sir, are you Captain Samuels?"

"Yes, Staff Sergeant, and this is my platoon sergeant, Staff Sergeant Grier." Another Marine approached and asked Quarry to follow him while the two N.C.O.s talked.

Where Colonel Brodrick had been huge and imposing, Lieutenant Colonel Dillion was streamlined and plain. Dillion stood about five-eight, and was thin and balding.

"Good evening, Captain Samuels," Dillion said in a mild voice. Quarry stepped forward to meet his new commanding officer. To his surprise, the hand he shook was rough and callused; the grip, like a vice. Quarry sat down when directed, and was asked what he knew about the company. Quarry gave the textbook answer but was wrong, again. Dillion corrected him.

"Intelligence Company consists of the Marine All Source Fusion Center, the Fleet Imagery Intelligence Unit, the Topographic Platoon, Sensor Control and Management Platoon, Psychological Operations Platoon, and now Scout Platoon." Quarry felt pretty good when he heard his platoon mentioned without hesitation in the table of organization. "We are experiencing some difficulty with the Saudis. Currently there is no Host Nation Agreement normally associated with U.S. Forces deployed overseas. Some of the Royal House don't want us here at all. Thus, our mission right now is to establish a relationship. The two ground forces in the kingdom are the Royal Saudi Land Forces, who fall under the command of the Minister of Defense and Aviation or MoDA and the separate and more elite force is the Saudi Arabian National Guard or SANG. Ultimately, both are under the command of Prince Khalid, who coordinates all Arab coalition forces. Units from both MoDA and SANG are in front and to both flanks of us. The majority of SANG is to the east, as the coast will probably be the point of effort should the Iraqi army continue south. We are working with every unit we can get a liaison team to. Force Recon is working with the Saudi Marines at the port of Ras Al-Mishab. The majority of ANGLICO went to the Joint Forces Command under the control of Major General Sultan Adi AlMutairi. ANGLICO will most likely stay in place as permanent liaison cells. That's where you come in. In the next few days, I'm going to get you and your platoon in with a SANG unit. If I can pass you off as an ordinary unit—no insult intended captain, I realize what your Scouts are capable of—I can get you closer to the border. The fact that you come from an armor battalion may just be the angle we need." Quarry's heart was beating a mile a minute. "We are greatly in need of human intelligence on the border. We've only been getting haphazard reports at best, from our hosts."

Quarry cleared his throat to ask a question.

"Sir, don't we know what's going on via satellite imagery and signal intelligence?"

The colonel had been asked that same question many times before.

"I can show you the battalion, brigade and division location of every Iraqi unit along the border. In fact, I'll actually do that, the day after tomorrow around 0900. Bring your squad leaders and platoon sergeant. We've conducted an intelligence preparation of the battlefield and know all the hard facts. What we don't know is the Iraqis' determination and resolve. That takes people on the ground."

The interview over, Grier met Quarry outside the main entrance.

"What's the new C.O. like?"

"That man has forgotten more about the Iraqi order of battle than you and I put together will ever know."

11 December 1990, Kuwait, North of the Saudi Border

"We travel west," *Muqaddam* Rahama told his company commanders. "The Corps is on line the entire length of the Kuwaiti border. We will travel behind the 8th, 42nd and 29th Infantry Divisions. When we get to the end of the 29th we will turn north. 1st Brigade will take a position behind the westernmost position of the 29th. 2nd Brigade will take their position north of 1st and 3rd north of 2nd. We will move in two days. That will give us time to complete maintenance on our vehicles and fill them with fuel." Aziz had hundreds of questions, but it was obvious the battalion commander didn't have any more information.

Three

13 December 1990

The Scouts had no trouble claiming their vehicles. Little was disturbed and nothing, surprisingly, was missing. Equipment checks were completed and nothing had been damaged during transport. Being attached to a group that had two communication companies and an entire radio battalion had its advantages. With little to no trouble, Quarry was able to preset every imaginable frequency in the command Hummer's radios. Of the 20 available presets, five were dedicated to air support, five to artillery support, five to tactical command nets, two to administrative and logistics nets, two to other supporting arms, and one remained unfilled.

At 0900 the Scout leadership met in a closed room inside the rear-most portion of the H.Q. The entire room had been turned into a terrain board of Kuwait, thanks to the efforts of Topo Platoon. The walls were covered with corresponding maps. Quarry noted that most of the Republican Guard units were pulled closer to Kuwait City, all oriented east in anticipation of repulsing a Marine amphibious landing.

"These images were taken four days ago," the colonel explained. "These will probably be the last satellite images we get of front-line troops. CentCom reoriented the track to focus on Baghdad. Any further real-time images will have to come from our own R.P.V.s. Other than that, we rely on the photoreconnaissance the Air Force trickles down to us." No one said anything to that comment.

* * *

It had taken two days, but they were finally ready. Every brigade recovery vehicle had worked frantically to pull tanks and B.M.P.s out of their fighting positions. Every brigade mechanic had worked feverishly to get vehicles running. The combination of the longest road march ever conducted by the division and an extended period of no activity had taken its toll on many vehicles. Some never started again. Aziz once again thanked Allah; only two of his vehicles did not start immediately, but eventually they were brought to life. His was the only company in the brigade with no mechanical failures.

The brigade commander made a huge show and drew attention to himself as he mounted his tank. When it turned west, Aziz's battalion commander followed. The entire division started moving west, in a single column, navigating by keeping the rear of the infantry units 100 meters to their left. When they pulled out, the soldiers of the 8th Infantry Division waved good-bye and wished Allah's blessings upon them. Somewhere in the distance was the 42nd Infantry Division.

Aziz saw something in front of him, but distance is deceiving. It took longer to reach the edge of the 42nd than one would have imagined. Even after they passed behind the 42nd, his brigade continued west. Infantry battalion and brigade boundaries became easier to recognize. After a very significant gap, Aziz called down to a solider on the ground. They were now behind the 29th Infantry Division.

The brigade commander continued west towards what appeared to be another unit. The setting sun was in their eyes making details difficult to see. As they got closer, objects became clearer. It was not another unit, but oil wells, and the Al-Wafrah oil processing plant.

The brigade commander's tanks came to a stop without warning. Aziz's battalion commander dismounted his tank and approached the brigade commander. From his cupola, Aziz watched a lively and heated exchange until the brigade executive officer drove up in a jeep and pulled alongside the brigade commander's tank as well. With map in hand, the executive officer pointed to a processing plant, then at two large sets of exposed pipes that ran north a few feet above the ground. An obviously frustrated brigade commander climbed back into his tank and started driving west, again.

When the brigade commander's tank stopped next, it was in the middle of an oilfield. Aziz's battalion commander drove past it and continued for another kilometer. When he stopped, he turned to face south. Aziz continued to drive west until his last platoon radioed they were 25 meters past the battalion commander. Aziz stopped and turned south, as did the rest of his company, as did the rest of the battalion. As the sunlight started to disappear, far behind them 2nd Battalion continued to set in on line before they turned and faced south as well. 3rd Battalion used this line to set in 500 meters north of, and centered between the two.

At dawn, everyone saw the horrible position they were in. Pipelines ran to and from pumping stations at every conceivable direction and angle. Originally built above ground, most of the pipes were now half or fully buried from years of shifting sand. The ground was so crisscrossed and intertwined with pipes that many tanks couldn't see the vehicles beside them. Most of the tanks had no clear field of view and few had a field of fire that would support tank main-gun engagements.

1st Brigade remained among the pipes as 2nd Brigade, with its two battalions of infantry and one tank battalion, moved parallel to them. Navigating by keeping the rear of 1st Brigade 1,500 meters to their left, they formed their own line. Aziz never saw 3rd Brigade. Engineers started making the positions permanent by digging tank fighting positions. Unbeknownst to Aziz, their new location placed the brigade about seven kilometers north of the Saudi border and about 40km from the coast. Right in the middle of the Al-Wafrah oilfields.

* * *

It was late evening when the Scouts finished putting their map packets together. Each team had a complete set of 1:50,000 tactical maps. The series covered the entire country of Kuwait, the top 25km of Saudi Arabia, and most of the Iraqi coast. The Scouts had marked every known enemy position. Thanks to the Fusion Center and Topo Platoon, aerial photos depicted the right and left lateral limits and the depth of each unit, weapon systems, and their direction of orientation. As important, the map also portrayed wadis, gullies, and dry beds, all just waiting to suck the life out of a ground unit sneaking through at night. Although the Scouts still didn't have orders to go north, they were ready.

19 December 1990

The Scouts finished their fifth lap around the compound. Not that the distance meant anything, but the hour-long run chewed up time. Frustration was the biggest enemy now, and time was its lieutenant. Days became routine: out of the rack, morning run, showers, morning chow; language training, weapons cleaning, equipment maintenance, afternoon chow; language training, Iraqi order of battle and equipment training, evening chow; weight lifting, language and cultural training and rack.

As the Scouts turned the corner to their area, Quarry saw the lance corporal from company admin. Calling quick time, Quarry stepped to the side of the formation and was told the colonel would like to see him sometime that morning.

"Any indication what it's about?"

"You know the way we operate around here, sir, everything is on a need-to-know basis and I don't have a need to know that. Even if I did, we couldn't talk about it out here in the open."

"Did Lieutenant Colonel Dillion say what time this morning?"

"No, sir. No ASAP, or now, or anything like that."

"Thank you."

"You're welcome sir," the Marine said, saluting. As he turned to leave, he paused and turned back to face the Scout Commander. "Who knows sir, maybe today will be the day."

* * *

It was 0900 when Quarry entered the company office. Now that he was a familiar sight, the Marines merely greeted the new captain as he made his way towards the rear of the trailer. The first door to the right belonged to the All Source Fusion Center. The walls were covered with maps and armed Marines monitored stacks of every conceivable radio ever designed. Frequencies were dialed into every outpost, listening post, liaison unit, and intelligence collecting agency on this side of the world, and then some.

Quarry knocked on the frame of the only open door in the building, and received an invitation to enter.

"Good morning captain," the colonel said from behind a large cup of coffee. "Let's go next door." The two entered the Fusion Center from the colonel's private entrance. The watch chief rose from behind his desk as the colonel came over and looked at the summary of morning messages. They bypassed the enemy map and looked at the friendly forces.

"Take a good look of where everyone is, Captain Samuels," the colonel said, handing the clipboard back to the master sergeant. "Keep a separate log of each unit's call signs and frequencies." Being the astute fellow he was, Quarry realized this was an operational brief. He drew the note pad out of his cargo pocket. "As you already know, since August, I MEF's mission was to defend in-sector and on-order pass lines with the Royal Saudi Land Forces and Gulf Cooperation Council Forces. As you can see on the map, our northernmost point is 3rd Battalion, 9th Marines. They're affectionately known as the 'Speed Bump Battalion' because they are opposite two Iraqi divisions. The rest of MEF is set up in mechanized and armored task forces as far north as Manifah Bay. I MEF also has the 7th British Armored Brigade, the famous 'Desert Rats' attached to it, here," the colonel said, pointing on the map with a laser pointer. "Their 170 Challenger tanks and 72 155mm artillery guns are the MEF's heavy force. North of 3/9 is the Army's 3rd Armored Cavalry Regiment, who are screening directly behind SANG units.

SANG is concentrated closest to the beach and stretch west. This places the bulk of their combat power defending the coastal highway leading into the city of Khafji. The further west you go, the more spread-out SANG becomes.

"SANG has taken a defensive line about fifteen clicks south of a five-meter high earthen berm, constructed years ago, that separates the Saudi northern border from Kuwait and Iraq, and extends the length of the country. About every fifteen clicks along it are police posts. Some of them we own, some of them the Iraqis own. The ones the Iraqis own are in red." Only the ones closest to the coast were blue. "All of the observation posts are within range of the Iraqi D-20 152mm howitzers. The D-20 is capable of delivering biological weapons, the most likely of which will be highly concentrated anthrax. If that isn't bad enough, the outposts are also within range of their multiple rocket launchers and Soviet 'FROGs', free rocket over ground. None of the observation posts are currently under a U.S. artillery umbrella.

"You can see which SANG units have Force Recon Marines and Army Special Forces with them." Quarry gave another quick look at the map; Marines were primarily along the coast, Army Special Forces worked inland. *Makes sense*, Quarry thought, *Marines augmenting SANG with naval firepower support, a nice touch seeing how one SANG division is arrayed opposite three Iraqi infantry divisions with two mechanized divisions behind them. The Berets could help in the west by calling upon army attack helos.*

"The westernmost SANG unit is the 2nd Armored Brigade. Equipped with U.S.-made M60A3 tanks, they are on the heel of Kuwait. After that, it's up to Army Special Forces to provide observation along the border. It isn't until you come up to the westernmost borders, where Kuwait, Saudi Arabia and Iraq intersect, that we pick up more coalition forces again. This is where you come in." Quarry's heart started pounding. "You are going to be our liaison to 2nd Armored Brigade SANG. Your official mission will be to liaise with the SANG commander. Unofficially it's your job to keep an eye on the border and report anything of value. You may take whatever defensive measures are necessary to ensure the safety of your unit and your mission."

"Sir?" Quarry interrupted. "If I'm officially attached to the 2nd Armor, am I authorized the use of NATO assets in the event of defensive operations?"

"Absolutely. Ask for the world, see what you get. Most likely though, you'll end up fighting with what you have." After a moment, the colonel continued. "Try and gain the Saudis' confidence but don't push too hard. You'll be up there for Christmas but, per the code of Sharia, there can't be any display of any religion other than Islam. You also won't be allowed to display any American flags. As you become integrated into the unit, take a look around and get back to me with what you find. Only on my order will you conduct operations north of the berm. Is that clear?" The official manner in which the colonel addressed Quarry left no doubts of where the line was drawn.

"Perfectly, sir," Quarry answered without thinking.

"The route you will take is here." The colonel traced a laser line from Jubayl to Mishab, then along an east/west-running pipe-line until it intersected a north-running pipe-line. "You'll find the 2nd Armored SANG here," he said, circling the laser south of the border, "somewhere in the vicinity of grid 1040. I can't tell you where the brigade headquarters is, but I suspect it will be somewhere around here, where the pipe-lines run north toward the Al-Wafrah oilfields."

By 1500, three different sets of passes, orders and permits had been given to Quarry by various individuals. Meanwhile, Grier and the squad leaders took the vehicles to the ammo dump, supply, comm, and the fuel farm. By 1700, they were all back at the hooch. Despite the cold, most of the Scouts had beads of sweat on their foreheads. As Quarry walked into the building, his driver, Lance Corporal Dole, announced his arrival. The Scouts came to attention. While the gesture of respect was unnecessary, it was appreciated. Quarry looked in the eyes of Grier and the squad leaders and found what he was looking for.

"Seats," Quarry ordered. The Scouts sat down. Some were on their racks, some on the floor, some climbed to sit on a top bunk. "Report."

"We're ready, skipper," Grier started. "I'll let the squad leaders start the brief. 1st Squad, Corporal Marion."

"If you've noticed the vehicles, sir," Marion started with a shit-eating grin, "they've changed color. We struck a deal with some guys at supply for 25 gallons of tan paint. All vehicles were painted. We also swapped out our green cammie nets for tan cammie."

"2nd Squad," Grier ordered.

"I headed up ammo, sir," Sergeant Caine started. "We have more TOW 2-B missiles than we can carry. Every TOW vehicle has full racks. Staff Sergeant Grier has six spares in his Hummer. Each 50-cal Hummer has 400 rounds; the staff sergeant is carrying another 400. Each squad automatic weapon has 1,000 rounds; the staff sergeant has another two. Each Scout has 210 rounds of five-five-six on his person for the M-16s; each vehicle has an additional 2,000 rounds; Staff Sergeant Grier has two more. Each 9mm pistol has 60 rounds. You and Staff Sergeant Grier have an additional 200 in your vehicles. Each vehicle has enough grenades, frag and concussion, for five per Scout. None have been broken out of their containers yet. Each vehicle has two green, white and red star clusters, same for colored-pyro parachutes. You and the staff sergeant have about ten of each. Each vehicle has a mix of different colored smoke, white, yellow, green, and everyone has at least one red. You and Staff Sergeant Grier have what's left of a couple cases. What we didn't get was match-grade 7.62 for the sniper rifles."

"Don't worry," Grier said with a smirk. "A little old-fashioned smuggling took care of that. We have some. Dole is holding on to yours, sir."

Quarry ran through the inventory in his head. "I'm impressed, Sergeant Caine. Thank you."

"All encryption gear is on the radios," Sergeant Ogdon, 3rd Squad Leader, said next. "All are up in both the red and green, both encrypted and plain language transmission. Everyone uses red. We can talk to everyone. We have ten spare batteries for the P.R.C.77 radios. Because everyone is in the red, and MEF doesn't feel the Iraqis have a significant direction-finding capability, we are operating with straight call signs; 1st SRIG, MEF Main, MEF Rear, 3/9, that sort of thing. We'll answer up as Scouts since the Light Armored Reconnaissance Battalions are going by their task force designators. If we meet someone on a net we don't recognize, then we use the alphanumerics in the codebook. From there, we go back to straight call signs."

"Thanks, Ogie."

"We have full fuel tanks and 15 extra gallons of extra J.P.5 per vehicle, skipper," Grier finished. "Every canteen is topped off, and we have 15 gallons of water per vehicle. We have five days of chow on each vehicle. I have an additional five days per vehicle in mine. Other than that, boss, there is no room for anything else. If you want something, it's gonna have to ride in your lap."

Quarry tried to suppress a smile. He handed Dole a 1:250,000 scale map to hang on the wall.

"Squad leaders, prepare to copy."

Four

20 December 1990

There was no use getting up at zero dark; the trip was only about 180km from start to finish. Quarry estimated five hours' travel time, half again as many hours going through checkpoints. Most of the Scouts got up early anyway and took prolonged hot showers. For all they knew, these would be the last ones they would have for quite some time. The Scouts went through the breakfast line, many twice. Even if they weren't hungry, there was something ceremonial about "the last supper." At 0800, the pre-combat checks were complete. Quarry turned the corner of the company head-quarters with Lieutenant Colonel Dillion and the "morale officer." Under Sharia, chaplains weren't to be addressed as such, so morale officer was the next best title. As the small group approached the vehicles, the Scouts came to attention.

"I've asked the Group chaplain to come over this morning." Quarry said. "He'll give us a few words and lead us through Communion. If you don't want to participate, feel free to wander off for ten or fifteen minutes." No one moved. "Scouts, this is Chaplain Porter." He didn't feel the need to use the "morale officer" title. Although in theory, if a Saudi "religious police officer" observed any "unauthorized" religious activity, he had the legal right to beat offenders with a two-inch-diameter rattan club until he felt the punishment fitted the crime, it was curious that none ever seemed to come around.

The chaplain delivered a non-denominational service, mostly from the Old Testament, mostly Kings and Judges. The Scouts added their favorite prayer or scripture. Everyone shared something. The Communion was M.R.E. crackers and water from a canteen. At the final "Amen," an easy silence came over the platoon.

"Thank you for coming, Chaplain," Quarry addressed their guest. "I don't want to steal any of the chaplain's thunder," he added, turning to the Scouts, "but I'd like to share my favorite two verses with you. Psalm 144, verse one: 'Praise the Lord, my rock, who trains my hands for war and my fingers to do battle.'" Quarry let the silence run another few moments before turning the formation over to the colonel. After his words of support and motivation, Quarry called the Scouts to attention. The Scouts snapped to with the precision of a drill team. Quarry turned, faced the colonel and came to attention.

"Permission to carry out the plan of the day, sir," he said, saluting.

"Permission granted, Captain Samuels," the colonel said. "Good luck and God's speed."

Quarry faced his men: "Mount up, comm checks in two. Move!" The Scouts gave a loud "Oorah," as they broke the position of attention.

The first checkpoint was north of the Camp Five compound. The check was an easy one, a simple look at the Group orders and a wave through. As the Marine area of responsibility was divided between the different task forces, every time the Scouts traveled along the coastal road to a new area, there was a checkpoint. Task Forces Grizzly, Papa Bear, Ripper, and Shepherd required validation of the orders. The last checkpoint was at Mishab. From this point on, there might or might not be Saudi or friendly forces between them and the Iraqis.

As they moved, Quarry continually read the G.P.S. and ticked off their location on his map. In the open sea of continual sand, the Scouts had an endless, flat tabletop on which to play.

"Open the interval between units and squads," Quarry transmitted. The Scouts didn't acknowledge the order on the radio; they just did it. The platoon's dispersion interval was now doubled. But in an area where you can see from horizon to horizon with nothing in sight, it still seemed too close. Used to operating in woods and forests, the Scouts would take a while to get accustomed to operating in the open terrain. They practiced changing formations and immediate action drills as they drove.

It was late afternoon when the platoon started seeing signs of a military unit. Tire tracks, inches deep in the sand, indicated transports and supply trucks. Multiple tracks indicated a unit.

"Cut speed in half," Quarry ordered over the radio.

Minutes later, the radio broke squelch.

"Six this is One. Observing a military logistics unit in defensive positions, continuing mission, over."

"One, Six, roger, out." Quarry pulled the C.E.O.I., a code book that dangled on a lanyard around his neck, from inside his flak jacket. On the last page of the list of organizations and their corresponding radio frequencies, Quarry found the call sign of 2nd Brigade, SANG. Quarry pushed the second preset button on the top radio.

"*Thaani* Brigade, *Thaani* Brigade, *ana naqeeb* Samuels, Scout Platoon, *Amreekiyya*."

Within seconds, the radio came to life.

"Welcome to 2nd Brigade, Scout Platoon. This is Sergeant Stevens, 1st Group. That's the worst Arabic I've ever heard, but come in anyway."

Quarry looked over at Dole, who was looking at him.

"It wasn't that bad."

"If you say so, sir," Dole said, turning his head back to watch where he was driving.

Sergeant First Class (S.F.C.) Stevens, U.S. Army Special Forces, met the Scouts at the rear of the brigade area and escorted them in. The Green Beret sat in the passenger seat of a vehicle that was best described as a heavily armed dune buggy. It wasn't long until Quarry and Grier were standing inside a massive tent at 2nd Brigade headquarters.

"I have a meeting with the colonel," Stevens told a Saudi corporal in perfect Arabic.

"*Itfaddal, ya Raqeeb, al-aqeed mawjood*," the corporal said, getting up from his chair. Please come in, Sergeant, the colonel is in.

Stevens, Quarry and Grier were escorted to the rear of the tent which was sectioned off by heavy hanging rugs. Stevens made the introduction.

"*Masaa' al-khayr, ya aqeed* Ahmed. *Uqaddim laka naqeeb* Samuels." Good evening Colonel Ahmed. May I introduce Captain Samuels.

"*MarHaba bil'akh* Samuels. *Itsharrafna. Anta tahjee 'arabi?*" Welcome, brother Samuels. Do you speak Arabic? the colonel asked, stepping forward.

"*Mit'assif ya aqeed* Ahmed. *Maa afham arabi.*" I'm sorry colonel Ahmed. I don't speak Arabic.

The colonel gave a huge laugh that brought the attention of everyone in the room.

"Well then, we'll have to work on that," he said in perfect English, still laughing.

"The colonel graduated from Cornell," Stevens put in. "Class of '63 wasn't it, sir?"

"Exactly," the colonel said, slapping Stevens on the back and calling for tea.

The 2nd Brigade was modeled after a U.S. Army armored brigade, which was no surprise as the Saudis had sent their officers to the U.S. for military training for decades. The brigade consisted of two armor battalions of M60A3 tanks and a battalion of mechanized infantry with armored personnel carriers. The colonel further task organized the battalions into tank-infantry teams, so each battalion had a combination of armor and infantry. To the east, he had reinforced his infantry heavy battalion with a TOW platoon to give it an increased antitank capability. The tank heavy battalions stretched on line toward the west. The colonel stated they also had two batteries of artillery, of 16 tubes, ten clicks behind the front lines, and the rest of their supplies were another five clicks behind that. He gave Quarry a list of the staff officers who spoke English well and authorized him to call them directly at any time for any assistance. Later that night, when the meeting was finished, the colonel presented Quarry a set of orders, written in Arabic, authorizing the Scouts full access to anything they needed at supply.

During the tour of the command post, Quarry met every officer, and Grier met the sergeant major. Quarry was briefed on the Iraqi situation, which amounted to significantly less than his own knowledge. Stevens informed him that if it weren't for the CentCom updates he provided the brigade, the Saudis wouldn't have a clue what was going on across the border.

That evening, Quarry set up camp ten clicks west of the 1st Battalion, close enough he could make easy liaison with the Saudis but not so close they would get in his way. Quarry sold the idea to the colonel by pointing out that he and the Scouts could screen his exposed flank. The colonel agreed as it was sound tactics, but in truth, he really didn't want the Americans poking their noses around his camp.

Once finished setting up camp, Quarry asked Stevens to give them the real scoop on what was happening.

"We've been hanging out to the west of here, Captain," Stevens started. "That police post you see to the west is the last Saudi post. That's where I operate out of when I'm not making contact with the colonel here. Other than that, we screen the border and wait for missions."

Quarry was taken back by the sergeant's aloofness.

"Have you checked out anything north of the berm yet?" Quarry asked.

"That's classified," Stevens said in a tone that indicated that nothing else would be said on the matter.

Quarry took a minute to ponder what just transpired. Here they were, U.S. forces miles away from any backup or any real firepower, closer to the enemy than to friendly units, no direct logistical or artillery support, low on the air-request priority, and this son of a bitch wants to play the "that's classified" game.

"O.K.," Quarry said, taking a map out of his flak jacket, like Stevens' answer made perfect sense. Spreading the map out on the hood of his Hummer, Quarry pulled a red-lensed mini flashlight from his web gear. "Here we are now." Quarry started by drawing an incomplete circle on the map. In the back of the circle, Quarry placed three dots, indicating a platoon battle position. Grier took a quick side-glance at Stevens. The moment didn't go unnoticed on the other end of the service spectrum. By a simple circle on a map, Quarry told the Sergeant First Class Green Beret there was a new sheriff in town. Grier read Stevens' face and suppressed a smile.

"Tomorrow, Five," Quarry addressed his platoon sergeant using the call sign normally assigned to an executive officer, "we'll start digging hull-down positions. I want supplementary and alternate positions for the squads here, here and here," Quarry said, making smaller circles with dashed lines but only two dots in the open space. While he made a series of other circles, Quarry continued.

"My orders, sergeant, are NOT classified. I am NOT to conduct operations north of the berm. I AM, however, to conduct defensive operations in support of host nation and U.S. interests. That includes defensive patrolling in my ENTIRE area of interest." By stressing a few doctrinal words and by using the term area of interest, not area of influence or operations, Quarry was making it clear he owned everything south of the berm. "I will not permit enemy activity to go on in an area that is vital to the survival of my men or the security of the unit I liaise with." Quarry had just reprimanded the Special Forces team leader for not giving him additional information on the enemy observation posts. It would have been embarrassing had the S.F.C. not just made a complete ass of himself with the "that's classified" statement. Grier suppressed another smile.

Stevens assessed Quarry. *Tough little shit*, he thought. He decided he liked the captain. Taking a map out of his own blouse, the sergeant unfolded it and placed it beside Quarry's. The scale was larger so more terrain was visible.

"A couple nights ago, there was a lot of activity in the oilfields. Something big ran through there. Someone is currently in the processing station area, but we don't know who or in what strength. That's a little too far north for our concern. My team and I spend a lot of time keeping an eye on the border and the 29th Infantry. We haven't neutralized the first Iraqi observation post because they're no threat. The guys there now are pretty lax. A squad that gives a damn could disrupt our lines of supply so we simply skirt that O.P. at night as we come in and out. It works to our advantage, them being there."

"Can we count on 2nd SANG to resupply us?" Grier asked.

"Absolutely. Colonel Ahmed may not want us telling him what to do, but he's a team player. He realizes they can't pull this off by themselves and welcomes our input, as long as it's input, not orders. In exchange, he gives us fuel and fresh food. The Saudis don't have stocks of M.R.E.s like we do. They operate field kitchens. Not bad either."

"Get the specifics for me later, Five," Quarry said. "All right, here's what I propose." Quarry took a few minutes and drew some more lines on his map. The three went on for quite some time, planning events for the next few days.

21 December 1990

Just before dawn, the Scouts confirmed radio checks.

"We can talk to everyone in the world this morning," Dole told Quarry as his platoon commander and the Green Beret jumped into the Hummer. "Group, Intel Company, the Fusion Center, you name it, we have a button for it."

"Thank you Dole," Quarry answered. Then, ensuring the frequency was set to the platoon tactical net, Quarry keyed the mic. The squads answered in sequence. When all was ready, Quarry gave the order to move.

The first operation was a zone reconnaissance. The night before, Quarry, Grier, and Stevens had planned a simple orientation to the area. While Stevens was comfortable moving in and out of the area at will, Quarry still wanted to take a look for himself. Because there was no friendly artillery available, the Scouts would depend solely on air support for support. If the Scouts needed immediate help, Quarry would call the Direct Air Support Center. Already preset on the bottom 526 radio, the DASC coordinated all offensive air operations within the MarCent area of operations. If needed, Quarry had the standardized "nine-line" air support request written on the inside of the windshield in permanent marker. Based on the morning's operation, he took water soluble markers and filled in as many of the details that applied. The call for close air support would take less than fifteen seconds to finish and another ten to transmit.

Quarry also wrote down a few lines in case they worked with Marine attack helicopters. A new organization for the Marines, Task Force Cunningham, concentrated a large number of Bell A.H.1W Sea Cobra helicopters into a maneuver unit. Quarry didn't want to leave any asset uncovered when it came to the security of the platoon. Lastly, Stevens gave Quarry the call sign and frequency of Army Aerial Scouts who worked in support of Army Special Forces, organized into reconnaissance and attack platoons. Quarry could count on the laser-designating O.H.58 Kiowa Scouts and their big brothers, the A.H.64 Apache attack helos. The frequency had its own preset button on the bottom radio.

The first stop on their sightseeing tour lay due north. While the berm was clearly visible from their battle position, Quarry wanted to get a warm and fuzzy feeling of what lay beyond. Using the TOW thermal sights, Marion's TOW gunner Lance Corporal Botsford and Caine's gunner Lance Corporal Guy reported negative contact the entire distance to their destination.

Despite its plain and ordinary appearance, the significance of this mound of dirt wasn't missed by anyone. The anti-tank TOW missile Hummers drove up the back of the berm until only the optics on their sights rose above the top. From where they were, the oil wells and processing center of Al-Wafrah were in view.

"Sir," Lance Corporal Tellado, the TOW gunner for 3rd Squad, called for Quarry. "You better take a look."

Quarry walked over, climbed the berm, jumped up on Ogdon's Hummer and looked through the TOW optics.

"Holy mother of God," Quarry said, barely audible. The spontaneous utterance drew everyone's immediate attention. "Sergeant Stevens."

Looking through the TOW sight, Stevens let out a few choice words. Climbing down and turning the optics over to Ogdon, he voiced his thoughts: "Seems we have company." Indeed they did: an Iraqi brigade.

"As far as neighbors go, this is as close as we can get until MEF gives us authorization to go north of the berm," Quarry explained to his squad leaders.

"I'm not exactly thrilled about having a thousand Iraqi troops and a hundred tanks within optic range of me, skipper." Marion voiced the opinion of everyone present.

"Nor am I, Mary," Quarry answered. "But let's take a closer look at what we have. First of all, we don't have artillery pouring down on us. That's a good thing."

"Yeah, no shit on that one, sir," Caine chimed in.

Quarry smiled.

"That's exactly my point. Sergeant First Class Stevens, when did you say this unit moved in?"

"Just a few days ago."

"And how many times have you moved in and out of this area from your normal op area?"

"Once in and out. Came back in two days ago when we heard you guys were going to be the new liaison to 2nd Brigade."

"So what we have here," Quarry started, "is a failure to communicate." No one chuckled. "Oh come on, that was a little funny." Still nothing. Quarry continued: "So we have an estimated Iraqi combined arms brigade that hasn't put one defensive patrol out yet and by the looks of it, hasn't even ventured out of the oilfields."

"How d'ya know that, skipper?" Corporal Hauser, Team Leader for 3rd Squad's Second Team, spoke up.

"Take a peek, Howie," Quarry said, passing binoculars. The two, immediately followed by the squad leaders and just about every other dismounted Scout, low-crawled to the top of the embankment. Looking through the ten-powered binos, they made out vehicle movement, but not the type of vehicle.

"We have at least fifteen open clicks before the oil wells." Quarry paused, letting Howie and the others scan the area. "Does anyone see even one set of tracks the entire distance between us and them?" A few seconds of analysis later and everyone confirmed what Quarry was thinking. The ground before them was undisturbed. Not a boot print, tire mark, or tank track had been left in months. "If these guys have been here for a week, that's exactly the type of unit I want across from me," Quarry commented.

The group made their way back down their side of the berm and back to the vehicles. At the Hummers, the leaders gathered.

"O.K., change of mission. Dole. Work with Tellado. Get me a vehicle count. See if you can distinguish boundaries. Send a sitrep to the Fusion Center. Get confirmation that I-Six gets it," referring to Lieutenant Colonel Dillion. "Ogie. It was your gunner that saw them first; you get the first watch. We'll set up an O.P. here. We'll designate it O.P. Berm. We'll rotate in and out in 24-hour intervals starting today. Rotate in at 2100. Mary will relieve you tomorrow night. Mary, bring your cammie nets back with you. Ogie, start digging in as best you can. Don't draw attention to yourself, keep an eye on 'em. Continually monitor our tactical net and the DASC net. Radio checks every half-hour on tac. Should they ever remember to put a patrol out, use your best judgement. Stay in place as long as you can, break contact if you have to, call for everything in the world if you're discovered. I'll work up a fire plan for 2nd SANG's artillery, only as a last resort engage with direct-fire weapons."

"Yes, sir."

"From here," Quarry said, facing Marion and Caine, "I want to pull back about seven or eight clicks. We'll head west until we come across Sergeant Stevens' O.P. Once there, we'll move forward only until our TOW gunners can make out the top of the next O.P. As soon as that happens, we'll mark our position using G.P.S. We'll continue to make a series of bounds until we trace a huge arc of observation, radiating out from the enemy O.P. By plotting the positions and adding a click or two for safety, we'll have an area we can move around at will without being detected. Any questions?" There were none. "Mary, Caine, go brief your people. Meet back here in 15. We'll do a leaders' rehearsal but I specifically want the TOW gunners present."

Dole was creating a sketch of what they discovered. A bird's eye view showed a series of lines that intersected a small circle.

"Sir," Dole started, "this is the central processing plant. These lines are the different pipelines radiating out of the plant. To be honest, from this angle, there are too many pipelines to count, well over a dozen running in and out with as many crossing back and forth connecting the mains. They're using the pipelines for cover and concealment. From this one location though, Tellado and I can count over forty vehicles. Twenty-six of them are definitely tanks, older models, most likely T-55s." Dole presented Quarry with the map they had drawn.

"Battalion or brigade?"

Dole thought for a moment.

"At least two different battalions in the pipes. Probably more behind them. Can't tell boundaries because there is no logical order to where they put the vehicles. Some are totally masked, some in keyhole positions, and some right out in the open. Doesn't make any sense how they set in."

"Works for me," Quarry replied. "Get on the horn, tell Company what we have. Tell 'em our intentions for keeping one squad here and two squads heading west. Ask for any additional instructions."

"Consider it done, sir."

"Ogie. Take this," Quarry said, handing him the map Dole had provided. "Stay behind the berm but send flankers out a few clicks. Work the angles; see what else you can add."

"Yes sir."

* * *

Since the elevation didn't rise or fall more than six feet from horizon to horizon, there wasn't much to the terrain model. Five small mounds of dirt represented the police stations. There was a half circle drawn in the sand around the second one.

"Sir?" Marek asked after Quarry finished the brief. "Why do it during the day?"

"Due to the curvature of the earth, when you watch a ship approach from over the horizon, the first thing you see is the mast. As it gets closer, you can make out the superstructure and so on until you can actually see the hull. By doing this op during the day, our TOW gunners will be able to make out the very top of the enemy O.P. before the Iraqis in the tower can see us. As soon as the gunners see the top, we stop there, plot the position and bound. By doing the op in daylight, there won't be any mistakes about what is the top of the tower and what isn't. I estimate that arc will be about ten clicks before we are hidden by the curvature of the earth."

It took less than a half-hour before Sergeant Stevens saw the other dune buggy at what was now being called O.P. Tower. The station itself was a one-room building with an observation tower next to it. Stevens called on his own radio to verify the site was secure. It was, and the Scouts picked up the pace.

Later, at the camp, the Saudi military police, Stevens' 2nd Team, and the Scouts became one big happy family over bottles of cold water taken from a refrigerator. Once in the tower, Quarry looked at the next police station to the west through binos. It was located almost exactly on the berm. Stevens explained that the post was on the Khabari Umm Jathjath flats, just north of the Ash Shaqq wadi. The Bedouins had used the flats as a navigation aid along the camel trade routes for hundreds of years. The route was clearly known, because the few inches of rain that fell annually made the ground permanently darker than the surrounding sand.

It didn't take long for One One to return. On the map, Lance Corporal Botsford showed Quarry the location of where he saw the top of the enemy tower. The distance was 22 clicks. Quarry's stomach turned. At that distance, the enemy O.P. could see almost anything. The thought of fighting a war where the enemy had essentially unlimited observation gave him chills.

Spreading his map on the hood of the Hummer, Quarry plotted five points, 22 clicks out and equal distance apart, in an arc around the enemy observation post. He looked up and saw his squad leaders and Stevens around him.

"Here we go. If the terrain is uniformly level, the distance the enemy tower can see should be consistent. Bots already located the first point of the observation arc for us. Here are four more I want to verify," Quarry said, pointing to four dots on the map. "Mary, Caine, I want you guys to make a speed run due south. Somewhere about here," Quarry said, drawing a rectangular shaped box on the map indicating a release point, "Mary will turn back to the northwest and verify our first point on the arc. Caine, cut due west until you come up from and behind the next point. Once you make your cuts, turn the vehicle over to the TOW gunners. Creep up only as far as it takes Bots and Guy to verify the top of the tower. Once you do that, back up a couple clicks and start your next run. Mary hit point three; Caine, four. Here are a few checkpoints, call them all so I can track your progress. I'll remain here. I'll be monitoring platoon tac and have the DASC on the other radio. Break contact immediately on any observation other than the tower, call in what you have, and I'll get some air on station if you need it. Questions?"

"Would you like me to help, captain?" Stevens asked.

"Your offer is greatly appreciated, Sergeant Stevens, but the arc is based on the height of the tower relevant to the height of the TOW launcher. Those dune buggies of yours would give us a false distance. Besides, I'd like you here with me. If my boys get into any trouble out there, I'd like to call your attack helos."

Mary and Caine mounted up. The squad leaders performed radio checks, Botsford and Guy conducted prep-to-fire checks on the TOW missiles, and Peterson and Stone made sure there were rounds in the chambers of the 50-caliber machine guns. Even though they were still on the Saudi side of the border, the operation was directed against a known enemy target. The Scouts were ready for their first combat mission.

A speed run sacrifices security for time. But in the open desert, where you can see 20km in any direction, it isn't nearly as big a risk as in the woods or jungle. If the Iraqis changed their minds and wanted to engage the Scouts with artillery, the speed run itself would be a form of protection. As soon as an enemy call for fire was placed, the Scouts would be out of the impact zone. This still didn't make Quarry feel any better as he watched his men pull out without him.

It took three hours from start to finish. The points were plotted, the tower observed, and no contact was made. All in all, a successful mission. A short and to-the-point debrief followed.

"Caine," Quarry turned to his squad leader, "you've got the duty."

"Am I staying here tonight, skipper?"

"Yep. Mary will return to base camp with me tonight. Mary will replace Ogie tomorrow night. Ogie will come here. You'll rotate back after tomorrow's mission."

Caine's face lit up.

"For a second there I thought you weren't going to let me play."

"Not on your life."

"Thanks for putting it like that, sir," Private First Class Orsini, Marion's driver, said under his breath. Caine punched him in the arm in no friendly manner. Stevens and Quarry turned away and suppressed a smile. That had to have hurt.

It was midafternoon when Quarry and 1st Squad returned to their Command Post on the flank of 2nd SANG. The sounds and sights of a Saudi bulldozer digging fighting holes greeted them. Grier was talking to a Saudi *raqeeb* when Quarry and Marion walked up.

"*Yawm jayid,*" Quarry greeted their guest. Good day.

"*Masaa' al-khayr,*" the Saudi sergeant replied politely.

Grier noticed they were a few squads short of a full platoon.

"Did we lose something?" he asked his platoon commander when the Saudi sergeant was out of earshot. Quarry smiled. As the two looked at the fighting position already dug, Quarry brought Grier up to date. Grier, in turn, informed Quarry they were expected at the colonel's after noon prayers. As Saudis commonly use their five ritual daily prayers to refer to meeting times, they would see the colonel anytime from noon to 1700.

Grier showed Quarry their new home, a dug-in underground C.P. The Saudi corporal behind the bulldozer had obviously made a few of these before. After digging a fighting hole for the two Hummers, the backhoe dug out the middle, forming a large "H." Two large pieces of corrugated tin were placed on the sides, support timbers driven into the ground and more tin bolted on top. The top was then covered with three feet of dirt. A makeshift table was placed in the middle with enough room that all headquarters and team leaders would fit easily. Cammie nets were spread over the top of the openings. A 292 radio antenna was remoted 100 meters away and tied into Grier's Hummer. On one of the walls, Grier placed large-scale maps of Kuwait covering the heel to the coast and tactical-level maps covering the

2nd Brigade's frontage. Grier had also snagged a 50-pound bag of rice, a few 25-pound bags of potatoes and numerous cans of dried meat, accompanied by a few large pots and a five-pound can of coffee.

"You've been busy," Quarry said.

* * *

Quarry, Grier and Dole mounted up. Fifteen minutes later, they pulled in behind the 2nd SANG's headquarters. Quarry and Grier went inside the massive tent.

"*Ana Naqeeb* Samuels. *Indi maw'id ma'a l-aqeed* Ahmed, *min fadlak*," Quarry greeted the *areef* behind the field desk.

"*Itfaddal, istareeh ya naqeeb*," the corporal said, rising from his desk. Please have a seat, Captain.

Moments later, the booming laugh of Colonel Ahmed was heard coming from behind the draped rug. Seconds later he emerged.

"*Assalaamu alaykum Naqeeb* Samuels." Peace be upon you, Captain Samuels.

"*Wa alaykumu ssalaam Aqeed* Ahmed." And upon you peace, Colonel Ahmed. Quarry immediately responded to one of the traditional greetings without hesitation.

The colonel was taken back for a second and continued, "*Kayf haalak?*" How are you?

"*Tayyib, walhamdu lillaah*." Fine, praise be to God, Quarry continued the traditional greeting.

Colonel Ahmed gave out another belly-busting laugh.

"You have such wonderful manners, Captain Samuels; one would think you are Muslim."

"You are very kind, Colonel."

"Come in, come in. We must have some tea." The colonel held open the curtain to his "reception" area. Thick heavy carpets covered the floor and walls of the divided-off area. Sitting down on the carpet and leaning up against a pillow, Quarry just got comfortable before an *awwal* brought four small cups and poured sugared tea. He waited until his host was served and took a sip. It tasted like shit.

"*Ash-shaay mumtaaz*," Quarry said, thanking his host. The tea is excellent.

"Glad you like it," the colonel replied, smiling.

They sat in silence for a while, drinking their tea.

"Thank you for your generous hospitality," Quarry said at last, finishing his cup.

"You're welcome."

The *awwal* brought the pitcher of tea back towards Quarry but he shook his cup from side to side.

"*Mashkuur, kaafi.*" Thank you, enough, he said, handing his cup back to the private. Grier choked down his last swallow and also expressed his gratitude. The colonel smiled at them broadly. Placing his own cup back on the tray, he stood up.

"Come, I will show you my command."

The three exited the tent and approached the colonel's jeep. Colonel Ahmed offered the passenger seat to Quarry but Quarry politely declined, citing military courtesy. Again the colonel beamed and Quarry climbed in the back with Grier.

The brigade headquarters was three clicks behind the main body of Ahmed's forces. He task organized his force by mixing infantry and armor units. Of the three battalions, the two armor battalions each gave up one armor company and received one mechanized infantry company in return. The infantry battalion retained only one infantry company and received two armor companies. From where they were, as far as the eye could see from west to east, were dug-in tanks every 100 meters. As they got closer, Quarry saw infantry-fighting positions dug in between and behind every tank position. As they got closer still, Quarry noted these positions were empty. As they finally rolled up on line with the tanks, the reason for the empty holes became clear. Twenty-five meters in front of and between the tanks were more infantry fighting positions. In each position was a four-man fire team. Quarry looked over to his host.

"I can see by the look on your face, Captain Samuels, you are impressed."

"Indeed I am sir," Quarry said. And he was. The amount of effort put into the defensive position was incredible. By placing the infantry forward of the tanks, Ahmed prevented infiltration by Iraqi reconnaissance. By placing fighting positions behind the tanks, the infantry could fall back in case of an Iraqi armored attack. The close proximity of the infantry positions allowed the infantry to move back and forth without compromising a tank's fighting positions. The close proximity of armor and infantry positions ensured mutually supporting arms. Behind every third infantry fighting position was a dug-in armored troop carrier. In extreme emergency, the infantry could quickly fall back to the protection of armored cover.

"The colonel will make an excellent guest speaker at the U.S. Armor conference next year, sir," Quarry said, turning from the 4,500-meter battle position in front of him. "Your emplacement of mutually supporting positions will be a topic for discussion. I'll submit the subject to the Advanced Armor School next time I am at Fort Knox."

"*Mashkuur, ala karam iddiyaafa, Naqiib* Samuels."

The three drove the length of the defensive position, stopping at each of the battalion headquarters where Quarry and Grier met the battalion commanders and some of the troops. Quarry climbed up on some of the tanks and talked to the tank commanders. He was impressed with their professionalism. The tankers' battle-carried ammunition, range cards, and maintenance logs were all immaculate. At the ends of the defensive position, Ahmed had placed TOW squads in depth, protecting the exposed flank of the brigade. The third squad of TOW missiles was held in reserve near the brigade headquarters as a combination of palace guard and mobile reaction force. The squad could reinforce anywhere on the line within minutes, the entire length of the battle position. Again, Quarry was impressed.

When the three returned to the main tent, Quarry once again expressed his sentiment. Colonel Ahmed glowed with pride.

"Come, we will eat now," he said, holding back the entrance to the tent himself. Entering the reception room again, they all sat down and an *awwal* brought a pitcher of water and a towel. Quarry held out his hands and the private poured a small amount of water. The ritual was repeated for Grier before the private approached his colonel.

"Where did you learn so much about our customs and our language, Captain Samuels?" the colonel asked.

"From books and language tapes, Colonel," Quarry answered. "I hope Staff Sergeant Grier and I bring honor and respect to your command."

The colonel let out another one of his gut-born laughs.

"Indeed you do, young *naqeeb*." After the *awwal* withdrew with the water pitcher, he returned with a large brass pot filled with coffee. The coffee was hot, unsweetened and flavored with cardamom. Quarry blew on it softly, took a sip, and repressed spitting it out.

"*Al-qahwa mumtaaza,*" Quarry informed his host. The coffee is excellent. The colonel smiled, raised his cup to his guests and took a drink. Moments later, the main course was brought: lamb, covered by a large amount of rice, served on a large platter. The dish was placed in the center of the three, and the colonel invited his guests to start. Quarry reached out with his right hand and manipulated the rice around a portion of lamb until it made a small pasty ball. Quarry leaned back on the pillows and popped the ball in his mouth. It was fantastic.

"*Al-akl tayyib waayid,*" he said truthfully. Grier reached over and started his own handful, as did the colonel from the other side of the platter. Quarry reached for and broke off a piece of bread, similar to pita, and dipped it in a sauce. Except for the damn coffee, dinner was one of the most memorable meals Quarry would ever have. As the three ate and talked into the night, friendships were made, and bonds of trust created.

The evening came to a close with the call for evening prayers. The colonel excused himself but invited Quarry and Grier to stay. Knowing this was only a polite invitation, Quarry said he and Grier had to check on their men. Again, the colonel smiled. The three leaders exited into the main tent. Several senior Saudi officers were present, waiting to be led in prayers by their commanding officer. When Quarry and Grier gave the traditional thanks and good-byes as they departed the tent, the colonel smiled and hugged Quarry good-bye. They had been accepted.

Five

23 December 1990

All three squad leaders checked in on the platoon tac at midnight. The Saudis at O.P. Tower were dead asleep and the one who was nodding off at the radio didn't care what the Americans were doing. The operations order had been written and disseminated yesterday and squad and platoon rehearsals conducted that night.

Orsini pulled his Hummer to the west side of the Saudi outpost. Guy took a few seconds to look through the thermal sights of his TOW launcher. When he removed his eye from the optics, he looked down through the turret and nodded.

"This is Two, all clear," Caine transmitted over the platoon net. Upon hearing the report, 1st Squad headed due north. Dole pulled in behind them as Two Two came up and parked alongside their squad leader. With the new moon overhead, it didn't take long for One and Six to disappear in the night. The sounds of the Hummers gave away their positions long after the eye no longer detected them. The night-vision goggles Caine wore corrected that. When the sound of the Hummers finally faded away, Caine shot them with the laser: 1,734 meters.

"One point seven five," he reported over the radio. Seconds later, One, Three, Five and Six acknowledged the transmission. Then all was quiet again. Caine watched 1st Squad continue north. With N.V.G.s and Guy's thermal TOW sights, 2nd Squad was able to watch 1st all the way to the berm.

When Marion turned his vehicles west, he transmitted, "One set." Caine looked over to Corporal "Specter" Speckman, his Team Two Leader, and nodded. Moving west at a pace that kept the engine just above idle, it took 2nd Squad about ten minutes to travel one kilometer. When the image of the Hummer took up the first two hash marks in Botsford's sights, he let his squad leader know. Marion confirmed the distance with a laser shot of his own and picked up the hand mic.

"Two set in. One is Oscar Mike." With nothing to hide behind, 2nd Squad merely came to a halt. Guy scanned ahead with thermals, Caine and Orsini, Specter and his spotter Lance Corporal Peterson with night-vision goggles. With nothing out there to see, four kilometers north of them, 1st Squad started their bound toward the enemy O.P. Dole let 1st get 100 meters ahead, took his foot off the brake and gradually accelerated to match the pace.

Grier and Ogdon continued to listen to 1st and 2nd in silence. It wasn't until they reached their own checkpoint along their speed run to the south that Grier made their first transmission: "This is Five, checkpoint five, Charlie Mike." Grier looked at his watch; so far, so good. Twenty-two clicks to the north, Quarry was doing the same thing.

The platoon, minus Three Two, which was still at O.P. Berm, was now all heading toward the enemy O.P. on three different axes. It was after 0230 when Grier called in: "Six, this is Five, delta papa, negative contact, Charlie Mike, over." Ten clicks to the north, with his right tire on the side of the berm, Quarry acknowledged the transmission. 1st and 2nd held five kilometers from their objective.

When the southern teams were a mere three miles from their destination, Grier and his driver, Lance Corporal Slayer, Ogdon and Mathews took to the ground. They had ten minutes to close as much distance as they could on foot until 1st, 2nd, and Six did the same. Tellado took one final look through the TOW optics. All he saw was the heat signature of friendly Scout vehicles.

"All clear. Go," he whispered. With all four wearing night-vision goggles and stripped down to the bare necessities for combat, the two snipers, armed with M-40s, and their spotters took off at a quiet run. Grier set the pace; they would go only as fast as silence allowed.

As his watch counted down, Quarry held the mic to his lips.

"This is Six, Charlie Mike." Despite the 46-degree temperature, he was sweating. Along the berm, Marion and Marek exited their vehicles and teamed up. Davis and Kantner stayed in the driver seats, ready to make a rescue run if necessary. In the turrets, Botsford kept a keen eye on the enemy O.P. with his thermal optics and Stone sat poised behind his 50-caliber, scanning the area with his night-vision goggles. Four clicks to the southwest, Caine and Guy also dismounted while Orsini climbed up into the TOW turret. Speckman and his driver, Lance Corporal Throop, dismounted and took an extra second to adjust their equipment. Only when both Orsini and Botsford gave a final "all clear" over the radio, did Quarry give the final order: "This is Six. Move." In the north, the teams took a low crouch and silently started moving next to the berm on foot. To the south, the two teams moved more methodically. In the ten minutes that passed, Grier and the south team closed almost another two kilometers.

At one-minute intervals, Botsford gave updates: "No movement." "Looking good." "Negative contact." "Nothing seen." The reports became monotonous but were better than having a high pitched "Oh my God," come over the radio.

Finally, the radio reported a different voice.

"Six, this is Five, set, negative contact, out." The simple transmission reported a world of information. Grier and Ogdon were now somewhere between 300 and 500 meters directly in front of the enemy O.P. If the occupants of the tower were awake and/or attentive, the southern team would have been detected by now.

The next phase of the operation began even though the northern team was still 1,000 meters away from its objective. In the south, Grier and his men settled down in the sand. Though there wasn't enough light to see by, the scopes of the snipers' rifles were trained on the O.P. The spotters placed their scopes in the sand and watched for any changes in shadows. The reports from Botsford continued to confirm that all was quiet.

It took another 15 minutes for the north team to close the distance. Caine and Guy were first to arrive. They took position at the base of the ladder to the platform above. Guy placed his back to one of the supports and aimed his rifle straight up. Caine knelt down beside him facing due north. Nothing. Caine closed his fist and made a pumping motion with his arm. Speckman and Throop quickened their pace and took positions on the far side of the platform. Caine looked to his left and confirmed his men's position. One more check north and the second hand signal was given. Quarry whispered into the mic, "Move." Marion and Marek silently slipped in and around the berm, and disappeared from sight.

Quarry and Dole moved to the edge of the opening in the berm. They placed the medical stretcher they carried against it and waited. It seemed to take forever, but then the signal came in. Marion turned a dial on his goggles and admitted an infrared beam. To the naked eye, one couldn't see a thing. To someone wearing goggles, it was like a torch being lit. The beacon caught Caine's attention immediately. He flashed Quarry his own signal and the two teams converged.

As the four turned the corner of the berm, they saw what Marion and Marek had already inspected in detail. An infantry squad supported the observation post. Quarry counted eight soldiers lying on the ground, next to a B.M.P., asleep under threadbare blankets. It took another ten minutes for the two additional teams to negotiate the obstacles of sleeping bodies. Quarry was more afraid the soldiers would wake from being cold than from any noise the Scouts created. As the two teams closed in, Quarry saw what Marion determined to be their objective. The senior ranking soldier was easily identifiable compared to his subordinates. He was alone in the back of the B.M.P., lying on cardboard boxes that insulated him from the metal floor. The sergeant had placed prayer rugs over the cardboard for cushioning, his blanket was new and his uniform was not tattered. Quarry scanned the inside of the vehicle. There wasn't anyone else inside the passenger compartment or inside the turret. Quarry gave a nod and Marion and Caine slipped inside like shadows. Like a stalking cat, Caine moved to the head of the unsuspecting Iraqi. Marion controlled his muscle-ripped frame inside the confined space with the grace of a dancer. Marek and Guy covered sleeping forms with their M-16s, which were set on three-round bursts. Quarry surveyed the area one more time, looked inside the B.M.P. and gave another nod. In a flash of movement so quick Quarry didn't see it, even though he knew what was about to happen, Caine delivered a blow to the side of the soldier's neck, immediately followed with a morphine injection, courtesy of the N.B.C. supply satchel, delivered through the blanket. The sergeant responded to the needle but soon mellowed into peaceful sleep. Dole passed the stretcher inside. Marion lifted the soldier as easily as a young girl would raise her doll, then placed him on the stretcher. Dole and Caine adjusted the weight of the stretcher and nodded to Quarry. Dole stepped out and Marek took hold of a side. Marion came out and supported the opposite side as Caine also stepped down out of the B.M.P.

Quarry took a few additional critical seconds to reenter the infantry fighting vehicle. Using a red lens on his flashlight, he scanned the inside. In seconds he found what he was looking for, a logbook and a map. Quarry snatched the prizes and turned to exit. In the process, he was surprised to notice the ammunition for the 73mm cannon was merely snapped in place around the turret. But there wasn't time to analyze his finding at the moment, it was time to leave.

Quarry exited the vehicle and took the lead. The stretcher team fell in behind their leader while Guy brought up the rear. As they neared the opening to the berm, Quarry flashed an I.R. signal. He got the countersign, and the teams turned the corner. They continued to make as good of a pace as possible but if the teams made anything above the slightest rattle, Quarry slowed them down. Now was not the time to hurry. The snatch team continued due east along the berm another 500 meters before Specter and Throop eased out of the supports of the tower. Grier and Ogdon watched as the cover team also melted into the east. Only when Tellado reported "Clear" did the sniper teams rise from the sand and disappear to the south.

At the 500-meter mark, the Iraqi soldier's hands and feet were bound with duct tape. Next, he was cocooned with duct tape to the stretcher. Lastly, a piece of tape was placed over his mouth so any chemical-induced dreams would remain muffled. The Scouts picked up the pace and quickly brought their guest back to the Hummers. Once there, the stretcher was secured to the back with cargo straps. Mounting him over the hood like a deer hunting trophy wouldn't have been neighborly. As soon as everyone had a handhold or climbed in a Hummer, the northern-most team was off. Orsini remained behind the sights of the TOW and Peterson behind the 50-caliber until Grier reported in.

"Six this is Five, mounted, Oscar Mike." Upon hearing the report, Orsini dropped into the driver's seat. The vehicles of 2nd Squad turned around and moved slowly and quietly out of the area.

Quarry picked up the platoon tac.

"Five, this is Six, roger, switching, out." Quarry breathed a sigh of relief upon hearing his platoon sergeant was on the way. Quarry pressed the second preset button on the top radio. The dials spun and settled on the appropriate frequency.

"I Six this is Scout Six, over."

The response was immediate: "Scout Six, this is I Six, over."

"Mission successful. Have a Christmas present for you, en route to post office, over."

"Acknowledged. Good job, looking forward to unwrapping the present. Need anything from postman? Over."

"Negative, all in the green, over."

"Roger, Bravo Zulu, I Six out." For centuries, Bravo Zulu has been the abbreviation for good job based on naval signal flags. Quarry smiled, took a deep breath, and fished for the G.P.S. They continued slowly and quietly, due east.

At a designated waypoint 30 minutes later, Dole started slowing.

"Five, this is Six, you out there?"

"Roger, have you in thermals, be there in ten."

Another five minutes and the G.P.S. told them they were at the designated location.

"One, this is Six, box it up." Dole continued to pull forward a few hundred meters and then came to a stop. From where Quarry gave the order, Davis turned east, Kantner west. Minutes later, Grier pulled up, dug a hole in the sand and placed a flashing beacon in the middle of the cross formed by the vehicles. Dismounting from the Hummer, Grier stayed with the beacon while Slayer moved north and completed the cross. Seeing all was going as planned, Quarry lifted the mic to the bottom radio.

"DASC, this is Scouts, over."

The response came back quickly: "Scouts this is DASC, meet traffic on button three, call sign Spud, over."

"This is Scout Six, roger, transferring now." Quarry put down the hand mic and picked up the very high-frequency radio. He dialed in the setting for the third tactical frequency assigned to groundair operations and keyed the net.

"Spud, this is Scout Six, over." Quarry waited for a few seconds, and the radio came to life.

"Scouts this is Spud, have you in sight."

"Spud, this is Scout Six. Line seven, 400-meter L.Z., no obstacles, no wind, friendlies on perimeter in Hummers. No known enemy. Line eight, flashing beacon. Terminal control provided by controller on the ground with one green, one red chem light, over."

"Scout Six, this is Spud. Damn son, do you think you're back at Quantico?" Quarry dropped the hand mic and looked over at Dole who merely shrugged.

The Huey came in and settled on the flashing beacon. Grier let them know they were on profile by waving them in with the chem lights. As soon as they touched down, Dole was heading toward them in the Hummer. Fifty meters away from the helo, the Scouts exited the vehicle and pulled the stretcher from the back. As they approached the side of the helo, Quarry recognized one of the passengers as a gunny from SCAMP platoon. Quarry didn't know the Marine's name but said hello and shook his hand as the flight crew took charge of the passenger.

"Here's a little something for you guys," the gunny said, handing Quarry two large postal bags.

"Thanks, Gunny," Quarry yelled. Then moving forward and to the right side of the helo, Quarry met the pilot.

"What's this Quantico shit?" Quarry yelled into the cockpit. The pilot extended his hand through the sliding window.

"Hey, skipper, I'm Spud."

"Quarry," he said, shaking the pilot's hand.

"Don't worry about that zippo brief and nine line out here, Quarry. We're totally in the red and no air threat. Just tell us what ya need next time."

"You got it, Spud."

"That was some ballsy shit Quarry," the copilot yelled from the opposite side.

"It gets better," Quarry yelled before he backed away from the helo and joined Grier 20 meters to the front. Quarry stood behind his platoon sergeant as Grier held his arms out and level. The pilot increased power and lifted the skids off the ground. Grier brought his arms up indicating it was clear for the pilot to take off. In seconds the helo was breaking left and climbing into the night. When the roar of the rotor blades subsided, Quarry and Grier congratulated each other on their first successful mission.

25 December 1990

The night dropped below 40 degrees as the squads rotated to their new assignments: Caine to base camp, Marion to Berm, and Ogdon to Tower. At 0600 in the morning, Quarry and Grier loaded the Hummer and made their rounds. Starting with 2nd Squad, Quarry delivered the mail they had received the night before. In addition to letters and packages from home, dozens of small gifts came from the States, addressed to "Any Sailor or Marine." The fewer packages a Scout got from family and friends, the more Quarry and Grier balanced the numbers with the generic presents. In addition to packages, each Scout also received three or four letters from persons unknown. Of course, every Scout hoped for the steamy letter from some beautiful young lady, but all were just as happy with the endless pile of cards from elementary school children.

Quarry and Grier spent an hour with both Caine and Marion. Once they got to Tower, however, they changed tactics. Quarry went inside and greeted their hosts. Ogdon rotated each of the Scouts back to the command Hummer, which was further back than usual. When all the gifts and letters had been handed out, Grier eventually joined Quarry and Ogdon in the tower. The day before, the Scouts had set up a defensive line facing both west and north, but no retaliation for their raid occurred. Today, the Scouts continued to keep a close eye on the west.

It was noon before the command Hummer pulled back into its fighting hole. From ground level, it disappeared under the cammie net.

"You got a message, sir," Slayer informed Quarry, as he and Grier entered their underground headquarters.

Grier was busy taking the remaining packages and letters from the postal bag.

"Merry Christmas," he said, handing Slayer five letters and three packages.

"Thank you, Staff Sergeant," Slayer said, taking the gifts and placing them on the table. "Actually, captain, I think that's what your message is all about." Quarry stood after getting some coffee. Handing a canteen cup to Grier, he turned to the table. "You are expected at Colonel Ahmed's C.P. after evening prayers," Slayer told him.

"Think the colonel heard about our little tea party?" Grier asked Quarry.

"No way."

"Religious stuff?"

"Most likely. But I think we've been pretty good about keeping our host ignorant of the Ghost of Christmas Present."

"Agreed," Grier said, taking the few remaining boxes out of the mailbag and handing them to Quarry. "Merry Christmas, skipper."

"Merry Christmas, Five," Quarry said, taking the gifts from his platoon sergeant. Turning to their drivers, Quarry continued, "Merry Christmas Marines. If we can't be home with our families, I can't think of any others I'd rather be with. I'm glad we're here together. You two make Staff Sergeant Grier's and my job a lot easier. Thank you."

The simple compliment meant more to Dole and Slayer than their gifts. The pride swelled in their chests.

"Merry Christmas, sir." "Merry Christmas, Captain Samuels," they replied.

Quarry changed the subject: "Let's see what we got."

Grier opened a box from his wife Ann.

"Chocolate chip cookie anybody?"

* * *

It was after five when the Hummer pulled up behind the SANG command tent. The Saudi clerk was standing outside; it appeared as if he were waiting for them.

"*Al-aqeed mawjood, ya naqeeb* Samuels," he said holding back the flap that lead into the tent.

"*Shukran,*" Quarry thanked him.

Taking off his boonie cap and entering the tent, Quarry and Grier were welcomed by the booming voice of Colonel Ahmed.

"Is that my American brother Captain Samuels?"

"*Aywa, ya aqeed* Ahmed. *Assalaamu 'alaykum,*" Quarry answered with a traditional greeting.

From behind the entrance to the "reception" area, the traditional "*wa 'alaykuma ssalaam*" response was followed by, "*Mawjood, itfaddal.*" Quarry and Grier looked at each other, then following the request of their guest, entered. The colonel was leaning up against pillows, drinking coffee. Instead of his uniform, Ahmed wore a white silk *thoob*, the traditional long, loose-fitting garment that covers the body from shoulders to the ankles.

"Come in, come in," the colonel offered. "Please, make yourselves comfortable."

"Guess we're not in trouble," Grier said to Quarry under his breath. Quarry and Grier removed their flak jackets and gear harness. Several unseen heaters warmed the room. Knowing that it would be rude to ask what the occasion was that brought them here, Quarry and Grier made themselves at home and started in with the mandatory small talk. The private brought the hand basin and towel for them to wash. Coffee was poured from the *dalla* and the three talked about nothing in general for the good part of 20 minutes. During the course of the conversation, dinner was brought. Quarry and Grier caught each other's eye, wondering what the hell was going on. The meal was the traditional lamb over rice with a few side dishes. The two Scouts eased back further into their pillows, knowing it was going to be a long night.

It got close to nine o'clock. They talked about going to school at Fort Knox, their homes, families and goals. Ahmed told the Scouts about his three wives and how he was blessed with eight children. They talked about tactics, the Iraqis and the possibility of future operations. It was an unexpected but very enjoyable evening. Finally, Ahmed said he must meet his officers for prayers, but before he would let them leave, he had something for them. When the colonel clapped his hands, the private brought two large packages, wrapped in brown paper and tied with twine. The *awwal* placed one in front of each of the Scouts. The colonel waited for the private to leave.

"Merry Christmas, *Naqeeb* Samuels. Merry Christmas, *Raqeeb* Grier." Quarry and Grier were absolutely stunned. "Please, open them." Momentarily overcome by surprise, Quarry and Grier tugged on the stings. On top of folded material was an *igaal* and brightly checkered red, woven *ghutar*. Under the headdress was a cotton *thoob*.

"*Aqeed* Ahmed," Quarry stumbled, "I don't know what to say. We are greatly honored. *Mashkuur 'ala karam iddiyaafa*." Thank you for your generosity.

Colonel Ahmed beamed.

"*Bil-hana wa sh-shifaa*." Glad you like it. Changing back to English, he continued: "When I was at Cornell, it was hard enough adjusting to a different culture, especially on the first Ramadan away from home. Having friends made it easier. Next time you come to visit, it would give me great pleasure if you wore your *thoob* and *ghutar*."

"*In shaa' Allah*," if God wills it, Quarry added. Since it was bad manners to refer to anything in the future that God won't allow, the phrase recognized that events occur only if God allows it happen.

"*Aywa. In shaa' Allah*." Ahmed corrected himself, pleasantly surprised his guest corrected his bad manners. "Now, if you don't mind, I must see to my staff and battalion commanders."

"*Fi amaan illah, ya aqeed* Ahmed," Quarry said, standing. Go in the protection of God.

"*Fi amaan ilkareem, ya naqeeb* Samuels," Go in the protection of the generous One, Ahmed replied as he exited the room smiling.

Both Scouts stood in silence a second before walking to their equipment. It had been a remarkable day.

Six

27 December 1990

"Contact!" Stone's voice came down the ladder. It was 2130 at O.P. Tower. In the Hummer below him, Cat jumped from the driver's seat into the turret to turn on the battery to the thermal sights. The clicking started, indicating the system was cooling down, but it would be precious minutes before the optics revealed anything. Marion half climbed, half flew up the ladder. There was a flurry of organized chaos. In less than two minutes, Marion, Stone, and a sleepy-eyed Saudi sergeant manned the tower. Davis warmed up his Hummer with Bots behind the 50-caliber machine gun. Marek moved Cat's Hummer south of the O.P., until the enemy was in sight. It was a quarter moon and only those with night vision knew what they faced.

At headquarters, Quarry came running to the Hummer and took the top handset from Slayer.

"1st Squad reports contact, sir. Time delay 20 seconds since first transmission, nothing heard since then."

"Thank you, Slayer," Quarry said, taking the microphone. Looking across from him, he saw Dole on the bottom radio getting radio checks with Stevens, who would in turn be asked to make radio checks with the attack helicopter brigade and the Army's multiple rocket-launcher company, should it be needed. Grier was in his Hummer, monitoring the platoon net and checking in with DASC.

A hundred meters away, Ogdon heard the contact report over the platoon net, readying Hummers and weapons. To the north, Caine upgraded his defensive posture to Readiness Condition One, to see if anything happed from another direction. Now came the hard part, waiting for additional information. Quarry fought back the temptation to ask for a report; Marion would transmit the situation report as soon as he was able. Another heart-pounding 37 seconds went by before the next transmission came in.

Marion looked through the night-vision goggles and raised the radio's microphone.

"Six, this is One, over."

"One, Six, send it," Quarry answered immediately.

"Observing three Iraqi infantry soldiers, approaching from west to east, on foot, south side of the berm, weapons slung over shoulders or carried at the side. Distance about a click out, they're walking straight up, and right towards us. Negative aggressive actions, no offensive posturing, nothing tactical at all, over."

Quarry thought a second before transmitting.

"Acknowledged. Report contact to north and south, over."

Marion looked to the cardinal directions.

"Initial contact negative. Stand by for additional, over."

"Roger, standing by. Break, Two, this is Six, report all contacts."

To the north, Caine looked 360 degrees around him.

"Six, this is Two, negative contact, over." Quarry wanted to ask if anything was moving around the oilfields but the report he received already told him there wasn't. Caine would have mentioned even the slightest movement.

The next transmission from Marion would be critical. Eventually, it came in: "Six, this is One, over."

"One, Six, over."

"Negative contact, north and south. No new contacts west, continuing to observe, over."

Quarry, still holding the handset to his ear, looked over at Dole.

"Roger, keep me advised, over, break. Three this is Six, over." As Quarry keyed the net calling for Ogdon, Dole gave Quarry a thumbs-up, indicating he was in radio contact with Stevens and his Berets.

"Six, this is Three, over," the platoon net squawked.

"Three this is Six, reinforce One, over."

"Six, this is Three, wilco, over."

"Three this is Six, out, break. Five, this is Six, over."

"Six, Five, go."

"Send what we got to higher, over."

"Six, Five, roger, out." In the logistics Hummer, Grier handed the DASC radio to Slayer and picked up the top radio to let Company know what was happening. While Quarry could have yelled over his shoulder to Grier, transmitting the request over the radio let the squads know they weren't in this alone.

To the west, Marion had a second P.R.C. radio brought up to the tower so he could monitor the squad and platoon nets simultaneously. With Stone on platoon, Marion started to choreograph the next set of moves. Within seconds, the plan was put into action. The three Iraqi soldiers were 900 meters away.

"Execute," Marion said into the squad radio. Along the berm, Davis floored the accelerator and let the Hummer build up speed. To the south, Cat was doing the same thing. Seconds later, the two Hummers came screaming out of the night toward three terrified soldiers from two different directions. With Bots behind the 50-cal and Marek supporting the squad automatic weapon from on top of the other Hummer, the Iraqi soldiers didn't have to hear "*Inta shajean*" (you are a prisoner) before dropping to the ground with their hands in the air. Thirty seconds later, the three were stripped of their weapons, duct taped, and in the back of Marek's Hummer.

"Six this is One, over."

Quarry wiped the sweat from his brow despite the 44-degree temperature. "Send it."

"Six, this is One. Secured three E.P.W.s. I say again, three E.P.W.s. No casualties, friendly or enemy. No rounds fired. Returning to O.P. Awaiting orders, over."

Quarry raised his arms over his head and let out a yell. Regaining his composure, he keyed the net.

"One this is Six. Great job! En route to your pos. Maintain separation between your host and your guests."

"Roger Six, over."

"Six, out." Quarry raised his arms and let out a war cry. Grier came from across the headquarters area. The two gave each other a high five. It took a few moments before it was back to business.

"There's no way we are going to be able to keep this one quiet, skipper."

"Yeah, you're right on that one, Five." Quarry thought a moment as he turned and picked up the handset to the platoon radio. "Colonel Ahmed will hear about this in the morning. If not sooner," Quarry added as an afterthought. "Let's do this." Leaning against the Hummer, Quarry gave his ideas another few moments before speaking.

"Make a run over to the colonel's tent. Tell him we had three Iraqi soldiers give themselves up. Our colonel wants them in the rear so we're going to take them back immediately but we will gladly share whatever information they reveal."

"On the way, skipper." Then, turning back towards his Hummer, "Crank it up Slayer," Grier called out.

"Dole, bottom radio. Tell Stevens what we have and thanks for being there if needed." Quarry got on the top radio and changed the freq.

"I Six, this is Scout Six, over." The radio watch took the call but it didn't take long to hear Lieutenant Colonel Dillion on the other end.

"Scout Six, this is I Six, over."

"I Six, this is Scout Six. Have three E.P.W.s. No casualties, over."

"Scout Six, this is I Six, wasn't expecting another Christmas present, over."

"I think he's pissed, skipper," Dole said under his breath.

"This is Scout Six. They came wassailing into camp, over."

There was a pause before the reply came back.

"Acknowledged, Scout Six. Didn't mean to imply Santa flew the sleigh again. Personally escort EPWs via ground to this pos. Have additional information for you. Good job, I Six out."

Quarry heard Grier's Hummer pulling out. "Pull the wires and back 'er up Dole. Let's go look into the face of the enemy."

The three guests were eating M.R.E.s when Quarry drove up. Ogdon kept the Iraqis under a watchful eye. As Quarry walked up, he introduced himself to the prisoners as a Marine captain and the commanding officer of the Scouts. From their sitting position on the ground, the three attempted to kiss Quarry's feet and hands. Revolted by such actions, Quarry merely backed up and told them to continue eating. The three again thanked all the Scouts and went back to their dinner eagerly.

"What ya got Mary?" Quarry said, walking around to the other side of the Hummer.

"I had our Saudi sergeant ask a few questions. It seems that their sergeant just up and disappeared a few days ago."

"You don't say," Quarry replied in a sarcastic tone.

"It gets better. Because none of them knew what channel to transmit on, they didn't get resupplied. They've gone two days without food, a day without water. Only when they were two days late calling in did anyone come to check up on them. When the new sergeant found out what happened, he started beating the shit out of just about everyone there. The new sergeant called it in and has assumed command of the O.P. These three got tired of the daily beating and decided to strike out on their own."

"Parent unit?"

"The 29th, sir."

"Any maps or log books?"

"Nothing but what they had on their backs. A few personal items in their pockets, nothing else. Oh, and skipper, no spare ammo magazines for their guns."

"Interesting. Good job Mary."

"Thank you, sir, but Marek and Bots pulled it off." Marion took a few minutes to describe the operation.

Quarry listened without comment. When the tale was told, he made a few mental notes and changed the subject.

"Ogie. Let me borrow the Three Two Hummer and two Scouts. The rest of 3rd will keep Mary company tonight. Keep an eye to the west. Let Caine know we won't rotate tonight. Grier will join you for the night. He is currently letting Colonel Ahmed know what's going on. I'm escorting our guests to the rear. Questions?"

48

"None, sir."

"Mary, have our Saudi sergeant tell our guests to make a head call. They're going on a little ride and I don't want to have to stop at every gas station along the way. After that, explain to them we're going to tape their hands together, but if they don't get squirrelly, nothing will happen to them."

"You got it, skipper," Marion said, turning to carry out his orders.

"Any idea what the colonel has planned for us, sir?" Ogdon asked as Marion turned the corner.

"Not a clue, Three."

28 December 1990

It was after midnight when the Scouts returned to friendly lines. They moved through checkpoints without complication. Many of the Marines were more interested at looking at the Iraqi soldiers than checking the papers of two lonely Hummers returning to Jubayl.

"I Six, this is Scout Six, over," Quarry transmitted. The Intel Company master sergeant answered. "We are an hour out, request instructions, over."

"Roger Scout Six. I Six hit the rack. You are to drop off your presents to me. Will meet you next to your old billeting when you arrive, over."

"This is Scout Six, roger out."

The remainder of the journey passed without incident. True to his word, the Top was waiting for the Scouts. On each side of him were two non-distinct Marines. On each side of them however, were two of the largest jarheads Quarry ever had ever seen. Dressed in full combat gear, flak jacket, helmet, and M-16s with bayonet attached, these two made even Marion look small. Quarry got out of his Hummer and approached the master sergeant.

"Hi, Top," Quarry said, shaking the hand of the Intel Company chief. "Who are your friends?"

"Two from Interrogations and Translation, two military police for visual effect. Take a guess on which ones are which." The master sergeant paused. "So where are your friends, sir?"

"In the back of the Three Two Hummer. Corporal Hauser tells me they slept the whole way. Even the checkpoints didn't rouse them." The two from IT made eye contact with each other but didn't say anything. "How do you want to play it?"

"Sir," the gunny from I.T. asked, "Can you give us a little more on how you got them and what's gone on since you took them into custody? I'd specifically like to know how they were treated and how they acted." Quarry gave them the story with emphasis on getting the soldiers food and water. The gunny made a few quick comments to the sergeant beside him, then turned to one of the monsters and gave a few additional instructions. When the gunny sensed all was ready, he turned to Quarry.

"Sir, we'll take it from here."

"All yours, gunny."

The two I.T. Marines approached the Three Two Hummer. Seconds later, Hauser and his driver, Lance Corporal Carleton, were standing by their platoon commander. Quietly, without undue speaking, two of the sleeping soldiers were woken and removed from the Hummer. The movement and voices woke all three but only two were escorted toward the main office; the third was ignored. As his anxiety increased, he started babbling, his voice increasing in volume and pitch as the seconds passed. The two M.P.s let the soldier get worked up, and when he attempted to exit the vehicle, they almost ripped the door off the hinges and extracted the now terrified soldier. Each Marine grabbed the soldier under an armpit and carried him off in the opposite direction than his comrades. The two Marines were so much larger than the Iraqi soldier, the Iraqi didn't even touch the ground as he was carried, screaming, into the night.

The Scouts stood there for a few moments in utter silence.

"What's going to happen to him?" Carleton asked.

"The technique is simple," the Top explained. "Since all three came in at the same time, IT has to make sure they get what's going on, not some made-up story. For all we know, these three could be planted with the mission to get caught and give us some disinformation. Of the two that went over to headquarters, one will be treated real well and then asked some questions. The more he talks the better and better he'll be treated. The second guy will be asked the same questions but won't be given any more perks than the food and water you guys gave him. The third guy, well, let's just say he's going to have a long night and leave it at that. The two gorillas in uniform over there started setting the stage by adding a certain level of uncertainty to his life.

"Sir," the Top continued, "your old rooms are still vacant. Go grab some shuteye. No one will wake you until tomorrow morning. Captain, you have a meeting with the colonel at 1300 tomorrow."

"Any clue as to what that might be, Top?"

"Not really, sir. I can say this though, a lot of people are real happy with what you've been doing up there. Even got a call from the G7 saying Colonel Ahmed thinks you're the greatest thing since toilet paper."

"Coming from an Arab, that's a compliment!"

"Other than that, sir, head to supply. They got a few things for ya."

"Roger that. Thanks, Top."

* * *

It was after 1000 when Quarry rolled out of the rack, and another 30 minutes before he got his butt out of a hot shower and changed into a clean uniform.

A trip to the washing machines took up the rest of the morning. Lunch was chilimac, but even that tasted good. Then a visit to the situation room filled in the rest of the time before he met the colonel. Dole went to Supply. The Scouts were to receive a new night-infiltration suit, a pattern of tiny white and green checks that claimed to make a Marine almost invisible on the desert sands.

The map on the walls of the briefing room hadn't changed much. The only difference was the red-dotted rectangle around the Al-Wafrah oilfields. The dots indicated an unknown size and composition of the enemy forces. Quarry smiled as he looked at a small black triangle, mere clicks to the south of it. To rear-echelon types, it was just another observation post; to Quarry, it was one third of his men. *Funny,* Quarry thought, *how simply life can be reduced to mere symbols.* Nonetheless, Quarry removed his series of maps and updated everyone, based on those symbols.

The door behind him opened and closed. Quarry finished what he was doing before he looked up and into the face of Lieutenant Colonel Dillion. Quarry almost wrenched his back out by standing up so fast. The rapid movement startled the colonel.

"My God, son, relax!"

"Sorry, sir, I was pretty engrossed on what I was doing."

"I could tell. Sit down, Captain." Quarry sat down in one of the plush briefing chairs facing the main map. Dillion sat on the edge of the table in front of Quarry. "Skipper, what we're going to talk about for the next few minutes is classified Secret. Even though your Scouts have clearance, it will still be treated on a need-to-know basis. Understood?"

"Perfectly, sir."

"As you know, the MEF has been postured defensively. We have reinforced the Saudis which gave us time to build up our offensive capability. On the 19th, CentCom started planning offensive operations." Quarry was feeling the rush. "The plan will consist of a breach of Iraqi defenses, a link-up with Marine amphibious forces and a push into Kuwait. Several high-level staff officers, however, adamantly oppose the plan because it pits the Marines against the heart of Iraqi defenses. The Naval Analyses Center has estimated Marine casualties at over 10,000." Quarry's initial rush sank to the pit of his stomach. "To reduce casualties, we will undoubtedly attempt a breach where the Iraqis are weakest. This is where you come in. We're going to take your little corner of the world and make it appear that this is where our main effort is going to be. Phase One: Neutralize the Iraqi outposts." The colonel used a laser pointer to indicate a number of outposts on the map. "Colonel Brodrick wanted a Force Recon Team to take this one out," Dillion said, using the laser pointer again on the map, "but I told him you were capable of handling the mission. You can handle it, can't you, Captain?"

A nonemotional "Yes sir" came from Quarry.

"Good. In Phase Two, we take Iraqi eyes off of friendly forces by conducting deception operations in the corner of Kuwait. This will focus Iraqi signal intelligence and any remaining ground reconnaissance away from where the actual breach will occur. During Phase Two, you will assist a number of other units, providing them security, escorts, et cetera. Phase Three provides assistance to the air campaign. Are you equipped with a MULE?"

"No sir," Quarry said, referring to the ground-mounted laser used to designate targets for laser-guided smart bombs.

"Do you have personnel qualified in its use if I get you one?"

"Yes, sir. Many of my Scouts are T.A.C.P. qualified. But don't we need a wing-wearing pilot on the ground to act as a forward air controller?"

"Not during war. Captain Samuels, I want you to plan for a number of contingencies," the colonel said, getting back on the original subject. "First, on order, neutralize the enemy outpost designated Enemy O.P. Three. Second, be prepared to conduct security and screening operations in support of friendly deception forces. Three, on order, conduct ground reconnaissance north of the berm. And four, on order, conduct ground operations in support of offensive air operations. Any questions?"

"Estimated time of execution of contingency operation one, sir?"

"Within the week."

"Rules of engagement for neutralization of E.O.P. Three, sir?"

"Taking of prisoners is secondary to the accomplishment of the mission."

"Understood, sir."

* * *

Grier sat on a stack of empty burlap potato sacks while Quarry drew pictures in the sand.

"You're the boss, skipper," Grier pointed out the obvious, "but I still say that plan puts you in the thick of things. I read somewhere once, that commanding officers and platoon sergeants supervise the entire battle. If the shit hits the fan, who's going to call for air, arty and the whole fucking U.S. cavalry?"

Quarry looked up from the diagram.

"Right again, as usual, Five." He played with the stick and retraced the circles and arrows. "O.K., how about this…"

It had been a long day, but the two continued working well past midnight.

Seven

30 December 1990

"Here we go again," Kantner said to no one in particular. He moved to the edge and called down to the bottom of the tower: "Corporal Marion. Contact!"

The P.O.W. drill, as it came to be known, was practiced two times a day, per squad, since their last encounter. After Quarry returned from headquarters, the leadership had conducted an intense, in-depth, after-action review on how the first event went down. The lessons learned were discussed and developed into a standard operating procedure. In less than 30 seconds, Marines manned posts. The few that were on "sleep plan" were now awake and in flak jackets and helmets. The TOW thermal sights were cooling and the first radio transmission went out.

Quarry was sitting on his makeshift rack, a medical stretcher propped up on some M.R.E. cases. In front of him were ten empty potato sacks; to the side were strips of burlap, torn two inches wide by 24 inches long. By the light of a gas lantern, Dole sat on the hood of the Hummer, weaving the burlap strips into cammie netting sewn onto the back of a pair of blouses and trousers.

"Six, this is One, contact, out." The headquarters group paused only for a split second as reaction became action. Dole tossed the cammies to the side and bolted for the radio. Quarry did the same on the passenger side of the Hummer. Grier and Slayer made a mad dash for their own Hummer.

From within the tower, Marion saw infrared shapes. Nothing moved to the north or south.

"Six, this is One, over."

At the platoon headquarters, all was ready. Thumbs up from everyone indicated they were prepared for the worst.

"This is Six, send it."

"Observing three soldiers, approaching from west to east, on foot, weapons slung over shoulders, no offensive or tactical movement, continuing to observe, P.O.W. drill in effect, over."

"Six, this is Two, negative contact, out."

"Six, this is Three, Oscar Mike in three, out." Quarry turned off the radio for a second while Dole started up the vehicle. With the radio back on, Quarry contacted Company as Dole pulled out of their hole.

Botsford was in the TOW Hummer using thermals to track the contact. A squad automatic weapon sat on top of the roof within easy reach. Cat covered the target with the 50-cal and night-vision goggles. Marion watched the three soldiers from the tower, one hand on the squad radio handset, the other on a rifle. Davis and Stone waited for their guests to arrive, in a fighting hole 50 meters to the west of the tower.

In the darkness, the three Iraqis walked toward the tower, making no attempt to hide themselves. With hands in the air, they were softly calling out greetings and prayers. Only when they were ten feet in front of the fighting position did Stone call out in Arabic. The three were so startled they didn't immediately comply with the order. Fingers started taking the slack out of triggers. When the adrenaline wore off, the three soldiers dropped to their knees. A few more orders and the three were sprawled out, face down in the dirt. With "secure" coming over the squad radio, Marek, Cat and Bots pulled up in the Hummers. Within seconds, they were at Davis and Stone's side. Seconds after that, three Iraqi soldiers were duct taped, searched, and transported. Marion changed handsets.

"Roger," Quarry said, acknowledging Marion's entire report. Changing handsets, he informed Company of the situation and asked for instructions.

Fifteen minutes later, the master sergeant came back on the radio. "Set Lima Zulu, from, Alpha four niner, south three point seven, break, east four point two, break. India Six inbound, break. Will take your packages, E.T.A. 20 mikes, over."

Quarry wrote down the coordinates but Dole one-upped him. After shifting from a known point on the map designated by a cross hairs and A49 in the upper corner, Dole already had his finger pointing to where the Top wanted the landing zone.

"Echo Eight Hotel, this is Scout Six, hard copy, out."

"Guess the boss wants to see how we live," Quarry commented.

"Guess so, sir," Dole replied, removing his hand from the map. The location Dole pointed to was right behind the platoon headquarters.

At 2200, the U.H.1 set down. But instead of idling, the pilot shut down the engines completely. Quarry looked over at Marion who shrugged.

"He's a lieutenant colonel, he can do what he wants to." *No arguing that,* Quarry thought. Turning back to the helo, he watched Lietenant Colonel Dillion exit the side door.

"Welcome to our part of the world," Quarry said as the colonel cleared the rotor blades. A moment later, the gunny from I.T. climbed out of the helo as well. "He looks a little pale, sir," Quarry said to Colonel Dillion as the gunny approached the Hummer. "Does he get air sick or is this his first time to the front?"

Dillion gave only the smallest semblance of a smile.

"We all have our jobs to do, Captain Samuels," the colonel replied. The problem with Colonel Dillion was Quarry couldn't read him. "I thought he was going to throw up when I called for him to come along," Dillion added with a gleam in his eyes. Quarry lightened up, realizing he hadn't screwed the pooch with that last comment.

"Sir, you remember Corporal Marion," Quarry said, as a way of introduction.

"Of course," Dillion said, shaking Marion's hand.

"It was Corporal Marion at our O.P. both times the E.P.O.W.s were taken, sir. I had him personally bring them down tonight in case you had any questions for him."

"None whatsoever. The gunny from I.T. will probably have a few though. Turn your prisoners over to him, Corporal."

"Yes, sir."

The helo engine was completely off now, but the rotors were still turning. Grier was talking to the pilot.

"Got time to show me around your command, skipper?" Being of sound mind and body, Quarry knew damn well that wasn't a request.

"Right this way, sir." Grier looked over from the helo. "We're going to tour the area, Five. Meet ya back at the C.P. when we finish."

"Roger that, sir." Grier excused himself from talking to the pilots and walked over to the logistics Hummer.

"Fire it up, Staff Sergeant?" Slayer asked as Grier approached.

"Not yet. Drop down to the individual squad nets. Let them know I Six is on the way. Do not, under any circumstances, use the platoon net."

Slayer leaned over and hit 1st Squad's preset button.

"I get it, Staff Sergeant."

Dole headed to O.P. Tower first.

"I'll show you where all the activity comes from, sir," Quarry told the colonel.

"Sounds fine," Dillion replied nonchalantly. "Have you given any thought to the topics we discussed the last time we were together, skipper?"

"A great deal of thought, sir."

"Good, I look forward to hearing your ideas."

There were three Hummers at O.P. Tower when they arrived. Stone and Kantner were in the One Two 50-cal Hummer on the north side of the tower covering from north to west. Ferrado and Carleton were in the Three Two 50-cal Hummer, covering from south to west. Laumeyer and Tellado were in the Three One Hummer, scanning due west with thermals. Quarry caught Dole's eyes as they exited the vehicle, but neither showed any sign of emotion. A few of the Scouts were at the bottom of the steps, as if on guard duty. Quarry greeted them all and showed Colonel Dillion to the base of the ladder.

When Quarry cleared the ladder, the tower looked as if it were a DDay bunker. Sandbags sat in the openings of the glassless windows. Radios were behind sandbags as well. A map showing enemy locations hung from a wall. A solid black line labeled "Kansas" was drawn around the enemy O.P.

"Good evening, Colonel," Ogdon said dryly. Then, not waiting for a response, he turned toward Quarry. "Sir, no additional contact since Corporal Marion left. Patrols show no movement out to our limit of advance. Permission to decrease to readiness condition three."

"Granted. Sir, Sergeant Ogdon, 3rd Squad Leader and Lance Corporal Marek, team leader for Two Two."

"Good to see you again Marines. Why Kansas, Sergeant Ogdon?"

"Our limit of advance is based on the arc of observation from the enemy's perspective, sir. Like the song, it's our point of no return."

"Clever, I like it." The two officers looked around a little while. The highlight was the colonel getting to see the four Saudi soldiers fast asleep in their racks. "Guess all the excitement wore them out," Dillion said.

"Yes sir," Quarry said facetiously.

The meeting at O.P. Berm was much less formal. The colonel greeted 2nd Squad and asked the typical commanding officer types of questions: getting enough to eat, mail coming regularly, any comments, gripes or complaints? There were none. Caine commented that the Iraqis weren't accommodating enough; Marion seemed to be having all the fun. The colonel ensured them they would have their share before it was over.

The third stop was the platoon C.P. Dole stopped short of pulling into their hole and left the Hummer running.

"I'll stay here and monitor the radios while you show the colonel around, sir."

"Thank you, Dole, we won't be long." The two officers got out. Quarry showed the colonel their operation.

"Not much to look at, sir, but we call it home," Quarry said, offering the colonel a chair made out of M.R.E. cases. The colonel sat behind the desk and looked around the area. Quarry caught his eyes as they landed on three Ghillie suits and a partially completed suit still lying on the ground.

The colonel shifted his eyes from the suits to Quarry and then to the map on the bunker wall. Of particular interest was the dotted red rectangle in the Al-Wafrah oilfields.

"How soon would you feel comfortable executing Plan One?"

Quarry thought for a moment, the mood turned deadly serious.

"I'd like to get a quick brief on what our latest E.P.O.W.s have to say, sir. If it's as simple as they're hungry and tired of being beaten, we can run our op in 24 hours. That way, the Iraqi gungho sergeant will be exhausted from beating the shit out of those remaining and any reinforcements wouldn't have arrived yet."

"Give me your concept of the operation." The colonel sat in silence while Quarry outlined what he and Grier had come up with. When Quarry finished the basic plan, the colonel rose up from the chair. "Let's go see what our new prisoners have to say."

The helo was only a couple hundred meters south of the C.P. The I.T. gunny had the three soldiers sitting at different points around the aircraft. Grier, Slayer, and the helo crew chief each kept one company. Upon pulling up, the gunny left his charges and approached the colonel. Quarry eased up to his side to listen. After the gunny finished, the colonel contemplated the new information, "I will expect to hear from you soon, Captain Samuels."

"Yes, sir."

31 December 1990

At 2200, the moon was extremely bright. Quarry and Grier walked into the open desert. At 500 meters out, Quarry keyed the net.

"Delta, this is Six, start now." Dole started walking back and forth while Slayer stayed in place. From where they were, Quarry and Grier saw the movement plainly. "O.K., put 'em on." Both Dole and Slayer put on their infiltration suits and repeated the drill. For all practical purposes, they were invisible. "We're a go," Quarry commented.

1 January 1991

The final rehearsal had occurred at 2000. Everything went like clockwork. By 2130, the moon was already up, shining down with its three-quarter-full brilliance.

"Get 'em together, Five."

"Yes, sir."

Grier didn't have to go far. All the Hummers were in their dug-in C.P. positions. In minutes, everyone assembled. Some were already in desert face paint; others had the groggy look of sleep. Quarry and Dole climbed up and out of the command bunker in their Ghillie suits. Cradled over his left arm, Quarry carried his M-40 as if going hunting, which was exactly what he was about to do. As he approached his platoon, all became quiet.

"It's about that time, guys," Quarry paused. "Does anybody have any final questions or anything to say?" No one said a word. "If nobody has any objections, I'd like to read a few verses from the Bible." No one objected; most favored the idea.

"Psalm 18, verses 32–39." Most of the Scouts took a knee; all took off their helmets or boonie caps. "It is God who arms me with strength, and makes my way perfect. He makes my feet like the feet of deer, and sets me on my high place. He teaches my hands to make war, so that my arms can bend a bow of bronze. You have also given me a shield of Your salvation. Your right hand has held me up. Your gentleness has made me great. You enlarge the path under me, so my feet did not slip. I have pursued my enemies and overtaken them. Neither did I turn back again till they were destroyed. I have wounded them; so that they were not able to rise; they have fallen under my feet. For You have armed me with strength for battle." There was a chorus of "amens" around the platoon.

* * *

"There it is, skipper," Corporal Marion said, indicating a hole in the berm. "A Saudi corporal brought a backhoe up this afternoon. It took him about an hour but he said Colonel Ahmed personally told him to do whatever we asked. Guess those dinners with the Saudi brass are paying off."

"Trust in Allah, Mary, but tie up your camel."

"You worry me sometimes, skipper." Quarry and Marion shook hands. Botsford exchanged a few final insults with Davis. Moments later, the blacked-out One One TOW Hummer crossed into enemy territory. "Good luck, boss," Marion said into the night.

It took less than thirty minutes to reach the pipeline intersection.

"Negative contact, sir," Botsford reported for the hundredth time. Quarry passed the two hand mics up. Quarry strapped the P.R.C.-104 radio to his back, and Dole helped adjust the Ghillie suit over it. Quarry returned the favor with Dole's P.R.C.-77. Quarry and Dole checked each other's equipment a final time.

"No napping, Bots."

"That's not funny, sir."

"See ya in the morning." Quarry and Dole slipped under and moved 100 yards away from the pipe. The moon was so bright Quarry didn't need the illuminated dials to read the compass heading. Quarry then looked up into the night sky. "That's our heading, Dole, the left star in Draco's head."

"I don't know which one that is, sir," Dole said, looking at the evening's kaleidoscope.

Quarry started walking as if he were on a nature trail at the planetarium.

"See the two end stars of the Little Dipper?" he said, pointing upwards. "Now follow them to the left. The first star you see is in the middle of Draco's body. Go past that to the four bright ones. That's Draco's head. See 'em?"

"Sir? Aren't you the least bit scared?"

"Terrified. Now, as you look past Draco's head, you run into Hercules' body ..." Quarry continued as the two Scouts walked into the open desert.

Five kilometers out, Quarry and Dole started walking at a crouch. Grier pulled Marion and the security group out of the C.P. Ogdon packed two squads into two Hummers.

At 1,500 meters out, Quarry and Dole were on hands and knees. The security group was located outside phase line Kansas. Ogdon was putting the assault group through one more rehearsal at O.P. Tower.

The last 600 meters they went in on their bellies.

"This is Six, set, negative contact, continuing to observe, out."

"Six, this is Five, acknowledged."

"Assault group, mount up," Sergeant Ogdon ordered as he snapped the chinstrap to his helmet.

"Shit!" Dole let out a barely audible whisper as a light flared inside the tower. They watched as an Iraqi soldier shook a match that lit a gas lantern.

"Scouts, this is Six, contact, one Iraqi soldier in the tower, over."

"Six, this is Five, roger. He's lit up like a Christmas tree in thermals, over."

"Six, this is Three, we have the tower in visual, continuing to observe, over."

Quarry looked at his watch: 0210.

"Let's have a closer look," he said as he started crawling forward again. From the light of the lamp, Quarry and Dole watched the Iraqi soldier bend down out of sight and then stand back up with a blanket. Wrapping the blanket around him, the soldier sat down in an unseen chair with his back against the west wall. Quarry stopped his forward movement and grabbed the mic.

"This is Six, moving in, out." Quarry placed the mic back in the netting of his Ghillie suit. "That will work to our advantage," he whispered to Dole. "No one awake in the camp will have any natural night vision left." The two continued to crawl toward the light.

"Range," Quarry asked as they settled into their new position.

"Three hundred to the closest B.M.P., 320 to the tower," Dole barely whispered from behind the N.V.G.s.

"Concur." Quarry looked at his watch again: 0247.

"This is Six," Quarry whispered into the mic. "Significantly closer than planned. No new contacts, no observed movement. All teams, Charlie Mike, over." The security team acknowledged Quarry's transmission verbally, the assault team by a break in squelch. Quarry built up a small mound of sand in front of him and laid his left elbow on top of it. Gently, almost reverently, Quarry placed the M-40 in the crook of his elbow and sighted on the tower. He wiggled his elbow back and forth until the cross hairs of the reticle settled into place. A few minor movements and the cross hairs raised and fell over the height of the soldier with each breath Quarry took.

"Grab the mic." Dole slowly moved closer to his platoon commander and took the handset off Quarry's Ghillie suit and placed it between them. "Time hack?"

"0252."

"Give it to me by twos."

"0254," Dole reported, when his digital watch lapsed.

"0256."

"0258."

* * *

Laumeyer and Ferrado lay on top of the enemy B.M.P.s next to the open commander hatches. The moon to the north gave them enough light to coordinate their movements by. The light of the tower to the south, striking the commander's cupola, gave them enough shadow to live by. By the closed rear hatch of the first B.M.P., Hauser waited on the north side, his M-16 shouldered. Carleton crouched in front of him, pistol drawn. Twenty-four feet away, Ogdon and Tellado were stacked alongside the north side of the second B.M.P., M-16s shouldered, held in a low ready position. All members of 3rd Squad wore ear plugs.

On the south side of the berm, Two One and Two Two were arrayed in depth. Hiding in what shadows or folds in the earth they could find, each member of Two Two was in a prone firing position, sighting in on sleeping soldiers. Two One crouched behind them, ready to move.

Ogdon took his hand off the pistol grip of his M-16 and held it out, palm down, parallel to the ground. Above him, Laumeyer and Ferrado released the spoons of their grenades, tossed them into the fighting vehicles and rolled off the side. The night shook as the concussion grenades went off inside the B.M.P.s. 3rd squad button-hooked around the ends of the vehicles. Carleton yanked the hatch lever and flung open the door to the back of the first B.M.P. After the second explosion, the Scouts started shouting, "*Anta aseer.*"

It was dark inside the second B.M.P., but the shape of someone lying on the floor in a blanket was unmistakable. The distinctive outline of an A.K.47 lay on the bench, inches from a reaching hand. Ogdon put a three-round burst into the mound of blankets.

The soldier in the tower sprang from his chair. Where his head had been, within Quarry's scope, was now the soldier's chest. He placed pressure on the trigger as the cross hairs settled center mass. Somewhere between the blast of a .308 going off and the jerk of recoil, Quarry's elbow came off of the mound of sand. As he worked the bolt and settled the cross hairs back on the tower, nothing was in view.

Inside the B.M.P.s, movement under the blankets was frantic. One soldier rolled to his left with his rifle under him in an attempt to rise to his knees. The first round hit under his sternum while the second and third rounds crept up toward his throat. Speckman switched to a secondary target.

Caine led 2nd Squad toward the tower. Two Two secured the base. Two One reoriented their attack upward, not knowing if a threat remained in the tower above them.

There was movement in the back of the second B.M.P. Ogdon started to bring the muzzle of his rifle up to address the new threat as a single round went off to his right. The body of an Iraqi soldier slumped forward and fell to the bottom of the B.M.P. Tellado searched for a new target. Mathews watched over the front sight post of his rifle as a soldier curled into a ball and started jabbering. He shifted targets. Hauser and Carleton grabbed the arms of the first soldier and threw him on the ground. Even though they were yelling in Arabic, the soldier wouldn't have been able to hear them as blood oozed from his ears.

A second soldier was in the tower, standing between the lamp and Quarry's field of view; all Quarry saw was a black silhouette against a white background. The rifle spoke, the body dropped. Under the tower, at the base of the ladder, Throop and Surkein exchanged a quick glance.

Most of the enemy soldiers were on their knees with hands in the air, or sprawled face down in the sand. No one checked, but the time was 0300 and 17 seconds.

Ogdon could not discern any additional movement inside the B.M.P., but continued to cover it with his M-16 until help arrived for a detailed search. Hauser covered a soldier as Carleton searched him. Two One applied flex cuffs to some, as Two Two guarded soldiers sprawled on the ground. To the south, Grier and the security group were quickly closing the distance. Quarry kept his sights on the tower. As the Scouts secured the area, a three-round burst disturbed the night. Prisoners dove to the ground as Throop placed one more burst into the now nonmoving form. Rushing forward from where

Orsini had his back to a different soldier, Throop lifted a blanket with the barrel of his M-16. A dead Iraqi hand clutched the pistol grip of an A.K.47.

"Semper Fi, Bro." Orsini went back to searching and cuffing a prisoner.

After a detailed check of the driver's compartment, Ferrado yelled, "Clear." Ogdon, covered by Mathews, declared the second B.M.P. clear as well. Most of the soldiers were secured in the middle of the camp. Caine and Guy turned to the tower.

"Six, this is Two, over."

Dole picked up the handset as Quarry remained focused on the tower with the scope. "Two, this is Six Delta, you're clear to ascend, weapons are tight, over."

Caine and Guy opted for pistols.

"*Anta aseer*," Caine yelled into the platform but there was no answer. A quick climb and peek revealed two figures slumped on the floor. Caine covered the bodies as Guy squeezed by him on the ladder. Moments later, Caine leaned over the railing.

"Clear."

Ogdon made a visual inspection of the area and called for a radio. Tellado came running and handed Ogdon the mic from the P.R.C. strapped to his back.

"Six, this is Three, over."

"This is Six Delta, over."

"All secure, over."

Dole looked at Quarry who nodded his head. Dole took a red-lensed flashlight from his suit and flashed it three times in the direction of the camp.

"Got 'em," Tellado said, pointing into the desert. "Red flashes bearing zero six zero."

"Observed red flashes," Ogdon transmitted.

"Roger, identified." Quarry and Dole slowly rose to their knees and then stood up.

"Six, this is Three, have you visual. Come on in. Initial report: six E.K.I.A.s, two E.W.I.A.s, three additional E.P.W.s. Objective secure, no friendly casualties, over."

Quarry stopped walking, leaned his head back and looked up at the constellations.

"Thank you." He took a deep breath and exhaled loudly.

"This is Five, will send sitrep and medevac request to I Six, over."

Quarry nodded to Dole.

"This is Six Delta, roger." The Scouts remained at RedCon One for another hour, waiting for a counter-attack or an inquisitive patrol that never materialized. Observing from above, Spud told Quarry over the P.R.C.-109 there wasn't any movement anywhere on the far horizon.

When he arrived, Spud handed Quarry a sealed envelope and Grier a bag of mail. The Huey took the two wounded and the three P.O.W.s. Ogdon formed a work detail and took a Hummer to bury the remaining six.

Quarry climbed into the front seat of the One One Hummer. Bots looked down from the turret.

"I'm still awake, sir." Quarry looked up and smiled. Then he opened the envelope and read its contents. After a second reading, he folded it in half and placed it in the left breast pocket. He leaned his head back against the seat and closed his eyes.

Evening, 2 January 1991

"Praise Allah for your safety," Colonel Ahmed said for the tenth time during dinner. "Tell me again about your 500-meter shot."

Quarry looked over at Grier and smiled.

"It was only 320, sir. A stationary target, against a lit background. It's no big deal. All of it was all made possible because of your generosity of the use of your equipment, Colonel." Quarry popped another rice and lamb ball in his mouth.

"You are too kind, Captain." Ahmed turned and retrieved the trophy the Scouts had brought him. "Tomorrow morning we will go out to the berm and fire my new rifle." The A.K.47 was hardly new. The stock was pitted, the barrel rusty and the upper receiver needed bluing. But it worked, and for what it was designed for, worked damn well. "Tell me again how your brave sergeant battled an Iraqi squad of soldiers in a firefight to the death to retrieve my gift."

It was Sergeant Ogdon's turn to smile.

"Sir, you know it didn't happen like that."

"Ahhhh. Assuredly it did and my American guests are being too humble. Tomorrow, I will gather my entire staff, and we will fire my new rifle." Colonel Ahmed gestured and the steward came running with more coffee.

* * *

The Scout leadership enjoyed the colonel's hospitality well into the night.

"Would the colonel give us the honor of inspecting the observation posts tomorrow?"

You would have thought Quarry had offered him a week's vacation to Bahrain.

"I would be honored."

"The honor will be mine and the Scouts', sir. With the colonel's permission, I will send my driver over in the morning after prayers. He will be at your disposal."

"Allah has blessed me with such a friend and ally." The Scouts and the colonel said their final formal farewells and the Scout leadership packed into the command Hummer.

When they were a safe distance away, the topic was breached.

"I swear, skipper," Sergeant Caine started out, "you're Ali Baba reincarnated."

Eight

3 January 1991

"So the idea is that if we have the colonel over at a time of our choosing, he won't stumble over when he wants to?" Hauser asked.

"That's right," Ogdon said, then briefed his squad. "Captain Samuels and Staff Sergeant Grier will remain at his C.P. so we can continue to run over to the Saudis for food and fuel. Sergeant Caine is at O.P. Berm. 1st is at O.P. Tower, and we'll be here at O.P. Three for the next two days. The rotation will take us to the C.P. by teams for resupply before we occupy Berm. Now, if there are no other questions," Ogdon said, indicating there weren't.

* * *

It was after noon when the command Hummer was sighted. Laumeyer and Tellado manned the tower; all others were at its base. When the Hummer came to a stop, Colonel Ahmed and his executive officer exited. Quarry was right on their heels.

"Squad, attennn-tion." The Scouts popped to attention. Sergeant Ogdon faced the Saudi officers.

"*Sabaah al-khayr, ya aqeed* Ahmed," he greeted the inspecting officer.

"*Sabaah an-noor, ya raqeeb* Ogdon," Colonel Ahmed replied, beaming. Quarry stepped forward and introduced each member of the squad to the two officers.

For the next hour, the colonels asked each squad member about their part in the attack and had them walk through it. The two B.M.P.s had been cleaned up, moved to the south side of the berm, oriented north and integrated into the squad defensive fire plan. Quarry walked the Saudi officers through the vehicle, pointing out intricacies in the fire control and weapon systems.

"As you see here, sir," Quarry pointed out to Colonel Ahmed, "the ready ammo for the 73mm is clipped around the inside of the turret. The turret itself is a single sheet of steel. If you aim for the turret, you can get a sympathetic detonation of the ready ammo. My guess is you could probably penetrate the turret with a 7.62 if you could get a 90-degree angle." The two officers started speaking to each other at a rate Quarry couldn't pull a single word out of.

After a minute, the Saudis switched back to English for the benefit of their host.

"This is very interesting. Thank you for bringing it to our attention, *Akh* Samuels," the executive officer said.

Quarry smiled at the compliment of being called brother.

"Well gentlemen," he said, waving Carleton over, "shall we go for a ride?" The two officers looked at each other in confusion as Carleton climbed up and into the driver's seat. Quarry passed out the leather-and-cloth helmets. "We won't be patched in over an intercom, but it's really not that bad," he yelled over the starting engine.

Carleton took them on a 15-minute ride. Both officers drove the vehicle and played with the firing control system of the cannon and the missile launcher. At the return of the outing, Quarry nonchalantly mentioned they would have made it longer, but they were running low on fuel. The comment immediately received the desired response: an invitation to bring the B.M.P. over and fill it up. In return for "such a generous offer," Quarry counter-offered to take the vehicle around to the different units and allow the colonel's troops to learn about their adversaries' equipment. Colonel Ahmed was beside himself.

On the return trip, the colonel rattled on. He was quick to point out that Quarry and Grier were neglecting their language training and insisted they come by more often. Quarry ensured the colonel he would. By the time the command Hummer dropped off the Saudi officers, Quarry pointed out it would soon be time for afternoon prayers and he couldn't delay the colonel from further responsibilities. Traditional greetings were exchanged and Dole turned the Hummer westward. As they pulled out, Dole broke the silence.

"You've got something up your sleeve on this one, sir." It was a comment, not a question.

"That I do, Delta," Quarry answered. "That I do."

4 January 1991

The responsibility for the dog and pony show fell upon O.P. Tower. Quarry and Grier figured that if their flanks were secure, fewer eyes were required in the middle. Plus, if the Saudi soldiers stayed awake, they'd augment the remaining Scouts in the tower. Grier and Slayer also went over to help. This allowed 1st Squad to take the duty the first day. Starting with the furthest west unit, very detailed and specific coordination was made prior to bringing the Soviet equipment anywhere near the Saudi line of sight. Each Saudi company got a capability and limitation briefing and then was allowed to climb in and around the vehicles. By the end of the day, Marion had presented the equipment to well over half of the brigade. That night, Marion, Bots, Marek and Stone camped out in the B.M.P. in the middle of the Saudi battle position. Soldiers from every company came to visit and to get to know their American *Akhes*. Quarry and Colonel Ahmed visited after evening prayers, to be seen together as a show of unity.

The next day was more of the same. Marion finished the demonstrations by midafternoon. The highlight of the day occurred in the middle of the brigade area with a live-fire demonstration. The Scouts had easily figured out the fire-control system. Having tested and dry-fired the weapons several times in the last few days they were pretty sure they knew what they were doing. What better way to test their theories then to fire the weapons in front of the very people who would ask the most questions?

The two B.M.P.s were placed in the center of the brigade area. Two plywood targets were set up at 300 and 500 meters in the direction of the berm. The brigade officers made a semi-circle around the two B.M.P.s, followed by N.C.O.s and some of the troops.

"Let's hope this works." Quarry patted Marion on the back.

"Oh ye of little faith."

Quarry climbed out of the back of the vehicle. Looking to the east and west, Bots and Stone gave the thumbs-up, indicating the range was clear.

"Sir, with your permission, we will now attempt to fire the machine guns." Colonel Ahmed gave his permission, and Quarry nodded to Marion. The 7.62mm rounds burst from the coaxially mounted machine gun. Firing only ten rounds to conserve ammo, Marion nodded to Marek. Marek's gun then sprang into life. A hail of shouts came from the spectators. Quarry didn't quiet the crowd, as it gave Marion and Marek time to adjust the zero of their weapons.

"Next we'll try the 73mm cannon, sir." Hearing the cue, Marion opened the breach and loaded a high-explosive round in the chamber.

Dropping down to the gunner's position, Marion yelled out the turret as best he could, "Fire in the hole." Sighting in on the nearest target, he pulled the trigger. The 73 fired and splinters flew from the plywood. Again, cheers went up among the crowd. Another nod and Marek repeated the procedure with the same results.

When the yells of the crowd died, Quarry played ringmaster one more time.

"Sir, for the last demonstration we will attempt an A.T.3 Sagger antitank missile. We have no idea how the ammunition has been stored or treated so I hope we don't disappoint you and your men."

"It is Allah's will, *ya akh naqeeb* Samuels. You can not disappoint us, please continue."

Smiling again at the honor of being called brother, but this time in front of the colonel's command, Quarry turned and gave the signal to Marion. On a rail mounted atop the 73mm gun, Marion slid the missile into place. Next, the firing wires were connected at the top of the mount. Marion then dropped down into the turret and turned a switch on the fire-control panel from Gun to Missile. He climbed into the gunner's position.

"Fire in the hole," Marion yelled. Marek had also dropped out of sight. Seconds later, the missile accelerated down the rail with a loud roar and a huge cloud of gray smoke. Nine seconds after that, the plywood target was demolished. This time, the crowd's reaction was mixed. Some were stunned by the destructive power of the missile, some cheered. When the crowd realized its own mixed emotions, all fell quiet.

"As you know, sir," Quarry said breaking the silence, "the A.T.3 is very simple but also very lethal." He paused for translation. "Each B.M.P. carries four missiles. They are fired by a manual command to line-of-sight guidance system. This means the gunner must track both the missile and target. Once fired, it takes the gunner about 500 meters to acquire the missile before he can guide it. The missile itself is capable of engaging targets out to 3,000 meters. If it hits, it can penetrate up to 400mm of steel." Quarry paused again while the translations were completed.

"It doesn't mean that it's invincible," Quarry added. "Gunners," he paused and looked around at the soldiers, "you just saw the large smoke cloud this missile produces. If you see a smoke cloud, fire whatever you have in the tube at the base of the signature and then reengage with a high explosive. It will take this missile 25 seconds to travel 3,000 meters. If you can make the enemy gunner look away from his sights, he will lose line-of-sight with the missile. Tank commanders, hit your smoke grenades, drivers turn on your smoke generators and back up quickly. They can't hit what they can't see and they can't shoot the missile while moving."

Quarry waited to see what kind of response he would get. The troops were quietly talking among themselves, as were the officers.

Colonel Ahmed walked forward, joined Quarry behind the first B.M.P. and addressed his command in Arabic.

"*ya akh naqeeb* Samuels has taught us a very valuable lesson. Tomorrow we will practice the tactics that he has taught us. Tonight, go back to your tanks and discuss what you have seen here. Dismissed." Ahmed turned to Quarry and many of the colonel's senior officers joined them. "Tonight, you will eat with my officers and me. But for now, my officers and I will talk further on how to defeat the threat we face." The colonel spouted something in Arabic to fast too pick up on. "I will see you in my tent, my friends."

"Thank you, sir. The colonel is very generous. I will also see to my men first." Quarry had never seen the colonel like this before. He stayed in place as Colonel Ahmed rattled something else off and the entire staff fell in about him as they moved toward the operations tent.

Marion climbed out of the back of the B.M.P.

"Think we rattled his cage, skipper?"

"I think we gave him his first dose of reality," Marek said, joining them.

"Crap! I wanted to get that second missile tested," Quarry said under his breath and to no one in particular. Saudi N.C.O.s came up and shook Marion's and Marek's hands, patted them on the back and some kissed their cheeks. Quarry ordered Marion to fill up both B.M.P.s with diesel.

"And ask around; see what you can find out. Get Grier on the horn and have him get over here. Have your Scouts meet me at the colonel's tent during evening prayers."

"During, sir? Something's up. You got that look about you."

"Yep."

* * *

It was an absolute feast; lamb, vegetables, potatoes, a variety of breads. The meal was the best Quarry had eaten since leaving the States. The mood, however, was somber. Colonel Ahmed was not his usual self; his staff was quiet. There was little conversation. Finally, even though he knew it was impolite to discuss business over dinner, Quarry literally couldn't take it any longer.

"*Ya aqeed* Ahmed, please forgive my rudeness, but the air is heavy, and I feel that I am the cause."

Colonel Ahmed wiped his hands and sipped his coffee before answering.

"*Ya akh naqeeb* Samuels. Allah himself has sent you to us. Therefore, you cannot be a source of unpleasantness. We will speak of this no more."

"*Aywa, ya akh aqeed.*" Quarry looked around the room. Ahmed's staff looked like spanked puppies after wetting the floor. Evening prayers couldn't come fast enough.

* * *

They walked into the open desert. They were 200 meters from the colonel's C.P. but still Quarry strolled further south. Eventually, he stopped. The Scouts gathered around him.

"The word from the *raqeebs* and *areefs* is we can do no wrong," Marek started. "We have taken the time to learn their language, we honor their customs and most importantly, we sure as hell know what we're talking about.

69

Then to top it all off, we come riding into camp in captured Iraqi equipment. That little demo we put on, and you quoting Soviet field manuals? Not bad for infidels."

Quarry thought it over.

"We may have made the colonel lose face. We'll get a few things we need from Supply and lay low for a while. Five, get what we need."

"Aye, aye, sir."

"Now, to the reason I wanted to meet with all of you tonight." Quarry took out an envelope and opened it. "We're going to go on a little road trip," he said, handing I Six's orders to Grier.

Grier examined the orders and then went back to one particular task.

"Determine the size, strength and exact location of enemy forces in the oil refinery area of operations," Grier read to the others.

"And we're going to use the B.M.P.s," Dole thought out loud.

"And the demonstrations were weapons checks," Marek added.

Quarry drew some lines in the sand.

"Here's my idea ..."

Nine

6 January 1991

The combat checks were complete.

"I still don't like it, boss," Grier said as he handed out the black berets and olive drab tops. "I think they call this spying. And ya know, last time I checked, they hang spies in times of war."

"Ahh, Five, who would think twice about helping a lost brother in the big open desert? Besides, to hang us, they have to catch us first," Quarry retorted, trying on one of the black berets with the gold embroidered eagle, wreath and tank emblem. Grier wasn't buying it, so he continued. "No one is going to leave the comfort of their fighting hole to help us little lost Iraqi soldiers with directions. You know damn well there is never a patrol around when you need one."

"I still don't like it," Grier said, handing over the two laser range-finders and G.P.S.s.

"What you don't like, is not being asked to come along."

"Well, that too."

"We're ready, skipper." Marion joined in the conversation. "All gauges in the green, fuel tanks full, comm checks on all frequencies completed."

"See ya in a couple days, Five."

"Watch your ass, Six."

The B.M.P.s pulled out of the Saudi C.P. and traveled due west. At an unidentifiable point in the open desert, the G.P.S. indicated a right turn was in order.

"Waypoint One," Dole called down to the driver. Davis made a 90-degree turn and the lead B.M.P. was on the second leg of its journey.

"Two this is One, in-bound, over."

"Sergeant Caine. Got first squad in thermals," Guy said with the TOW sights turned 180 degrees from where they usually scanned.

71

"Hope this is the only time we see two B.M.P.s approaching from the rear."

"I hear that, Sergeant!"

Three minutes later, from the vehicle commander's position, Marion saw the Hummers outlined against the berm. A few minutes after that, Caine climbed atop the B.M.P.

"Glad ya gave us a call, One," Caine said, shaking Marion's hand. "Sure would hate using a missile on such an easy target."

"Funny, Two," Quarry said facetiously. "Report."

"Nothing, sir. No movement as far as thermals or binos can see. No contact whatsoever."

Quarry nodded. Reaching down in a storage box, he pulled out two pyrotechnics.

"One green-star cluster and one red-star cluster. We have another set on Marek's vehicle in case these don't work."

"We'll be waiting, sir."

The two B.M.P.s passed through the hole in the berm and turned west. Marion sat in the vehicle commander's turret, Quarry poked his head out of the troop commander's hatch, just behind Davis's driver's compartment. It took 15 minutes before the Scouts reached the first set of pipes and turned north. Another 15 minutes, another pipe intersection.

"Sure feels weird driving out in the open desert in the middle of the morning," Dole yelled to Quarry.

"That's a no-shitter!" Quarry yelled. "I was thinking the same thing." Marion looked down and smiled in agreement.

At the next intersection, with the smallest portion of the G.P.S. antenna sticking out of the troop compartment, Dole got a good fix and plotted their grid. He yelled to Quarry, "The map grid is only about 20 meters off from the G.P.S. grid. Tracking seven satellites."

Quarry gave Dole a thumbs-up and grabbed the microphone of the P.R.C.77 strapped to the inside of the B.M.P.

"Five, this is Six, checkpoint five, Charlie Mike, out."

"Fifteen miles per hour, all gauges in the green, sir. Marek reports the same," Marion advised.

"Roger, One." Quarry looked behind him. Marek threw him an Iraqi salute. In the troop compartment of the second vehicle, Stone and Botsford were plotting their own independent track. The two B.M.P.s turned northeast.

"Here we go," Quarry said out loud to settle his own nerves.

It was another five minutes before Marion reported contact. Quarry raised his binos in the direction Marion pointed. In front of them was the first vehicle in a line that stretched east as far as the eye could see. Marion used the intercom to give Davis a few specific directions. Quarry gave Dole a hand signal. Dole in turn opened the rifle ports on both sides of the B.M.P.

Marion picked up his hand mic and made sure Marek saw the vehicles. Quarry picked up his radio handset.

"Five, this is Six. We're here."

Quarry drew a line in water-based ink on the overlay of his map. Climbing back, then into the troop compartment, he tugged on Marion's leg. Marion looked down to see the line on the map, then looked to the horizon. He hunched down so his face was about a foot from Quarry's.

"Jesus Christ, skipper! Are you sure?" Marion yelled at a volume he thought was just loud enough to be heard over the engine.

"You know damn well if we get off the established roads we draw attention to ourselves."

Marion looked up and out of the turret again and then quickly dropped back down.

"You know something, Captain Samuels; you're one crazy son of a bitch!"

"Glad ya came along?"

"You bet your ass, sir!" Marion stood up in the turret and found the "road" he was looking for. The roads weren't black-topped, but over the years, the paths had been so well traveled and worn they were permanently discolored, indented, and hardened. Compared to the surrounding desert, they were well-defined thoroughfares. Quarry crawled back to Dole and showed him the line he had drawn. Dole looked up at his commander in disbelief, but it didn't take long before the young cool professional regained his composure. The next road intersection would take them within a hundred yards of the enemy position.

It was 1143. Davis turned due north on the road. Dole picked up the laser range-finder. Making sure the G.P.S. was set to "calculate," he aimed the laser down the row of tanks and took a laser shot. When he spun the dial on the G.P.S. to display, the reading came back 83856493. Dole placed a dot on the map corresponding to the grid.

Marion's head barely stuck out of the turret. With the black, cloth-covered helmet and eye goggles on, his face wasn't visible. Quarry's head was barely out of the troop compartment. At such close proximity and at this speed, it was hard to accurately count the vehicles. The pipeline hindered the view of many of the tanks, even though tracks led into the positions. Passing an Iraqi tank within 50 meters, Quarry was close enough to make out the shoulder boards of an officer.

* * *

The Iraqi captain noticed the B.M.P. driving too fast for safety. *Arrogant 2nd Brigade Infantrymen,* Aziz thought. As the B.M.P. passed within its closest point to the tank unit, Quarry raised up and saluted. *But then again, I don't want to be late for midday prayers either.* Aziz returned the young soldier's salute.

* * *

Five hundred meters further down the road, they came upon another small tank unit. This one was further to the east and appeared to be centered in depth between the first forward two units. Quarry made a quick count, Dole used his laser to shoot another grid, Marion consulted the map and Davis kept his eyes squarely on the road.

They continued north about 1,500 meters; another Iraqi unit appeared behind a new set of pipelines. Offset from the road at least 600 meters, this unit was made up mostly of B.M.P.s with only a few tanks immediately behind them.

"Slow down a tad, Mary," Quarry called over. The message was relayed over the intercom and Davis slowed down to 10 miles an hour.

This group was more concerned about unit integrity, which made it extremely easy to count individual vehicles.

"Marked," Dole called up from within.

"Jesus," Quarry uttered without even knowing it. There was one more unit at least another two kilometers further down the road. This unit was at least a full click to the east of the road they were on. "Bring it to a halt, Mary." The order was passed, and Davis stopped the B.M.P. at an intersection. Quarry brought the binos up: "T55 tanks."

"Holy Christ!" Marion exclaimed as he lowered his binos. "Skipper, those boundaries are between brigades."

"Marked!" Dole called up from the troop compartment again. Marek's B.M.P. pulled up beside them. His helmeted head fell into folded arms as the vehicle came to a complete halt. When he looked up, his face was pale.

Quarry considered the risks, but only for a second.

"Here," he said, pointing to a spot on the map. "Two and a half clicks down the road. Put us behind that small hill." Marion looked at Quarry's map and then looked out over the terrain. A quick intercom message and they turned around, moving south again.

They were about ten clicks north of the Kuwaiti border, over twenty-seven from the nearest friendly line. The position Quarry chose was off of the beaten path by a good 500 meters. The B.M.P.s parked next to each other facing opposite directions.

"Everybody take a few minutes to clear your heads. We'll debrief individually and consolidate reports when we get clear of here. One, over here, please." Quarry led Marion to the back of the troop compartment.

Dole climbed up in the turret and placed the binos to his eyes. "Comments," Quarry quietly requested.

Marion took a deep breath, paused and looked around the inside of the vehicle. He reached up and touched a rocket-propelled grenade launcher strapped to the side of the compartment. Quarry didn't rush him.

"Jesus, sir, you know I'll back whatever decision you make."

Quarry smiled. He put his hand on his subordinate's shoulder.

"I know you will, Mary, but I value your opinion."

Marion took his time before answering.

"We have a hell of an opportunity here," he started off. "On one hand, we proved we can come and go as we please. On the other, if we get our asses in a sling, we're out of arty range, and I sincerely doubt they would send air in here." He paused again. "We've fulfilled our mission sir. I guess the question you'll have to answer is, is the risk of running around the enemy's rear outweighed by whatever further intel we can gain?"

"Thank you, my friend," Quarry said, patting Marion shoulder again. "I'll need a second or two please."

Marion's face showed concern, but his eyes sparkled. He turned to take his position in the turret. Quarry took a deep breath and studied the map and the ground. Three and a half clicks to the south, there was a small hill. At 224 meters above sea level, it was the highest terrain in this immediate area. Quarry climbed up from the troop compartment and looked toward the south. All eyes were on him. He waved Marek over.

"Mary, Dole, stick around also." Quarry waited for the 2nd Team leader to join them. Atop Marion's B.M.P., Quarry spread a section of map in front of them.

"We're here, at Hill 183," he said, pointing to the map. "Over there is Hill 224. What I want to do is work our way down to 224 using this roadway here," Quarry traced the route with his finger. "This will let us know what kind of flank security our friends to the east put out, and give us a commanding position for further observation of the brigade to the east and to the AlFawarais police station to the south. There is a saddle we can place the vehicles between, and put dismounted O.P.s on the reverse slopes. We'll conduct debriefs there while the information is still fresh in our minds. If we make contact with any enemy units, we keep on driving like we own the road, due south, until we break contact. If we don't run into anyone, Corporal Marion will pull us into position. Weapons status remains Hold. Questions?"

Marion looked at Marek as he answered, "No questions, sir."

"Let's move."

Marion reconnected the internal microphone and moments later the B.M.P.s lurched forward. They traveled over open desert until they picked up the first road of a detailed network, black-topped years ago to support construction vehicles. On this surface the B.M.P.s made good time. The maps were up to date and navigation was easy. Dole continually updated tick marks on the map corresponding to the G.P.S. readings. In less than ten minutes, Hill 224 loomed ahead. Old tracks that indicated someone had been up the hill before, but the wind-blown sand over them also indicated that hadn't been any time recently. The B.M.P.s pulled up behind the center of the hill, their view screened to the east and south. "Shut the engines down, send Davis up the back of the hill and take the first watch to the east. Have Marek send a dismount south. We can watch the west and north from turrets."

"Roger that, sir," Marion said picking up the squad net.

"Five, this is Six, over," Quarry transmitted over the platoon frequency. Dole was busy making notes and placing graphics on his overlay.

"Six, Five, over," the radio immediately responded.

"Set, from Lima one eight, north eight point three, west one point four. Continuing to observe, over."

Grier took a second to trace coordinates from a target reference point.

"This is Five, acknowledged. Report status."

"Cat One, all green, continuing mission, over."

"Roger, over."

"Roger, out." Quarry looked at the handset before replacing it. "Ready Dole?"

"Yes, sir," Dole stated as he laid his map on the floor of the compartment. "Here's our track sir." He traced the pipelines they followed in. "We came up this pipeline and then turned north here. Our first contact was a T55 tank unit on line from west to east, from grid 816650 well beyond 821649. We only counted 24 tanks though. After the tanks, still on the same west-to-east line was a B.M.P. unit. We didn't get an accurate count as our line of sight was disrupted by the oil pipes and then came to a complete stop at the processing plant. What we can see is a lot larger than a single battalion, but if it's a brigade, it's hurting. I guess they're conducting a hasty defense. A defense of what I don't know because there is no tactical advantage, key terrain or any other reason for them to be where they are." Quarry laughed to himself. *There are some colonels that could learn a lot from this kid*, he thought.

"Next is a B.M.P. unit. The first subordinate unit was from grid 823850 to grid 830854. Another continuous line, all B.M.P. model ones, just sitting out in the open. No signs of infantry digging fighting holes or defensive positions. No antitank or antiair emplacements either." Quarry thought about that for a moment: *Dole is absolutely right, there were no combat support vehicles.*

"There was another B.M.P. unit further to the east." Dole pointed to a business area crisscrossed with hundreds of smaller pipes on the map, "A location deep within the oilfields. This one had some tanks with them.

I estimate this is part of a mechanized infantry brigade." *Another very good observation,* Quarry thought. "Then there is that unit still a couple clicks to the north of us. What we don't see are engineers, medical, supply, or N.B.C. assets. Also should have seen some one-twenty mortars and maybe some artillery, but nothing. My guess, sir, is we're looking at an Iraqi mechanized infantry division at about half strength." *This kid is really sharp!*

"What do you recommend, Dole?"

"Sir, the fact that we rolled right up here on the high ground without even encountering an O.P. shows they don't know what they're doing. These guys are third string at best. Hell, skipper, we could hang around here until the war is over." Quarry smiled; Dole's face showed a moment of terror. "I mean, Captain Samuels, sir."

"You keep calling it the way you see it, Dole, and we'll get along just fine. Now if you don't mind, let me use your map. Go relieve Marek's O.P. so I can get his input." *Not that I'm going to get any better analysis short of calling Colonel Dillion.*

"On the way, sir," Dole said, grabbing his M-16.

Quarry debriefed each Scout using a standard reconnaissance patrol format. Working his way from the troops to Marek, he didn't hear anything that even came close to Dole's report. Finally, Quarry plopped the map on top of the B.M.P. and solicited Marion's input. When everything was said and done, Quarry added a few notes to the margin of his own map. With few exceptions, he copied Dole's graphics to his own. Then at last he keyed the net.

"Five this is Six, over."

The radio answered immediately, "This is Five Delta, over."

"Get Five on the horn, Delta. And have him bring a note pad."

* * *

Now that they had some room and high ground between them and the Iraqi division, nerves settled and 1st Squad was interested in hanging around a while. A three-man watch was established on the ground, with a fourth man in the turret manning weapons and monitoring radios. Not that anyone could sleep, but B.M.P. One took the first four-hour watch. Quarry got comfortable but continued to watch the division also.

They rotated the watch at 1600. Marek sent his people out and Quarry asked Marion to join him. The two sat on the sunny side of the vehicle and warmed themselves like desert reptiles in winter. Quarry unfolded his map.

"Here's what I'm thinking."

"Let me guess, skipper. Low crawl down there and check the tire pressure in the tank wheels to determine their maintenance readiness?"

"Not quite that drastic, Mary. But I will consider it as a contingency operation." The two grinned. "Actually, what I was thinking was taking a little road trip." Marion pulled out his own map. "We're here at 224."

"Check."

"This road behind us runs due south until it cuts towards this 'Gathering Center,' whatever that is. After that, it turns due south again until it comes to within a click and a half of the AlFawarais Police station."

"And you want to just go drive around, and in the process, we might be able to see what kind of manning strength is at the police station. And if there's a shitload of Iraqis, we just keep driving down the road and wave, because it's night and we're little lost Iraqi soldiers trying to get back to our unit."

"Actually ... yeah, that's exactly it."

* * *

The mission was as easy as packing up the kids after school and going for a drive in the family car. Quarry and Marion agreed they wanted the op to start shortly after dark. That way, anyone watching a B.M.P. drive by their position would assume the crew was late coming from somewhere. Nineteen hundred hours was good enough. The area was lit up like a Christmas tree from the light of the moon so N.V.G.s weren't needed. Davis started the engine and B.M.P. One moved to the road.

The Gathering Center was a single-room building once used as a mosque and business hall. Since the opening of the oilfield refinery complex it saw little use. B.M.P. One circled around it and they didn't see any signs of life. They continued south.

In the five clicks they traveled south, not once did they encounter anyone. When the road started to turn east, Quarry nodded to Marion. He spoke into the intercom and the B.M.P. left the beaten track and angled into the desert.

The police station had a flickering light, but no sign of movement came from within the tower. A blacked-out and powerless B.M.P. sat in silent watch in front of the main door. No guards were posted; no sign of movement was detected. Marion gave Quarry a thumbs-up. Quarry nodded his head "yes," and Marion passed another intercom message.

They didn't slow as they approached the building. Davis continued directly for it but veered off at the last second at 15 miles per hour. He drove the B.M.P. around the station as the three remaining Scouts yelled insults in Arabic: "Alli sleeps with goats."

"Alli kisses the sergeant's butt."

"Alli wants to be an officer." Quarry looked over at Marion in surprise. "Sorry boss, it's the only thing I could translate off the top of my head."

Inside the building, and unbeknownst to the Scouts, an Iraqi soldier lifted his head out from under his blanket: "Pigs."

They returned to the paved road. Quarry, Marion and Dole continued to watch for any reaction from the building. They saw none.

They continued eastbound for a click and a half. At the second road intersection, they could turn 90 degrees to the north, or 45 degrees to the northeast. "Checkpoint five again, sir," Dole called out over the sound of the engines. Quarry gave him a thumbs-up.

They paralleled the northbound road they had used earlier that morning. This time, however, they were a comfortable two clicks to the west of the Iraqi division, close enough to see there were no signs of security, but far enough they could joke about their adversaries.

"One One Bravo to One Two. Making northbound run, over." Marek didn't say anything as he keyed the net twice.

The second half of the trip was uneventful. No one was out. As they approached Hill 224, the appropriate combinations of flash-light flashes were given, received and returned. B.M.P. One pulled in for the night. As the watch rotated, Dole told the story of driving around the police station with such enthusiasm that Marion reprimanded them for noise discipline. The story was retold throughout the shift, as evidenced by the sound of muffled laughs.

The Scouts stayed at Hill 224 the rest of the night and through the next day, watching routine traffic come and go from the division. Jeeps and trucks drove back and forth, delivering supplies and personnel. Not once did a combat vehicle pull out of position or conduct a patrol. Not once did they see infantrymen training. Not once did the unit at the police station mount its vehicle and screen the flank. If it wasn't so pathetic, it'd be funny.

An hour after dark, Quarry reviewed the route with the Scouts. Dole and Bots confirmed the waypoints in the G.P.S.s. In teams, Marion and Davis, Marek and Cat conducted final inspections of the vehicles. Quarry got on the radio and informed Grier of the change of mission.

The two B.M.P.s started their engines and backed off the hill. They started south, but instead of continuing toward the Gathering Center, at the first road intersection, B.M.P. One turned due west into the open desert. It was marked as a trail on the map but one would be hard pressed to prove it when looking at the ground. Dole tilted the G.P.S. for Marion to see: they were heading home.

Ten

9 January 1991

"Link-up completed at Contact Point Three, sir. Visitor positively identified as Psy-Six. Specter is bringing them in now," Caine reported.

"Sir," Guy called down from the tower, "I'm observing four Hummers and four trucks approaching from the south."

Quarry looked over to Grier, who shrugged his shoulders. "This should be interesting," Grier commented.

Chief Warrant Officer Macey pulled his Hummer next to the tower. The crusty old infantryman had been in the Marine Corps since Christ was a corporal. Now a C.W.O.4, he was the commanding officer of the Psychological Platoon of Intel Company.

"Captain Samuels?" he greeted Quarry as he climbed out of his Hummer.

Quarry extended his hand.

"It's Quarry to my friends, Gunner. This is Staff Sergeant Grier, my platoon sergeant, and Sergeant Caine, my 2nd Squad leader." Handshakes were exchanged all around.

"I have orders for you from Lieutenant Colonel Dillion," Macey said, reaching inside his flak jacket for a sealed envelope.

"Seems like we have to provide PsyOps with security for some joint operations," Quarry paraphrased the operations orders moments later.

Macey looked around.

"So this is home?"

"This, and others. Come on in. I'll show you our situation map."

"On January 5th," Macey informed them, "CentCom placed Element 91 of the Army's 8th Psychological Operational Task Force in general support of MarCent. An Army major who is still at Camp 15 commands the unit. What we've done is form Army, Marine, and Kuwaiti linguists into 26 loudspeaker teams. I have four teams with me now. We're going to set up sites, co-located up here with you. The teams will use prerecorded tapes to simulate a division's worth of noise and direct them at the 29th, 42nd, and your mystery unit in Al-Wafrah."

Grier whistled out loud.

"Damn, sir. We usually don't like drawing attention to ourselves, and now you want to set up loudspeakers in the direction of three known Iraqi divisions?"

"Sounds fun, doesn't it," Gunner Macey chimed in.

Quarry looked at Grier and then back at Macey.

"Around here, gunner, we're going to change your call sign from Psy-Six to Psycho Six!"

"Like I never heard that one before."

"Well, let's get started on some detailed planning," Quarry said, standing and facing the map.

11 January 1991

The patrols worked well. Three times a day, every day, Psycho's and Quarry's Marines mounted up together. A Scout 50-cal Hummer and a loudspeaker-equipped Hummer departed at irregular intervals from O.P. Three and O.P. Tower.

The next phase of the PsyOp began when Master Sergeant Amos climbed down from his truck. A communicator by occupational specialty, Amos and the Radio Battalion detachment set up remote antennas to transmit false information over unsecured radio frequencies toward the enemy divisions.

O.P. Tower had more electronics than Radio Shack. Macey's men ran a generator 24/7 to power 12-inch reel-to-reel tape players and amplifiers that put any rock concert to shame. Amos had twice as much. The Marines from Radio Battalion operated electronic equipment Quarry had never seen before.

"It's getting entirely too crowded around here," Grier pointed out. Quarry agreed.

With Amos's introductions came another set of sealed orders. On the top and bottom of each page, stamped in half-inch high, red letters was the word SECRET. It didn't take long to read the two pages. Upon completion, Quarry asked Dole to have Grier, Macey, and Amos join him. Minutes later, when the four were assembled, Quarry took them for a short ride into the desert. Quarry read a portion of the orders out loud.

"Scout Platoon. Establish O.P./L.P. vicinity Hill 224 no later than 2359 15 Jan. Ensure O.P. is MULE equipped to support Phase 3 of larger operation." Quarry paused. "Phase 3, gentlemen," he said looking up, "is the start of the war."

14 January 1991

The plan had been finalized with all five Scout leaders, Macey and Amos in agreement. There was only one wild card: Colonel Ahmed. The plan would work without him, but Quarry would feel better if the Saudi colonel would buy in. So he had arranged a social call.

O.P. Berm was abandoned. At his old C.P., Quarry shook hands with a Saudi lieutenant as five tanks pulled into position. Colonel Ahmed and his operations officer were present, as another lieutenant set the last of an infantry platoon into forward fighting positions.

"You have no need to worry, *ya akh naqeeb* Samuels," Ahmed said in all seriousness. "*Al-mulaazim* Anul is a graduate of your own armor officer course at Fort Knox, Kentucky. *Al-mulaazim* Anakeeb is a member of our royal family. These are two of the finest officers I have. When I asked for volunteers to help keep Marines safe while you are on a mission, there wasn't an officer or a unit that didn't request the honor."

"It is I who am honored, *ya akh aqeed* Ahmed. Allah has graced me with your friendship and support."

Ahmed beamed a great smile.

"But all this talk is entirely too serious. Come, we will go back to my tent for dinner."

15 January 1991

It was just after dark when the Scouts saddled up; 2nd Squad manned the B.M.P.s; 3rd Squad manned their Hummers; Marion and the Scouts of One One mounted up in the TOW Hummer. That left One Two—Marek, Stone and Kantner—with two 50-cal Hummers and a TOW Hummer to provide security to the Marines of PsyOps and Radio. Marek was heard clear across the compound, even over the noise of the generators, when Marion gave him his orders.

O.P. Berm was now mere tire tracks in the sand, but the Saudi platoons provided a secure flank for the SRIG Marines. Macey kept a TOW and 50 Hummer at O.P. Three while Kantner provided O.P. Tower with a 50-cal Hummer. With the radios, tapes, and amplifiers running, the Marines of PsyOps and Radio provided the manpower while the few remaining Scouts contributed the firepower.

Grier got off the P.R.C.-109 radio.

"Just talked to Spud. Company has him also working with PsyOps. Seems they mounted four large speakers on his helo, and he's running up and down the border transmitting propaganda: 'No need to die, Come over to our side,

Come get something to eat,' that kind of stuff." Quarry smiled. "He's working the west side of the heel now, but he ran the gap between the two divisions. Says we have open desert. No patrol from either unit."

"Let's move."

* * *

Less than an hour later, the radio came to life: "Six, this is Two One, clear." Caine reported the road north of Hill 224 empty. As they approached the hill, Marion turned in the same tracks they had departed from days earlier. The column of Hummers followed, and in seconds they were concealed from view. Specter turned behind them, careful to run over the tire tracks with the B.M.P's tracks. Caine's B.M.P. turned around and also rolled over the tire tracks leading up the back side of Hill 224. After entering the saddle, Caine's B.M.P. changed direction and closed off the entrance. Anyone driving up or down the west road would only see a B.M.P. sticking out from the entrance to the high ground and hopefully think nothing of it.

On the far side of the saddle, where the low ground opened to the southeast, B.M.P. Two stuck its nose out. The Hummers took position on the west side of the saddle, which kept them from being observed by anyone on the road. Dismounted Scouts crossed the opening and lay prone on the reverse slope of the east side of the saddle. With eyes and weapons now facing every direction, the Scouts watched the division to the east and the open terrain to the north, west, and south.

The Scouts maintained their position for a full hour. There was no sign of movement in any direction. Quarry informed I Company they were set. The radio watch acknowledged the transmission with no emotion.

Grier took charge of the consolidation. The two TOW Hummers were moved to the east side, in a reverse slope defensive position, and covered with tan cammie netting. This position allowed the sights of the TOW system to see over the top of the sand dune without exposing the vehicles. Their positions angled so that they could watch the center of the Iraqi division as well as north and south. The 50-cal Hummer watched the open desert to the west with the headquarters Hummers in close proximity but hidden behind the crest of the hill. The two B.M.P. locations filled the gaps and blocked the entrance to their position. Hide positions for two-man observation teams were dug in between the vehicles and covered with nets. A directional antenna was rigged facing south. As morning broke, nothing moved on Hill 224. As far as the Iraqi division was concerned, it was business as usual.

* * *

It was too far to walk to the gathering station; so once again, Aziz led prayers at the side of his tank. His lieutenants and 1st sergeant joined him of course, but so did many of the officers and senior enlisted men of his battalion. When they finished, Aziz looked to the east. It was an impressive sight. Combat vehicles stretched as far as he could see. Beyond his own company, the only tank company in the brigade at full strength with ten tanks, 2nd Company had eight tanks and 3rd Company had seven. After them, the B.M.P. infantry fighting vehicles of Second Battalion continued the line. The 22 tanks of 3rd Battalion were centered and behind 1st and 2nd Battalions.

Of the 47 tanks and 22 B.M.P.s of his brigade, Aziz knew that after maintenance losses, the true strength of his brigade was even lower than the 70-percent of what it should be. Still, this was an impressive sight.

0800, 16 January 1991

"Company on the horn, sir. Actuals to be standing by on the net at 0900 for I Six."

Quarry looked at Grier and Dole, then to Grier's driver.

"Thank you, Slayer. Pass the word for me please, squad leaders to report at 0850."

"Think it's show time, skipper?" Grier asked.

"We'll find out in an hour." Quarry stuck a spoon back in an M.R.E. omelet with ham and continued with their conversation.

An hour later, the Scouts leadership was ready and waiting.

"India Company, this is I Six." The numerous platoons and detachments answered in sequence. Being the new guy on the block, Quarry waited his turn on the list. After acknowledging his C.O., however, he was surprised to hear a couple more units report in on the net after him. Dole picked up a note pad. "As of 0900 this date, Iraq failed to comply with UN deadlines. Phase 3 to commence in, I set, Zulu Echo November, Foxtrot Whiskey Foxtrot Foxtrot. All units set appropriate RedCon and N.B.C. level. Good luck and God bless you all."

Quarry looked over.

"Got it sir," Dole said, looking up from his pad. Grier was busying himself going through the C.E.O.I., decoding the colonel's message. Quarry waited for his turn and acknowledged the orders.

Quarry looked over to Grier.

"Zero three hundred tomorrow morning."

Quarry looked around at his leadership. Faces were somber at best.

"Well, it looks like we didn't come all this way for nothing." The comment didn't draw any humor or crack the resolved faces. "O.K., check all weapons, RedCon One at 0230. I don't think they'll slime anything this close to their own units, but let's put some M9 chemical agent detection paper on a few of the vehicles, check gas masks and have N.B.C. suits, boots, and gloves within easy grabbing distance. Anything else?" Quarry waited for a second but there were no questions.

"Sir?" Slayer asked from inside the logistics Hummer.

"Yes, Slayer."

"Can we get together and read another passage from the Bible?"

"You bet we can. Services at 0200."

Eleven

0305, 17 January 1991

There weren't any signs to indicate anything out of the ordinary. Around the post, every Scout looked at his watch a dozen times a minute and to the skies a dozen more. Still nothing.

"Jesus Christ!" Ferrado said a little too loud from inside his hide position 15 feet from the 50 Hummer.

"Quiet down, shit-for-brains!" Hauser softly called down from on top of the 50-cal turret.

"Corporal Hauser, we're bombing Baghdad!"

"Awww, bull shit."

"No, Corporal. I'm listening to British Broadcasting Corporation on the short-wave, Armed Forces Radio Network. Some guy is hiding under a bed somewhere in Baghdad, watching the whole thing."

Hauser slid down the back of the Hummer and knelt down by Ferrado for less than a minute.

"Shit! Ferrado, take the 50. I'll get the captain."

The 50 Hummer was less than 25 feet from the command Hummers. As Hauser slid from the Hummer turret, the movement drew attention.

"Captain Samuels, Staff Sergeant Grier," he forcefully whispered as he approached.

Quarry stuck his head out of the command Hummer.

"What's up Howie?" he said as his own radio came to life.

"I Company, I Company, this is India Charlie, Echo Eight Hotel. Units be advised, Phase Three in effect, report status and observations, over."

"Take that for me please, Dole," Quarry said over his left shoulder. "What's going on, Howie?"

"Sir, we're bombing Baghdad! Ferrado's listening on short-wave. It's happening now, sir."

Quarry looked over to the other Hummer.

"Anything on DASC or AirCom?" he asked, referring to the two aviation frequencies Grier monitored.

"All quiet. Not even a radio check."

"Howie, have Ferrado bring his radio over here, please. Slayer, make the rounds, let the squad leaders know that Phase Three is on and you'll update them as events happen."

"All squads report no movement, no contact, sir. Company informed," Dole reported. Ferrado closed the distance, bringing his radio. The radio correspondent was describing the rounds fired into the night air as fireflies. The four listened to the radio until the correspondent was forced to conclude his broadcast. Then, as if on cue, the night sky came to life with the sounds of high-pitched shrieks directly over the heads of the Scouts. The sudden noise made everyone flinch, and any who were standing dove to the ground.

"What the hell was that?" Slayer asked with a slight rise in his voice.

"Wasn't air or helos," Grier said as a statement of fact, not an answer.

"Stealths?" questioned Dole.

"Cruise missiles?" Grier wondered out loud.

"Could be. Though I've never heard one to compare it to. Makes sense if you think about it. The first wave of missiles takes out radars, command and control nodes, communication centers, and their headquarters." Quarry paused and then turned to his Scout. "Thanks for the radio, Ferrado. I think we can figure out what's going on from here. Return to your post please. Dole, handle the radio for me," he added, referring to answering routine radio traffic. "Let's go take a peek, Five," Quarry said to Grier as he reached inside the command Hummer for his rifle.

The Iraqi position appeared as quiet as normal. Quarry popped the cover to his scope and settled down into the sand. Grier climbed up on Ogdon's TOW Hummer and relieved Tellado at the sights. Using the starlit sky as his only light source, Quarry scanned the enemy position. Even without infrared or thermals, he could see the Iraqis had no idea of what was going on. Quarry looked to Grier. The platoon sergeant removed his eyes from the sights, looked down to his commander, and shook his head. It appeared the soldiers were more curious then concerned; they were not starting vehicles or aiming machine guns into the night sky. Most were simply looking up.

"Hell of a way to fight a war," Grier commented as the two continued to watch the inactivity below them.

"Let's go find Ferrado again," Quarry suggested.

"Whoever's in Baghdad, sir," Hauser reported as Quarry and Grier approached, "the radio service lost contact with 'em."

"Recapping events," the A.F.R.N. announcer stated, "US missiles and bombers struck Iraq and Kuwait in a massive, pre-dawn attack, firing the opening shots of the war, now named Operation *Desert Storm*."

"At least we know what we're calling it now," Grier commented.

Carleton's youthful ears picked up the sound first.

"Sir, do you hear something coming from the south-west?" Ferrado turned off the radio.

Within seconds, Grier confirmed it: "Helos. Lots of 'em!" A second later, Quarry picked up on the sound too. In no time at all, the aerial armada was visible.

As fast as they came, the helos were gone equally as fast. The night returned to normal. Less than ten minutes later, the curtain rose on the next act of the aerial ballet. Dozens of jets streaked over like a roar of thunder. Where the helos took minutes, the fixed-wings took seconds.

"Make any of 'em out?" Quarry asked. All shook their heads, no.

* * *

"Skipper, Sergeant Ogdon reports movement," Dole softly called over to the small group surrounding the 50 Hummer. Quarry looked at his watch: just after 0400. Quarry and Grier turned without saying a word and walked over to the other side of the O.P.

"They're sending out a few patrols, if you can call them that," Ogdon reported, as the two approached. They took the same positions as last time, Quarry on the ground and Grier behind the thermals. Ogdon was right. One would be hard pressed to call a few B.M.P.s driving behind their positions a patrol. None of the vehicles ventured as far west as the road.

"Doesn't make any sense to me, skipper."

Caine and Marion came over to join the party.

"What if it's not the coalition air strikes they're worried about?" Marion suggested. "Maybe they just want to see how their own soldiers are reacting?"

"Go with it, Mary," Grier said.

"Well, it's been an hour since the fly-over. We know by the short-wave radio that targets in Kuwait were hit in the opening shots. We know that the units around Kuwait City are in a different corps than the three infantry divisions facing south. But with no reaction from the mechanized unit in front of us, we now know they don't belong to either corps."

Quarry looked at Grier and then back to Marion.

"Damn, Mary!"

"It was just a thought, sir," Marion said with a slight hint of disappointment.

89

"Are you kidding?" Quarry said, getting up off the ground. "Get your ass over to the command Hummer. Get Intel platoon on the net. Ask for the watch commander. Tell him what we're watching and your analysis." Marion's expression changed to uncertainty. "Mary, you single-handedly hit on the reason our lone division here is out in the middle of nowhere, not moving, with no organic artillery behind them."

Marion still didn't realize what he'd hit on. "I get it, skipper," Caine chimed in. "We know 3rd Corps is strung along the coast and the southeast border of Kuwait. But they're all infantry divisions. Up until a few weeks ago, these guys weren't even here. We know that from the old satellite imagery in the Company situation room. So now, we have a task-organized armored division in the middle of an infantry corps."

"And what's an armored division doing so far from home?" Ogdon asked to keep the brainstorming going.

"To provide offensive capability to a dug-in infantry corps behind multiple obstacle belts and minefields," Marion answered.

"If we're striking targets around Kuwait City," Quarry interjected, "there aren't any high-payoff targets unless they found the armored division of the Republican Guard." He paused, unconsciously stroking a day-old beard with his thumb. "Also ask them if the 5th Mechanized Infantry Division moved south in 3rd Corps' zone yet. Lastly, when the air bubbas return, see if any of 'em happened to notice an extra artillery regiment hanging around behind the 8th Infantry Division."

"You thinking counter-attack forces, skipper?" Grier asked.

"Or continuing attack forces."

"You still here?" Grier asked Marion.

* * *

"The battle has been joined. The world will wait no longer," the President said to his nation and to the world. The Scout leadership listened in silence, hanging on every word. After the speech, all five turned and walked across the O.P. As they watched the division to the east, the sound of high-performance aircraft continued to streak overhead. The wave of northbound planes hadn't stopped for the last hour. At irregular intervals, a squadron or group would hurl itself into the night. Still no reaction from the unknown division.

As dawn broke, a new sound came to the Scouts' ears: a high-pitched buzzing.

"O.V.10 aircraft to the south, Captain," Carleton reported from behind binos. The dual turbofan propeller-driven observation plane preceded A.V.8Bs, the Marine Corps vertical take-off and landing jet. Both squadrons traveled north to join the carnage.

As Quarry watched the planes go by, Dole called out from the command Hummer.

"Update from Company, sir. ANGLICO units at Khafji report artillery strikes against the oil refinery. No Marine casualties. Marines at Mishab report three separate rocket strikes. No damage, no casualties, but some incredible fireworks."

To their east, the Iraqi division was waking up. For the first time since the Scouts arrived, they saw more than just complacent activity. Due east, soldiers of what the Scouts called the "B.M.P. Regiment," were finally getting off their asses and digging fighting holes. The regiment to the southeast, what the Scouts called the "Tank Regiment" sent out a mounted patrol: one B.M.P. that traveled west to the north/south-running road. It first turned south and traveled for half a click until it came up the road intersection with what the Scouts called the "hospitality tank." But instead of continuing to the south and patrolling in front of the regiment, it merely turned around. The last regiment to the northeast, what the Scouts called the "Hard Luck Regiment," also sent out a B.M.P., but this one merely came to the edge of the unit before it also turned around.

Quarry remained at the top of the hill, watching the Iraqis for the better part of an hour. It wasn't until Slayer came to get him that he looked up from behind his rifle's scope.

"Ferrado says you might be interested in listening to the radio, sir."

"Even in these earlier hours, the Pentagon is announcing that the Iraqi Air Force has been decimated," the radio reported. Quarry sent Slayer to inform the rest of the platoon of the results of the first waves of the Air War, as it was now being called. Quarry and Grier excused themselves and walked back over to the hill.

The rest of the day continued as it started. Friendly aircraft continued to fly north. Quarry downgraded the Readiness Condition to Two. Those not currently on watch or asleep gathered around the short-wave radio. Quarry and Grier continued to watch the Iraqis and talked about future operations. Periodically, Company came across the net, asking for updates. There were none to give.

The course of the day changed around 1700. Dole came running over to where Quarry and Grier watched the Iraqi inactivity.

"Company on the net, sir. I-Six for you in ten."

"Have answers to your questions," the colonel said minutes later. "2nd Corps seems to be missing an armored division. We suspect your friends are the 108th Armor Division. 3rd Corps' 5th Mechanized Division is positioned just behind 8th Infantry Division. We suspect a dual-pronged attack in the near future. Outstanding job Scouts. Over."

"Will introduce you to the man who came up with it, over."

"Will look forward to it. Heavy Metal Six went feet-dry today," Quarry's heart sank. Instead of sending individual companies, 2nd Tank Battalion was now in Saudi Arabia.

"Acknowledged Six. Any additional orders? Over."

"Yes, but not what you're thinking. You're not going anywhere yet, over."

"Sounds good to me, over."

"Your orders are a change of mission. Can you find your neighbor's arty and antiair units?"

"Will try our best, over."

"Then I'll consider it done. No time requirement. Safety has priority, acknowledge."

"Hard copy, Six, over."

"Good hunting, I Six out."

Quarry turned to Grier with a shit-eating grin on his face, "Let's go watch those patrols some more."

* * *

Quarry knelt at the head of the sand table: "Any questions?"

"What about air support?" Ogie asked.

"Marine attack helos are in general support of the division," Grier answered. "Some are operating from forward landing zones. There are also two stacks of fixed-wing overhead at any given time. If a call comes in for an immediate air request, the Airborne Command and Control Center can divert birds from a preplanned mission to FastFACs, the forward air controllers flying around in O.V.-10s or the two-seat F/A18. The FastFAC has as many as four aircraft every 15 minutes for close air support. If we can't designate ourselves, which we can with the MULE, the FastFAC can. The pilot in the back seat will control the inbound flights as he talks to us."

It was 1930 when the Scouts went over precombat checks and immediate action drills. The quarter moon wouldn't rise for another five hours. It was as dark as it would get. With thermals and N.V.G.s tested and ready, the Scouts owned the night.

The mission was based on four assumptions. One, that the armored division possessed self-propelled artillery, typically the 2S1 or 2S3 howitzer. Infantry divisions possessed the D-20, or the D-30. Two, with a maximum effective range of 15,300 meters for the 152mm ammunition, the Corps commander would mass the artillery where two thirds of its maximum range covered the forward divisions. This placed the artillery north of the infantry divisions, but between the 5th Mechanized and the 108th Armor. Three, the 108th wasn't coordinating its position or fires with 3rd Corps. This lead to the fourth but riskiest assumption: that no one would be looking behind them.

At 2000, Caine pulled his B.M.P. back to let Ogdon creep up to scan with thermals. When the "all clear" was given, 3rd Squad pulled out and took the lead.

"Bring me back a souvenir, Boss," Caine called down from the commander's turret of the B.M.P. Quarry touched the rim of his boonie hat as the command Hummer followed 3rd Squad. In the back seat, Grier and Slayer balanced the MULE between them. Marion and 1st Squad brought up the rear. Offsetting to the west, but running north, the Scouts continued to the same latitude as the westernmost vehicle of the Hard Luck Regiment. Then they continued north another three clicks. Turning east, they continued in darkness, using the thermal signature of the back of the 108th as their guide.

The Scouts anticipated the westernmost artillery to be at the end of the Hard Luck's eastern flank. Ogdon's findings, or in this case, the lack thereof, were a greater cause for alarm than a comfort.

"They should have been here," Dole spoke out loud. Quarry looked at his map. If they continued east, they would come to their first danger area, another Gathering Center.

"Get us closer to Three." Dole inched their Hummer up to Three One until Quarry's window was inches from Lance Corporal Mathews'.

"Hold up a second," Quarry called softly over to Ogdon. "Tellado, what's in front of us?" When the lead Hummers stopped, Grier motioned to Marion, who quickly joined them.

Quarry looked to the south. To the naked eye, he didn't see anything. Through thermal imagery, Tellado reported, "Signatures to the east. Can't make out specific vehicles though."

"Range?" Quarry asked just above a whisper.

"Eighteen hundred meters."

Quarry looked to his platoon sergeant.

"That's probably the 108th's Division C.P." Quarry remained quiet, deep in thought. "They don't know we're here, skipper," Grier continued. "We have the advantage at night. Moonrise isn't for hours."

Quarry considered the recommendation of the man whose opinion he valued so highly.

"Phase line Kansas."

"How's that, sir?" Ogdon asked.

"It might be a division command post Ogie, but it's still only another O.P. Give me a fish hook around it, open the interval back to three clicks, let's keep going."

* * *

"Six, this is Three. New contact. Many vehicles south. Continuing mission, over."

"Roger Three, keep me posted."

Minutes later, Botsford distinguished the vehicles and Marion called it in.

"Six, this is One. Massed artillery, direct front, over."

Quarry's heart pounded.

"Acknowledged One. Form line, halt, actuals to the center."

The four leaders met in front of Quarry's Hummer.

"Confirmed, sir," Ogdon agreed with Marion. "Contact continues until the thermal can't return specific targets."

Quarry was hastily drawing lines on his map. They were too far east to see Hard Luck or B.M.P. Regiment, and they were about a dozen clicks south of the division's C.P. Quarry looked up from his map and to the south.

"I can't see shit!"

"That's our safety blanket," Grier calmly reassured his commander.

It was one thing to play cat and mouse with a division they'd watched for days; it was quite another to creep up on a corps' artillery. "Check in with the air bubbas, Five. I'm going to see if there are any other friendlies out there."

"Same drill, different unit," Quarry began minutes later. "The support and ammunition trucks should be a couple clicks behind the front-line artillery. Continue east behind them, so we can get an actual count of artillery pieces and units' boundaries."

And that they did.

It took over an hour, but they traced the line of artillery until a new contact report identified B.M.P.s to their front: the 5th Mechanized Division.

"Well that's just dandy. An armored division behind us, a mechanized infantry division in front of us, and a corps' worth of artillery to the flank. Considering the 108th is at half strength, and assuming the 5th is at full strength, that's only about 23,000 Iraqi soldiers verses 14 Marines." Quarry paused. "Think they have a chance?"

It took 15 minutes to close the distance.

"Range, 2,500 meters," Ogdon updated his report barely above a whisper. Quarry couldn't see the vehicles Botsford lazed, but didn't need to. They were on N.V.G.s and thermals; Grier and Quarry were on the radios. Quarry didn't take his eyes off the invisible unit to the south and forced out a lungful of air.

"Five, let Company know we're in the gap, west of the 5th, north of the 42nd and east of the arty. Slayer, give him grids." Slayer hit a button and silently showed Grier the display.

Quarry got back on the horn.

"This is Six, form tight coil." Dole slowed his vehicle to a stop. It took only seconds for the other vehicles to close around each other.

The leaders gathered in the center of the vehicles, placed the map on the ground, and covered themselves with a poncho liner to keep any red light from their flashlights from escaping.

"With all due respect, Captain," Ogdon said, "You're one crazy son of a bitch!"

Quarry smiled and pointed to a spot on the map.

"Here is where the line of arty began," he started briefing.

As he talked, the Company net broke squelch. Dole replied and Grier went back to the mic. Grier listened for a few seconds and then told the person on the other end to stand by.

"They want to know if we're in a position to laze for an air strike."

Quarry considered it for a moment, looked at his watch, and gave it a second thought. "Tell 'em we can be in 40. I'll give them a five-minute window. They have to come in on 270 magnetic with no possibility of reattack. If they can live with that, I'm pretty sure we can too."

"I hate it when he talks like that," Slyer said, leaning over to Dole.

Grier relayed the message. A moment later, he again played middleman: "It's a go."

The mission was simple. Head west, drive over their own tire tracks, double their speed, and get back to the beginning of the arty before the arriving aircraft checked in on station.

"The abort plan is to make a speed run due north then egress west," Quarry continued with the brief. "Ogie, you're probably on your last nerve. Mary, you got the lead home. I don't want to be anywhere around here when that moon crests. Questions?" There were none. "Let's do it."

The leadership turned towards their vehicles.

"Ogie?" Quarry softly called out. The squad leader stopped and turned. Quarry placed a hand on the other's flak vest. "Outstanding job, Marine." Ogdon gave Quarry a rare smile in return, and touched the brim of his boonie hat.

It took less than a minute for the leaders to brief their people and check in on the radio. Quarry gave the order and the Hummers moved. Grier was busy on the Company net giving updates; Slayer was using the range-finder and G.P.S. As soon as one function was completed, Slayer changed equipment, plotted the results, and immediately started the process over. Quarry put the platoon mic against his left ear as he talked to someone else on the high-frequency net in the right. His transmissions were short but the responses were long. When he finally put the net down, Dole asked, "Who was that, sir?"

"That was Lone Warrior Three Six, Dole. The U.S.S. *Missouri*, and all nine of her beautiful 16-inch guns." Knowing his platoon could be supported from a navy battleship allowed Quarry to breathe a lot easier. He changed mics and let his leaders know their situation.

At 2347, about a half an hour before moonrise, the Scouts were parallel to B.M.P. Regiment and south of the 108th division command post.

The command vehicle faced north, so Grier could place the MULE on the hood of the Hummer facing east. Quarry gave the formal nine-line brief to the FastFAC including the laser frequency of the MULE they were using. The Scouts would laze for the FastFAC who was 30 seconds in front of a flight of four F/A-18s and six A6 Intruders, loaded to the gills with dual-purpose improved conventional munitions. The Scouts would illuminate the first vehicle in the line of self-propelled artillery, the FastFAC would acquire and acknowledge the MULE laze, then take over with his own assets. This gave the Scouts one minute and 30 seconds to mount up, and start the reverse fish hook around the 108th C.P. It was hoped that a quick exit, covered by the night erupting to the southeast, would provide safe passage.

At 2349, it was show time. Quarry held the P.R.C.-104 mic in his right hand, while looking at his watch on the left.

"Stand by, Five." Quarry paused no more than 30 seconds. "Grier, in five, four, three, two, one, laze!" Grier depressed a single switch that looked much like an ordinary toggle. To the unaided eye, it appeared that nothing happened. The laser did its job for 30 seconds. "Cease fire. Let's get out the hell of here." Grier picked up the MULE and dove into the open rear door. Quarry did the same in the front. Marion was already on the move. Dole pulled in behind One Two as his leaders closed their doors.

"Fifteen seconds," Slayer announced as he looked at his watch.

"Thirty seconds," Slayer updated his commander.

"Twenty-five miles an hour," Dole reported their speed.

"Forty-five seconds."

"Speed 30." Quarry had the aviator's frequency on the radio's speaker and listened to the H.F. net.

"One minute." "One fifteen." "One …" The flashes behind them lit up the night and Slayer's report was drowned out by the sound of explosions seconds later.

Quarry looked at his watch and let another minute and thirty seconds pass.

"This is Six, ease down." Dole took his foot off the accelerator and matched Marion's speed. Undoubtedly, thousands of enemy eyes were now open, and the Scouts didn't want any on them.

* * *

The distant rumble woke Aziz out of a sound sleep. *Why would the 29th register artillery at night?* Aziz thought. *Bastards.* He rolled over and went back to sleep.

* * *

"Airborne Command wants to know if we're in a position to give them battle damage assessment?" Grier said from the other side of a radio mic.

"Tell 'em to go to hell," Quarry answered, still looking into the black of night.

"Thought as much," Grier said before returning to his radio.

* * *

Ogdon reported "clear" and Marion angled northwest, giving the rear of the 108th a wider berth. Caine reported the road in front of them was also clear.

The next transmission occurred 15 minutes later.

"Six, this is Two. Have you in I.R., path still clear. Welcome home."

* * *

As they went through the standard post-operation procedures the familiar lack of movement from the 108th was a welcome sight. Debriefs were conducted and the information consolidated. With adrenalin now burned off, the exhausted Scouts were soon asleep. It was well past four in the morning when Quarry and Grier hit the bags.

"That was one hell of a night, skipper," Grier softly commented. Quarry didn't answer; he was already asleep.

Twelve

18 January 1991

The flight of A.V.8Bs screamed 200 feet above ground level, two clicks to the west. Quarry sprang straight up, getting caught in the desert cammie net in the process. Grier rolled quickly to the side, bringing his Beretta 9mm pistol into a ready position. As soon as the adrenaline dump ceased, the sight of his commander tangled in the netting immediately changed the mood, and Grier's heart returned to normal. Quarry, fully awake, started extracting himself. Guy, who was sitting behind the radios of the command Hummer, was doing his best to suppress a laugh.

"Go ahead, let it out," Quarry said with a bit of embarrassment in his voice. Guy gave a grunt but continued to smile. Grier, on the other hand let out the first hearty laugh Quarry had heard in a while. "When you are finished having a laugh at my expense, would you be so kind as to point that pistol in a safe direction?"

"Sorry," Grier said, bending over, picking up his 782 gear and holstering his pistol. By now, Quarry was free, and Grier was as fully awake as someone with only two hours' sleep in a couple days could be. The jets cleared the area, bound for targets to the north.

Quarry looked around the camp as the high-pitched sound of O.V.10s followed their faster brothers. Heads were sticking out of the B.M.P.s, while 1st and 3rd Scouts looked from behind weapons.

"Anything?" Quarry asked Guy.

"No patrols this morning, sir," Guy reported. "All three regiments are sending vehicles out and around their position, but they're not really patrols. They don't go 500 meters from their own position at any time. Hard Luck never bothered to tie in with B.M.P. Tank Regiment still isn't going forward." Quarry looked at his watch: 0615; it would be light soon. As if on cue, the quarter-hour reports started coming in. Quarry listened: negative contacts.

99

"It's good to be home," he commented. Then he looked over at his platoon sergeant. "Well, now that I'm not in fear of getting shot, I think I'll brave a baby wipes bath and put on a clean set of underwear," he said, shivering in the morning cold.

"Ouch, that hurts, skipper. You know I'd never shoot you. Not on purpose."

"That's reassuring, thank you, Five." The two leaders and Guy all smiled.

Quarry washed his hair in the left-over shaving water in his helmet. The old steel pots were better for washing but when Kevlar was all you had, one made do. Baby wipes made a great bath cloth and in no time Quarry finished washing his chest, back, and arms. After a liberal helping of baby powder, Quarry put on clean underwear, undershirt, and sweatshirt.

"Sir, Company needs to know if we are in a position to observe the arty we lazed last night," Slayer asked from inside the Hummer.

Quarry thought the question strange but also knew there would be a legitimate reason for it.

"Tell them negative. Tell them we are all set on 224." Quarry carried on getting dressed as Slayer continued to listen to the message.

"Roger, will advise, Scouts out." Slayer stuck his head out of the Hummer, his face pale. "The reason they wanted to know if we were still in a position to observe is because one of our O.V.10s was shot down last night."

Quarry's heart sank.

"Let Grier know."

* * *

It was afternoon when Quarry got off the radio with I-Six. The leadership and a good number of the Scouts were patiently waiting nearby.

"It was the commanding officer of Observation Squadron 2 and his copilot. They went in to assess the damage on the arty and were hit by a surface-to-air missile. They successfully ejected but were captured. They're being listed as P.O.W.s."

"Why fly over the divisions, sir?" Hauser asked.

"MarCent places indirect-fire weapons second only to command and control nodes in priority. When we found the combined artillery regiments of three different divisions and the 3rd Corps reserves, it shot right up on the air-tasking order. With no fast-moving aerial reconnaissance and a shortage of Pioneers, it was up to the O.V.10s to get the battle damage assessment."

"Why not just keep hitting them?" Speckman asked.

"Duplication of effort," Grier answered. "The air bubbas don't mind taking risks, but not to blow up the same target twice. At least we learned that much since Vietnam. In reprisal for last night's love peck, the undamaged Iraqi arty opened up on every known front-line position this morning. Didn't do a whole lot of damage, but imagine what could happen if they used forward observers to adjust rounds like we do?"

"That was a good introduction into tonight's mission, Five," Quarry said, breaking the silence. "Squad leaders, prepare to copy."

* * *

Caine had the duty; Marion and Ogdon were catching up on sleep.

"Got a second, skipper?" Grier asked, lifting up the cammie net and entering the command area.

"Well gee, Five, I was waxing down the ol' surf board, ready to go hit some gnarly waves but I think I can find some time for you before I go on safari." Dole looked up and smiled, then put his eyes back into the Soviet ground equipment manual.

"We're getting pretty low on water. I need to make a resupply run to O.P. Three."

"When do you want to head out?"

"Tonight, after dark. I'll take Marek and the 50 Hummer with me."

"Sounds like a plan."

"All personal canteens are full. We've consolidated all remaining water into two five-gallon jugs. We'll take everything else that holds water. We've topped off all Hummers and will refill our gas cans as well. I'll grab as many M.R.E.s as I can carry. We're still green in ammo and pyro. Can you think of anything else?"

Quarry smiled at his platoon sergeant: "How about a B.B.Q. grilled hamburger with all the fixings and a keg of beer for the men?"

"I'll see what I can do," Grier said, returning the smile. Quarry wouldn't bet against his platoon sergeant not coming back with the goods.

* * *

It was 1545 when the B.M.P.s started their engines. Marion gave a thumbs-up, indicating the coast was clear. Caine ordered Orsini to pull out, Speckman close in trail. Since tracking the rear of the 108th had worked, tracking the rear of the 29th should work as well. They would head south, using the westernmost possible road for about a click. At a waypoint that only the G.P.S. satellites would recognize, the two B.M.P.s would head east, passing the Gathering Center, until they picked up the rear support units of the 29th Infantry Division. This would put them in front of the 108th, but what the hell; they were all one big happy family. It would also eventually place them in front and south of the westernmost Iraqi artillery regiments. They would travel at 20km an hour the entire trip. After a 32km journey, the Scouts would arrive at their destination before dusk. To a casual onlooker, they would appear to be just another resupply run or another lost patrol looking to get home. They would take both B.M.P.s, since the Scouts didn't know how well the vehicles were maintained. It was better odds that both wouldn't break down on the same mission. The crews were simple enough: Two One manned a B.M.P. with Peterson adding another set of eyes. Quarry and Dole jumped in the back of Two Two.

The journey began without incident. The patrol drove down the paved street, as if at home on the main drag, cruising in daddy's Mustang. Their approach to the Gathering Center was cautious but also without incident. It wasn at a point in the middle of nowhere that Caine called Quarry on the squad frequency: "B.M.P. to our front."

Quarry aimed his binos east. In front of them, about two clicks away, was a B.M.P., all by itself. Quarry dropped down inside the vehicle and looked over Dole's shoulder at the map and their location. The lone B.M.P. was at the end of a single road that abruptly stopped in the middle of nowhere. Two kilometers further south was another police post and at least a dozen other buildings. The Scouts were easily within observation range of the post. Anybody standing on a second floor and looking through binos was probably watching them now. But the lone B.M.P. was the prime concern.

The Scouts had a contingency plan for this type of encounter. While they were hoping they wouldn't have to use it, they began taking their places within the vehicles. The drivers were already wearing green Iraqi blouses. In the turret, Marion and Speckman quickly donned theirs. For those in the exposed positions, cloth communications helmets covered their heads; neckerchiefs came up as goggles went down. Vehicle commanders energized their weapon stations. Quarry made sure his rifle was on safe and chambered a round. Peterson checked his full magazine in his M-16. Quarry gave a thumbs-up to Speckman, who relayed the signal to Caine. Caine returned the gesture.

At 20 clicks an hour, it took four minutes to close on the enemy B.M.P. As the Scouts approached, the vehicle commander of the enemy vehicle waved. Marion waved back. The Iraqi vehicle commanders waved more rigorously. So did Marion. It was obvious the commander wanted the Scouts to stop, but they kept right on going without changing speed or direction. When another Iraqi stepped to the side of the vehicle and started waving down the Scouts, Marion, Specter, Orsini and Surkein all returned the gestures. The Scouts passed within 75 feet of the enemy vehicle and kept going. Marion returned his view to the east as if nothing of importance had occurred, though sweat was trickling down his neck.

When two B.M.P.s failed to comply with his orders, the Iraqi corporal merely yelled insults at them and returned to his business. The Scouts continued east. Through rifle ports, five Scouts continued to watch the checkpoint's every move. When there was no sign they were going to be followed, Quarry sent a single word over the squad net: "Clear." Every Scout took a breath.

They didn't encounter another vehicle for the remainder of the trip. They used the back of the inverted V trenches as their guide south, as blown-up, destroyed and mutilated equipment started to appear to the north. In the back of both vehicles, Scouts recorded the status of every artillery piece. They slowed their pace as they moved toward their objective, a small rise on the desert floor, known on the map as Hill 81. Hardly enough to be called a hill, it was nothing more than a rise of dirt a few meters higher than the surrounding elevation. As they made their approach, activity, clearly visible about three kilometers away was the beginning of the artillery units that were still intact after the previous night's air strike.

Caine pulled his vehicle up the slightly rising slope, even though he could already see over the top. Speckman pulled his vehicle next to Caine's. The Scouts waited.

As the sun sank towards the horizon, Quarry caught Caine's attention. The two B.M.P.s started their engines and headed east one more time. They drove in column until a gap, about a click wide, appeared between a destroyed and a functional artillery unit. Quarry looked at his map: this would be a gap between regiments.

"Thirty-two, sir," Dole said, looking up from his own map and a notebook of sequential grids. Because the Iraqis follow Soviet battle doctrine, 32 annihilated artillery tubes represented almost two full battalions of artillery and the 460 men who operated them.

Quarry looked over to Specter and made a circle with his finger in the air. Specter keyed his internal vehicle microphone, and Surkein turned the vehicle around and stopped. Quarry opened one of the back hatches of the B.M.P. and placed the MULE against a hole in a burlap cloth they strung across the opening. With the MULE stabilized on the floor by sandbags, Quarry sighted in on the first intact tube to the east as Caine talked to the FastFAC on the P.R.C.109.

Dole relayed Caine's hand signals.

"Five minutes out, sir." The minutes ticked by. "Caine reports two minutes out. Mission is a go."

"Roger, mission is a go," Quarry mimicked.

"Aircraft are in the pop," Dole said with a hint of excitement in his voice. Seconds later: "Wings level." A heartbeat later, "Laser on."

Quarry held his breath and squeezed the trigger as gently as he would his M-40. He held it for 15 seconds until the first of four F/A18s screamed overhead. An instant later, the Scouts heard the first explosion caused by a 250-pound laser-guided bomb ripping into metal. Quarry turned off the MULE. As the first F/A18 continued to pickle off bombs, his wingman came in behind him, continuing on the same gun target line. Then there was a pause as the FastFAC came in between the flights. The Scouts enjoyed watching the first set but sure as hell didn't wait around for the second. Iraqi units mobilized, a few surface-to-air missiles were fired and every wheeled or tracked vehicle drove off in different directions. In all the chaos, two nondescript B.M.P.s drove west as fast as they could, blending into the confusion.

Quarry lifted his head out of the top of the troop compartment slightly. He made out the reflection of canisters releasing over six hundred bomblets of dual-purpose improved conventional munitions. Though he couldn't see the individual explosions, Quarry knew damn well scores of Iraqis were meeting Allah. Hundreds more would soon follow.

* * *

Grier was still gone when the patrol returned home. Quarry received a non-surprising report on the 108th from Marion and Ogdon. With the other two squad leaders in attendance, Quarry and Caine conducted a quick debrief of the day's events. The return trip had seemed to take no time at all. The only time they slowed was to strike a deeper path than their outbound tracks around the north entrance of the police outpost.

While the leaders debriefed, Dole got the real work started. Quarry passed the confirmation of the 32 pieces of scrap metal and the location of the day's raid to both Company and the targeteers at the Air Command Center.

19 January 1991

Quarry woke violently to the "thrump" of distant explosions. Though the morning was still dark, the eastern sky was lit like a flashing beacon. Ducking under the cammie net, he saw over half the platoon watching fireworks.

"Morning, skipper," Grier greeted his commander. "Better put your boots on; we killed two scorpions this morning."

"What's going on?"

"Arc light mission. Seems somebody found a shit load of artillery between the Iraqi 42nd Infantry and the 5th Mech. Rather than individual fighters, the flyboys are giving them a B52 wake-up call."

Quarry looked at his watch. Indeed it was a wake-up call. It was quarter to six in the morning. "You look like shit, when did you get in?"

"You don't look all that wonderful first thing in the morning either, oh fearless leader. But thank you for your concern. Slayer and I got in about an hour ago. Brought you a present too." Grier pointed to the opposite side of the O.P. In previously vacant locations now sat a 50 and a TOW Hummer, pulled in and cammied up. "We're at full strength." Changing their view to the east, Grier continued to update his boss.

"We'll get all the leaders together later, so you can update us on the entire friendly situation," Quarry said after the light show came to an end. Quarry and Grier walked the perimeter before going back to the command Hummer. "It's good to have ya back, Five," Quarry said, climbing back in his sleeping bag.

"Missed you too, dear."

"Good night, John Boy."

"Good night, Mary Ellen." Listening to his two leaders, Dole smiled and shook his head in the darkness of the command Hummer. It was indeed good to have everyone back.

* * *

Just past noon, Quarry woke. After baby wipes, baby powder and teeth brushing, he opened the door to his Hummer. On his map board in the passenger side were two large sandwiches wrapped in wax paper and two cans of soda.

"What's this?" Quarry asked, eyeing the booty.

"I have failed you, oh Great One," Grier said, doing his best impression of Colonel Ahmed. "You asked for hamburgers and beer," he continued in his normal sarcastic tone, "but I was only able to produce fresh lamb sandwiches and canned soda." Quarry opened the first and took a bite out of the two-inch-high stack of lamb and fresh bread. "When we went over to SANG to gas up, I guess the colonel heard we were coming. He wouldn't let us out of there until my Hummer was so full with fresh food I couldn't pack any more. Everyone got sandwiches and fresh fruit. I have a dozen or so cases of soda in my trailer." Quarry looked over at the back of Grier's Hummer. There was a small trailer attached to the back, piled high and tarped over. "Everyone is overflowing in water and gas. We've got enough food for about a week without ever touching the M.R.E.s and mail call sounded." Dole looked up from a magazine he was reading and smiled. Quarry opened a can of soda and washed down a bite of sandwich.

"What time is briefing?"

"Whenever Allah wills it or you command it."

All of the Scouts not currently on watch attended the briefing, each with chocolate chip cookies or other treats in hand. Using a series of 1:50,000 tactical maps taped together, Grier laid out the entire front line. The structure and locations of the Coalition Forces had changed: a number of Arabic countries had taken positions alongside the Saudis; Marines manned the rest of the northern border. The Army had moved west. Numerous allied countries provided ground troops, and O.P. Three was now a powerful forward outpost, which explained why the Scouts and a few Hummers were no longer deemed necessary. Grier answered everyone's questions as best he could, until everyone was satisfied with what was going on. When there were no additional questions, the Scouts returned to their duties.

0358, 20 January 1991

"Skipper," Dole quietly called from the other side of the cammie net. "Skipper? Company's on the horn, wanted to ensure we were all at 224. I told them we were. The duty officer wouldn't give me any specifics."

Quarry unzipped his bag. The cold morning air shocked him into being fully awake.

"What time is it?"

"Zero four, sir," Dole said as Quarry grabbed his boots from beside his makeshift pillow of dirty laundry rolled inside a soiled shirt. After beating his boots together and dumping them upside down to make sure nothing had found a home in them, Quarry swung his feet out of his bag.

The movement and muffled noise woke Grier.

"What's going on?"

"Dole was kind enough to wake me out of a perfectly wonderful out-of-body experience to let me know Company called. I was going to shoot him, but you woke up and provided him a witness."

"Sorry, sir," Grier said, rolling over and facing away from them. "I'll go back to sleep." As Grier covered his head with his bag, the night sky to the east lit up. It took a while for the first of hundreds of "thrumps" to be heard.

Quarry sprang to his feet, slid under the cammie net and jogged to the east side of the O.P. By now, the light was sufficient to make out the lines on Mathews' face as the Scout sat in the turret of the TOW Hummer. In no time, the majority of the platoon was crouched down around them and watching the show. Quarry reached down to retrieve the compass in the outside pocket of his flak jacket, only to realize he wasn't wearing it.

"Mathews, azimuth."

The young Scout slew the launcher in the direction of the light and looked at his range card. The light provided by the bombing was enough to read by, "070, sir."

"Time from the sight of the first explosion to the first sound."

"Less than a minute sir."

"Map," Quarry said, to no one in particular.

Ogdon extended his map out the passenger side window to his platoon commander. A few of the Scouts gathered around him. Quarry found their position and turned two pages on the Australian nine-fold map board. At a distance of 45km on an azimuth of 070 was a red rectangle with three vertical lines and a filled-in circle.

"I'm not sure of the combat load of a B52, but I'd venture to say more than one artillery regiment just got their asses handed to them."

The light lasted 30 more seconds before it went out. Smaller individual explosions lasted two more hours as artillery ammunition continued to go off as secondary explosions. True to his word, Grier slept through the whole thing.

* * *

At 1000, the Company net came to life. Slayer took the report and walked over to Quarry, Grier and Marion as they watched the lack of movement of the 108th.

"Sir, Company sent you a message."

"What ya got, Slayer?"

"R.P.V.s confirm 80 percent of two artillery regiments destroyed in B52 strikes earlier this morning, thanks to the accurate detection, plotting and reporting of Scout Platoon. Bravo Zulu, I Six sends."

"Congratulations, skipper," Marion said. Other accolades worked their way around the squad. Quarry accepted the praise in silence; it was a team effort.

Later that afternoon, Quarry and Grier sat in the command Hummer listening to an update. In retaliation for the morning's air strike, the Iraqi artillery attacked several front-line outposts along the Saudi border. Several Marines were wounded, one seriously. But considering the amount of firepower the Iraqis still possessed, the retaliation was light and ineffective.

Slayer climbed in the driver's seat to take his turn on watch.

"Sir? Do I remember you saying you had friends in Israel?" he said, closing the driver side door.

"Sure do. Why, what's up?"

"We were listening to the B.B.C. Iraq launched ten SCUD missiles at them this morning and afternoon. Five hit Haifa and Tel Aviv." Quarry's face blanked at the news. "I'm sorry, sir. I thought you would want to know."

Quarry took a few beep breaths.

"Thank you, Slayer. I appreciate hearing it from you rather than over a radio. Did they say anything about casualties?"

"Twelve injured. One died later of suffocation when her gas mask failed to operate correctly."

"A chemical attack?"

"No, sir, but the Israelis had their citizens mask until they gave the all clear."

"Kinda puts a whole new twist on things, doesn't it?" Quarry commented to no one in particular.

Slayer waited a moment before asking, "How's that, sir?" Quarry heard the question but didn't realize he was being talked to. His mind was elsewhere.

Grier answered for him.

"By launching SCUDs on Israel, Saddam is trying to get Israel to enter the war. If they do, several Arab nations currently in the coalition will side with Iraq to defend against the Jewish nation. Think of where the Arab forces are physically located in the Coalition. Now imagine that some of those forces change allegiance. One minute friend, one minute foe."

"Oh my God," Slayer said in disbelief.

"Exactly," Grier agreed as Quarry dug out a copy of *FM 100-23, The Soviet Army; Troops, Organization and Equipment*, from under the rear passenger seat. Quarry opened the book to the motorized infantry division and cross-referenced the chapter to find artillery regiments. "Skipper," Grier said with a rising inflection in his voice, "you've got that look in your eyes again."

"Just some wishful thinking, Five. I sure would like to add a SCUD missile launcher or two to our kill list."

"Skipper," Grier said not all jokingly, "you're scaring me. Remember me? The nice platoon sergeant who brought you fresh lamb sandwiches and canned soda?"

"Relax, Five," Quarry said looking up from the manual, "there are no SCUD launchers anywhere near here. Besides, we'd never get authorization to go after one anyway." Slayer watched Grier visibly relax. "But there are still a number of FROG sites out there launching against our brother Marines, though," Quarry added in all seriousness.

0300, 21 January 1991

"Sir, Company on the horn," Dole spoke from the other side of the cammie net. "They want us at RedCon One." Quarry paused as he heard a new sound and looked through the net at his driver.

"That wasn't air," Ogdon said as a matter of fact.

"Wasn't outgoing," Grier commented, meaning it wasn't Iraqi artillery fire.

"Marine 155 artillery?" Marion asked.

Quarry looked at Grier.

"I'll monitor Company and Intel. Five, air ops and DASC. One, arty regimental ops and F.D.C. Two, arty command and safety. Three, arty admin/logistics and MEF Command. Anybody hear anything of interest send a runner back here."

Ten minutes later came the undeniable sound of Iraqi D30s firing outbound rounds. To the west of the Scouts, even at this distance, the duel of artillery was unmistakable.

Company allowed individual units to set their own RedCon at 0700. With the 108th sleeping soundly through the night, Quarry downgraded the posture to Three. For Hill 224, it was a night of wasted sleep and not much more.

* * *

Ogdon was bent over a joint operational graphic air map, the large-scale type that pilots use to navigate. Grier was in the back seat of the Hummer, listening to the P.R.C.109.

"Here's what we came up with, skipper," Grier said as Quarry climbed in the back passenger side. "They sent O.V.10s and R.P.V.s out over the heel." He indicated the southwest part of Kuwait where the country boundary turns northwest. "Ogie plotted the track of the R.P.V. on the map. My gut tells me we conducted an arty raid against the Iraqi arty somewhere between the Qalamat and the south-west Umm-Gudair police stations." Ogdon pointed out the specifics as Grier talked.

"Why an arty raid when air can come and go at will?" Quarry wondered out loud.

"To show them that we can," Ogdon pointed out dryly.

"I can buy that," Quarry said, still looking at the map. "Why the increased RedCon, Ogie?"

"Company wanted to see the 108th's reaction. If they reacted rapidly and defensively, we would know they're in communication with the 29th. Our sitreps say the 108th is still a wild card, not listening or caring much about what goes on around them."

"Nice analysis, Ogie. Help yourself to a can of soda."

"Gee, skipper. A whole can? I better drop what I'm doing and write home about this!"

"Smart ass," Quarry said, smiling.

"What's happening on the short-wave?" Grier asked, turning off the P.R.C.109 and changing the batteries.

"The Army's 101st is moving closer to the border in what the B.B.C. is calling 'more aggressive posturing,'" Ogdon answered.

"No shit. Think we should send them a road map?"

"Now, now, Five. Division commanding generals have to follow orders if they're ever going to be corps commanders."

"That's true. What's happening in the rest of the world, Ogie?"

"Marines raided nine oil platforms off the coast. They secured five and took about another dozen prisoners. Seems these are the first reported prisoners taken during the war," Ogdon answered.

"Don't worry, Six," Grier interrupted Ogdon, "You'll get your picture in the paper someday."

The two waited a second before chorusing, "NOT," in unison. Both smiled and smirked.

"Lastly, it seems that our Army friends are going to get to pull a few libs in Israel," Ogdon finished.

"How's that?" Grier asked, returning the 109 to the rack.

"The U.S. is deploying Patriot antimissile batteries in and around Tel Aviv. The State Department assured them that everything that can possibly be done is being done. The Israelis seemed to have bought it and so far won't enter the war. The Patriots sweetened the deal."

"That is a good deal, not only for Israel, but those poor Army doggies that will be comforted and thanked by beautiful Israeli vixens. Maybe by a couple you know, skipper?"

Quarry looked over at his platoon sergeant who had a smirk on his face.

"You know, Five, I haven't killed anyone for a couple days now. Don't make me hurt you."

Grier smiled and threw his commander and Sergeant Ogdon a soda.

Thirteen

22 January 1991

On the horizon, a dust cloud rose from a moving vehicle. "Go around and pass the word quietly, RedCon Two," Caine ordered. "Orsini, hand me the spotting scope."

"Do you want me to wake the skipper?" Guy asked as his feet hit the ground.

Caine looked over to where the cammie net covered the command Hummer.

"Not yet." Guy took off at a trot.

"What ya got, Caine?" Ogdon asked.

Through the 45-power spotting scope, Caine watched as he answered, "Armored vehicle. Unknown type. Moving southeast. Estimated speed, 15–20."

Marion grabbed a map from within the commander's turret.

"Azimuth?"

"Three one zero magnetic."

Marion placed the map on top of the B.M.P. and oriented it north. "Three one zero puts it on an improved road running parallel to the power lines heading in this direction."

"Fuck that!" Ogdon said, jumping out of the back. "I've got the east side. Mary, reinforce the west, go to RedCon One. Orsini, wake the C.O."

Dole didn't wait for Orsini to make it up to the command Hummer.

"Skipper?" he called out in a normal voice. It only took a single word to wake Quarry out of a sound sleep. "We're in contact."

Quarry threw boots and vest on as Orsini finished giving the information he knew. He looked around the camp. Everything was being done he would have ordered, so he simply grabbed his rifle and jogged over to Caine's B.M.P. It was just after 0900.

From the slight rise in the ground by Caine's position, the approaching vehicle was already in view to the naked eye. Quarry and Grier both looked around the camp. Only the two Iraqi B.M.P.s stood out. Scouts were either behind steering wheels, at weapons, or in dug-out fighting holes.

"Range, five clicks," Orsini announced after looking at the readout of the laser range-finder. Quarry, Grier, and Caine all checked the map simultaneously. The distance and direction placed the now easily identifiable B.T.R.60 on the hard surfaced road northwest of their position. While classified as an armored personnel carrier, the B.T.R. is nothing more than a battlefield taxicab, manned by a crew of three, armed with a 14.5mm and a 7.62mm machine gun, and a carrier of up to eight infantrymen. None of this concerned the Scouts. What scared the hell out of Quarry was that it also carried a couple radios.

"Shit! It turned south," Caine said from behind ten-power binos.

"Aloha drill," Quarry called out. Guy got on the platoon net and passed the order. Picking up the green blouses and black berets, Orsini and Caine started getting in costume.

It took a few minutes for the B.T.R. to make its way to the base of Hill 224. The road the Iraqis traveled was 200 meters west of the Scouts.

"Here they come, skipper," Caine announced. In the B.M.P.'s driver position, Orsini slumped his head in his arms as if asleep, his M-16 leaned against his knee. Caine looked up from on top of the B.M.P. command turret as the B.T.R. drove by. From the road, the B.T.R. commander looked at the vehicle on the hill and waved. Caine returned the gesture as if bored and unconcerned. The B.T.R. continued south without slowing. From inside the B.M.P., Quarry, Grier, Guy, Tellado, Mathews, and Ferrado all gave a collective sigh as they listened to the sound of the vehicle pass by. They placed their weapons on safe.

"Losing sight of 'em," Caine called down. "They're still heading south."

"I want eyes and optics on them until we find out exactly what they're up to," Quarry said, exiting the back hatch. Caine caught Peterson's eye. With a few hand signals, Peterson had Throop back out of their primary fighting position and occupied their supplementary position. This placed Two One's TOW Hummer and Hauser's 50 Hummer in position to clearly observe the AlFawarais police station.

Peterson relinquished the TOW turret to his platoon commander. Quarry climbed up, looked through the optics, and acquired his target. For minutes, Quarry watched the B.T.R. continue south until it stopped at the police station. Through an assortment of different optics, the Scouts also watched. While exact numbers couldn't be made out, at least half a dozen troops unloaded supplies.

"Skipper," Grier said an hour later as he looked through his binos, "I'd bet my left testicle fewer troops got in that thing than originally got out."

"Well I'd hate for Annie to blame me for you coming home half a man, Five, so I won't take that bet. Stand by for another Aloha drill everyone," Quarry said a few seconds later.

The minutes seemed to hang in the air.

"Here they come," Caine called down from the turret as he handed the microphone to Guy. "They're coming north …. Still coming north. They're parallel to us. Oh shit! They stopped!" Every head in the troop compartment looked towards the turret. "They stopped … the vehicle commander is looking over …. He's looking over … oh God, the vehicle is turning."

Quarry reached over and grabbed the microphone from Guy's hand.

"This is Six, hold your fire!" Quarry thrust the microphone at Grier. "If things go wrong, give the command!" Pushing his way to the back of the troop compartment, Quarry called over his shoulder: "Two, report!"

"They've turned off the road, they're heading in this direction."

"If they close to within a hundred, wave to them to come around and behind the B.M.P., then drop down out of the turret and get your ass back here. Orsini, drop down now, use the vision blocks and let us know where they are."

Following his commander's orders, Orsini lifted his head, stretched both arms and patted his mouth as if yawning. He then dropped his seat and looked out the thick slabs of glass that allow the driver to see outside when he drives with the hatch closed.

"You gonna let us in on your little plan, skipper?" Grier's voice rose.

Quarry looked around, grabbed a blanket, and shoved it in Ogdon's chest.

"Close quarters combat, use pistols," Quarry said, looking in Ogdon's eyes. Turning back to Grier, Quarry continued. "Let them come in close. Depending on how many come, Caine and I will take them out. If more than a few come, rifles out the firing ports. If a shit-load come, the platoon supports by fire, the B.M.P. will protect us." Dole grabbed a blanket and extended it to Quarry. Quarry looked down, drew his own pistol and handed it to his driver. "I'll need that back soon."

Dole didn't say anything.

"They're coming," Caine said as he dropped into the troop compartment, making his way to the rear. Ogdon wrapped the blanket around his hand and pistol. Caine drew his pistol and handed it to Tellado. Caine and Quarry took a final look at each other, stepped down and out of the troop compartment. The troop doors of a B.M.P. open in the middle and swing out, so the two Scouts were concealed from view behind each one.

"They stopped 50 feet from us," came a whisper from the front.

"*MarHaba*," a voice called from the B.T.R.

"Two getting out from the side door," Orsini whispered.

"*Sabaah al-khayr*," the voice called again.

Quarry took a deep breath, held it, and called out, "*Sabaah an-noor*." The Scouts in the troop compartment looked at their commander in shock and disbelief.

"One has a pistol in his holster. Looks like a sergeant. The other is a private, carrying his rifle like a golf club," Orsini reported. The humorous visual image of an Iraqi soldier carrying a golf club in the middle of a war momentarily made Quarry lose focus, but the lack of enemy discipline made his decision obvious. He drew his K-bar fighting knife from its sheath.

"*Hayyaak Allah*," he called out. "*Itfaddal*." Be my guest.

"The sergeant is coming to starboard, the one with the rifle to port," Orsini whispered another update.

A few seconds later, Quarry heard each Iraqi footstep in the sand as clearly as a gong. He mentally imaged the distance. When the sergeant was at the front of the B.M.P., Quarry called out, "*Marhaba*."

"*Min fadlak?*" The man had reached the middle of the vehicle.

More footsteps. He was on the other side of the hatch.

As the Iraqi sergeant turned the corner, Quarry's right arm shot out. The K-bar disappeared in the victim's throat, just above the larynx. Quarry pivoted on his right foot, bringing his left arm up and behind the Iraqi's neck. His left hand wrapped around the Iraqi's mouth, stifling any further sounds. The Iraqi's body convulsed a few times, slumped in Quarry's arms, and sank to the sand.

When the private turned the corner of the opposite hatch, he couldn't comprehend the significance of a pale- skinned man, in a strange uniform, holding his sergeant. Caine's arm wrapped around the unsuspecting victim's throat. Caine quickly pulled the man in towards him and locked his own arm with the opposite hand. A quick flex of the biceps and a tug towards the ground voided any remaining blood inside the soldier's carotid arteries. The private passed out immediately, but Caine held his grip, until he could no longer feel the man's pulse.

Quarry made a series of rapid hand and arm signals, praying desperately his intent and the Scouts' training would let them live though the next few minutes. The two bodies were passed up and into the troop compartment and Quarry took his pistol back from Dole. The Scouts readied themselves, and waited.

It took some minutes for the rest of the Iraqis to become curious. Quarry used the time to silently pass on details of the ambush.

"Three getting out of the back," Orsini whispered. "Vehicle commander climbing down .... Driver still in the hatch .... Three moving towards us ..."

A few of the soldiers called out and Quarry invited them for tea.

"Twenty feet away .... Two more getting out .... Just in front of the vehicle ..."

Quarry raised a hand with fingers spread: *Five*. He rotated his thumb in: *Four*; little finger down: *Three* …

They turned in unison. Quarry took out three on his side with one head shot each. Ogdon took out two on his side. Orsini brought up his M-16 and fired a short burst on automatic into the enemy driver. The assault team rushed forward and cleared the inside of the B.T.R.

"Clear," came from several Scouts, from several directions. Then all was quiet. It took moments for everything to sink in.

"Five, check the perimeter," Quarry ordered. As an afterthought, he continued, "Dole, sitrep to Company! Ogie, police up the bodies."

Grier checked the perimeter. Either the sounds of gunfire hadn't reached the 108th or they just didn't care. The Scouts remained at their highest readiness for the rest of the day; still nothing moved within the 108th.

"We need to get that vehicle of here," Quarry commented as dusk set in.

"We can triangulate a position equal distance from the far eastern boundary of the 29th, the police station, and O.P. Three. Ogie can dump the B.T.R. right in the middle. No one should run into it for quite some time," Grier suggested. "I'll coordinate our move with Company and inform DACS we are moving an enemy vehicle. Maybe they can run an air strike on it when we send them the final grids to help cover any questionable tracks?"

"Do it!"

0053, 23 January 1991

Quarry woke abruptly to the sound of artillery from the west.

"Arty is getting some tonight, sir," Dole said, looking over to his commander. He continued with the reports and messages of the day. "Howie said minutes after the first rounds went off over the 29th, the Iraqi outpost went to general quarters. We count six soldiers there, three in the tower, two walking around outside, and one in or near the B.M.P. They didn't move more than a few feet from around the building."

"Thank you, Delta. Why don't you turn in and get some shuteye. I'll take the duty." Minutes later, the "thrump" of incoming artillery woke everyone. This time, the sound came from the east. Seconds later, the platoon net came to life. Both Marion and Mathews observed explosions to the east-northeast. Marion guessed the rounds were falling on the westernmost Iraqi artillery regiment on the far side of the 108th. Quarry trusted Marion's guess more than an "intelligence assessments" from Company and thought an unannounced arty raid in his A.O. was rude and un-neighborly. He picked up the Company net to report the platoon's sightings, but was also looking for some answers.

Apparently, to the west, 5th Battalion, 11th Marines was conducting artillery raids along the "heel" of Kuwait. Last night and this morning, 2nd Battalion, 12th Marines, got in on the act also. The arty raids deceived the Iraqis on the exact locations of forward friendly units, disrupted Iraqi command and control, and all but annihilated specific targets. More importantly, when the Iraqis retaliated, they often did so with rockets. Once the rockets were located with counter-battery radar, a flight of F/A18s came in after them. Quarry liked the idea, but he let the duty officer at Company know, in no uncertain terms, that he didn't like surprises.

* * *

When I Six got on the horn, the platoon leadership was already around the command Hummer. After acknowledging the order, Quarry looked at his notes, his map, and his men.

"We've done it once. We'll do it again, essentially the same way. Grier and I will finalize the plan and bring you in on it in an hour. Meet back here at twenty-one hundred. Dismissed." The squad leaders departed without saying anything. They would receive their orders soon enough.

Fourteen

0010, 24 January 1991

Except the Scouts specifically designated to watch the police station and the 108th, everyone was at the briefing. Taking out his red-lensed pen light, Grier updated the friendly situation.

"CentCom, and therefore I MEF, is moving more units toward the border. The number of artillery raids has increased east and west of us. Light Armored Vehicle Battalion increased the number of raids and reconnaissance missions across the border. Hundreds of sorties are running both close and deep-air missions. At any given time, there are over fifty aircraft either inbound, on target, on call, or egressing. This morning, at 0400, an arc light will conduct blanket bombing of the arty regiment immediately east of the 108th. They will be supported by a FastFAC who will control a flight of two Navy A6s armed with antiradar missiles, and a flight of four Marine F/A18s will target FROGS, air defense artillery and any other units who try to engage the bombers.

"The op is designed to destroy indirect weapons capability but I MEF is using it to divert the attention of the 108th and the 42nd from a simultaneous ground operation. At 0400, we, along with elements of LAV, Force Recon and ANGLICO, will neutralize the remaining Iraqi forward observation posts from the coast all the way to the heel. This will decrease the Iraqis' border observation capability and increase friendly forces' freedom of movement. The targets from the coast to the heel are the AlHazam police station," Grier pointed to the station with the pen light, "located south of the 1st Brigade, 8th Iraqi Infantry; the Al-Jilaidan police station, south of the 2nd Brigade, 8th Iraqi Infantry; the AlMaziam Station, south of the 1st, 42nd; our own AlFawarais station; and lastly, the AsSur police station, located south of the 3rd Brigade, 29th Infantry. The police stations in the heel of the country are not being engaged by ground forces at this time."

"Thank you, Five," Quarry said, taking over the brief. "As of three minutes ago, Marek reported that there are two in the tower, the rest are in the support building. No lights have been seen for over an hour and a half. The op will be run in three phases. Phase One, the control group sets in. Phase Two, the infiltration of the assault team. Phase Three, the relocation of the evidence. Team leaders will now brief their assignments."

"Stone, Cat, Davis and I will watch the tower through N.V.G.s and thermals," Marek said. "Any movement will be relayed to Six on the platoon net. Staff Sergeant Grier will be with us in the One One Hummer. Staff Sergeant Grier has abort, and all contingency plan authority."

"Captain Samuels and I make up the control group," Dole said from under a heavy burlap-laden Ghillie suit. "We are going to leave from here in the Three Two Hummer, manned by Tellado and Ferrado, and stay mounted for four clicks. We will then infiltrate as close as we can, staying on the west side of the building. At no time will we get closer than 300 meters to the tower. I will carry and monitor the platoon tac. We'll check in when set. Silence is consent for the remainder of the operation."

"3rd, minus Tellado and Ferrado, is the security group," Ogdon continued. "We'll use B.M.P.2 to move the assault team to within two clicks of the station unless the control group calls us off. The dismount point will be the low ground in the wadi in the vicinity of Hill 197. If Five calls Foxtrot, we take out their B.M.P. and then put a missile in the building. Fifty-cal will only be used on positively identified threats. Missile fire has priority as it should be concealed by the arc light strikes. During Phase Three, Three One will pick up Six and Delta and escort the enemy B.M.P. to the triangulation point. Three Two will mount the assault team and return to base."

"After dismounting, we'll make our way to the building," Caine finished. "Me and Guy, Marion and Botsford will take the back, located on the east side, which we are calling the main entrance. Kantner and Davis will cover the front from the north. As soon as I hear the air strike in full effect, we use grenades. The east teams will enter, clear the inside, and show a chem light when secure. Cat and Davis have anything that tries to get away to the north, Captain and Dole anything heading west or south. Davis will use the radio to indicate the start of Phase Three."

"We'll keep an eye on the station, the tower, control group, and the 108th," Grier concluded. "Every team has walked through contingency plans. The abort plan is for the primary plan only. Foxtrot is the alternate. As stated in the situation, this op is part of a larger plan. It will go down, one way or the other, questions?" There were none. "Skipper?"

"Anybody have anything they want to say?" There was silence. "See ya in a few hours." As Quarry and Dole got up, many of the Scouts came over to help adjust their suits, offer a final drink of water or check of their gear, a warrior's silent tribute and unspoken "good luck."

"I don't see why the skipper always gets to be in the sniper's position," Marek grumbled to his spotter while Quarry and Dole were being tended to.

"Stone, turn to your Hummer, get me an update. Move," Marion ordered. When Stone was out of earshot, Marion turned to his second team leader and moved in close. "This isn't a fucking game!" Marin forcefully whispered. "Now get your ass over to the Hummer and carry out your mission." Marek silently turned to carry out his orders. "And Marek?"

"Yes, Corporal Marion," Marek said solemnly.

"If I ever hear anything like that again, you won't like results."

Marek swallowed hard before answering, "Yes, Corporal."

It was about six clicks from Hill 224 to the station. Quarry and Dole had planned to infiltrate the entire distance, but Grier, Ogdon, and Caine and Marion adamantly opposed the idea, as the route would take them to close to Gathering Center 10. While no Iraqis had used the center the entire time the Scouts had been in position, that didn't mean a worst-case scenario wouldn't find the control group caught in the middle of a last-minute patrol. Quarry finally agreed to the overwhelming opinion of his leaders and accepted the mounted ingress for the first four clicks.

Quarry and Dole took the two passenger-side seats in Three Two. After confirmation from Marek, Cat, and Grier that all was quiet, Carleton pulled out. Ferrado was on the 50 with N.V.G.s while Hauser rode shotgun on top of the turret. Averaging a maximum speed just above idle to keep the noise to an absolute minimum, it took the Hummer 20 minutes to reach its turn-around spot. As Carleton maneuvered the Hummer into the two-foot drop of the wadi, Quarry and Dole opened the doors and rolled out. The Hummer made a wide arc and headed back in the direction of Hill 224. Quarry and Dole remained in place without moving.

It took over an hour and a half for Quarry and Dole to reach the station. The morning's temperature was in the upper thirties, but beneath the yards of shredded burlap, the two Scouts sweated profusely. They tolerated the discomfort, knowing that from 280 meters away the shredded burlap blended in with their surroundings without an edge. Even in the increasing moonlight, the only way they'd be detected was if stepped on. Dole transmitted, "Set." From their vantage point, the two watched and waited.

"They're inbound, sir," Dole whispered. Quarry shifted his attention from the B.M.P. to the building. Nothing moved. There was no indication anyone inside was awake. Eventually, Quarry thought he saw dark silhouettes creep into his field of view, but the shadows blended with those cast by the station itself and were lost from sight.

"Any second," Dole informed his commander. Quarry clicked the safety off his rifle and sighted in on the tower.

The first bombs of the B-52s either struck further east than Quarry anticipated or they were only using 250-pound bombs. The difference in what he heard and what was expected made little difference; it was the signal to commence their ground assault. Three seconds later, the unmistakable sound of four grenades came from the police station. Half a breath later, the silhouette of a body rose in the tower. Quarry squeezed the trigger and the shape fell from sight. By the time Quarry reacquired his sight picture from the recoil of the shot, a second target presented itself. A quarter of a second later, it too was neutralized. A shot came from within the building, then all was silent.

"Chem stick," Dole announced. Quarry took the word of his spotter without coming off target. "Scout coming out." Quarry picked up the movement in the lower left portion of his scope. The dark shape slung his rifle over his back, withdrew a pistol and started to ascend the ladder leading to the tower. Seconds later, a second chem stick illuminated the back of the platform.

"Target!" Dole called out in a high-pitched voice, "B.M.P., driver's hatch!" Quarry shifted his point of aim a few minutes of angle. Where there had been horizon and stars, was now a perfect black circle of an open driver hatch.

"On," Quarry announced.

"Echo Five Charlie, contact, soldier in the B.M.P.!" Dole transmitted feverishly over the radio.

An unidentified voice yelled from the building. Even at that distance, Quarry could make out the words "Caine" and "B.M.P." Quarry watched a dark outline drop from the observation post onto the top of the combat vehicle below. The Scout never stood but bent over the turret. It took a second but Quarry realized the Scout was disregarding the danger to himself to break the vehicle's radio antenna at the back of the cupola. Another shadow, rising from the B.M.P., caught Quarry's eye. Like the outline of a snowman, a small circle appeared, rising above the larger circle of the driver's hatch. Knowing Caine was low, Quarry fired high. The shape dropped from sight.

Quarry sprang from his firing position and started sprinting towards the station. Momentarily surprised, Dole pursued his platoon commander.

In the minute it took Quarry to close the distance, the assault team cleared the rest of the B.M.P. When Quarry was close enough, voices confirmed the worst had not happened. Supported by Marion, Caine was sitting up.

"Secure the vehicle! Set a perimeter!" Quarry yelled angrily. Guy and Bots jumped down and headed toward the back of the troop compartment.

"Caine?" Quarry asked gently, looking at the blood-splattered face of his squad leader and friend.

"I'm fine, skipper," Caine said, still slightly out of breath from the adrenaline dump. After a second, he continued: "I can't believe you shot me."

Quarry's heart skipped a beat as he looked from the smirking Scout to the dead Iraqi soldier. Quarry reached down and grabbed the body and pulled it backwards. An A.K.47 with the bolt locked forward fell to the B.M.P.'s floor. The single entry hole in the back of the soldier's head was barely visible.

The exit wound had literally blown out the entire front of the soldier's face. A face that was now splattered all over this squad leader. Quarry looked back at Caine in confusion. With a smile on his face, Caine patted the outside of his flak vest until he found what he was looking for. Reaching up and pulling his knife from its scabbard, Caine made a small cut in the outer lining of the Kevlar vest and retrieved a small mushroom-shaped object. He stretched out his arm.

"I believe this belongs to you," Caine said, depositing the now deformed and still warm bullet in Quarry's open hand.

Quarry looked at it in disbelief.

"You keep it," he said, handing the spent slug back to his squad leader. "And the next time you do something so stupid as to jump down off a tower to play radio operator, it just may be your ass I shoot instead!" The two paused, laughed, and hugged each other.

"I hate to break up this Kodak moment," Marion said. "but the building and B.M.P. are secure."

"As is the tower," Caine added. "Nice shooting by the way. Three more confirmed."

Only minutes had passed since the first B-52 started dropping bombs. Quarry once again became aware that the air war was still being conducted northeast of them. "I doubt anybody paid us any attention but let's police up the compound and get the hell out of here." As if on cue, Ogdon's Hummers pulled up. "Can you stand?" Quarry asked and assisted his squad leader.

"My ribs will be a little sore tomorrow but considering the alternative that's a small price to pay." Quarry helped Caine to the edge of the B.M.P. and then to get down. As Caine climbed in the back of Three One, Quarry noticed the slick film of blood and tissue on his hands. Quarry looked back at the B.M.P. where the enemy soldier's body lay sprawled on the floor. A cold shiver ran down the length of Quarry's spine, but when he looked back to Caine, talking to Ogdon, the feeling disappeared.

Around the station, Scouts removed bodies and placed them in the back of the B.M.P. Guy started the enemy vehicle. In less than two minutes, the small convoy departed for the open desert.

26 January 1991

"*Ya naqeeb* Aziz," 1st Sergeant Zamir called out as he approached the tank. "The refueling trucks have come."

"How many gallons do we get today?"

"Sir, every tank is being filled!"

* * *

"The refueler is spending ten to 15 minutes at each tank, sir," Marion commented.

"Going right down the line. Everyone's getting topped off," Ogdon added.

"I think what we have here is what the spooks call an indicator of enemy intent," Quarry said from behind the binos. "Keep an eye on 'em Ogie," he added, handing the binos back to Laumeyer. "We'll let Company know what's going on."

27 January 1991

"*Ya naqeeb* Aziz," the 1st sergeant reported. "Battalion maintenance is here to fix the two tanks that didn't start yesterday."

"Thank you, *ya raqeeb awwal.*"

"Any word from battalion yet, sir?"

"Not yet. Have patience and trust in the will of Allah."

"*Hayyaak Allah,*" Zamir replied.

* * *

"Jeep!" Tellado said from behind the TOW sights.

"Got it!" Laumeyer said, adjusting the dirstion of his binoculars.

"Go get Sergeant Ogdon; he'll want to see this."

* * *

"Remember that Iraqi captain you saluted during your drive-by a few weeks ago?" Ogdon asked Quarry.

"Sure do."

"A jeep came and picked him up. One driver, no others, departed east down the line, in a big hurry."

"And in the ten days we've been here Sergeant Ogdon, have you seen anything that's been done in a hurry?" Quarry asked.

"There is a first time for everything, sir."

Quarry looked at his squad leader and smiled.

"I'll be on the horn with Company. When they come back, call me over."

* * *

"The plot thickens," Quarry said from behind the TOW sights. "Looks like an orders group. Five?"

"The captain, three officers, one enlisted, most likely the company gunny or a first sergeant," Grier said, from behind a 45-power spotting scope on sandbags on the top of Marion's turret. "Drawing some lines in the sand ... pointing south."

Quarry watched the Iraqi officers get in line and walk behind their company commander. "I'd call that a rehearsal. What do you say, Five?"

"I'd say they have more practicing to do."

"Now, now, Five. Here they are showing us everything they have and you want more. You're always thinking about yourself. You can be so greedy."

* * *

"The division continues in column," Aziz said over his shoulder to the officers and 1st sergeant walking behind him. "*Al-aqeed* Karim will give the signal by radio. 1st Brigade will slow down to allow 3rd Brigade to move and take position to our left. We will continue at a slow pace until 2nd Brigade moves between us and 3rd Brigade."

"Will we see the B.M.P.s of 2nd Brigade behind us, *naqeeb*?" the 3rd platoon commander asked.

"We will not, but to the east, our 3rd Battalion will. The tanks of 3rd Brigade will be too far to our left to see." Aziz walked them a few more paces. "When *al-aqeed* Karim gives the order, the brigade will form a line. Battalions in both lead brigades will move in column. Our 2nd Battalion will come to our right, our 3rd Battalion will come to the left." Aziz walked them a few more paces. "*Al-muqaddam* Rahaman will then give the next order by radio and by flare. When you see the first flare, it will be the signal for companies to form line," Aziz held both arms out to his sides. The platoon commanders moved to each side of Aziz and the 1st sergeant continued to walk behind the 3rd platoon commander.

"When we are ready for the final attack, the battalion commander will fire two flares. Your platoons will come on line with you." The 1st sergeant moved to the 3rd platoon commander's left without having to be told. "We will continue to close with the enemy. We will begin firing at maximum effective range, 1,000 meters. We will attack through the enemy line and allow the infantry of 2nd Brigade to break any enemy resistance. We will continue on line until we see the third set of flares. We will then wait for further orders."

28 January 1991

Marion watched tanks pull in and out of their fighting holes.

"Get the skipper, Staff Sergeant Grier, and all team leaders over here," he ordered.

It took only a minute for the Scout leadership to assemble.

"What ya got, Mary?" Grier asked as he and Quarry approached.

"Lots of movement but nobody going anywhere," Marion commented, handing Grier the binos. Quarry relieved Botsford at the TOW sights.

In front of them, as far as the eye could see with ten-powered optics, vehicles were moving back and forth from their fighting positions, ensuring they were free from the dirt that had entombed them earlier.

"See anybody moving on the road?" Quarry asked.

"Nothing, skipper. No moving to alternate or subsequent positions, just back and forth."

Quarry slewed the TOW system to the left. The B.M.P. Brigade was dancing the same dance. A small dust cloud even further north suggested Hard Luck Brigade was probably doing the same.

"Five, let Company know what's going on. See if any of the other O.P.s have anything to report."

Grier returned a short time later.

"Nothing, boss. But they're sure as hell interested in what's going on here though. They want updates every half-hour."

"Roger that. Mary, give Company what they want until they get tired of hearing it. If it gets too stretched out, Ogie and you can trade off." Both squad leaders acknowledged their orders.

* * *

"Hello. What do we have here?" Marion wondered. Then the tone of his voice changed. "Get the skipper."

"On it," Davis said, leaving the area.

Less than a minute later, Quarry and Grier were also watching the jeep.

"It came from Tank Brigade," Marion reported, "hit the hard ball and turned north. Now it's just sitting there."

Quarry took the compass out of his flak jacket pocket.

"Range?" From inside the Hummer, Davis plugged the range-finder into the G.P.S, pointed at the jeep, and pulled the trigger.

"Three thousand, four hundred, seventy, sir."

"Zero four seven magnetic," Quarry added.

Davis added the direction into the G.P.S. and turned the dial to calculate. "Grid, 8042 6910."

Ogdon found the grid on the map.

"That puts them on the road intersection northwest of the Gathering Center." Quarry looked over Ogdon's shoulder to where his finger plotted the enemy jeep.

"New contact," Mathews spoke up. "Jeep coming out of the B.M.P. Brigade, moving directly toward Jeep One."

Every leader turned binos or sights toward the new movement. "Five, get on the spotter scope." From within the Hummer, Davis handed the scope up through the turret immediately followed by a sandbag.

Grier climbed up and positioned the optics.

"The first jeep has a driver and three passengers. Unable to tell much more than that." He paused. "Second jeep taking position on the first. Salutes by the drivers. None of the passengers exchanging salutes."

"New contact. Another jeep coming from Tank Brigade," Mathews sang out. "One driver, one passenger."

"Got another one coming from Hard Luck Brigade," Botsford announced.

"Turning out to be quite a little party," Quarry commented.

"The second jeep from Tank Brigade pulled up with the others," Grier reported. "The first three saluted the newcomer. The passengers from Jeep Two and Three rendered salutes."

"New contact, from B.M.P. Brigade area, one driver, one passenger."

"Another one coming down from Hard Luck."

Grier continued to watch.

"Mary, did the first jeep pick up the tanker captain?"

"No, Staff Sergeant. Came from further east and drove right by the first tank."

"Skipper, I'd bet a month's pay we're looking at three brigade commanders and nine battalion commanders."

"Shall I get the DASC on the 109, sir?" Ogdon asked.

Quarry looked at his squad leader and then back towards the Iraqi officers. On one hand, an F/A-18 could take out the better part of an entire division's leadership. On the other hand, without the division commander present, any operation would probably go on anyway after the X.O.s took command. Bringing in a fast-mover now against a mere cluster of jeeps would compromise the Scouts' position. Quarry considered his options before answering: "Let's see what they're up to first, Ogie."

A division-level rehearsal without the division commander? Quarry thought. The jeeps married themselves up in twos. The first couple moved in front of the others.

"Tank Brigade C.O. followed by his battalion commanders," Grier guessed. The second and third pair moved into column behind the first set. After a few minutes, the rear-most jeeps moved to the left of the first pair. When they were on line with the lead jeeps, all moved south simultaneously.

"Why have a rehearsal all the way over here?" Caine asked from behind a pair of binos.

"Probably to stay out from under the division commander," Ogie guessed.

"Fewer oil pipes to run into?" Marion commented.

"All getting on the same sheet of music?" Quarry added. In front of them, the second group of jeeps waited until the first two sets moved, followed the first pair for a few minutes, then angled left and centered themselves between but behind the front sets.

The triangle of jeeps continued until the first two sets stopped. The center-rear pair continued until they were on line and parallel with the others. When all the jeeps stopped, the occupants got out and gathered together, all less than 2,000 meters in front of the Scouts.

Fifteen

29 January 1991

Throughout the morning, every Iraqi vehicle within view was started, pulled out of position, returned and shut down. Maintenance teams moved among vehicles like ants at a picnic. Refuelers moved about too. Just after 1200, the first of several jeeps moved into what the Scouts were now calling the training area.

"1st Battalion's turn, skipper."

"How's that, Bots?"

"The jeep that came out stopped by the first tank of the Tank Brigade and picked up one person. Now the three are paying attention to the one in front." Quarry turned his binos in the direction of Botsford's missile launcher. Directly in front of them, no more than two clicks away, was a group of three soldiers taking orders from a fourth. The three walked in column for a while and then moved on line with each other. Quarry and Bots watched the drill repeated three times. After each practice, the fourth officer critiqued the three. "Doesn't have much faith in his company commanders does he, sir?"

The observation by the young Scout was right on the money.

"Kinda makes you wonder who's training who," Quarry replied.

The Scouts continued to watch the commanders for most the afternoon. It wasn't until the onset of evening prayers that the last group departed the area.

"Wonder what's on the schedule for tomorrow?" Quarry mentioned.

* * *

"Get Captain Samuels, now!" Dole called to Slayer. Without questioning, Slayer ran to Caine's B.M.P. where the leadership was listening to the latest B.B.C. broadcast on the short-wave.

As Slayer approached, Guy stuck his head out of the driver's compartment and called over to his squad leader.

"Sergeant Caine!" When Caine looked to his driver, Guy continued. "Six Delta ordered RedCon Two." As he finished his sentence, every head turned toward to Slayer.

"Sir, Dole told me to come get you. Didn't say what it was."

Everyone moved with a purpose. Squad leaders returned to their vehicles as Quarry and Grier ran to the command Hummers. When they arrived, Dole sat intently behind the radio.

"Sir, O.P. Four was attacked."

"Who's at Four?" Quarry asked.

"2nd Platoon, Alpha Company, 1st Recon," Grier answered.

"O.P. Four, wasn't that Stevens' old hang-out?"

"Yes, sir, but they haven't been in the A.O. for a while now." Reports started coming in on the platoon net, the Scouts exceeded RedCon Two, but still the 108th didn't budge. Quarry looked at his watch. It was 0726.

"Is there anyone out there to assist?" Quarry asked.

"Yes sir, Task Force Shephard is right behind them."

"Three companies Light Armored Infantry?"

"Yes, sir. Company D, 3rd LAV, and A and B Company, 1st LAV. I think they also have two batteries from 5/11 in support."

"Any indication of the size of the enemy force?" Quarry directed his question to Dole.

"First report is an estimated fifty vehicles sir."

"No movement from our friends?"

"No movement from the 108th, sir."

"Roger that. Let's not go to general quarters yet. Let's see what happens." Grier turned on the Tactical Air Control Party net. Air support was being directed against the enemy column of approximately thirty B.M.P.s supported by at least five tanks. The initial air strike did little to stop the Iraqi advance, but more assets were being called to support the Marines fighting for their lives. It was 0800.

* * *

"Davis," Laumeyer softly called. "Davis?"

"Yeah?" the Scout behind the thermal sights of Three One called back.

"Hear anything?"

"Yeah. A few engines cranking over. Why?"

"Sounds like more than a few to me."

"I think you're right," Davis agreed. "You want to run or watch?"

"I'll run," Laumeyer said, leaning half way out of the turret.

In the moonlight, Laumeyer's motion caught Ogdon's attention. By the time Ogdon crossed the camp, Laumeyer was no more than ten feet from the Hummer.

"Lots of engines starting up, sergeant. Standing orders say bring anything out of the ordinary to your attention. This is the first time they've started this many engines at one time at night." Ogdon stopped and cocked his head to one side in the direction of the 108th. He turned and made eye contact with Marion. A quick nod in the direction of the command Hummers was all it took. Marion was off at a trot.

Quarry and Grier were sitting next to the Hummer under the cammie net, listening to as many radios as they possessed. As Marion lifted one side of the net, Quarry and Grier's ears also perked up to the sound.

"Lots of engines starting, skipper."

"Let's take a look." It took less than thirty seconds for the three to get over to Ogdon's TOW Hummer. "How many warming up?"

"Most of them, sir."

Quarry climbed in the driver's seat.

"Three Two this is Six on your push, over," Quarry said on 3rd squad's radio frequency. Quarry looked through the Hummer to where Stone sat in his turret. "Report contacts to the south, over."

"Negative contact, Six, nothing all day, over."

"Roger, Six out." Quarry climbed out of the Hummer and grabbed a set of N.V.G.s. Nothing was moving, yet. "Go to RedCon One," Quarry ordered.

"I don't see anything out there, skipper," Marion commented. "What'd ya catch?"

"Nothing, Mary. That's the problem. No soldiers walking around, no cooking fires, no one loitering behind tanks. Five?"

"Shit!" Marion said under his breath.

"RedCon One being set. Guy reports negative contact to the west."

"Roger that. I'm going to get Company on the horn. Ogie, if even one vehicle backs up, let me know immediately."

"Aye, aye, sir."

Quarry and Grier wasted no time getting back to the command Hummer. Quarry called Company and asked if there were any other significant developments reported in the company's area of interest.

The master sergeant simply answered, "Nothing yet," and asked why. Quarry summed what was happening and gave his estimate of the situation. He started to say something else when Ogdon's voice over the platoon net interrupted him."

"Six, this is Three, movement."

"Watch the store for me," Quarry said, exiting the vehicle. In seconds, he was back at Ogdon's Hummer. He didn't need night-vision goggles to see the first tank of Tank Brigade facing west and pulling towards the road intersection. The second tank in line was backing up and pivoting; the third was backing out of its fighting position. As Quarry looked down the line, the other tanks were also backing up.

"Get my Hummer over here," Quarry ordered. Ogdon made the appropriate hand signals in Dole's directions. In only took moments for the command Hummer to pull up. Dole handed both handsets out the passenger window. Quarry grabbed the Company mic and stood where he could see the formation. "I Six, this is Scout Six, over."

"Send it Scout Six," the Top answered.

"Tanks lining up. Lead tank on M.S.R. facing south. Tank Brigade staging, over." Quarry turned to the northeast. "Bots, what's B.M.P. Brigade doing?"

"Engines running, glowing hot in thermals. Haven't pulled out yet."

"Hard Luck?"

"Running and glowing. Hard to tell anything else," Bots said, his eye pressed firmly against the optics. Quarry passed the additional information to Company as well.

When the other end answered, the voice was different and unmistakable.

"Hard copy Scout Six. Continue to observe. Report first southern movement by lead tank. Will get some eyes over that way. I Six out."

"Sir?"

"Yeah, Bots."

"I can't tell because of the distance, but I'm pretty sure Hard Luck is moving east."

Quarry considered the report.

"Makes sense, sir," Grier commented. "We watched them practice doctrinal formation drills in daylight. How about this? Hard Luck moves east now, to get east of Tank, before both move south in a two-up one-back formation."

"That means they go from the march formation to a pre-attack formation, right from their fighting positions," Quarry thought out loud.

The Scouts continued to watch the lack of movement in Tank Brigade for another 30 minutes. "Hard Luck is out of their positions and lost in the thermal clutter to the east, sir," Bots reported. "I can't pick them out at all anymore."

"Thank you, Bots." Still, the Tank Brigade showed no indication of movement.

Thirty minutes later, Tellado reported a new contact.

"Bulldozer, behind Tank Brigade's old line, moving west."

"Confirmed," Bots said. Moments later, he sang out again, "Got two more."

Quarry put N.V.G.s to his eyes. The first vehicle was a commercial bulldozer and sat at the road intersection. In a few more minutes, the other two dozers caught up with the first. When the three bulldozers started south, the lead tank followed behind them. Quarry looked over his shoulder and called out to Grier. "Enemy tank brigade, attacking south." Grier relayed the information to Company.

"Sir," Dole called out from inside the Hummer, "Joint Forces Command East reports two Iraqi brigades crossed the border into Saudi Arabia and are approaching the city of Khafji."

"Roger," was all that Quarry said in acknowledgement. It was just before 2300. "Five," Quarry said, gaining the attention of his platoon sergeant, "gather the leaders." With a simple look from Grier, Slayer was off.

Quarry placed his map on the hood of his Hummer.

"We're going to track them, try to find out their intention," Quarry started. "We're here," he said, pointing to Hill 224. "We'll follow the west-most road, the one that leads down to the police station. We'll continue south from there using G.P.S. That will give us over three and a half clicks' separation. Should be far enough that they don't notice us. If they do anything, and I mean anything that would indicate we've been compromised, we beat feet due west. If they're in the attack, they shouldn't pursue us. We'll only take the TOW Hummers. The rest stay here. Sergeant Ogdon, Three Two will also go for point defense. You and Three Two, take the lead. I'm next, offset to your right. Caine, you've got the camp. Keep Company up to date, based on our platoon traffic. Two One will follow me followed by One One. Mary, maintain contact with Marek on your net, have him watch our ass close. Questions?" There were none. "Let's move."

The Scouts were ready in minutes. Ogdon moved his Hummer to the west of the hill with Hauser close behind. Dole pulled the command Hummer behind Hauser and in less than two minutes, Two One and One One were ready to go also. Marion gave an "up" on the platoon net, and Ogdon started forward.

The Scouts held their position at Gathering Center 10, while they watched the column of tanks turn southeast. Slayer lazed one of the tanks and calculated their position. "They're at the road intersection at 815 648, moving southeast at ten kilometers an hour."

Caine's voice came over the platoon net: "Six, this is Two, over."

"Send it," Quarry responded.

"ANGLICO reporting two Iraqi brigades overran Khafji, over."

"Roger, out." Quarry looked at his watch. It was 2315.

Slayer lazed another tank.

"Lead tank now at 827 648, heading due south, speed still ten clicks." Quarry checked the enemy position on his map and motioned Ogdon to continue as planned.

Minutes later, the Tank Brigade turned again, this time to the southwest.

"Scouts halt, wedge formation, move," Quarry hurriedly transmitted over the radio. In seconds, the Hummers complied with the orders.

"By turning southwest, it confirms they're still on the road," Grier added.

"But why would they do that?" Quarry asked no one in particular. He brought the microphone to his lips again. "Three, lead us to the north side of the police station." Without verbal confirmation, Three One moved.

It took only ten minutes for the Scouts to set their vehicles around the deserted police station. Two Hummers faced south and watched Tank Brigade. Marion faced east and watched the B.M.P. Brigade follow the 3rd Battalion of Tank Brigade. Hard Luck Brigade was nowhere to be seen. Quarry, Grier, and Dole climbed into the tower. In the moonlight, Quarry made out two dark stains on the floor, indicators of his marksmanship days before. He lifted the N.V.G.s to his eyes and concentrated on the mission at hand.

"Grid."

Dole shot the laser and calculated the exact point.

"They're still on the road, right at the berm."

"Ogie, report," Quarry said over the P.R.C.77 set on the platoon net.

"Bulldozers working on the berm, over."

"Five, get on the 109. Get me some air support." Grier balanced the extra P.R.C.-77 on the sill and climbed down the ladder.

At four clicks away, the sounds of the bulldozer were easily heard.

"Dole, get Colonel Ahmed on the radio." Dole read Quarry's mind and quickly dialed in the frequency for the Saudi Brigade. It took five minutes of calling before anyone on the other end answered. When they did, Quarry grabbed the handset. "This is Captain Samuels," Quarry said over the radio in perfect Arabic. "This is an emergency. Get Colonel Ahmed on the radio immediately."

"The colonel has gone to bed, Captain Samuels," the voice answered.

"Wake him now! You are going to be attacked! Go!" There was no response from the other end. "Think he got it?"

"Sounded good to me, sir. I didn't realize you'd been studying Arabic that much," Dole said with a mic pressed to each ear.

"Neither did I," Quarry answered. A minute later, a different voice came over the Saudi net and identified himself. Quarry recognized the name as the brigade operations officer.

"Colonel, an Iraqi attack is taking place along the entire border. There are two Iraqi brigades currently at 805 599. They are about to break through the berm. They will be able to attack you in less than thirty minutes, over!"

"*Ya naqeeb* Samuels. Is this true?"

Quarry moved the hand set to in front of his face and stared at it in disbelief.

"No you stupid fucking son of a bitch. I'm making the whole thing up to make you shit your dress!" Quarry yelled at the handset in front of him. Dole couldn't hold back a burst of laughter. Quarry returned the microphone to his ear and clearly and simply transmitted, "Yes, sir," in Arabic. "This is an unsecured net, don't ask me how I know, but it is true. Please hurry."

"Thank you, Captain Samuels," the colonel responded in English, his voice a higher pitch.

"Six," Grier called up from the Hummer.

"Yeah."

"All green, blue and purple air is running missions or being diverted to either Khafji or Task Force Ripper."

"Try arty." Both Quarry and Grier knew damn well any artillery in the area would be out of range, or supporting green forces, but they had to try. From his vantage point, Quarry watched the first bulldozer open a hole in the berm.

Quarry continued to watch as the second dozer assisted the first, effectively halving the time it would take to finish a breach.

"No arty, Six." Quarry contemplated the consequences of Grier's last statement. A man Quarry had come to know and respect might soon be dead.

"Roger, Five. Get your butt up here."

As Quarry yelled to Grier, the radio broke squelch: "*Assalaamu alaykum bil'akh naqeeb* Samuels."

"Jesus Christ!" Quarry blurted, recognizing Colonel Ahmed's voice. *This guy is about to be run over and he's stringing out traditional greetings.* Lifting the receiver, taking a deep breath and keying the net, Quarry gave the traditional response: "*Wa alaykumu ssalaam, bil'akh aqeed* Ahmed."

Quarry heard the colonel laugh as he keyed his side of the net.

"No doubt you are wondering if I plan on continuing small talk and greetings," Ahmed said, switching to English. "I assure you, brother Samuels, I am not. I want to thank you for all that you have done for us. We are prepared."

"That is good news, sir. May Allah smile upon you and your men tonight."

"He already has, brother Samuels. We will feast at my home when this is all over. I must go now."

"*Hayyaak Allah, bil'akh aqeed* Ahmed."

"*Allah yahayyeek, bil'akh naqeeb* Samuels." A lump developed in the back of Quarry's throat. He truly hoped they'd have that dinner.

"I don't get it, Five," Quarry said somberly. "We watched the drills: Brigades to battalions, battalions to companies, companies to platoons. March, preassault and attack formations. Now this."

"Don't read too much into it, skipper. They don't have G.P.S., no history of training at night, and there sure as hell aren't any traffic signals that say no left turn on red. Someone screwed up."

"In this case, I hope so." Whatever the original plan was, the 108th was now divided. The three Scouts watched in silence as the bulldozers finished and moved to the side of the breach.

* * *

The horizon was clear, the stars were bright, but the lights Aziz had been told to follow, the ones that would guide him into the city, were not there. He could see the lights and hear the sounds of combat, but they came from the east. There were no cities to the west, only along the coast. The division was supposed to be heading toward the coast. The brigade commander climbed off the back of the bulldozer and stood to the side of the berm. *Surely there was a change of orders. Maybe the commander did not transmit them to maintain radio silence.*

"Drive toward the stars shining in Jidda's belt," Aziz told his driver over the tank intercom. The driver started forward. As they went through the breach in the berm, the brigade commander stood at the side and shouted encouragement as his men passed.

* * *

The Iraqi division's chief of staff was chewing the ass of the support platoon commander.

"Where are all the other bulldozers?" he screamed at the young lieutenant. The lieutenant tried to tell the colonel that five of his vehicles weren't running and that he didn't know where three of the operational ones were. He pled his case but it fell on deaf ears. With only one bulldozer attempting to make a dent in the berm, 3rd Brigade was backed up and massed in a very small area, waiting to go through a hole that didn't exist and wouldn't for some time. After another round of answerless questions, the colonel got back into his jeep.

"Drive me towards the coast," he told the driver. "Maybe 1st and 2nd Brigades missed a turn."

* * *

"Why are you leading us in this direction?" the battalion commander yelled across the tank as it came to a stop.

"*Aqeed al-Karim* pointed me in this direction, *muqaddam*," Aziz answered.

"This is not right. I will go and confirm the colonel's intent myself." The battalion commander's tank turned around and proceeded back down the column. Aziz kept his tank moving just enough for forward momentum. It would take another 40 minutes for 2nd Battalion to pass through the gap and another hour for 3rd Battalion to clear the berm. It wasn't for another two hours until Aziz got the order to move at normal speed. Aziz keyed the intercom and told his driver to move at ten kilometers an hour. He would wait until 3rd Battalion was on line with him before he would order the increase to double that speed.

* * *

134

"Give 2nd SANG another update," Quarry ordered. "Tell them all Iraqi vehicles of the lead brigade have cleared the breach: two tank battalions, one B.M.P. battalion. Additional B.M.P. Brigade following in trace. Estimated speed, ten kilometers an hour. Estimated time to their position, one hour. Five, I'm taking 3rd Squad to go see what's happening to the east of us."

"Don't you mean, we are going to go see what's to the east of us?"

"I need you to stay here and let 2nd SANG know of any changes. Dole will keep you company." Dole looked up from his radio, clearly displeased.

By the look on Grier's face, he wasn't too happy with the change of mission either.

"Ya know, skipper, the Saudis have thermals in their A-3s. Two more missile shooters here would be a lot better if one or two of those tanks turned tail and came back through the breach."

"That's why you're the man while I'm away," Quarry said, punching Grier in the arm. "You are highly qualified to watch my ass to the east, two Iraqi brigades to the southwest, and smart enough not to confuse the two."

Even Dole smirked on that one. Grier knew that further discussion was out of the question.

"Well, at least take this," Grier said, holding out the P.R.C.-109. "If you get in a shit sandwich, give air a call. There's a hell of a stack waiting to get in on some action."

Quarry took the radio.

"Thanks," he said as he climbed down the ladder.

* * *

"Where in the love of Allah is Colonel Karim!" the chief of staff yelled as he pounded his fist upon the hood of the jeep. With no one around to answer, the driver simply looked away. They were already half way to the coast. No one from either the 42nd or the 8th Infantry Divisions saw a lost colonel, let alone over seventy tanks and 140 B.M.P.s. "Take me back to the berm."

* * *

"They're still just sitting there, sir," Tellado said to Quarry from behind the TOW sights.

"Get us another 500 meters closer," Quarry called down from the turret.

* * *

When the chief of staff returned to the berm, his anger turned to rage. "Why haven't you moved your command through the breach, Colonel?" he roared at the commander of Hard Luck Brigade.

With only one bulldozer working, the breach had opened just enough to move a single tank through.

"We were about to move as you pulled up, sir." The colonel moved the mouthpiece towards his lips and keyed the net. The chief of staff watched in disgust at the incompetence.

* * *

"Someone in the jeep got out and approached a tank. Stand by …. The lead tank is starting to move, sir."

Quarry shot the laser range-finder one more time to confirm the grid. He brought the microphone to his mouth and keyed the net.

"Alpha November Lima 36, this is Mike Romeo Foxtrot 17, over."

"Mike Romeo Foxtrot 17, this is Alpha November Lima 36, over," the net responded almost immediately.

"Alpha November Lima 36, this is Mike Romeo Foxtrot 17, fire mission, over."

"Mike Romeo Foxtrot 17, this is Alpha November Lima 36, roger. Authenticate Whiskey Oscar, over."

"Golf!" Ogie called up from his passenger seat as his red penlight danced on the pages of the C.E.O.I.

"Alpha November Lima 36, this is Mike Romeo Foxtrot 17, I authenticate Golf, over."

"Mike Romeo Foxtrot 17, this is Lone Warrior. Use of abbreviated call signs is authorized. Send your request."

* * *

The Iraqi command came over the radio: "Form battalion on line, companies in column." Aziz's tank never went above five kilometers an hour as it waited for 2nd Company to come alongside. Aziz looked over his shoulder; his 1st Platoon lieutenant waved in recognition. Deep to the left and behind him, he heard tank engines increasing their speed. *Forming companies on line should be conducted in less than five minutes*, Aziz thought, *but tonight, the battalion would do well if we did it in less than twenty.*

* * *

As the enemy tanks started maneuvering into "pre-battle" formation, the Saudi squad leader atop the M113 armored personnel carrier recalled his infantry from their forward observation post. The squad leader made a count of his men as they entered the vehicle. The forward-most enemy tank was

1,500 meters away from them. That placed the enemy armor just over seven kilometers away from the 2nd SANG's defensive line.

From inside his M60A3 tank, Ahmed keyed his net.

"Battalion commanders. Reconnaissance unit number two confirms Captain Samuels' report. The enemy armor is now in prebattle formation and moving toward us. Have every tank change its monitor to the brigade frequency. When the enemy is 1,200 meters from us, I will order the brigade to fire. We will use the frontal fire pattern. If the enemy continues to move against us, I will give a second command. If any enemy armor closes to within 1,000 meters, tanks may fire at will. May Allah bless us and have mercy on our Arab brothers. Relay my message to all of your soldiers. Ahmed out."

* * *

Quarry reshot the grid of center mass of vehicles stacked up on the north side of the berm.

"Lone Warrior, this is Scout Six," Quarry said, keying the net. "Target One, grid 885 594, altitude 138 above mean sea level, break. Direction 087 magnetic, range 3,000. Iraqi armored brigade in the open, over."

The target acquisition officer held the microphone away from his ear.

"Damn, this guy sounds familiar," he said as he quickly looked at the map on his tactical display. "Scout Six, this is Lone Warrior, confirming grid 885 594, direction 087, range 3,000, over."

"Lone Warrior, this is Scout Six. Hard copy, shoot straight you fucking squid, over." This told the battleship the Scouts were directly in the line of fire, 3,000 meters past the target. If the Navy overshot the target, 3rd Squad would never know what hit them.

"I swear I know this guy," the T.A.O. said. "Roger, Scout Six, stand by." Lowering the handset, the Navy lieutenant looked at his map again. "Do we have a firing solution, Chief?"

"Turrets One, Two and Three, locked on."

"Recalculate and confirm solution," the lieutenant ordered.

The chief gave a look of disapproval, but knowing a Marine squad was on the other side of the gun target line made pressing a single button worth the effort. "Confirmed, Lieutenant. Turrets loaded and ready."

"Weapons officer, I have a firing solution. Request permission to fire."

The Navy commander looked at the tactical display, the weapons status board and the digital firing solution readouts. "You have permission to fire."

"Scout Six, this is Lone Warrior, shot, over."

"Lone Warrior, this is Scout Six, shot, out." Quarry and 3rd Squad waited 27 seconds before the earth erupted before their eyes. The concussion and blast, even at 3,000 meters, staggered the Scouts. Quarry wondered if an erupting volcano was as powerful or as deadly.

* * *

"Jesus Christ!" Marion blurted out as his head snapped to the east. "What the hell was that!"

* * *

Aziz heard the distant explosion. *Finally*, he thought, *artillery support to whatever it is we are supposed to be fighting.*

* * *

"My God," Laumeyer asked, "where'd they go?" Indeed, where over a hundred vehicles, their crewmembers and troops had been seconds earlier, was now only a crater filled with twisted metal as turrets, tracks, and hulls rained from the sky.

Quarry was stunned by the devastation. Quickly shaking it off, he continued to perform his duty.

"Lone Warrior, this is Scout Six, target. Open sheath. Repeat! Repeat! Repeat!" The *Missouri* changed the gun data so every 16-inch gun would hit a new location in the same area, and fired again.

There must be a Heaven, Quarry thought, *because right now we're witnessing Hell.* "Lone Warrior, this is Scout Six, target. Adjust fire, over."

"Scout Six, this is Lone Warrior, target, adjust fire, over."

"Lone Warrior, target two, guns one and two, grid 887 596. Target three, gun three, grid 887 592. Remaining vehicles of the brigade, over."

It only took the Navy 20 seconds to make the minute adjustments and apply the new data to the guns. Thirty seconds later, with the exception of some scattered vehicles to the north and the remnants of the company that passed south through the berm, 3rd Brigade of the 108th Iraqi Armor ceased to exist.

* * *

It took a few minutes for the Scouts to realize the totality of the obliteration. Quarry tried to speak, but his mouth was void of moisture. Having to take a drink from his canteen prior to keying the net, he transmitted the battle damage assessment.

"Lone Warrior, this is Scout Six. Target annihilated. Nice shooting, Navy. Scout Six out." Aboard the U.S.S. *Missouri*, in the combat information center, a hail of applause and cheers went up. The moment of rejoicing for a job well

138

done was short lived. The guns shifted in support of Marines fighting for their lives on the outskirts of the city of Khafji.

* * *

Aziz watched 2nd Battalion move to his right. Moving at only five kilometers an hour made command and control easier, but was grossly inadequate for tactical maneuvering. Aziz never saw any indication of 3rd Brigade to the east, but 2nd Battalion's B.M.P.s were starting to deploy. Aziz did not feel confident about this operation.

* * *

"Range, 5,000, sir," the Saudi gunner reported to Ahmed.

* * *

3rd Battalion increased speed and closed the gap. Five minutes later, the lead company of 3rd Battalion's tanks pulled up, on line with Aziz.

* * *

"Five, this is Six," Quarry radioed. "Is it clear to return, over?"
    "Six, Five, roger, all clear." Lau pushed the gas petal as far as it would go.

* * *

From their vantage point, and with the use of night-vision goggles, Quarry and Grier watched Iraqi forces close the distance to the Saudis. "I don't think the Iraqis have a clue the Saudis are out there," Quarry said, since the Saudis tanks were dug in so only their turrets were above ground level.
    "I gave Ahmed a call about fifteen minutes ago," Grier added. "The Saudis have them in thermals. They're waiting for the Iraqis to either I.D. 'em or make the first aggressive move."

* * *

"Captain Aziz," the gunner transmitted in a high-pitched tone over the intercom, "I think there are tanks in front of us." Aziz dropped down out of the cupola, gently pushed the gunner to the side and looked through the gunner's sights. Against the backdrop of a starlit night was the unmistakable void of dozens of blank spaces in the constellations. Aziz contorted his way back into the commander's hatch and keyed the net.

"This is First Company, enemy tanks to the front."

* * *

"Range 4,000, sir."

* * *

Quarry and Grier watched as the Iraqi red flares went up, arced over the sky and fell toward earth.

"Let's get ready to rummmmble," Quarry said from behind the N.V.G.s.

* * *

"Range, 3,000, sir. Pre-battle formation complete. Battalions are on line, companies in column."

"Thank you," Ahmed acknowledged his gunner.

* * *

Aziz looked to his left and right. His brother company commanders were to each side of him now. Behind him, his own company followed in column, patiently waiting for the next order. They didn't wait long until the next set of flares shot through the sky.

* * *

"Range, 2,000, sir."

* * *

His platoon leaders brought their tanks up flawlessly. Aziz made a mental note to make tea for them after evening prayers tomorrow night. The company was now on line, with platoons in column. Aziz felt the pride in his chest when he looked to the right and left of him and saw three full platoons of three tanks each.

* * *

"Range, 1,500, sir."

* * *

The final flares went up. Without having to be told, the platoon commanders deployed their tanks to their left and right. The final jostling for position was tight as the battalion was deployed too close together. The final outcome: mere meters between tanks. Nonetheless, the sight of hundreds of tanks and B.M.P.s in close formation was enough to strike fear into the heart of any infidel. *Surely,* Aziz thought, *they would flee in panic.*

* * *

"Range, 1,200 meters, sir."
"Brigade, this is Colonel Ahmed, prepare to fire ... FIRE!"

* * *

The kinetic energy sabot round that ripped through the hull of Aziz's tank created a pressure wave so forceful it launched him from the open hatch. The fireball created by the spontaneous combustion of hydraulic fluid didn't have time to fully engulf him. Aziz was actually outside the tank and still accelerating above the ground when his own tank rounds started to explode inside the hull. Unconscious from the blast and smoldering from the heat, Aziz fell to earth like a rag doll as the turret of his tank reached the zenith of its own upward trajectory.

* * *

The bellow of flame emitted from dozens of tanks at the exact same moment, blinded the Scouts who didn't have on N.V.G.s and temporarily washed out the view of those who did.

Quarry ripped off his goggles to witness the carnage. The Saudi gunners traversed and acquired new targets. There was little duplication of effort as the 2nd Brigade fire command came over the radio in each Saudi tank. A split second later, all remaining tanks and scores of B.M.P.s were destroyed. The remaining B.M.P.s were not aware their sister unit had been devastated. While the distance from the lead Iraqi line to the Saudi position was still slightly over 1,100 meters, Saudi gunners adjusted fire on the remaining B.M.P.s. Within minutes, hundreds, if not thousands of Iraqi soldiers died. Quarry continued to watch the Iraqi vehicles explode. White, red, green, silver; streaks of yellow and gold and solid walls of light. Quarry wondered if he would ever be able to watch another Fourth of July display without reliving this night.

"Let's get the hell out of here."

Sixteen

30 January 1991

Aziz realized he was alive. Were his eyes were open or closed?

"I am here, my captain," a distant voice wavered on the brink of reality. Aziz saw a light above him and concluded he was lying on his back. This light seemed to focus and then spiral away. Aziz was also aware of a great weight upon his lower body. He couldn't move his legs, his feet hurt, but at the same time, he really didn't care.

"Wherrrmi," he heard a voice say.

"You are at Gathering Center 5," 1st Sergeant Zamir answered. "It has been turned into a hospital. You were injured in the battle but will be fine."

Aziz's head started to clear and his mind began to focus.

"*Raqeeb-awwal*?" Aziz asked meekly as he placed the voice. The events of last night started rushing back, like a nightmare that he couldn't wake up from. "*Raqeeb-awwal*, you're alive," he heard the voice say, finally realizing it was his own. "Praise Allah. What happened?"

"We were hit by units dug into the earth," Zamir began. "In seconds, the entire battalion was on fire. My tank took a sabot round directly through the turret. The round deflected downward and came to rest inside the engine. I had time to evacuate my crew before the engine caught fire."

"How many? The company."

"Seven in the company survived, *naqeeb*."

"Seven tanks?"

"Seven soldiers," the 1st sergeant answered.

The shock brought Aziz out of morphine-induced stupor.

"How did I get here?" he asked through tear-soaked eyes.

"My crew ran behind the destroyed tanks. We pulled survivors from wreckage where and when we could. When we came upon you, I thought

143

you were dead. Your uniform was on fire. I put out the fire around your legs." Aziz looked down the length of his body. From his waist down, he was wrapped in bandages, and his legs were strapped so they could not move. At the end of the bed, his toes stuck out of the bandages. He wiggled them. It hurt, but they worked. Zamir traced the direction of where Aziz was looking. "Your boots protected your feet, *naqeeb*. But your legs were badly burned. The doctors say you will be fine, but they must get you to the hospital in Basra soon."

"Please continue with what happened, *raqeeb awwal*."

"When we found you, we stopped and dragged you behind a tank that was not on fire. Minutes later, a B.M.P. from 2nd Brigade came driving by, also using the line of tanks for protection. I stopped it by pointing my pistol at the driver. We loaded the vehicle with everyone we gathered and drove back toward the opening in the berm. Gathering Centers 2, 5 and 6 have been converted into hospitals."

"How many vehicles made it back?"

"Twenty-two."

"For the battalion?"

The 1st sergeant paused before answering.

"For 1st and 2nd Brigades, *naqeeb*. We don't know where 3rd Brigade is."
The shock was too much for Aziz's body to handle and he drifted back into unconsciousness.

* * *

Quarry and the Scout leadership listened as Dole summarized the I Company morning brief.

"Eight Gathering Centers were turned into temporary hospitals," Dole continued. They already knew about Gathering Center 10, a mere 2,000 meters away from Hill 224. One Two reported a steady stream of trucks moving back and forth between the center and the refinery area throughout the night. "Company also suspects the same for Gathering Centers 2, 3, 4, 5, and 6. We learned that LAVs took care of what remained of the Iraqi company that got through the breach east of here. There are still Marines inside Khafji. They got caught up on top of a building, and a mounted Iraqi patrol stopped right underneath them for a while."

"Some people have all the fun," Quarry joked. "Company have anything for us?"

"Nothing yet, sir. With Khafji still hot, we've pretty much been forgotten."

"Situation normal."

* * *

Every truck and jeep had been turned into a stretcher carrier. Once an hour, a group of trucks would muster at the division headquarters before transporting their human cargo north to the hospitals in Kuwait City. Next to the division H.Q., 1st Sergeant Zamir said good-bye to his commander.

"I will see you when we get back to our barracks in Basra," the 1st sergeant said to the stretcher-bound captain.

Aziz looked up with pain of body and soul, the pain of a warrior who could not protect his men.

"*Aywa, ya raqeeb awwal.*" The corpsmen lifted and placed the stretcher on the back of the truck. "Wait," Aziz commanded. Zamir stepped closer to his commander. Reaching up, Aziz removed the cloth rank insignia from his shoulder epaulettes. "A commander must earn respect," he said to his 1st sergeant as he removed one of the epaulettes of four diagonal and one horizontal stripe, and replaced it with the three stars of a captain. The two said nothing more to each other. The medics put the stretcher in the truck bed, lashed it down, and closed the tailgate. Zamir stood as the truck pulled out from the headquarters. No one in the immediate area said a word.

* * *

"Skipper, ditch diggers. Three of them. Escorted by two B.M.P.s."

Three ditch diggers, each immediately beside but behind the other, made a wide trench the entire length of the oilfield. "Kinda late in the game to be making a defensive network," Marion said from behind binos.

Quarry watched the activity from the TOW sights.

"Straight line a few clicks south of the main refinery. Doesn't make any sense to me," he said, removing his eye from the sights. "Keep a dedicated eye on the diggers. Let me know if there is any change in their ops."

* * *

"They knew we were there," the 1st sergeant said to the operations major.

"And how do you know that, *ya raqeeb?*" The major paused, not knowing where Zamir's battlefield promotion came from. "And how do you know that, *ya naqeeb?*"

"1st and 2nd Brigades were destroyed by two direct-fire salvos. The enemy on the other side of the berm knew exactly where we were and waited for us to close to 1,000 meters before firing."

"Interesting theory, *ya naqeeb*. I will bring it to the attention of my seniors."

"There is no one here senior to you, *ya raa'id.*" True enough: throughout the day, with every medical evacuation truck that departed for Kuwait City, the number of staff officers around division headquarters decreased exponentially.

"I assure you, *ya naqeeb*, I will personally bring this to the attention of the general. Until then, how is your mission going?"

"Fine, sir, the trench is coming along fine. I have assigned two B.M.P.s to provide them security."

"Do you think that is wise, *ya naqeeb*? I doubt we will get fuel again."

"I think it is very wise, *ya raa'id*." Zamir did not attempt to disguise the disgust in his voice.

"If you think so," the major said with arrogance in his own voice. "Report to me, here, when the trench is completed. Dismissed." Zamir came to rigid attention and saluted sharply, not out of respect or military courtesy, but as an act of defiance. The major noticed, but didn't care.

* * *

The ditch digging continued well into the night. Except for refueling from siphoning off other vehicles, the diggers never stopped. Drivers rotated in and out, allowing the work to continue. The Scouts watched in curiosity.

31 January 1991

Now why would they be doing that? Bots asked himself. Dropping down inside the Hummer, he retrieved the laser range-finder and the G.P.S. After calculating a grid, he pulled up a couple of maps until he found the right one.

"Oh shit." Bots shot another azimuth with his compass, input the direction, lazed to a new target, and calculated the grid. "Oh shit! Corporal Marion!" The yell attracted everyone's attention. Everyone not currently on duty rushed to the east side of the camp, ready for the worst. What they saw were a few trucks moving among the Gathering Centers and the ditch diggers making individual trenches.

Marion came running up, quickly surveyed the routine activity to the east and then looked over at Bots.

"Look at the ditch diggers, Corporal."

Quarry and Grier came running up.

"O.K., and?" Marion questioned.

"They're working as individuals. They're connecting the main trench with individual feeder trenches." Bots looked to his corporal and then to Quarry and Grier. He placed the map on the top of the Hummer so his chain of command could see. Taking a pencil from his blouse, he pointed out specifics.

"The triple wide trench runs like this," Bots said, penciling in the starting and ending points and connecting the dots. "Then these," Bots pointed to where the trench ran through paved streets. "That doesn't make a bit of sense unless you plan to use the streets as an obstacle and not as a road. The three diggers broke off and are now *here*," he pointed on the map, "here, and here. These are oil pump transfer sites. Now look at where the triple wide trench goes. Both ends lead into oil run-off pits."

Quarry looked at the map and then grabbed a set of binos.

"Nice work, Bots. Five? We got any sodas left to reward our bright young petroleum engineer?"

"I think I can find something, skipper," Grier said with a smile.

"Keep an eye on 'em, Bots. Let me know when they decide to open 'em up. I'll let Company know."

"Yes, sir." The leadership departed leaving Lance Corporal Botsford grinning from ear to ear.

"I don't get it. What the hell are you looking at?" Davis asked.

"They're going to fill the trench with oil, shit-for-brains. Probably rig it to blow."

* * *

While members of the support platoon manned the ditch diggers, members of the Demolitions Platoon, Combat Engineer Company, worked at selected sites a kilometer to the north. Most of the leadership from the division's engineering battalion was "reassigned." Once this final task was complete, the technicians would also report for duty with the corps' engineer brigade, in northern Kuwait.

* * *

It wasn't hard to find; all one had to do was care to look. Zamir traveled south from the division headquarters until he found hundreds of tracks heading east. He followed 3rd Brigade's tracks until they turned south and passed between the 29th and the 42nd Infantry Divisions. A few kilometers south of that, in front of him, was the berm and the second breach site. Among the torn and twisted steel were shredded flesh and disfigured bodies. The main crater, 200 meters north of the berm, was more than 10 meters deep and 35 meters in diameter. Vehicles on the outskirts of the blast area appeared as children's toys thrown around and left to be picked up. The vehicles furthest from the center contained the most horrid scenes. Intact vehicles contained gelatin statues, still molded and resembling human forms. Bodies, once friends and companions, had been instantly pulverized from the concussion and blast of whatever did this.

A second crater, to the north and east, was not as big. Zamir paced the distance off from the edge of the first crater. The distance was too precise and too perfectly located in the center of a second group of vehicles to be a coincidence. While looking at the second crater, he noted that the eastern side of both craters had a more predominant slope than that on the west. That meant that the rounds had been fired from the east.

The third crater was the smallest. But like its big brothers, it too was exactly in the center of a concentration of vehicles. Zamir walked the short distance and climbed the berm. While standing on top of the berm and facing west, he turned his head to the right. Over his right shoulder, he saw the hole in the ground to the north. As he turned his head in the opposite direction, the smallest crater was exactly over his left shoulder. Zamir waved to his driver, and the B.M.P. pulled up to him. "Drive me west, along the berm."

Seventeen

1 February 1991

Zamir rose just after daylight. Although he was a devoted Muslim, he hadn't participated in daily prayers these last few days; he had lost patience and trust in the will of Allah. This morning was no exception. As the Zamir walked around the empty division headquarters, not an officer, N.C.O., clerk or even a radio was present. Then he walked through the support buildings that acted as the division staff's barracks. No one was present and everything of value was gone. A quick drive to the division engineer battalion headquarters building revealed the same thing. Division supply was still in place though the soldiers knew nothing of the whereabouts of any of their N.C.O.s. Most of the food stores were still in place but there was precious little fresh water. The refueling trucks were gone, as were the cargo and transport trucks from the division motor pool. Everywhere he went, Zamir found the same thing: he was the senior officer. After giving orders to find the most senior soldier in each of the remaining sections and commodities, Zamir stormed off towards his own company area. When asked where he was going, he replied, "I'm going to go find something."

* * *

It was no surprise that just before daylight, four B.M.P.s departed the division headquarters. In anticipation of a trench and two lakes of oil being ignited, Hill 224 was at full alert.

* * *

Zamir took his vehicle, three other B.M.P.s, and as many infantrymen as he could muster. Since the roads leading south were cut by the trenches, the four vehicles travelled east before rounding the spillover pits, which now contained fresh oil. Zamir led them to the berm, west past the craters and to the site of strange tire tracks. Continuing west, he momentarily lost the tracks as they crossed the second breaching site but easily found them on the other side. The he looked to the horizon. The tracks headed toward a supposedly abandoned police observation post.

* * *

"Get Six on the net," Marek said from behind his binos.

* * *

Zamir didn't see any signs of movement, enemy or friendly. He ordered his driver to stop. After briefing the other vehicle commanders and a corporal who was the senior ranking infantry soldier, he ordered the B.M.P.s to continue toward the police station, missiles armed, a round in the cannon, and machine guns ready.

* * *

"They're on line," Stone narrated from behind the spotting scope for the benefit of those who didn't have binos. "Correction, there is one B.M.P. out in front of the others. The other three are on line but behind and centered on the lead. They're heading toward the Gathering Center. Stopping. All four on line now. Infantry dismounting the B.M.P.s."

* * *

The vehicles stopped 100 meters from the police station. The three squads maintained 25-meter intervals between fire teams and continued toward the building. Zamir led the formation with an A.K.-47 in hand. When the infantry made it to the building without incident, he nodded to the corporal. The platoon leader motioned to the right-most squad which threw the door open. Before the first soldier entered, Zamir already knew there was no one inside.

"*Ya naqeeb*," the corporal called from outside the door. "There was a battle here."

* * *

Quarry and Grier were more interested in the enemy's numbers.

"Four vehicles," Quarry commented quietly.

"We should have had eight grunts coming out of each B.M.P.," Grier added. "I didn't see any come out of the lead vehicle and only five or six from each of the remaining three."

"I count … 15 on the ground." Quarry said.

"They're forming up," Stone continued. "All squads on line. Now starting an envelopment of the Gathering Center."

* * *

"The building is clear, *ya naqeeb*. There is no sign of struggle, but there is blood and dirty bandages everywhere."

"Of course," Zamir answered, "it was used as an aid station for the wounded." he looked around. To the north was a hill, the same hill he had looked at from his tank many times. "Corporal, put your men in the vehicles. We are going to check one more place."

"*Aywa, ya naqeeb.*"

"Corporal, you are from 2nd Brigade, are you not?"

"*Aywa, ya naqeeb.* 3rd Company, 2nd Battalion, 2nd Brigade."

"Did 2nd Brigade ever put security on that hill?" Zamir asked.

"Not that I was aware of, *ya naqeeb.*"

* * *

"They're forming up again." This time it was Sergeant Ogdon giving the narration. "Column formation. Same vehicle taking the lead. Moving around the Gathering Center. Getting on the road. Moving on the road towards us, range 2,000. Continuing to move north on the hard ball," Ogdon continued. "Range, 1,750."

* * *

"Stop the vehicle." The driver didn't ask questions but brought the B.M.P. to an immediate halt. Zamir turned in the cupola and gave the hand signal for the vehicles to stop. Looking down, he changed the frequency on his radio and transmitted a message.

* * *

It was 15 minutes until the next sitrep, this one from Speckman.

"Six this is Two One, over." Quarry was standing next to Marek's Hummer with Ogdon and Grier. Kantner handed the platoon net mic out the window.

"This is Six, send it."

151

"Observing new contact. Six B.M.P.s pulling out from the old B.M.P. Regiment position. Moving west in column, over."

Quarry looked to Grier and Ogdon.

"Be right there," he said, keying the net. Quarry, Grier, Ogdon and Marion were at Speckman's B.M.P. in less than twenty seconds. Caine was already there. In the same amount of time, the six B.M.P.s moved past the old 2nd Brigade flank position and turned south on the main road. "Seventy-seven," Quarry ordered. Throop took no time in handing down the spare radio. Quarry made sure it was on the platoon net and transmitted. "One Two this is Six, any change of your four B.M.P.s?"

"Negative, Six, over."

"Roger, stand by." Quarry and the other leaders watched the six B.M.P.s continue south. Quarry's darkest fear began to materialize. The six B.M.P.s stopped on the road directly east of them.

* * *

Zamir radioed the soldier he had placed in command of his 2nd Platoon. While the vehicles didn't have infantry, they still had full firepower.

"Do you see a B.M.P. at the top of the hill?"

"*Aywa, ya naqeeb.*"

"I am going to approach him from the south. Have all your vehicles turn right. Continue on line up the hill until I tell you to stop. Do you understand?"

"*Aywa, ya naqeeb.*"

"Driver," Zamir switched to the vehicle intercom, "continue up the road at five kilometers an hour." He then looked behind him. As he pulled away, he gave the hand signal to the B.M.P.s behind him to follow.

* * *

"Specter, Aloha drill. Now!" Quarry called up. "Five, take charge here! Get Ogdon's and Caine's TOWs, keep Speckman's B.M.P. I'll take Marion's TOW and Caine's B.M.P. If those six B.M.P.s close to within 1,500 feet, light 'em up. Caine!" Quarry didn't watch as a green-bloused, black-bereted man waived from atop his B.M.P.; he was sprinting back to Marek's vehicle.

* * *

"*Ya naqeeb.* A soldier is standing on top of his vehicle, waving to us," the 2nd Platoon commander reported over the radio.

The Zamir breathed a heavy sigh of relief.

"That is good news. Continue up the hill and I will meet you there."

"*Aywa, ya naqeeb.*"

* * *

"Range, fifteen hundred," Marion reported over the net.

"Skipper," Dole said beside him, looking through his spotter scope. "There's a captain in the cupola."

"Range?" he asked.

"Fourteen."

Quarry stepped forward, and flopped down into a prone firing position. As the smallest mil dot on the vertical cross hairs of his scope passed over the B.M.P., Quarry steadied the sight's picture as best he could on the figure in the cupola. At this distance, the smallest mil dot covered the entire top of the B.M.P. and the person in the cupola was completely obscured. The B.M.P. continued to advance. Quarry paused, then started a gentle trigger squeeze. Somewhere in the continuous gradual rearward pressure, the firing pin released and his shot rang out. From across the O.P., Grier spun around to see what had happened. Dole's near immediate reaction answered his question.

"Target! Driver! Holy shit! What a shot! 1,375 meters!" The B.M.P. slowed to a stop. The driver slumped forward in the open hatch. Quarry immediately realized he'd missed his target and aimed the smallest mil dot to the left of the vehicle commander. A second shot rang out.

* * *

"Driver, why are you slowing down?" Zamir spoke into the intercom. Even with the volume all the way up, it was difficult to hear anything over the noise of the engine. "Driver!" Zamir yelled into the intercom as he felt an intense searing pain in his right shoulder. Instinctively, his left hand went to the source of pain, and came away covered with blood. As he looked up at the hill in disbelief, Quarry chambered another round. The second 7.62, 168-grain boat-tailed hollow-point bullet, now traveling at 2,600 feet per second, entered below the right clavicle and continued unchecked by the soft tissue until it shattered the 1st sergeant's fifth thoracic vertebra. The terminal ballistics of the round drove the Zamir's body backwards. Nerves in the lower back tried to correct the angle of the body, not realizing the rest of his body was already dead.

* * *

"Target! Vehicle commander! Range 1,350," Dole called out as a father would call out a son's high-school touchdown. Quarry simply looked up and chambered another round.

* * *

"Range 3,000," Tellado called out from behind the TOW sights while watching the six B.M.P.s. "On line, moving toward us."

"Let Company know what's going on, Slayer," Grier said calmly.

* * *

The other three B.M.P.s slowed to a stop. Quarry watched the commander in the second vehicle play with his microphone on his helmet. He saw the frustration continue to mount until the vehicle commander made hand signals telling the other vehicles to form a line.

"Dole. Our section. Low sky," Quarry ordered.

"One One and Two One, this is Six Delta, low sky." The two squad leaders pulled their vehicles out of hide positions until the gunners could see their targets in their sights, although the rest of the vehicle was not yet exposed to the B.M.P.s. Being taller than the Hummer, the B.M.P. needed to move only a few feet. Marion continued to move his Hummer forward until Botsford called he was on target.

"Frontal fire on my command," Quarry quietly said to Dole.

"One One and Two Actual, this is Six Delta, standby. On command, frontal fire, acknowledge, over."

"Six Delta this is One One, target, left B.M.P. standing by, over."

"Delta, this is Two, target, right B.M.P., standing by, over."

* * *

"Range, 2,000," Tellado reported.

* * *

From his position, the B.M.P. vehicle commander couldn't figure out why the captain stopped. *He must be talking on a different net or his radio broke.* The commander dismounted his vehicle and walked toward the captain's.

Quarry settled back into position, placed the smallest mil dot on the side of the B.M.P. and waited for the soldier to move forward.

The vehicle commander walked up and next to the captain. The blood on the captain's left hand was immediately visible and the tilted head confirmed the commander's suspicions. Looking up in confusion, he called the captain's name.

Quarry pulled the trigger.

The commander was turning to look toward Hill 224 as the bullet entered his body between the left shoulder and chest. The bullet continued through the left atrium and the right ventricle before exiting through the commander's liver.

Quarry removed his eye from the scope and looked at the two remaining B.M.P. vehicle commanders.

"Fire."

"One One and Two, fire!" Dole relayed the order. A second later, two missiles streaked down range. Hearing a "swoosh" from the north, the vehicle commander of the third vehicle looked from the body of his friend to a smoke cloud that was increasing in volume. Confusion caused indecision.

The Soviet Sagger anti-tank missile impacted the front slope of the vehicle and exploded. As the molten stream of heat and pressure ripped through the thin layers of steel, the TOW-II-B detonated on the eastern-most B.M.P. The concussion and blast instantaneously killed the exposed commander and driver of the center vehicle. Botsford wasn't interested in economy of effort. As soon as the first missile hit, he cut the controlling wires and immediately set a second missile in the launcher. Eight seconds later, the second missile impacted the undamaged B.M.P. It took Caine a few seconds longer to reload, but he sent a second missile down range, into the B.M.P. Quarry had neutralized. The missile worked as designed: few infantry soldiers exited the back of the B.M.P.s. Those who did, came out with hands in the air.

* * *

"Range, eighteen hundred," Tellado reported.

* * *

The 2nd Platoon commander was confused. A large smoke cloud was drifting up from the other side of the hill. Even at this distance, the sound of an explosion was unmistakable. The platoon leader yelled into the microphone: "Get to the top of the hill. All vehicles increase speed!"

* * *

"Range, seventeen and closing. Vehicles increasing speed and loosing formation."

Grier was standing between Three One and Two One. Speckman's B.M.P. was 20 meters to the south. "Frontal fire," Grier said into the net. Seconds later, the squad leader reported they were ready. "Fire," Grier said into the mic.

* * *

The back-blast of three missiles launching made the Scouts on the south side of the hill flinch. Quarry looked east.

"Dole, command Hummer. Drop nets, we're getting the hell out of here. Give Company an update and my intentions. Get Slayer moving too."

The Sagger missile is slightly faster than the TOWs, but not as lethal. Against such lightly skinned vehicles, however, the impact had more than satisfactory results. A second after the Sagger hit, the two TOW-II-Bs ripped through their targets. Quarry heard the explosions and got to Grier in time to see some spectacular secondary explosions from the ammunition inside the vehicles. The TOW gunners automatically reloaded. The three remaining B.M.P.s prepared to return fire, but to no avail. Two more disintegrated from TOW missiles, while Specter's 73mm cannon caught the sixth B.M.P. mid-vehicle. The gunners scanned the area: nothing moved. They reported "mission complete."

"Mary's gathering prisoners, Dole and Slayer are dropping nets. Let's get the fuck out of here."

"I hear that, boss," Grier said, still looking east.

No additional combat vehicles departed the division headquarters. They had witnessed the destruction of half of their remaining combat power, but without a leader, the soldiers were happy to stay in their holes.

* * *

It took only minutes to break camp. The Scouts rigged the B.M.P.s to explode minutes after their departure. Hummers staged to the west as 3rd Squad continued to watch east. The surviving Iraqi soldiers were stripped of weapons, searched for intelligence, and treated for minor wounds. Their hands were duct-taped together before they were told to walk back to their headquarters. Most didn't want to go back and asked to be taken prisoner. A corporal and an older soldier were selected to be taken back with the Scouts to Company, to be turned over to the interrogators. As secondary explosions continued to cook off in the B.M.P.s, the remaining Iraqi soldiers headed back toward the refinery. The Scouts departed Hill 224.

Quarry updated Company as they traveled southwest. Grier coordinated the passage of lines with O.P. Three. The Scouts, for the most part, traveled in silence, each lost in his own thoughts. They reflected on events, and actions, and bonds that cannot be explained to those who haven't been there, done that.

Eighteen

Evening, 1 February 1991

When the Scouts arrived at Company, the prisoners were turned over to the M.P.s. The Scouts got hot chow, hot showers and racks to sleep in. Quarry, Grier, Marion, Caine, and Ogdon were immediately separated and taken to different areas for debriefing.

That evening, Quarry was ordered to attend an additional debrief at MEF headquarters. After a panel of a half-dozen freshly laundered, cammie-wearing lieutenant colonels second-guessed Quarry's every action, and armchair-quarterbacked his every decision, Quarry was finally dismissed. In place of "well done" or "good job," Quarry was given orders cutting him loose from MEF and reassigning him back to 2nd Marine Division. After a short drive to division headquarters, Quarry's "welcome back" consisted of a chewing out by some full-bird colonel for not having a helmet on in a combat zone, not having any rank insignia on the pocket of his flak jacket and for slinging a sniper rifle over his back like he was John Fucking Wayne. Quarry was then given orders reattaching the Scouts back to 2nd Tank Battalion and told he better square his ass away, he was in a combat unit now. When Quarry stepped outside division headquarters, his ride was gone. Because the ride he caught was from MEF, and Quarry was now a "Division" Marine, he found himself having to walk back to where the Scouts were billeted.

When Quarry entered his old room, he found his sleeping bag already laid out and his laundry washed, folded and stacked at the end of the rack. A note on top of it read: "Skipper, the duty will finish up the laundry. Leave all your dirty gear outside the door when you crash. You have a meeting with Lt. Col. Dillion at 1000, then with Colonel Brodrick at 1100. Get some sleep, we'll compare notes tomorrow morning. Everything else is being handled, Semper Gumby, S.S.G."

Quarry smiled and placed the note back on the rack. He looked at the clean laundry at the end of the rack, and thought of the outstanding officers he had had the pleasure of talking to earlier. "REMFs," he said out loud. Finding his shaving kit in his backpack, Quarry grabbed a towel at the bottom of the folded clothes and stripped down. He spent the next 30 minutes in a hot shower.

2 February 1991

"Rise and shine sleepy head," Grier said, holding a cup of coffee under Quarry's nose.

"Oh shit, what time is it?" Quarry said, gratefully accepting the coffee.

"After nine," Grier replied, sipping on a full canteen cup of coffee himself. The two compared notes. Grier's debrief had gone considerably better than Quarry's. Everyone at Intel and SRIG thought the Scouts were the greatest thing since automatic weapons.

Minutes before ten, Quarry reached for his rifle. It was in the same place he'd put it last night but in a slightly different position.

"Dole went over it with a fine tooth comb this morning." Quarry shook his head.

Quarry walked into the entry area of the company office. The master sergeant behind one of the desks stood and greeted him warmly. A few of the radio operators and Intel clerks also greeted the Scout commander.

"I'll see if the colonel is ready yet, sir," the Top said as he started down the hallway. A corporal offered Quarry a cup of coffee.

"Captain Samuels," a familiar and cordial voice came from down the hall. Lieutenant Colonel Dillion walked out and around the entry desks and extended his hand. "Welcome back," he said shaking Quarry's hand vigorously. "This way please."

Quarry's welcome was in stark contrast to the reception he had received yesterday, and he told Dillion as much.

"Pardon my French, Captain Samuels, but fuck 'em. Half the lieutenant colonels up there are officers that don't have a real job and busy themselves in 'planning cells.' Sure they perform a valuable service by war gaming and developing different courses of action, but most are reservists trying to advance their careers." By now, the two were back in the colonel's office. Dillion leaned back in his chair. After Quarry told the colonel what happened, Dillion asked a few specific questions. Quarry realized he had been "debriefed" again, but it was so much nicer being asked. He would truly miss working for this man.

After the debrief, Colonel Dillion invited Quarry into the situation room. The map symbols had changed drastically since the last time Quarry updated a map here. Colonel Dillion turned the show over to a staff sergeant who was the present Intel analyst on duty. Quarry was given a seat in the front, centered on several situation maps.

It took about five minutes to get caught up on all that had happened. After the formal briefing, the staff sergeant went off on a small tangent and projected what might have happened if the Scouts hadn't been where they were. Quarry wished Grier and the rest of the platoon could have been here, but except for Grier, the level of classification was higher than the Scouts possessed.

"My final question before we head over to see Colonel Brodrick," Dillion said, gesturing to the door. "Do you have any award recommendations you'd like to submit before you head back to 2nd Tanks?"

Quarry came back to reality quickly, but then again, it was inevitable.

"Off the top of my head, sir, four Bronze Stars with combat Vs, another five Navy Commendation Medals with Vs, and a dozen combat promotions."

"In the next few days, you write them up and get them to either myself or the master sergeant. I'll most likely endorse whatever you submit."

"Thank you, sir."

* * *

The meeting with Colonel Brodrick wasn't nearly as long or as informal.

"Do you have any award recommendations, Captain?"

"Yes, sir, I do," Quarry said, looking over to Dillion. "I'll get them submitted as soon as possible, sir."

"You write them and I'll look them over." Realizing his farewell speech was over, Quarry departed.

* * *

Everything was ready to go by noon. The squad leaders had 2nd Tanks' location plotted in the G.P.S. Waypoints indicated they were a short distance from Thunderbolt range at Assembly Area Crush. A final check of gear and people, and they were off.

* * *

The commanding officer of 2nd Tanks, Lieutenant Colonel Calhoune, hadn't developed a sense of humor while the Scouts were gone. Quarry's friends on the battalion staff walked around like they were whipped puppies. Tank Battalion was now designated the 2nd Marine Division's reserve, and the colonel kept both the Alpha and Bravo command groups busy on contingency planning. The primary contingency was a counter-attack, should the Iraqis break through the berm again. The colonel and Major Cranford, the operations officer, looked at the map and found a spot for the Scouts, a position seven clicks in front of Charlie Company and 12 clicks behind the division headquarters.

"Welcome to hell, skipper," Grier commented.

Evening, 3 February 1991

"All Heavy Metal units, this is Heavy Metal Three, over," Major Cranford's voice came over the radio. Quarry acknowledged the transmission when it was his turn and started writing down the order.

"It's a drill, skipper," Dole interrupted the radio. Quarry turned to his driver. "The route takes us past division headquarters, but keeps us behind 6th Marines' rear area. Quarry turned his attention to the radio and continued to write, but with vastly less enthusiasm.

The eight-kilometer tactical road march leading into a simulated counter-attack was good training for the tankers. Even in the largest training facilities in 29 Palms, California, tank companies, let alone battalions, never had opportunities to maneuver in doctrinal formations, if for no other reason than the vast amount of real estate required.

The Scouts were introduced to the mission of "pathfinder." They would lead the battalion from an assembly area to a release point, where the companies would bypass the Scouts and attack an objective. For the Scouts, the mission was no more than driving through a few specific G.P.S. waypoints in the middle of the desert, while 57 M1A1 main battle tanks blindly followed, trusting the Scouts to get them to the line of departure. The downside of the mission was that in real life, any enemy encountered along the way would chew up and spit out the Scouts with little to no effort.

Once the tank companies went into the attack, the Scouts would get the hell out of the way before they were stuck in the middle of armored combat. While they screened a flank, the Scouts would then wait for additional orders, such as seeking out additional enemy positions or finding alternate avenues of approach deeper into the enemy's rear. But this was only a training mission. The beneficiary of this exercise was the battalion staff, which coordinated command, control and communications. Even though the Scouts were bored off their asses, it was a necessary evil, being back with their parent unit.

Nineteen

7 February 1991

After three days of looking at a sea of sand, a radio transmission came over battalion tac: "All commanders report to Alpha command for orders."

With just friendly units in front of them, Quarry only required one Scout to be on watch per vehicle. Quarry happened to have the duty when the call came in and he acknowledged the transmission. Moments later, Dole ran up to the command Hummer, out of breath, having heard the order in the logistics Hummer.

"You could have walked," Quarry said, looking up from a novel. Dole only smiled as he stored his rifle in the vertical rack in the driver's compartment.

It took over half an hour for all the company commanders to assemble. When they did, the X.O. opened the meeting; the Three gave out graphics and went over the op order. Colonel Calhoune gave a weak version of a General Patton motivational speech. Quarry looked around at the company commanders, who were salivating like Pavlov's dogs. Maybe this was how he looked when he first received his orders from Colonel Dillion. Quarry hoped not.

* * *

"Anything important, skipper?" Dole asked as Quarry climbed in the Hummer.
"Just another road march."

* * *

"5646. That sounds familiar," Marion said, placing his own map on top of the command Hummer.

"It should," Quarry replied, placing the operations overlay where his squad leaders could copy the graphics. "We're going to man a contact point on the 1st and 2nd Marine Division boundary."

"That's where we were." Caine realized where the location was.

"Not exactly," Ogdon said, looking at the overlay and plotting points on his own map. "2nd SANG will still be ten clicks northeast of us."

An hour later, the companies reported RedCon One, and battalion gave the word to move. Five hours later, the Scouts were looking out over a familiar sight: same sand, different grid square.

9 February 1991

It was dark when the battalion staff meeting started. The word was the colonel had "big news." All staff officers and company commanders were present. Both Quarry and Grier were there, much to the displeasure of Captain Coleman. Coleman, commander of the TOW Company, which the Scouts belong to in peace time, told Quarry he didn't have to attend the battalion meeting and that he should come to the TOW Company meeting to get the word with the rest of the platoon commanders. But in war, Scouts work for the colonel, and report directly to the operations officer; that's why, as a captain, Quarry was given command of the Scouts. Quarry told Coleman to kiss his ass.

The staff portion of the meeting was well under way. When the X.O. called on him, Quarry simply said, "Nothing, sir."

The X.O. made a few other comments and the colonel was clearing his throat when a surprised communications officer's voice interrupted the routine: "Are you sure?" The radio watch waited. "Sir!" All eyes were on him. "The Scouts are in contact!"

"Which squad?" Quarry said, bolting out of his chair.

"I don't know."

"Go!" Quarry snapped, looking directly at Grier. Without saying a word, Grier grabbed his rifle at the side of the tent and disappeared. Quarry knew Grier would be able to get more information monitoring the platoon net than he could get on battalion tac. Quarry bounded up the lowered ramp of the command variation of the assault amphibian vehicle and pushed the radio watch out of the way, grabbing the handset. "This is Scout Six, over!"

"This is Three, contact, front, three soldiers approaching on foot, out." Having received a contact report and not a situation report, Ogie was effectively up to his ass in alligators and didn't have time to report the progress of draining the swamp. Quarry dropped the mic and started to make his way out of the back of the C-7 when he realized he and Grier had oame to the meeting in the same vehicle. Dole and Grier were clicks away by now, and Quarry wasn't with his platoon when they were in contact.

"Shit!" Quarry turned back to the bank of radios, picked one that didn't seem important at the time and dialed in the platoon frequency. "Scouts this is Six, Three is in contact. Go to RedCon One. Report all contacts."

It only took seconds for the net to respond.

"Six, this is One. RedCon One, negative contact over."

"Six, this is Two, RedCon One. Negative contact, over."

"Six, this is Three Delta, over," the net whispered back.

"This is Six," Quarry's voice turned cold. "Lau, what's going on, over."

"We're tracking three soldiers," the quiet voice replied. "We're using passive. We thought it might be only shadows. Sergeant Ogdon ordered confirmation with thermals. They must have heard the thermals cooling down, they stopped and haven't moved since. They're about 500 out."

"Five, this is Six, are you monitoring? Over."

"Roger, Six, over."

"Envelope from east to west, try to determine their intentions but take no chances, acknowledge."

"Roger, Six."

It was a long 16 minutes.

"Six, this is Three. Three E.P.W.s, no injuries, no wounded. Awaiting orders, over." There was a round of applause from inside the command post.

"Three, Six. Evac them in Three Two to battalion log trains, over."

"Six, Three, wilco, over."

"Three, Six, roger, Bravo Zulu, out." Quarry placed the handset back on the radio. He was going to dial the original frequency back in but he forgot what it was. No big deal. Quarry turned to see his peers and commander looking at him, shock etched on many faces.

10 February 1991

"The Scouts are in contact again!" the battalion radio watch announced in a high-pitched voice from behind the battalion tactical net.

Quarry didn't waste any time asking stupid questions, he merely took the handset. "Report!"

"This is Three, we're taking fire from the west. About twenty rounds went off around us."

"Six, this is Five. Observing a five-ton truck to the west."

Quarry thought for a minute and then made a mad dash for the operations officer's situation map. Seven clicks to the west of 3rd Squad's position was another contact point.

"What color were the tracers?" Colonel Calhoune called out in the direction of the radio operator.

"I don't know, sir."

"Ask the Scouts, you idiot!" the colonel yelled.

The radio watch started to transmit on the battalion tac net as the communications officer ran up to the radio Quarry was using. Moments later, the answer came back, "Red, sir." The answer sent a cold shiver to Quarry's heart. 3rd Squad was taking "friendly fire."

The communications officer realized what was going on.

"Samuels! Unit?"

From the map Quarry was looking at, the only other unit parallel to them, to the west, was a unit guarding the division's forward command post.

"24th Marines!" Quarry called back.

"24th Marines, 24th Marines, this is 2nd Tank Battalion. Cease fire, cease fire. Friendly squad in the vicinity of contact point ..."

"Seven!" Quarry called back.

"Seven. Acknowledge."

"3rd took another burst, sir," the radio operator relayed.

The ComO repeated the transmission. As the seconds ticked by, the 24th's regimental radio watch assured the ComO that there were no patrols that far north, but the word was passed to cease fire to all subordinate units. The entire command post stood in silence. Quarry felt nauseous not being able to do anything. An eternity later, which was actuality less than a few minutes, Grier's voice came over the platoon net.

"Six, this is Five. One U.S. five-ton truck, departing southwest at high speed. Do you want us to pursue? Over."

"Negative," the colonel said, breaking the silence. "All units remain in RecCon One until further notice." The ComO passed the word as the gathering reassembled in their seats and around the map boards. Quarry paid little attention to what the colonel had learned at the commanding general's meeting. He was too full of rage to give a shit. He wrote down his new orders only out of mechanical conditioning. The importance of his being appointed the divisional escort of six breach lanes didn't sink in.

12 February 1991

"What ya doing, Guy?" Quarry asked as he pulled up behind Sergeant Caine's Hummer.

"Listening to the B.B.C., sir," Guy said, sitting behind the Hummer and warming up an M.R.E. As Quarry looked up to the turret of the Hummer,

Orsini touched a forefinger to the rim of his boonie hat in a salty rendition of something resembling a salute. Quarry smiled and listened in.

"Iraq has issued a fresh call for Arab and Muslim militants to attack U.S. and western interests, stating there is no place for neutrality in the Gulf War. Syrian Foreign Minister Faroug Al-Shara says Israel must withdraw from occupied Arab land to ensure enduring peace after the war ends. French President François Mitterrand says an allied ground offensive against Iraq is inevitable and will occur this month. General Norman Schwarzkopf, however, says, it's too early to tell if a ground war against Iraq will be necessary. The U.S. has reviewed its aid to Jordan following a speech in which King Hussein appeared to abandon his neutrality and align himself with Iraq. And lastly, President Bush dispatched Secretary of Defense Cheney and General Colin Powell to Saudi Arabia to assess war progress, and determine when a ground assault might be launched. From Riyadh, this is Albert Green, B.B.C."

"Remember, Guy. Don't believe everything you hear."

"How so, sir?"

"The information that comes out of Riyadh has to be cleared. That information is most likely two or more days old. Bet ya Secretary Cheney and General Powell are already in country."

"Morning, sir," Caine said, waiting for Quarry's attention to divert from the short-wave radio.

"Morning, Two," Quarry said, moving slightly away from the Hummer. "Five and I are heading to division to get a brief on this breaching plan. Take charge for me, answer the radio, that sort of thing."

"No problem, sir." Quarry placed his hand on Caine's flak-jacketed shoulder, turned and got back in his Hummer.

* * *

The general-purpose tent was full to capacity, all seats taken and more people standing around its sides. Someone called "Attention on deck" and the tent became instantly quiet. The battalion commander of 2nd Combat Engineers led a small procession into the tent.

"The original concept of the ground war called for one breach of the berm," the colonel started. "The original plan called for 1st Marine Division to make an initial breach between the Al-Wafrah oilfield and the coastline. 2nd Division would then pass lines and become the MEF main effort after linking up with two brigades of Marines from an amphibious land. After the Battle of Khafji, the division staff developed plans for two breaches of the berm." The colonel switched to a different set of maps.

"2nd Marine Division will reposition to the west and north, around the 'heel' of Kuwait. 2nd Division, having more tanks, will be in a better position to meet armored counter-attack forces coming from the west. 1st Division will face the urban fighting in the east. Task Force Troy will conduct deception operations to make it appear that 2nd Division is still operating in the area. We will conduct the breach in the area of the Umm-Gudair oilfields."

Quarry and Grier looked at each other. The area the colonel suggested was the same one Stevens operated from.

"Division elements will wait in assembly areas and be called through the breach in serial sequence and waves. Colored approach lanes will lead from the assembly areas to the breach sites. These approach lanes will use colored plastic barrels placed every 250 meters along the route. The lanes will be marked from north to south, Red 1 and 2, Blue 3 and 4 in the middle, and Green 5 and 6 to the south. This is where you, the guides, come in. As the representatives of your units, you will work with Breach Force Alpha in a series of rehearsals. You will move your unit to the assembly areas, through the colored approach lanes and into the actual, correspondingly colored breach lanes. I'll be followed by the Breach Force Alpha commander who will brief the concept of operations."

A major stood and took over.

"Thank you, sir. Task Force Breach Alpha is task organized with units from Company B, 2nd Combat Engineer Battalion, Company D, 4th Combat Engineer Battalion, Provisional General Support Company, 4th Assault Amphibian Battalion and a detachment from 4th Tank Battalion. After they open the breaches, 6th Marines, temporarily reinforced by 1st Battalion, 8th Marines, will lead the division through the six breach lanes. 6th Marines will remain in the division center. 8th Marines will take the right boundary with 1st Marine Division. 1st Brigade, 2nd Armor Division, known as the Tiger Brigade, attached to us from the U.S. Army, will take the left. Tiger Brigade was specifically chosen for this mission as its heavy armor will protect our exposed flank from an Iraqi counter-attack. Tiger Brigade's boundary will be shared with an Arab coalition force to the west. 2nd Tank Battalion with its M1A1s is the division reserve and will follow in trace of 6th Marines.

"To deceive the Iraqis to the main effort, a total of 18 cuts will be made. Work will begin with nine cuts being made in Tiger Brigade's areas followed by three more cuts in front of 8th Marines. The remaining six are the actual breach sites and will be made in front of the 6th Marines' position at G minus 2. Units will check in and utilize the breach control frequency while they are in the breach. Units will remain on the breach frequency until they reach the breachhead at which time they will turn back to their tactical frequencies. Are there any questions?" There were many. When everyone was ready, the assembly walked behind the back of the tent where a scaled version of the breach had been made.

"At G minus 7, elements of division recon will insert to key points inside Kuwait. On G minus 4," the major continued, "engineers will start making cuts to the north of the breach area. At G minus 3, 2nd LAV will cross into Kuwait using known holes to the north of the minefields, attempt to identify gaps in the obstacle belt, and locate alternate breach sites in Tiger Brigade's area of operations. LAV's main mission will be to draw attention away from the location of the main breach site. At G minus 1, 3rd Battalion, 23rd Marines will also cross the berm and conduct security operations on the north side of the berm. This will further deceive the Iraqis to the location of the main attack. Lastly, on G minus 1, with LAV still screening forward, three of the division's six artillery battalions will move through the berm and set up on the far side. Guides for 2nd Battalion, 12th Marines sound off." They did. "Your assembly areas and lanes are here," the major said pointing not only to a map but to the terrain model as well.

"3rd Battalion, 10th Marines." Again, the major pointed out the areas.

"5th Battalion, 10th Marines will have an attachment of an M.R.L.S. from the Army," the colonel said, showing them their areas.

"6th Marines' guides."

"Here, sir," the lead guide answered up for the group.

"You'll be on the tail of the arty guides. As soon as they are through, bring up your units and stage in your assembly areas. At H-Hour," the major continued, "the lead elements of 6th Marines will pass through the artillery, cross the line of departure and follow along the lanes. When they reach the first obstacle belt, Task Force Breach Alpha will begin to reduce the obstacles. As they open the lanes, 6th Marines will assault through the breach." Questions were called for and answered. "Guides from 2nd Tanks."

"Here, sir," Quarry called out.

"You'll locate with 6th Marines the night before. After they assault through the first obstacle belt, your guides will mount up on six of Breach Alpha's assault amphibian vehicles. These A.A.V.s will follow the trail of the breach lanes while your guides place plastic barrels on each side of the lane," the Major said, holding up one of the plastic barrels that looked suspiciously like a plastic garbage can. "You'll place the markers the entire length of the lanes on your way down on your left hand side and throw a sand bag in each. When you turn around, you'll repeat the process, again on the left hand side on the way back to the berm."

"Yes, sir."

"When the marking A.A.V.s return, the general's forward command post will go through followed by 2nd Tanks, 10th Marines' forward command post, Tiger Brigade's command post and then Tiger Brigade. On order, the rest of the artillery units will move forward through the lanes. Any questions?" Again, there were many, some more important than others, but all were answered. When everyone was finished, a walk-through was conducted in an open area next to the sand table.

When the walk-through was complete, everyone returned to their parent units. When Quarry and Grier returned to their C.P., they briefed Colonel Calhoune on the day's events. Major Cranford, recently returned from his own briefing at division, added a few additional details. "Did anyone say when G-Day actually is?" the colonel asked.

"Not yet, sir," Major Cranford answered.

0700, 13 February 1991

The Scout leadership stood among a hundred others. Spread out in front of the Marines was a scaled sand table of the assembly areas and berm.

The engineer colonel called out unit designators, and Marines peeled away from the main crowd. When everyone was in place, the colonel continued.

"Immediately in front of the berm, the guides from 6th Marines will lead their units from their tactical assembly areas to the openings." Members of the breach control party gave the cue, and 6th Marines' guides stepped forward toward the scaled berm. As they did, six Hummers pulled up to the openings, representing the six "marking" A.A.V.s. Select members of the division either sat on the top of the Hummers or walked immediately beside it. Next to or on top of each Hummer was one of Quarry's Scouts.

Quarry and Grier stood in the area representing the staging area for 2nd Tanks. After the marking Hummers made their way down the lanes and back, the guides for 8th Marines moved forward. As the 8th Marines guides moved through the openings under the choreography of the colonel, Quarry and Grier moved forward to the final staging areas 8th Marines just vacated. As the colonel called out 2nd Tanks, the Scouts still at the berm stepped back to the final tactical assembly areas. The returning Scouts would pick up a tank company or commodity section and lead them to and through the berm.

The second phase of the rehearsal was a full-scale rehearsal of the 6th Marines assault. Once again, a scaled model of the breach lanes was painstakingly constructed. This one, however, was dozens of kilometers long so that every vehicle could take part.

Quarry and Grier took the time to get to know the guides who preceded and followed them. When 6th Marines started, Quarry and Grier, every now and then, caught a glimpse of their Scouts atop the "marking" A.A.V.s.

On the return trip, Quarry and Grier watched as the Scouts and guides from dozens of units placed the final garbage cans at the entrance of the mock berm on the left hand side.

The breach party control team took notes on the rehearsal and conducted a debrief upon the return of all six A.A.V.s. A few more problems were identified, and solutions were offered. The procedure proved simple, and effective.

Twenty

14 February 1991

While the Scouts created a scaled sand table for 2nd Tanks' breaching practice, "officially" Quarry went to check his positions. That Dole was driving north wasn't a mistake.

It took less than a half-hour. Quarry had Dole remain a respectful distance away from the main command tent while the Saudis finished their prayers. By coincidence, the colonel's clerk was the first to see the American Hummer.

"*Ya naqeeb* Samuels,'" the excited private yelled, standing up in the back row of soldiers.

Still kneeling on his prayer rug, Colonel Ahmed once again looked upon his infidel little brother.

"Allah be praised," he said, rising from his rug.

It only took a few minutes to close the distance. But by the time they did, easily over a hundred Saudi soldiers crowded around the Hummer. As Colonel Ahmed approached, the mass of soldiers parted and cheered as the two leaders embraced in traditional Arab greeting. After Colonel Ahmed stood back, dozens of his staff came forward, hugging Quarry and Dole.

"Come, we will have coffee and tea in my tent," the colonel said, gesturing towards the command tent. The crowd parted as they passed.

The colonel's entire primary staff was present, sitting on rugs or leaning against pillows. Quarry sat through what seemed to be hours of pleasantries but was in fact only a few minutes of small talk. Earlier than anticipated, Colonel Ahmed's American nurturing rose to the surface.

"Brother Samuels," he said in English. "You have done me and my command a great service, one that we can never repay. What can we do for you?"

Quarry simply smiled.

"Tell me, sir. How is your command? Are your men all right?"

There was a spontaneous burst of laughter from the colonel and then every other staff officer joined in. Quarry waited patiently for the laughter to subside. After a few moments, Colonel Ahmed regained his composure and wiped the moisture from his eyes.

"Brother Samuels," he started, "on January 29th, we destroyed hundreds of Iraqi vehicles, took over a thousand Iraqi prisoners and not one of my men received so much as a scratch. My command, Brother Samuels, is alive and well today because of Allah's gift of your friendship to us."

Quarry felt the lump form in the back of his throat and his voice cracked when he spoke.

"Allah is truly merciful." It was Colonel Ahmed's turn to be startled by the response, a response which started another series of hugs.

When the entourage exited the tent, several drivers were waiting to take them the short drive to the forward battle positions. As soon as Quarry and the Saudi leadership exited, the vast majority of Saudi tankers and soldiers swarmed the vehicles. It took over fifteen minutes to wade through the sea of soldiers. Most were very conscious of the rank of the foreign captain, but others still embraced Quarry and kissed him on the cheeks. Eventually, Quarry was physically lifted to the back of a tank to make a speech.

"*Allah yahayyeek*." Quarry continued, as best he could, in Arabic, "My friends, I am glad you are safe." A cheer rose from the crowd. When the crowd quieted down, Quarry continued, "I leave to take my position for the final battle. If Allah wills, we will see each other again when the war is over." The crowd cheered as Quarry climbed down from the tank.

"You make a fine Arab," Colonel Ahmed said to Quarry as he patted him on the back.

Quarry looked to the northeast. In front of the Saudi battle positions, the line of Iraqi vehicles could have been a picture from a Soviet training manual, if they weren't all mangled or burning.

It took only a few minutes for the Saudi leadership to reach the enemy's final resting place. Quarry exited his vehicle with a camera, taking internal and external pictures of a variety of destroyed Iraqi vehicles. Looking at the entry holes, Quarry and several Saudi staff officers got into a discussion of tactics, armor, ballistics, and weaponry.

While Quarry was busy down-range, Dole was climbing in and out of Iraqi tanks, recording ammo types and lot numbers. With the information the Scouts would provide, several Soviet armor publications would have to be rewritten.

Once back at the command tent, Colonel Ahmed had a special meal of lamb and rice prepared in honor of his guest. As they ate, every person told stories of where they were and how they had personally contributed to the victory over the Iraqis. Quarry told of how the Scouts saw the Iraqi movement and the call to Colonel Ahmed. When Quarry told how the *Missouri* engaged the enemy brigade to the east, every officer was riveted. Not one spoke or interrupted during the entire tale.

Just before 1100, Quarry announced the necessity of his departure. The mood changed quickly and hearts became heavy. As they rose to say their good-byes, Quarry shook the hand of every officer in the room, receiving hugs and kisses from many. Then it was time to say good-bye to Colonel Ahmed.

"When you come back to visit us, Brother Samuels," the colonel said, retrieving an object from his clerk, "you will wear this." The colonel placed the scarlet beret of the Saudi National Guard on Quarry's head. "That way, we will see you coming and know it's you."

Quarry took a step back and saluted the Saudi colonel.

"*Aywa, bil'akh al'aqeed* Ahmed." The colonel returned the salute, stepped forward and hugged Quarry, like a father would hug a son whom most likely he would never see again. The two officers patted each other on the back several times before releasing each other.

"God's blessing be upon you," Colonel Ahmed said quietly.

"*Wa'alaykumu ssalaam*," Quarry replied. Dole was waiting outside in the Hummer. Quarry silently got in, and Dole drove off.

* * *

Between the logistics trains and the command post, Grier and Three One made a three-kilometer terrain model with engineer tape and signposts. At 1300, the OpsO briefed the company commanders. When everyone was confident in the concept, the commanders staged their Hummers in one of the six tactical assembly areas identified by white engineer tape. Scouts came forward and picked up the leaders and guided them to the entrance of the makeshift berm. The Hummers then drove the route, with the Scouts explaining about the marking systems and what they could expect.

15 February 1991

Practice continued. Quarry dedicated a Scout section to each tank company. The Scouts would lead the tanks in their Hummers, the Alpha Command group would follow the lead tank company in Lane Four. The Bravo Command group followed a tank company on the far right flank in Lane Six. Quarry led in the middle, Lane Three, to control the pace and forward progress of all the Scouts.

At 1800, Quarry entered the C.P. The operations officer greeted him as he walked past the tarps between the A.A.V.s of the Alpha and Bravo Command groups.

"The division moved to the west side of the heel of Kuwait. We are the last units to move. Our new position will be here," the major said pointing to a spot on the map. "I suggest we use this route." The overlay showed a route in blue. "Tomorrow, conduct a route recon. Be back by 1800 tomorrow night with your report. You'll lead the battalion at 0600 on the 17th. Questions?"

Quarry looked at the suggested route.

"None, sir."

16 February 1991

As the crow flies, the distance was almost 40km. Unfortunately, within that straight line were two berms, two known enemy minefields, and a reinforced Marine Division. "So all we're doing today is a route recon to determine trafficability?" Caine asked.

"That's it," Quarry answered. "Essentially, all we'll do is chase G.P.S. waypoints. Do both G.P.S.s have the waypoints plotted?" The leaders shook their heads yes. "Then saddle up." The Scout leadership climbed into two Hummers. There was no need to pull shooters off line when all they were going to do was look at the ground and watch dirt go by.

* * *

Half a world away, a lieutenant colonel put down the phone in one of the many dark recesses of the Pentagon. An additional 1,758 Marine reservists were ordered to active duty. The total number of reservists called was now 24,703. As the colonel at manpower handed the memo to the captain of reserve affairs, he watched the status board update. The active duty strength of the Marine Corps was 200,248; the first time it had exceeded 200,000 since Vietnam.

19 February 1991

"Sir?"

The Scouts were performing no tactical mission whatsoever. TOW Company was a few hundred yards to the west. The gun companies were arrayed in a circle around the Alpha and Bravo command groups. To the east, an entire Marine Division lay between the Scouts and the bad guys, and the radio hadn't broken squelch for hours.

"Hey, Slayer, what's up."

"If you're busy, sir, I can come back."

"Of course not. What's on your mind?"

"A few of us have been listening to the short-wave. They say we're going to attack in the next few days." Slayer paused for a moment. "We were wondering, sir, if you've gotten any orders that we've haven't been told?"

Quarry got out of his seat, placed the remote speaker on the hood, and hoisted himself up next to it.

"Have a seat." Slayer looked confused but jumped up on the hood with his commanding officer. "I can honestly tell you, Slayer, that I haven't received a word that I haven't immediately passed onto the platoon leadership. As Grier's driver, you usually hear about it even before the squad leaders get the word. Now, what have you been hearing on the radio?"

"They say it's this weekend."

"Why's that?" Quarry asked only because he hadn't listened to the radio in a few days and was wondering what was going on in the world.

"The President said the invasion of Kuwait will end very soon. When he was asked about the timetable, he refused to answer but commented that we'll finish the job and do it right. A few minutes later, they were talking to the French Foreign Minister who said we were on the eve of the ground war and that G-Day was set. Some British commander stationed down in Riyadh made a press release and said he wouldn't give any hints on the dates, but they gave some pretty hard facts that make it seem like it's coming soon."

"What facts?"

"Like the moon, sir. Tonight is the smallest the moon will be. Minimal illumination from moonlight gives us and our night vision capability the advantage. The tides in the gulf are at a high point, an advantage for an amphibious landing. The Muslim holy season of Rajab ended Thursday. Ramadan doesn't start until 17th March. A British commander announced they took out two communications stations. He said the stations were the last link between Baghdad and troops in Kuwait. After that, a Marine general gave a summary of the effects of the air war. He said," Slayer took a piece of paper out of his flak jacket pocket, "that Iraq has lost 1,300 of their 4,280 tanks, 1,100 of their 3,100 artillery pieces and 800 of their 2,870 armored personnel carriers. He said that there are probably even more damaged and out of action."

What Slayer said made perfect sense.

20 February 1991

The engineering colonel exited the Hummer with a roll of maps under one arm and a determined look on his face.

"I've seen that look before," Grier said to Quarry under his breath, "this is it."

The crowd parted and made way for the colonel as he approached the easel.

"This morning, your commanding officers met with the general. They received Fragmentary Order 16-91. G-Day is set for 24 February with H-hour at 0530." The colonel gave the crowd a minute to murmur. "In front of you is a scaled sand table where the breaching lanes are going to be cut through the berm. You can see they lead to MEF and division objectives. Starting tonight, members of Breach Force Alpha and the 3rd Naval Construction Battalion are going to start cutting holes in the berm, north of the actual lanes. The next time we'll see each other in the morning of the 24th."

* * *

At 2000, the tarped area between the two command A.A.V.s was packed to capacity. The company commanders sat on the ground directly in front of the map board. Quarry was up front with the Three. The X.O. started with an overview of the proceedings. Major Cranford followed the X.O. with the operations order. Quarry followed the Three and briefed the concept of the guides. He called each Scout forward so the company commanders and commodity heads could make face-to-face contact with the Scout who would lead them through the minefields. After Quarry finished, the colonel stood and gave his pep talk. Battalion-level rehearsals would continue daily until H-Hour.

21 February 1991

The battalion conducted another tactical exercise without troops. A tank company's leadership packed into one Hummer. The Scouts assigned to a particular tank company drove to the holding point, picked up their designated company and escorted it to the simulated forward-assembly area. The guides paused as they simulated the hand-off to the breach control party and then continued through the simulated breach lanes. Quarry's role in the game was coordinating communications as Scouts left the platoon net for the breach control net. Individual Scout guides monitored the tank company's tactical net they were assigned to as well as the Scout platoon net. Since every Scout Hummer possessed dual radios and a number of portables, Quarry never lost communications with his men.

* * *

That evening, as Quarry entered the C.P., Major Cranford greeted him and continued: "Last night, a recon team had to be extracted by an LAV unit attached to 6th Marines. They were about to get detected by a unit of over thirty Iraqi infantry supported by five armored personnel carriers."

"Yes, sir."

"Starting tonight, LAV is patrolling on the Kuwaiti side of the berm. That should heat things up a bit more."

"Yes, sir."

"The Sea Bees identified an antiaircraft site at the northernmost cut in the berm, here," the major said, pointing to a small circle on the map. "They described what can only be a Z.S.U.-23-4 anti-aircraft vehicle as it shot at a flight of AV-8Bs. They said the stream of rounds looked like a waterfall of tracers going up into the sky. They never actually saw the Z.S.U. because it shot from a sinkhole, although the map doesn't show any depressions in that area."

Quarry leaned forward and took a closer look at the map.

"Most likely it's a wadi that has been dug out."

"Agreed. Tonight, take it out."

Quarry stepped back from the map.

"Doesn't that fall within 2nd LAV or Recon's area of responsibility, sir?"

"Yes, but division feels that moving a LAV unit that far north will bring too much attention to the division's frontage. It could ruin the whole deception operation," Cranford said, pointing to locations on the map. "LAV's mission is to engage the enemy and deceive them of the breach sites' true location. They're expected to get into it pretty heavy. That will allow a small team to move in undetected and neutralize the A.A. site. Recon is set in observation points along the actual breach site locations. As the division reserve, this mission has fallen on us. On you."

* * *

Two daylight and one night rehearsal were conducted before the platoon stood down for the evening. At 0100, reveille sounded and they ran through a final rehearsal. Quarry walked the length of his men, looking at their equipment as best he could in the starlight.

"Bring it in." The ends of the line collapsed around their leader. "Any questions?" There were none. "Any concerns?" None were spoken. They were ready. "Saddle up."

Marion and Davis, Marek and Kantner manned their vehicles, as did Hauser and Carleton. Grier climbed into Marion's front passenger seat while Quarry and 2nd Squad spread themselves equally among the three Hummers. Sergeant Ogdon handed Quarry his M-16 after everyone adjusted their seating and gear.

"See ya in a few hours, skipper." Quarry smiled.

From their assembly area at 2nd Tanks, the ten-click drive due south took little time as they were still behind the division. When they turned west at waypoint one, the pace slowed as the three Hummers formed a wedge with a TOW Hummer in the middle.

At the slower speed, it took 20 minutes to reach the Saudi side of the berm. Using thermal sights, Marion gave updates every two minutes and his "negative contact" was a welcome report every time. As they made their final approach, the Hummers slowed even more. At last they made a southbound turn, the passenger doors opened, and eight Scouts rolled out into the darkness. The Hummers continued south, increasing their speed.

The eight blackened shapes moved to the berm and waited. Two poked their heads over the top, one wearing N.V.G.s, one not. Ten minutes later, Quarry keyed the net twice but didn't say anything. He looked right and left, stretched an arm out level to the ground, and then raised it slightly above his shoulder. The eight shapes climbed over the berm without a sound.

The Scouts moved the first five clicks in two parallel columns, 25 meters apart. Every other Scout of the assault team was on N.V.G.s. Marion reported the lack of thermal imagery on the horizon from the TOW Hummer. That he couldn't see any signatures of vehicles or people was a good indication that the Iraqi anti-air position was lax. Grier and the rest of the support team on the Saudi side of the berm continued to monitor. Marion was ready to send a TOW missile into any vehicle that exposed itself from the hole. Hauser and Marek were ready to rush in with machine guns blazing, should the assault team need extraction.

At three three kilometeres out, the Scouts dropped to hands and knees. Marion easily tracked the figures that were radiating brightly in the mid-30-degree morning. With no other signs of life, Marion continued to update his commander.

At 1,800 meters out, the Scouts dropped to their bellies. Even though Marion assured Quarry there was no enemy movement, the assault team was taking no chances. Quarry continued to lead his team in a low crawl to where the darkness engulfed the ground, indicating the beginning of the hole. Quarry held up a hand and the two columns came to a halt. He and Caine continued forward. As the two approached the rim of the sinkhole, the starlight was bright enough to reveal the Z,S,U,-23-4 directly beneath them. Once a mere wadi, the hole was now at least ten feet deep and 15 feet across. The entrance to the hole was to Quarry's left, opening directly to the east. To the south of the pit was a B.M.P., with two of its infantry soldiers talking freely and playing with a small circle of rocks and coals that earlier had been a cooking fire. Quarry moved back a few feet; Caine mimicked his movement. Quarry pointed to Caine and indicated the direction of the B.M.P. Caine nodded and slightly raised a hand. A hundred meters behind, the two teams started low-crawling. One team moved to the two leaders, the other on a southern angle.

Team One arrived and spaced themselves ten meters apart and on line with Quarry. Marion continued to track and monitor the movement of Team

Two as they worked their way to the south. When they were in place, Caine raised his right hand at the elbow. Quarry saw the silhouette and raised his as well. The two teams independently readied themselves and gave each other a final visual check. Quarry raised his hand twice and Caine repeated the gesture. The two teams started to converge on the rim of the hole. Stopping a foot back from the rim of the crater, Quarry raised his right hand, which now contained a fragmentation grenade. The rest of Team One were similarly armed and copied the action of their leader. Caine looked over at Guy and Orsini, who readied themselves. Caine and Surkein also raised their grenades. Quarry pumped his hand three times and on third repetition, a hail of grenades rained into the sinkhole. The Scouts pressed themselves to the ground and within seconds the grenades did their job.

Raising themselves off the desert floor, Guy and Orsini each raised a 66mm light antitank rocket to their shoulders. The Scouts remained on the ground as the high-pitched squeal of the two rockets filled the air and hit the B.M.P. A second later, shots from M-16s completed the mission. All was quiet; no one heard anything over the ringing in their ears.

Team Two covered Team One as they entered the hole. Above them, a shot rang out as an Iraqi soldier attempted to climb out of the driver's compartment of the B.M.P. Team One swept the ground toward the vehicle. Speckman reached the back troop hatch of the B.M.P. first and placed himself nearest the handle. Peterson pulled the pin on another grenade and nodded. Specter opened the hatch just enough for Peterson to deliver it. Three seconds later, the explosion registered. Specter again opened the back hatch, and three Scouts sprayed down the inside with M-16s on full automatic.

Quarry and Dole checked the few intact radios to see what frequency they were on. The Scouts checked the bodies for maps, log books, and other intelligence. As the assault team withdrew from the wadi, Quarry threw two thermite grenades into the Z.S.U. turret. The heat would weld the metal of the turret together and cause secondary detonations of the rounds inside the magazines. They didn't have to wait long.

As the assault team double-timed away from the fireworks display, Marion reported there were no enemy reinforcements moving on the horizon. Grier ordered the support team to move to the closest point of intercept to pick up the ground unit. Thirty minutes and a high-speed run later, the Scouts were back at battalion.

23 February 1991

When Colonel Calhoune returned from division headquarters, the Alpha and Bravo command group were waiting. Accompanying the colonel was the company commander of Bravo Company, 1st Battalion, 8th Marines.

The entire staff was introduced to the infantry company commander who was now attached to 2nd Tanks. His hundred-plus infantrymen would arrive in their A.A.V.s in due time.

The staff worked frantically to update the operations plan with the new information and the additional asset. With infantry, the battalion could protect itself in close battle. The colonel further directed B-1/8 be task organized. The company commander detached one of his infantry platoons to Bravo Company, 2nd Tanks and received a tank platoon in return.

Two huge map boards were brought outside to accommodate all the Marines. Colonel Calhoune called the group to order, updated the friendly and enemy situation, and issued the operations order.

As the op order turned into back briefs and back briefs into rehearsals, the sky began to grow dark. For months, not a cloud in the sky had been seen. Now, the smoke generated from hundreds of burning oil wells, especially those in the Umm-Gudair and Al-Manaqish oilfields, loomed over the Marines. It was a bad omen.

* * *

The chaplain visited the Scouts late afternoon. As if inspired by divine intervention, the wind shifted and the sky cleared. Though it was a voluntary event, every Scout was present for Holy Communion, though saltines were substituted for bread and canteen water for wine.

The Scouts pulled three of their Hummers forward and lined up in two ranks. The chaplain took a picture of the entire platoon. After taking several shots with several cameras, he blessed them all.

Part II

Desert Storm: The Ground War

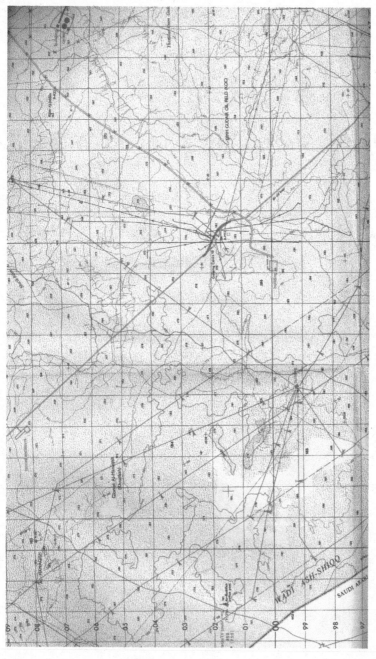

The Umm Gudair Oil Fields. The oil fields are located approximately 20 miles north of the southern-most border with Saudi Arabia, 30 miles from the Persian Gulf to the east, but only ten miles east and two miles south of the southwest portion of the "Heel" of Kuwait, at the V of present-day Highway 51. The site of 2nd Marine Division breech lanes near Wadi Ash-Shiqq, the mean elevation of this entire region doesn't rise or fall more than a dozen feet.

Twenty-One

24 February 1991

Quarry woke to what he thought was a practical joke. Rolling over in his sleeping bag, he pulled the cover over his head.

"Go away, it's not reveille yet." The patter didn't go away. Rising up out of his sleeping bag in the cold morning air, Quarry stuck his head out of the opening. "I said ..." He was pelted in the face by a full downpour of rain.

"I thought this was supposed to be a desert?" Quarry heard Dole say from within his sleeping bag next to the Hummer. Quarry looked at his watch: 0230.

The wind had shifted. Once again it came from the east, bringing with it the smoke of the burning oilfields. With the smoke came a complete change of normal atmospheric conditions.

"All right, ladies," Grier called out from the other side of the assembly area, "rise and shine. Break the weapons down and get some lubricant on 'em!" Fully awake, the Scouts dropped cammie nets and performed combat checks. Few had slept. Now, everyone was not only tired, they were cold and wet.

The rain lasted long enough to make everyone miserable. The Scouts completed their work and finally found the warmth and dryness of their Hummers. After changing into dry uniforms, Quarry, Grier, and the squad leaders performed the pre-combat checks. A protective biological and chemical suit was put on over the dry cammies. Looking like big green two-pieced jump suits, the N.B.C. suits were lined with activated charcoal. Over their boots, the Scouts strapped rubber booties and laced them half way up their legs. Lastly, rubber gloves were tucked in the strap of the gas mask carrier that went around their waist. Over the protective suit, the Scouts wore their normal flak jackets and helmets. If any chemical agents were detected, it would take only a few seconds to put on the mask and gloves and be protected. All Scouts carried a complete second set of protective clothes within easy reach. In the early-morning cold, the additional clothing was actually comfortable.

183

After the leaders determined everything was ready, the entire platoon gathered around the command Hummer.

"It's three thirty," Quarry said, "we might as well get started." There wasn't much else to say. Quarry looked upon his squad leaders and then on his men. "I'll see you on the other side." The leaders shook hands before the Scouts mounted their vehicles. The crescent moon didn't penetrate the low cloud cover. Those with superstitions were having a bad time.

Twenty minutes later, they had worked their way around the various formations until they were parallel with the cuts in the berm. Switching over to the breach control net, Quarry made radio contact with the radio operator. At a waypoint on the G.P.S., in the middle of the desert, in the darkness of the morning, the column of Hummers broke formation and headed in different directions. Quarry said a silent prayer for his men.

"Arty up front, skipper," Dole said, slowing down to almost nothing. They caught up with 2nd Battalion, 10th Marines, the direct support artillery battalion assigned to the 6th Marine Regiment. As planned, the bulk of the division's artillery moved across the berm at G minus 1. 3/10, 5/10, 2/12 and the Army's M.R.L.S. battery were already set, east of the berm. The Army's 1st Battalion, 3rd Field Artillery was on the west side of the berm, providing long-range supporting fire for the Marine artillery. They would displace and move later with Tiger Brigade. 2/10 would continue to move with 6th Marines in the assault and take position on the far side of the breach. While moving artillery forward of the division was a risky decision, if the artillery set up on the west side of the berm, the division would soon outdistance the maximum effective range of the M-198s' 155mm howitzers. Providing the artillery security was 2nd LAV Battalion to the front and 3rd Battalion, 23rd Marines to the flanks.

Dole followed the artillery until it came to the berm. Quarry continued to monitor the net until all the Scouts reached their designated lanes. As they waited, Scouts individually checked in on the breach control net, stating they had joined up with their particular marking A.A.V.

At 0430, every artillery piece on the west and east side of the berm fired. The initial volley scared the shit out of Quarry and Dole, who got out and watched the rest of the show from on top of their Hummer. Moments later, the low-lying clouds lit up as the M.R.L.S. rockets joined in the aerial attack. Their targets were the known remaining Iraqi artillery positions, a deeper target than the artillery's 30km rocket-assisted projectile could reach. At the same time, air strikes flew against targets in the vicinity of Phase Line Red, an east/west-running road north of the second obstacle belt. Quarry and Dole continued to "ooh" and "aahs" for over an hour.

At 0530, H-Hour, the last artillery rounds fired and lead elements of the 6th Marines crossed through the cuts in the berm. The ground war officially began to the sound of the Marine Corps' Hymn being broadcast over the loudspeakers, followed by the "Flight of the Valkyries."

The lead element of 6th Marines' attack was Task Force Breach Alpha. The A.A.V.s with the three-shot mine-clearing charges, and M-60A1 tanks with the M-58 line-charge trailers, led the way. The pressure from the exploding line charges blew up many of the Iraqi mines where they lay. Working under incoming Iraqi artillery fire, tanks with mine-clearing plows pushed the first few inches of soil to the side. Many Iraqi mines blew up in the churning soil, but not all. Tanks with mine rakes followed in the blown and plowed lanes, tumbling the few remaining mines to the side. Mines that tumbled back into the lanes had to be blown up individually by demolition teams. Small groups of Marines ran to and from any one of the 22 A.A.V.s dedicated to the combat engineers. Most of the plastic Soviet and Italian antipersonnel and tank mines were destroyed by the line charges. British "bar" mines proved more resistant and required engineers to place their own charges next to or on the enemy explosives to destroy them. Finally, specially equipped tanks with track-width mine plows, rakes and rollers, "proofed" the lanes.

At 0600, the main body of 6th Marines entered the breach. 1/6 was on the offensive. By 0615, 2/2 and 1/8 reached breach lanes Blue 3 and 4, and Green 5 and 6, respectively. The lack of early morning light, caused by the smoke-covered skies, meant Quarry and Dole lost sight of the advancing forces. A half-hour later, Quarry watched an A.A.V. drive through the cut in the berm that led to breach lane Blue 3. Among a stack of blue traffic cones, a gas-mask-wearing Marine saluted as they went by. Quarry returned the salute to the man whom he assumed was Sergeant Caine.

At 0656, the worst fear of every planner came true. The words "Gas, gas, gas," came over the breach control net. Quarry and Dole donned their masks, protective hoods, and gloves in less than seven seconds and waited for additional information. The information was too long in coming, and Quarry got impatient. Removing a 256 test kit from the readily available supply, Quarry exited the Hummer and broke the various capsules. Dole also exited the Hummer and applied M-1 detection paper to various parts of the vehicle. When Dole finished, he walked over to Quarry. His eyes widened when he saw the results of the test. The 256 kit had detected a nerve agent.

It took more than a half-hour for the initial N.B.C.1 report to be passed over the breach control net. A "Fox" nuclear, biological, and chemical reconnaissance vehicle, a vehicle specially designed and built for this mission, detected traces of mustard gas in Lane Red 1. The gas was thought to have been disbursed by a land-mine. Unbeknownst to Quarry and Dole, two A.A.V. crewmen suffered and were treated for blistering to their arms from the agent.

Quarry reported his findings over the control net. An N.B.C. specialist directed Quarry to a separate net and instructed him to conduct a second test.

The second reading also showed the presence of nerve agent. The specialist told them to sit tight and members of the N.B.C. monitoring team would be en route.

By 0724, 1/6 had passed through the first obstacle belt on Lanes Red 1 and 2. Iraqi units between the two minefields were quickly suppressed or neutralized. Shortly thereafter, 2/2 reported clearing the first belt on Lanes Blue 3 and 4. It wasn't long after that Quarry and Dole watched an antenna-laden command variant of a light armored vehicle pass through the cut in the berm. The commanding general was moving forward in his mobile command post.

To the south, 1/8 was having difficulty in the Green Lanes. Several engineer vehicles struck mines and were significantly damaged. The engineers reported a vastly different type, number, and array of mines than those of the minefield in the Red and Blue Lanes. Numerous acts of valor were observed as individual engineers set fuses on failed detonators, or ignited line charges that hadn't exploded.

At 0745, 1/6 passed through and exited the second obstacle belt. They met sporadic resistance, but brought to bear the full weight of the division's artillery on all that remained in their path. Cobra attack helicopters flew directly over the Iraqi trench lines and placed direct fire on those who chose to stay and fight. By 0850, 2/2 cleared the second obstacle belt on Lanes Blue 3 and 4.

At 0930, Quarry was contacted on the breach control net and had to give up listening to the division tactical net. The N.B.C. specialists stated the contamination on Lane Red 1 was either neutralized or dissipated to the point the blister agent was no longer be detected. The N.B.C. cell told Quarry to conduct another 256 test. Both Quarry and Dole performed the test at two separate locations; both kits reported negative, as did the M-1 paper strung over the top of the Hummer. The N.B.C. control team passed the "all clear" and the mission-orientated protective posture was downgraded. Dole and Quarry started to perform the selective unmasking drills.

As Quarry was in the process of exposing his eyes to the open environment, one of the many marking A.A.V.s returned through the berm with jubilant unmasked Marines riding on top. Quarry looked over at Dole in disbelief. Both simply shook their heads and took their gas masks off. As the marking A.A.V.s from the Red and Blue Lanes also returned, the guides reverted back to their parent commands. Marion and Caine checked in on platoon tac. With the Green lanes still in question, Ogdon and Hauser were still somewhere in the middle of a minefield. Quarry had Dole drive them to Lane Green 5 while Grier waited at Lane Green 6 for the return of their men.

By 1020, all three battalions of 6th Marines were in contact. The further the Marines pushed north, the more resistance they encountered. With 1/6 through the minefield, it took little additional fighting to reach, seize, and secure the left flank of the regimental objective, a location on the map that would be used for a link-up point once other units made it through the breach. 2/2 continued to fight its way north but met enemy tanks supported by artillery. Company A, 4th Tank Battalion, met the enemy head-on. In a series of armored attacks, the reserve tankers fought their way through enemy anti-tank and small-arms fire that came from bunkers and fortified trench lines. Their effort helped 2/2 break the enemy resistance and seize the center of the regimental objective. On the right flank, a bypass was cut from Green 5, south to Green 6. Another lane, further to the south, which was initially to be a return lane for westbound traffic, became the new Green 6. 1/8 continued the attack.

As soon as 1/8 cleared the first obstacle belt, they were engaged from buildings between the two minefields. A number of small-unit engagements killed many Iraqis; hundreds more chose to surrender. As soon as they cleared the first engagement, 1/8 ran directly into an entire Iraqi brigade. Outnumbered three to one and facing a well dug-in enemy, the battalion destroyed the enemy's heavy weapons emplacements and artillery with close air support. Harriers, F/A-18s, and Cobras screamed in, obliterating enemy armor and armored personnel carriers. As the smoke and dust cleared, only the Iraqi infantry was left to face the Marine battalion. After an initial slaughter, many Iraqis chose to surrender.

It took another hour and a half for Green 5 to open and allow 1/8 to fight its way through the second obstacle belt. With 6th Marines now in full control of their objective, 8th Marines poured through the berm. Quarry counted dozens of A.A.V.s and other combat vehicles pushing east. As Quarry continued to listen to the division tac and division Intel nets on the P.R.C. radios, Caine checked in on the breach control net. 2nd Tanks arrived at the breach lane assembly areas.

There was still considerable work that needed to be done on Green 6 before it opened. While the engineers were busy clearing mines, Hauser jumped ship and climbed up with Ogdon on his marking A.A.V. The two returned from the berm opening on Green 5 at noon.

With the Scouts back at full strength, they returned to the battalion assembly area and waited with the units they would lead through the berm. As 8th Marines cleared the first obstacle belt with only minor resistance, 2nd Tank Battalion was ordered from their rally point to the staging areas.

With enemy dismounted infantry still a viable threat to the south, Colonel Calhoune placed B-1/8 and the Alpha Command Group on Lane Green 6. Charlie Company would support them with long-range fires from Green 5. In the middle, the logistics trains would be covered by TOW Company in lanes Blue 3 and 4. The weight of the battalion would be to the north in the Red Lanes with Bravo Company in Lane 2 and Delta Company in Lane 1. The Bravo Command Group would follow immediately behind Delta Company.

When the order was given, 2nd Tank Battalion moved from their assembly areas and approached the berm. Dole moved the command Hummer into position and started down Blue 3. The time was 1250.

The battalion pushed through the breaches as fast as possible. Until Tiger Brigade crossed the berm, 2nd Tanks was the only heavy assault capability in the division. Designated the division reserve, 2nd Tanks encountered only minor resistance in the form of small-arms fire in the Green lanes. Two tanks hit mines and were temporarily damaged. As the crews exited the tanks, the blade tanks behind them dropped their plows and cut a safe path around their disabled brothers.

As the battalion went through the 16 kilometers of mine fields, Bravo Company came on line and took position on Charlie Company's left flank. TOW Hummers formed screen lines on each side of the tanks, while Quarry and the Scouts led the tanks north. As they cleared Phase Line Panther, the Scouts checked in on platoon tac. Quarry slowed the pace of the platoon to allow the logistics trains time to get behind Bravo and Charlie. Eventually, the rest of the "Box" formation caught up as Delta Company took position on the back left and B-1/8 on the back right.

"Contact! North, out!" broke the sound of silence on platoon tac.

"Shit!" Quarry exclaimed, reaching for the map by his left hand. "Who was that?"

"Sounded like Speckman sir! Lane 4," Dole answered.

"Break right. Get us over there!"

"Receiving small-arms fire from grid 652 076, enemy infantry in trenches, time now, returning fire with 50-cal, continuing to engage, over," Speckman reported seconds later.

"This is Six, hard copy. Be prepared to adjust arty, over," Quarry said, without looking up from his map where he plotted the enemy contact.

"Heavy Metal, this is Scout Six. Contact, grid, 652 076, enemy in trench line, Two Two returning fire. Switching to COF, over," Quarry transmitted, not waiting for a reply. He threw the handset with the battalion tactical net to Dole, switched on a P.R.C. with the platoon frequency, and hit button three on the top radio. The preset rotated until it stopped on the artillery conduct of fire net.

"Steel Rain, this is Scout Six, over."

"This is Steel Rain, over." Quarry was talking to the fire support coordinator of his own battalion. An artillery officer by MOS, he was a permanent member of the operations sections and someone Quarry and the Scouts knew well. He'd take care of them.

"This is Scout Six, adjust fire over."

"Adjust fire, out."

"Grid, 652 076, infantry in trench line, over."

"Grid, 652 076, infantry in trench line, out."

"Skipper, we're here!" Dole said with a hint of anticipation in his voice. As the command Hummer driver, Dole had never anticipated driving through the open desert, charging into an ongoing firefight at over 60 miles an hour in an unarmored Hummer.

Quarry looked up and saw the flash of the 50-caliber rounds from Peterson's M-2. A quick look at the G.P.S. showed they were less than 800 yards from where Peterson was firing.

"This is Scout Six, danger close, out!" Quarry yelled into the COF handset. "Pull in behind them. Offset so I can adjust," Quarry said to Dole without taking his eyes from down range. As he watched, Quarry was aware of the small wisps of smoke on the ground in front of them. The smoke was dirt being kicked up from the bullets impacting the ground. Looking down range again, Quarry watched as dozens of figures started climbing up and over the edge of the trench.

"Scout Six, this is Two Two, observing 20 infantry coming out of the trenches, continuing to return fire, over."

"Scout Six, this is Steel Rain, shot, over."

"This is Six, shot. Time of flight, over."

"Thirty-five seconds, over."

"Scout Six, out." Changing handsets, Quarry continued, "Two Two this is Six, roger, I'm right behind you. Observing and adjusting, out." Quarry heard Dole update the battalion on the tac net.

"Skipper! Did you see ...?"

Quarry cut him off in mid-sentence: "Holy shit!" Quarry watched a small but violent firefight. But the aggression wasn't focused on the Scouts. On the contrary, Quarry watched several Iraqi soldiers turn their weapons on their own. The incoming rounds stopped as the battle now raged within the trench. Then, as quickly as it had started, it stopped. As soon as it did, those who had fired into their own trenches dropped their weapons and put their hands in the air. Heartbeats later, the trench line was full of white cloth waving in the air.

"Skipper! Bravo Company!" Quarry looked past Dole and out the rear driver side window. The battalion had dispatched B company shortly after Quarry sent the report.

"Shit!" Picking up the platoon net, Quarry screamed into the handset. "This is Six. Cease fire, cease fire." Looking up at Peterson, Quarry saw his orders were being obeyed. As Quarry took a deep breath, his stomach turned. "Oh my God!" He changed handsets to the fire direction control net. "Check fire! Check fire! Steel Rain, Check fire!"

"Skip ..." Dole started to ask what was wrong.

"Drive!"

"Sir?"

"Drive toward them," Quarry said leaping out of the Hummer's door and climbing onto its hood. "Drive, damn it!" Dole didn't understand but started out slowly. Standing on the hood of the Hummer, Quarry frantically waved his arms.

Quarry signaled the A.A.V. to stop, but it kept going. Dole continued to drive forward, as Quarry watched dozens of Iraqi infantry soldiers come out of the trenches. Quarry started yelling "get down" in Arabic as loud as he could. He waved his hands frantically in hope the Iraqi soldiers would see and understand. They didn't. Seconds later, four, 155mm high-explosive artillery rounds landed exactly where called for. Speckman's estimation of the grid had been perfect.

Five hundred yards from point of impact, it wasn't the concussion that threw him, just loss of balance. Dole screeched to a halt and ran around to see his commander sprawled out, face down on the ground. He dropped down to see if Quarry was hit. As soon as Dole's concerned voice and gentle hand touched the back of Quarry's flak jacket, Quarry spoke in a broken voice.

"I'm fine Delta."

Dole helped Quarry sit up.

"They were shooting at us, sir. You did what you had to do to save us." Quarry allowed himself to be helped up.

One of the infantry's A.A.V.s drove by.

"Holy shit! That's the damnedest thing I've ever seen. Nice shooting Captain!"

"Yeah, nice shooting," Quarry said mockingly. Dole assisted Quarry to his seat, ran around the Hummer and turned away from the trench line. Dole picked up the COF net and called the mission was complete, and that Bravo Company would send the battle damage assessment. On the battalion tac, Heavy Metal Three asked for an update from Bravo as soon as possible and told the Scouts to continue to push forward. Quarry took a deep breath and exhaled sharply. Picking up the battalion handset, he acknowledged his orders.

The Scouts led the battalion north another five clicks to battalion Objective Foxtrot. When Quarry called it in, the battalion set up in a diamond-shaped formation with Charlie Company taking the point, Bravo Company, minus their attached infantry platoon, on the left; Bravo 1/8 on the right; the logistics trains and TOW Company to the rear; and Delta Company smack in the middle. The Scouts moved three clicks north of Charlie. At 1600, Tiger Brigade moved through the berm and three battalions of artillery set up in preparation for a night defense. The division was arrayed with regiments on a diagonal line from northwest to southeast. 2nd Marine Division had to hold where they were to allow 1st Marine Division time to catch up on their east flank. Having started further south, 1st MarDiv had further to go and participated in a particularly nasty battle around the Al-Jaber airfield. Until Tiger Brigade moved into position, the potential of a large and violent Iraqi counter-attack still loomed. 2nd Tanks, as the division reserve, remained at maximum alert.

The day was not without cost. The division lost seven M-60 tanks, two A.A.V.s, and one M1A1 tank to the minefields. Two Marines died and 12 were injured. The division captured over 3,000 Iraqi prisoners and inflicted unknown casualties.

For the Scouts, what started out as 20 soldiers in a trench line turned into 190 Iraqi infantry P.O.W.s for the battalion. Of the 190, 50 were injured. Thirty-five were dead. Neither Quarry nor Dole ever spoke a word of it again.

With the forward progress of the division stopped for the evening and a ring of armor with thermal imagery scanning every possible inch of open desert, Quarry reduced the Scouts' readiness condition. With the effects of adrenaline wearing off and the majority of Scouts having been awake now for over twenty-four hours, half of the platoon was asleep within minutes. Quarry told Dole he'd take the first watch. Five minutes later, Dole was snoring gently. Quarry climbed out of his seat and placed the radio speaker on the hood of the Hummer. He listened to the sounds of combat and watched the sporadic flashes of gunfire on the horizon as he relived the events of the day in his head.

0330, 25 February 1991

"Staff Sergeant?" Slayer said quietly after the radio transmission ended.

"Yeah, Delta?" Grier said without looking up from behind the map.

"Do you think we should wake the captain?"

Grier plotted the location where mortars fell in the 6th Marines' area. At this distance, the rumble was barely audible and the flashes were faint on the horizon.

"Nah," he said, looking over the open kilometer between the two command Hummers. "We have the watch. Let him sleep."

Tiger Brigade had discovered a bunker complex two kilometers north of where they stopped for the night. 3rd Battalion, 41st Infantry was ordered to attack the complex at first light. As dawn broke over the eastern horizon, the Army opened up with tanks and the 25mm gun of the Bradley fighting vehicles. While the western flank of the division unfurled, at 0620 the eastern portion heated up as well.

In what would later become known as the "Reveille Counter-attack," a battalion of Iraqi tanks and mechanized infantry charged full speed along the only black-topped road in the region and directly into 1/8's flank. The Scout leadership listened to the events on the division tac net.

"What d'ya think Dole?" Quarry asked, pointing to the location on the map where 1/8 was now decisively engaged. "Counter-attack or some poor Iraqi commander trying to get his unit out of the frying pan only to fall into the fire?"

Dole looked over at the map Quarry tilted in his direction.

"Winners record the results, sir. I think history will show that this was a full-scale attack, directed exactly at the exposed flank of the division, brilliantly fought off by the Marine defenders."

Quarry smirked. "You're a very perceptive young man," he said, tilting the map back toward him. As the two listened to the various radio nets, the lead battalion of an Iraqi brigade got chewed up and spit out. In the hours that followed, over thirty-nine tanks and armored personnel carriers were reported destroyed by Marine air, tanks, and TOWs. The final report stated the remainder of the brigade broke off the attack and fled north.

Quarry changed the radio frequency. After having met moderate resistance, Tiger Brigade captured over 400 prisoners. The highest-ranking Iraqi officer, a major, surrendered what was left of the 39th Brigade, 7th Iraqi Infantry Division.

Earlier in the morning, the remaining elements of 8th Marines crossed through Lanes Blue 3 and 4. Likewise, 5/10, the last Marine artillery battalion, crossed into Kuwait via Lanes Red 1 and 2. Additionally, 2/4 and 3/23 moved into position.

By midday, after repositioning several battalions, the division was poised to continue the attack north. Division Objective One was a complex known as the "Ice-Tray" and the "Ice-Cube" due to their appearance on the map. The objectives were only four kilometers north from where 6th Marines was located. At 1341, the division crossed the line of departure. In an unsettling omen, as the division started to move, the sky began to grow dark again. By the time 6th Marines reached the outskirts of the "Ice-Tray," day turned into night. Not a ray of light showed through the smoke-filled skies.

Under the cover of afternoon darkness, 6th Marines used air strikes and four of the five artillery battalions to soften up bunkers and dug-in tanks. 6th Marines moved into the eight square kilometers of buildings and defensive positions that made up the "Ice-Tray." On the right flank, 8th Marines simultaneously moved upon the one square-kilometer built-up area known as the "Ice-Cube." On the left, Tiger Brigade also moved forward. Immediately after clearing what once was the Iraqi 39th Infantry Brigade, the Tigers encountered another dug-in Iraqi position.

With the division in contact with the enemy within minutes of moving forward, many of the lead units bypassed the initial Iraqi resistance and left "securing" of the area to their regimental reserves. The advantage of the Marines' night-vision capability was negated since the light amplifying

N.V.G.s didn't have any light to amplify. The Marines and Tigers fought on in total darkness.

Since the regiments had only moved a minimal distance, 2nd Tanks was ordered to remain in place. As with their Tiger counterparts, the thermal imagery capability of the M1A1 tanks and TOW systems allowed the tankers to watch the combatants thousands of meters in front of them, often with more definition than those in contact with the enemy. As testimony to their ability, at 1536, the Tigers' commanding officer personally accepted the surrender of yet another Iraqi unit, the 116th Brigade, 7th Iraqi Infantry Division. As the Tigers' prisoners marched south, the brigade reached Phase Line Horse, the northern limit of the day's advance.

"Scout Six and Grunt Six, this is Heavy Metal Three, over," the battalion tac squawked into life.

"Scout Six, over."

"Grunt Six, over," the captain from B-1/8 replied.

"Change of mission. Report to C.P., over."

"Ahh, sir?" Dole said after turning the Hummer around.

"Yeah, Dole."

"I need a direction." In the pitch darkness, Quarry had to use the G.P.S. to get to his own command post.

* * *

"Have you been keeping up on the division's movement, Samuels?" the colonel asked, looking over his shoulder.

"Yes, sir."

"6th Marines' progress into the Ice Tray slowed considerably. They are now clearing bunker complexes and individual buildings one by one. 8th Marines is entering the Ice Cube. There is a small complex left unsecured, here," Calhoune said, pointing to a dot of red on the map, "bypassed by 6th Marines, but within their regimental boundary."

Quarry leaned forward and took a closer look at the map.

"That's only three clicks in front of 2nd Squad, sir."

"Exactly. That's why it got overlooked. Scout it out. If you find anything significant, report back, and we'll send Bravo 1/8 in to clear it. Captain," Calhoune said, turning to the infantry commander, "be prepared to support the Scouts. On order, seize the bunker complex 651 154. "

"Yes, sir."

"Once the complex is cleared, Scouts will establish a screen line there. The battalion will stay here. We'll use thermals to track anything that moves to the flanks." Both captains acknowledged the colonel's orders simultaneously.

Once clear of the security perimeter around the C-7, Grunt Six was the first to speak.

"Man, this sucks! If you need us, he says .... How do you want to pass lines?"

Quarry thought a moment.

"Infrared chem sticks. We'll place one on each of our helmets. That way we have a source of illumination for the N.V.G.s, and if things go bad, you take out everything that doesn't glow."

"Good luck, Scout," the captain said.

"Good luck, Grunt," Quarry answered. It was still too dark for the two officers to see each other even though they were only two feet apart.

* * *

"We don't have any troops or vehicles in front of us or Caine would have picked them up on thermals," Quarry briefed his squad leaders.

"Roger that, sir. There's nothing out there," Caine said from the rear right seat. All five of the Scout leaders were inside the command Hummer using pen flashlights to brief by. Sleeping bags around the windows and windshield prevented light from escaping. Dole and other drivers stood guard around the vehicle.

"Unless they're dug in so far that they're actually under the horizon," Ogdon pointed out.

"In that case, we don't have to worry about direct-fire weapons," Marion commented. "We'd still see anybody coming up and over the ridge of the fighting hole."

"If nothing else, at least we know they don't have anything larger that rifles pointed at us," Caine added.

"Unless, with all this shit in the air, the metal of the vehicles didn't absorb any heat from the sun," Grier stated. "There's wouldn't be anything to pick up on thermals."

"Could metal be so cold that we don't pick up anything at all?"

"Damned if I know, skipper. I never thought I'd have to use a flashlight at a midafternoon briefing. Who knows what this shit does to thermal radiation." The comment hung in the air as heavily as the smoke in the sky.

For positive identification, Grier suggested two chem sticks on every helmet. One stick placed in the helmet band horizontally, with the foil packaging opened at one end, would act as an I.R. flashlight. The second, opened only in the middle and placed vertically on the back of each helmet, would act as a friendly homing beacon for anyone coming up behind.

Caine picked up the M-16 next to him and held it out to his platoon commander.

"Here, skipper, take this." In the simple red light produced by the penlight, the Scouts saw the inquisitive look on Quarry's face. "It's Orsini's. He'll stay with the vehicle in the turret with the SAW. We all know there's no way in hell you're going to keep your ass in the command Hummer. The M-40 won't do you a damn bit of good in a trench line, so use this until the op is done." There were more than a few smirks as Quarry accepted the weapon with thanks.

At 1700, the Scouts moved. They closed the distance to the suspected bunker complex quickly. Minutes later, the first report came in on the platoon net.

"Scouts, hold! Six, this is Three. We're bent!" Ogdon reported. "The grid of the complex is off 300 meters to the south. Recommend you continue dismounted. We found the trench line by driving into it, over."

The situation would have been humorous if it weren't for the fact they had no idea what they were getting themselves into. Now, the platoon would be down a full squad as one vehicle assisted the other.

"Three, this is Six. Extract and report status. All others continue mission. Lead with dismounts." The Scouts acknowledged on the radio with breaks of squelch while Dole moved closer to Caine's flank. Within minutes, all the Scouts reported "set" at the base of trench line.

In the black of early evening, Quarry tracked his Scouts by their I.R. signatures. Similar to a laser show, streaks of infrared light bounced back and forth as the Scouts cleared trench lines and looked into fighting holes. When Quarry changed the N.V.G.s from I.R. mode to the normal light-amplification mode, there was nothing at all. Using I.R., however, was not without its risks. The Iraqis used Soviet equipment which had I.R. capabilities as well. They could be watching the same show Quarry was watching.

"Six, this is One Two, over."

"This is Six, send it."

"Five was right. Enemy vehicles didn't absorb any heat. Just cleared a T-55 tank near the trench line. One P.O.W., over."

"This is Six. Roger, all Scouts acknowledge." The Scouts checked in, acknowledging Marek's discovery. *Where in the hell are the other three crewmen?*

Minutes later, on the far west flank, Ogdon reported "up." The welcome transmission indicated the Hummer was out of the trench, there was no damage done, and that 3rd Squad was once again continuing the mission. Thirty seconds later, Ogdon made another report.

"Six this is Three. Command bunker located. Request additional squad for assistance." Three One was only a few feet from the entrance of the complex. Anyone inside not only knew the Scouts were there, they had had over fifteen minutes to prepare any additional defenses. Things were not good.

2nd Squad shifted left to support 3rd; Quarry and Dole exited the command Hummer. They took only a few paces before encountering the trench line. On closer examination, the trench had once been part of a larger fighting position. But with neglect, settling sand, bombs and artillery, portions of the trench were now almost completely filled. Quarry took the lead inside the trench with Dole immediately behind and offset to the left. Caine was behind them as the teams made their way toward 3rd. Less than 100 meters from where they started, Quarry came across the eastern end of the complex. 3rd was waiting to clear.

"Dole," Quarry whispered into the dark. Knowing what his platoon commander wanted, Dole held out the handset to the P.R.C. and touched it to Quarry's shoulder. "Three, this is Six. In position, to your east, at an entrance. Offset right, over." *This sucks!* With two friendly forces converging on the same location from opposite directions, they would be in each other's line of fire if anything happened. From the contrasting target drills the Scouts had practiced at Lejeune months ago, if the two friendly forces knew that if they had to mix it up, both would choose targets only to the right of what they would normally shoot at.

"Wilco, Six," Ogdon reported, "Oscar Mike." 3rd was going into the complex.

"Stack it up here," Quarry told Caine. "Bound by rooms." Caine acknowledged and passed the order back. Quarry brought the M-16 to eye level but squatted down. "Move," Quarry said, into the night. Dole pulled back a prayer rug that covered the entrance to the complex. Quarry's N.V.G.s, set on IR, were immediately overwhelmed by the light of a single candle which burned on a table not 20 feet into the complex. The candle was four inches tall and there wasn't much wax at the base. It hadn't been lit for very long. "Shit," Quarry said under his breath and took a step down and into the entrance.

Four feet into the complex, the first shadow indicated an entrance to a room to the right. *Shit!* Quarry took another step down and forward. Dole was a step back and to the side covering his length of the passageway. A second shadow indicated the presence of another room immediately behind where the candlelit table was. The complex was made of corrugated tin forming walls and a roof. Whoever was in there knew the Scouts were in there also. With the element of surprise gone, Quarry took a chance, "*Ana naqeeb Samuels, amerikee marine. Anta aseer! Ta'aal.*"

Ogdon evidently realized what his platoon commander was trying to accomplish and from the other side of the snaking tin passageway, another set of commands in Arabic were faintly heard: "I am Sergeant Ogdon, American Marine. You are a prisoner, come out!" From somewhere, far off in the darkness, an argument in Arabic took place, then, a single shot was fired. *Shit. Shit!* Hands, holding white pieces of cloth, extended from the second room.

Six soldiers came out and surrendered to the Scouts. The soldiers moved to the sound of Quarry's voice and were passed back and out of the complex. Quarry stopped an Iraqi corporal as he passed. He learned there were at least three more rooms and up to a dozen soldiers remaining.

Quarry button-hooked the corner, and Dole crossed the opening. Caine and Guy covered the passageway while Quarry and Dole searched the room. There were numerous prayer rugs covering the ground. Several makeshift tables had documents covering them, but there was no place large enough for a person to hide.

"Clear," Quarry announced. Caine and Guy moved past the opening and down the corridor. Quarry and Dole fell into line behind them. As they moved toward the next opening, the unmistakable sound of an M-16 filled the corridor. *Shit, shit, shit!* Quarry started to wonder if he had bitten off more than the Scouts could chew, and for a moment thought about pulling out and calling the grunts, but only for a moment.

Immediately after Caine and Guy disappeared into the second room, shots were fired. It took a few additional moments for Two One to announce "Clear." Quarry resisted the temptation to look into the room and continued to cover the corridor.

"Coming out," Caine called out from the room. As soon as his head came within feet of Quarry's, Caine reported, "One officer neutralized. None remaining." Quarry started moving down the corridor without comment.

Mere feet from where the second room ended, the corridor took a 90-degree turn to the right. Quarry waited a second to make sure Dole was in place and button-hooked around the corner. The passageway went straight 15 feet before turning left. Again, Quarry paused, then made his move. The room they entered was large and completely black. With two 90-degree turns behind them, the light from the single candle was now nonexistent. Using the I.R. chem light for illumination, Quarry started to make a detailed scan of the room. A sudden flash of light on the far left sent a shiver down his spine. Quarry snapped his head in that direction, only to realize what he saw was the reflection of an I.R. beam bouncing off the tin wall. His heart pounded in his chest.

"Three, this is Six," Quarry called out loudly. The room was full of overturned tables and chairs. Quarry's heart skipped a beat as his N.V.G.s revealed a body sprawled out on the floor. Whoever had killed the Iraqi soldier was still in here.

Quarry moved like a cat directly to the side. The prayer rug-covered floor kept his feet from crunching in sand. He made his way along the wall. A shot was fired inside the room. The flash of a pistol was answered by an M-16 and a body flopped to the ground. Quarry caught movement to the far left of his field of vision, and another burst from an M-16 came from the far passageway. "Passageway clear, Three coming in." When Quarry saw the I.R. signature coming from the opposite direction, he reached behind his helmet and grabbed the second chem stick. When he pulled the rest of the foil from off the stick, the room started to become clear. Taking the lead from their commander, the rest of the team used their chem sticks to light the rest of the room.

"Clear," Quarry called out from the north.

"Clear," Caine called from the east.

"Clear," Ogdon reported from where he was still standing in the southwest entrance.

Quarry covered the pistol-holding body with the M-16 while Dole examined it. "Down," Dole confirmed as he checked the pulse at the carotid artery.

"Same here," Guy reported with the Iraqi at the entrance of the room.

Quarry went to an overturned table and righted it. Dole discovered a few candles on the floor and lit a match. In the candlelight, the Scouts took off their N.V.G.s and examined the bodies. The pistol-wielding soldier was an Iraqi captain. The soldier the captain shot was a sergeant. The soldier in the corridor was a private.

"Caine. Get all P.O.W.s to Grier. Have him escort them to battalion. Have the Hummers cross over the trench and set up a screen on the north side. Give Tank Six a situation report. Dole, Sergeant Ogdon and I will look around here for any additional intelligence."

"On it, sir." Caine turned and issued some additional orders before replacing his N.V.G.s and departing the room.

Quarry looked down at the Iraqi captain.

"Thank you," he said, placing a hand on Dole's flak jacket.

Twenty-Two

26 February 1991

Quarry got off radio watch at midnight. It was now 0400.

"Sir?" Slayer asked from a safe distance. Quarry's head snapped up. "The division is in contact," Slayer said.

"Report," Quarry mumbled.

"Every battalion reports movement in their zones. LAV engaged and destroyed four tanks on the division's west flank. 1/8, on the division's right flank, is getting the brunt of it. They were hit by a dual-pronged attack where the two roads meet. Dismounted infantry and fighting vehicles from both the northeast and the northwest."

Dole turned over the engine.

"Lovely. Dole, pull out the C.E.O.I. Find 1/8th's tac net. Dial it in on a P.R.C. please."

"Already on it, sir."

"See, I don't care what Grier says about you. You are worth a shit. A small runny one with specks of corn, but definitely worth a shit." From inside the darkened Hummer, Dole grinned from ear to ear.

* * *

"The road intersection is the boundary between 1/8 and 2/4," Grier noted. Things were calming down. The enemy counter-attack was broken, and all that remained was the herding of over 200 Iraqi prisoners.

"Yeah, with a reserve tank company sitting right in the middle," Quarry said as he ate another spoonful of M.R.E. applesauce. "Ya know, Five. That particular tank unit was sent to 29 Palms and transitioned from the M-60 to the M1A1 before coming over here. They have the same exact tank as our battalion."

"Your point, skipper?" Grier said, dinning on a re-hydrated pork paddy.

"Some of the engagements reported were at distances as close as 75 meters."

"Again, skipper, your point?"

"A. The maximum return of the laser range-finder on an M1A1 using thermal imagery is over 9,000 meters. B. The maximum effective range of a high-explosive antitank round is over 3,000 meters. So C. Why were there engagements less than 3,000 meters at all?"

"Think somebody will get court-martialed for sleeping on duty?"

"Hell no! Some son of a bitch will probably get a bronze star."

* * *

"Well, will ya look at that," Quarry said in awe. After a day of complete darkness, the two leaders looked to the east. The sun was rising.

At dawn, 1st Marine Division reported being at Phase Line Red. 2nd MarDiv was still ten kilometers to their north. With the Kuwaiti International Airport to the front of 1st Division, it would take a while before the two divisions came abreast of each other.

Slayer alerted Quarry to the reports coming over DASC. Aircraft from the 3rd Marine Air Wing had detected Iraqis attempting to evacuate Kuwait City. As 2,000 vehicles tried to squeeze through the Mutlaa Pass, aviators attacked the leading formations. Hundreds of Iraqi vehicles fell prey to the aerial armada. The combined air power of the entire coalition was directed to what would later become known as "The Valley of Death."

The division commander was still expecting the "Mother of All Battles" to be fought as the division continued north. Thus, 2nd Tanks was again held in reserve with orders to follow in trace of 6th Marines. As 6th Marines attacked north with 1/6 and 2/2 abreast of each other, 3/6 mopped up bypassed Iraqi units. One particularly troublesome area, the "quarry," required the assistance of Cobra attack helicopters to destroy tanks, self-propelled artillery, and armored personnel carriers in their dug-in fighting positions, from above. It was through this same zone that the Scouts had to lead their battalion.

The Scouts were denied time to conduct a route or area reconnaissance. "Assured" that 3/6 had cleared the area, Quarry and the Scouts were simply driving ahead of the tanks through the quarry, using their G.P.S., an operation that didn't set well with them at all. Following three different sets of waypoints, Scout squads moved along three designated routes with tank companies following immediately behind each squad.

"I don't like this one fucking bit!" Quarry said as they entered a maze of holes in the earth and mounds of sand. With nowhere to move right or left and a battalion of friendly tanks crawling up his ass, if anything jumped out at them, the Scouts would be helpless. As Dole turned the Hummer left around a particularly large man-made hill, they almost rear-ended Two Two: Caine had stopped and dismounted to check the other side of the hill. To the right, Quarry's face was no more than four feet from the 100mm gun tube of a T-55 Iraqi tank that had been destroyed by a Cobra gunship.

"Shit!" Quarry jerked as a secondary explosion came from inside a second burning tank, about fifteen feet from the first, as the last remaining tank ammunition detonated due to fire inside the turret. Opening the door to yell at Caine to get back into his Hummer and move, Quarry wove a blanket of obscenities regarding his current situation. As he did, the platoon net squawked.

"Scout Six, this is Bravo Six on your push. You need to move!" Quarry looked at the radio in disbelief and then at Dole. Dole was as surprised. After looking back at the radio, Quarry opened the Hummer's door. Not 50 feet from the back of the command Hummer was an M1A1 main battle tank with Captain Smallings half way out of the commander's cupola.

"Listen you mother fucking son of a bitch!" Quarry started, and then proceeded to get nasty as he exited the vehicle and approached Smallings' tank on foot. "You want to lead this fucking battalion in a movement to contact you go right the fuck ahead. If not, get the fuck off my ass!" Smallings made some vain attempt to say something to calm Quarry down but it obviously wasn't working.

"Bypass Caine!" Quarry said climbing back into the Hummer. Knowing damn well he heard the order correctly, Dole resisted, with every fiber in his being, questioning the command. Dole drove to the left of Two Two, up and to the right of Two One and proceeded on the best route around the holes and mounds. "Scouts! Increase speed and maintain 15 miles an hour," Quarry ordered over the platoon net, with no sign of blood left in his face. Dole increased pressure on the accelerator, and the unarmed, unprotected command Hummer moved out in front of the battalion. "God. Please don't let us die like this," Quarry said out loud without realizing it.

There was no way to drive at 15 miles per hour in and around the quarry, but the intent of the order was clearly understood. Dole quickly outpaced the rest of the Scouts. Within minutes, the single Hummer was well out in front of the combatants. The act had the desired effect, and the Scouts pushed forward recklessly, extremely susceptible to ambush.

God answered Quarry's prayer, and in less than fifteen minutes, Dole broke out of the confined area into open desert. Dole heard Quarry give an audible sigh of relief as the Scouts called their positions. The battalion had entered the quarry at 1400. It was now 1443.

The operation order called for the Scouts to lead the battalion to Objective Kilo via checkpoints 49 and 633, but the battalion was now ordered to seize

Objective Lima, a location equal distance between 6th and 8th Marines and four kilometers south of the 6th Ring Motorway.

The Scouts completed their last pathfinder mission as they moved in and around Hill 112 and moved toward checkpoint 72. With numerous tanks burning and in various stages of meltdown, the Scouts slowed their pace by a few clicks per hour and continued to screen forward. Every nook and cranny contained destroyed Iraqi combat vehicles. The Scouts would be caught flatfooted and die horribly if even a single remaining Iraqi tank popped out of an unidentified fighting position.

As they got closer to the 6th Ring Motorway, the terrain became increasingly more agricultural with numerous buildings and structures. At 1700, the Scouts changed direction, east, to lead the battalion onto the objective. As the first set of tanks started to take defensive positions, the Scouts broke north.

They pulled under a set of power lines and Quarry gave orders over the platoon net. Marion went southeast to tie in with the north-most flank of 1/8. Ogdon went northwest to make contact with 6th Marines. Quarry pulled in with Caine to keep an eye on the cloverleaf a click in front of them, Division Objective Mike. With his Scouts strung out over a nine-click frontage, Quarry pulled out a set of maps and placed them on the hood of the Hummer in anticipation of plotting the locations of his squads. Due north, the city of Al-Jahra lay not three clicks away. As he looked over the first city he'd seen since Al-Jubayl, an unseen force spun him counter-clockwise. A burning sensation of searing pain registered in his right eye.

The next thing Quarry remembered was seeing Dole. His driver was shaking him by the shoulders. Dole's mouth was moving, but no words were coming out. *My God,* Quarry thought, *Dole was hit in the throat.* It took a few moments for Quarry to realize he wasn't hearing anything at all, including his driver who was less than a foot away from his face.

As Quarry lowered his right hand from his face, he was expecting the worst. To his pleasant surprise, the hand came away clean with nothing on it.

"Skipper, you got to get into the Hummer," a distant voice said. Quarry's hearing was coming back. As he looked around, what had been flat, level, open desert was now a cross-section of the craters of the moon. Quarry let himself be led to the Hummer. The front left tire was shredded, and the windshield was shattered.

Quarry focused on Dole as Caine and Peterson came running up. Peterson, a trained field medic, looked into his eye. Taking a pair of tweezers from a canvas bag, he removed the metal filing with little effort.

"You should go have the battalion surgeon take a closer look at this, sir," Peterson said, placing ointment in the corner of Quarry's eye and securing a padded dressing over it.

"I'm fine, Pete. Thanks." A few pieces of tape held the dressing in place.

"Put your goggles on, sir," Peterson instructed.

"Yes, Doc," Quarry said. "Anybody else hurt?"

"No sir," Caine reported. "Called it in. Probably rockets. They came in so fast nobody heard them. Didn't even have time to hit the deck before I realized it was over with."

"Get on the net, see what else is happening out there."

On the division's far right flank, 1/8 tied in with 1st Marine Division's 1/5. 3/23, 8th Marines' reserve battalion, was still taking sporadic fire and artillery. Whoever fired rockets on 3/23 only overshot by 12 clicks.

* * *

At 2250, the division was notified that the Arab forces on their left flank would enter Al-Jahra. Whoever made the decision was a crafty S.O.B. Arab fighting Arab in an urban environment would not only drastically decrease U.S. casualties; any "retaliation" would not be witnessed by "western" troops.

"Think we should wake the skipper and let him know?" Slayer turned and looked over at Dole who was on radio watch in the logistics Hummer.

"I turned all the radios off in the command Hummer," Dole answered. "Go anywhere near Six's Hummer and I'll hide all your baby wipes and powder."

"No need to get nasty about it, Dole," Grier said from deep within his sleeping bag.

27 February 1991

At 0555, Tiger Brigade made liaison with the Egyptians, the first Arab force that would participate in the liberation of Kuwait City.

"Six, this is Three, over."

"This is Six. Send it."

"Friendly forces moving from west to east on 6th Ring Motorway, and skipper, they're T-72s, over."

"This is Six, acknowledged, thanks, out." In less than fifteen minutes, Quarry and 2nd Squad watched the parade of Egyptian-used, Soviet-made tanks, moving east.

With Arab forces moving into Kuwait City, the Marines were not allowed to fire indirect weapons. Orders to "Clear enemy in zone" still provided 2/4 and 1/8 a full day's fighting. By day's end, 3/23 was ordered to move northeast closer to 1/8, receiving sporadic small-arms and more rocket fire on the way. One Iraqi ammunition truck was destroyed and a small number of soldiers were killed.

In the early hours of 28 February, the division's operations section started making contingency plans to send the division northeast of Kuwait City. Objectives were prepared; Al-Urthamah and the port of Al-Dohah were to be seized and secured. But at 0800, Headquarters, Marine Expeditionary Forces, ordered the two Marine divisions to cease all offensive actions. For the Scouts, Desert Storm was over.

Twenty-Three

1000, 28 February 1991

The word came, and to most, the word was unbelievable.

"We're not going to Baghdad?" seemed to be the underlying question. But by now, every radio in the free world was replaying the President of the United States' announcement: "Kuwait is liberated. Iraq's army is defeated. Our military objectives are met."

* * *

"This is Scout Six, Oscar Mike," Quarry reported on the battalion tac net. For reasons not explained, the Scouts were once again pathfinding for the battalion. This time their direction was almost due south. The battalion was ordered to move back to Objective Kilo. Quarry didn't bother asking why.

* * *

The battalion set up in its defensive circle with gun companies around the C.P., combat trains and TOW Company to the rear, and the Scouts a few clicks out in front. Quarry walked into the commanders' meeting at the C.P. that evening with his eye still bandaged and goggles on. The fire-support coordinator greeted him by calling him "Tonto" and asked where the Lone Ranger was. A few others asked why his eye was bandaged, but Colonel Calhoune didn't seem concerned. The Three debriefed the current and projected situations, the battalion X.O. stressed that the fight was far from over and not to slacken up. Either he wasn't paying attention to the Three, whose words came almost verbatim from division, or he had lost touch with reality. Either way, it was hard for Quarry to give a shit. As the Three continued, it appeared that the battalion wouldn't be moving any time soon.

* * *

The Three had been right: the battalion remained parked exactly where it was until March 14th. During their stay in the middle of nowhere, the Scouts were not totally idle. On March 5th, Quarry, Grier, and 3rd Squad escorted water trucks to the only source of potable water left in Kuwait, in the city of Al-Jahra. It was unnerving to pass T-72 tanks and B.M.P.s, when not long ago, Quarry and the Scouts had been blowing them up. Small Kuwaiti flags flew proudly from their radio antennas to identify their ownership. At every corner, Kuwaiti tankers kept a close eye on all visitors. There were still untold numbers of Iraqi soldiers who had remained behind in an attempt to defect, and the Kuwaiti soldiers were not taking any chances. While waiting their turn in line, the Scouts were lovingly assaulted by well-wishers. 3rd Squad eventually returned to battalion with the loaded water trucks; the Scout leaders took the "long way" and a not-so-quick look around.

The Valley of Death was starting to get cleaned up. Iraqi Army trucks were still full of the loot they had "liberated" from Kuwait City. T.V.s, appliances, and stereos were strung among the shredded and burned bodies. Numerous military and civilian wreckers worked among shot-up vehicles in an attempt to open the Mutlaa Pass. Everywhere the Scouts looked, among the military vehicles and stolen cars, they saw dead, burned, and torn-apart Iraqi bodies.

On March 7th, the Scouts were ordered to a location only distinguishable on G.P.S. in an area between checkpoints 53 and 55. The mission; mark unexploded ordnance. The route would eventually be used by the division to return to Saudi Arabia. Armed with dozens of rolls of engineering tape and stakes, the op only lasted until 1700 when the radio broke squelch. The Scouts had a change of mission. Once at the C.P., Quarry received new orders: recon a route back to Al-Jubayl.

The next day, the Scouts drove to Mishab, a port city located half way between Al-Jahra, Kuwait and Al-Jubayl, Saudi Arabia. The Scouts plotted a series of waypoints in the G.P.S. and checked the terrain as they went. Nothing would preclude a tank company from making this trip on its own, but the Scouts were told to escort them. In a two-pronged journey, a squad would lead a company from Objective Kilo to Mishab. At Mishab, the tanks would stop for the night, refuel, and perform maintenance. The next day, a different squad would escort them the rest of the way to Jabayal. Having no good reason to return to battalion, Quarry and Grier stayed at Mishab that night and set up some long-range communications. Caine stayed with headquarters, Ogdon returned to Kilo, and Marion continued south to check the rest of the route. If Quarry thought the 15km fronts were bad during their operations, by the time Ogdon and Marion reached their destinations, the Scouts would be strung out 240km.

On March 14th, while Quarry sat reading another Cornwell novel, the radio came to life.

"Scout Six, this is Heavy Metal Three, over."

Quarry put his book down and picked up the battalion tac: "Scout Six, over."

"Scout Six, this is Heavy Metal Three. Do you still have grid of division C.P.? Over." Quarry looked over at Dole who nodded his head.

"Unless it's moved in the last week, I still have it, over," Quarry transmitted.

"Report to division C.P. Scout Five and Two to remain in place. Additional refuelers will meet them there. Change of mission is for you only, over."

"Acknowledged, Tank Three. Any idea what this is about? Over."

"Was going to ask you the same question. You were asked for by name."

By the time Quarry replaced the handset on the radio, Caine, Grier and Slayer were standing at the side of the command Hummer. Quarry looked up in surprise.

"I have no idea."

* * *

When Captain Falagan, a reservist and lawyer by civilian occupation, was activated, he was assigned to the Civil Affairs Group. Now, Falagan was detached from 2nd Marine Division to assume duties with the Army's 352nd Civil Affairs Command, currently in Kuwait City.

"You'll find the 352nd at this address," the colonel said, handing Falagan another set of orders. "The captain from 2nd Tanks will give you a ride. Dismissed."

* * *

The drive to Kuwait City was uneventful. It took little time to hit the 6th Ring Motorway, and Quarry had Dole drive by the Mutlaa Pass to show Falagan some of what he missed.

"Shouldn't we be heading directly to the city?" Falagan asked.

"You got a date?" Quarry asked the passenger in the seat behind him. "Relax, Captain, we'll get you there," he added with a disgusted look on his face. Then after a moment's pause, Quarry looked over at Dole. "We *will* get there, won't we, Corporal?" Quarry asked, as he started to take out a stack of maps an inch thick.

Dole looked over at Quarry in disbelief, but it dawned on him what his skipper was doing, and he played along.

"I'm just going where you told me to go, sir," Dole responded dryly.

Quarry rustled through a number of different maps.

"We are going in the right direction. Aren't we?"

Dole looked around with a purpose.

"I think so, sir. See that over there? That's Al-Jahra. That means we're heading east. I figure if we head due east, eventually we'll see water. When that happens, all we have to do is turn left. From there, we go until we see water again. That will put us right in the middle of Kuwait City. From there we can read the street signs. Hope some are in English."

Quarry kept shuffling the maps.

"I don't know," he said straight-faced, "I think we should have turned left on that last cloverleaf."

"Oh for God's sake," Falagan said, reaching over and grabbing the maps. "Let me look at these!" As he sat back in his seat, Falagan looked at Dole and Quarry. It took a few moments to sink in. "Oh! Very funny. Ha, ha."

They traveled another 20 minutes until Quarry told Dole to stop the Hummer. Dole pulled over to the side of the road without asking why. They were already deep inside Kuwait City. Specifically, they were in a very nice shopping district. The majority of windows were broken, garbage lay piled in front of businesses, and damaged and wrecked cars were numerous. Quarry went to the back seat, tilted the cushion and removed four boonie hats that were still in plastic.

"I'll be right back."

"Captain Samuels?" Falagan said, getting out from his side and running around the front of the Hummer to catch up to Quarry. "Where are you going? What about my orders?"

"Relax, Captain," Quarry said as he walked toward a men's fine clothiers. "I need to pick up a souvenir for someone."

"What? Captain Samuels! May I remind you we are not on liberty here?"

Quarry wheeled about in a blink of an eye. Falagan, hot on Quarry's heels, was unable to stop in time and came nose to nose with the Scout.

"Mellow the fuck out, Captain!" Quarry said with a controlled and low-pitched tone in his voice and a finger in Falagan's face. Falagan didn't say a word but continued to follow Quarry towards the storefront like a little lost puppy.

"What are you going to do?" Falagan asked.

"Like I said, pick up a souvenir."

"With what? You don't have any Kuwaiti money?"

Quarry stopped dead in his tracks, turned, and looked at Falagan.

"You haven't been in this country very long. Have you, Captain?"

"Actually …" Captain Falagan started to answer, but Quarry turned and walked through the door of the store without care.

"*Assalaam alakum*," Quarry started out in the traditional greeting. The storekeeper was ecstatic not only that someone was in the shop, but that he was greeted warmly. After a number of minutes in the traditional greetings and a hug or two, the bartering began. The focus of Quarry's quest was two red, silk-lined berets of the Saudi National Guard, the type Colonel Ahmed had given him. After 15 minutes of haggling, Quarry walked out of the shop with the two berets as the shop dealer proudly displayed one of the four American campaign hats in the one window that was still intact.

"Shame on you, sir," Dole said, pulling away from the curb.

"Yeah, sometimes I even amaze myself," Quarry smirked, giving Dole one of the red berets.

* * *

Ten minutes later, Dole pulled up to the address he'd been given. An Army soldier looked in the Hummer and waved them inside the fenced compound. Once outside the entrance to a nondescript building, an Army sergeant eyed Quarry's M-40, looked at Falagan's orders, and picked up a sound-powered phone: "They're here, sir." After a few seconds, the sergeant gave Falagan his orders back, but addressed Quarry.

"You may go in now, Captain Samuels." Falagan was taken completely by surprise and got his feathers ruffled, again. Quarry turned to say something to Dole, but the sergeant spoke up first. "Lance Corporal Dole may go in with you, sir. Through the door, take a left, down the hall, last door on the right. They're expecting you."

"Thank you, Sergeant," Quarry said.

"Thanks, Sarge," Dole said following his commander. Falagan stood there for a split second, and then followed.

As soon as they entered the building, Dole asked, "Sir? How'd they know my name?"

Quarry stopped and looked at Dole. *You were asked for by name,* Quarry remembered Major Cranford giving him his orders.

"Let's go find out," Quarry said, leading them down the hall. Not bothering to knock, Quarry opened the last door on the right and stepped in. Toward the back, and in the center of the 20 by 20-foot room, was a plain gray desk with a large man reviewing some papers. Off to his side, two men leaned over the desk and looked at what the gentleman had in front of him. The entire left wall of the windowless room was covered with a map of the region. Two more men faced the map, studying it intently, trying hard not to be noticed. Instead of the desert cammie worn by everyone in Central Command, these men wore black fatigues and black berets with silver crests. The huge man behind the desk stood up.

"Orders."

Captain Falagan stepped up, came to attention and extended his orders.

"Captain Falagan reporting as ordered, sir." The mountain of a man looked at the orders for a second and then over toward Quarry and Dole. Quarry looked at man behind the desk and then at the two who were eyeing him. None wore Army unit designator, patches, or rank insignia. Quarry's hand went down and rested on the flap of his pistol holster. Dole picked up on the movement and gesture. His right hand tensed on the sling of the M-16 hanging on his right shoulder.

"I'm Colonel Hart, 352nd Civil Affairs Group," he said, extending his hand. "This is Mr. Jones and Mr. Smith," he said with a nod of his head to the two standing closets to the desk. "They are surgeons with Doctors Without Borders."

Falagan shook the hand.

"Captain Falagan, U.S.M.C.R., Assistant Staff Judge Advocate Corps, 2nd Civil Affairs, 2nd Marine Division, sir."

The man turned his attention to Quarry. Quarry curtsied.

"Bond, James Bond, of Her Majesty's Secret Service," Quarry said, without a hint of sarcasm. "And this beautiful thing next to me is Ms. Moneypenny. And if those two are surgeons and you're a colonel in Civil Affairs, I'm General Fucking Schwarzkopf." The moment was tense. Quarry thought Falagan was going to pee his pants. Finally the silence was filled with a burst of laughter from one of the two men standing next to the map.

"I told you he was a pistol, sir," the man said, turning towards the desk.

"A Beretta F/S-92 in 9mm. I know that voice," Quarry said, turning towards the wall, "you shit-eating Special Forces dung beetle!" Quarry and Dole wasted no time closing the distance on Sergeant First Class Stevens.

The two grabbed each other by the shoulder and shook hands. Stevens shook hands with Dole as Quarry greeted Stevens' section leader. After a quick reunion, Stevens turned back to the colonel.

"Captain Samuels goes by Quarry, sir. Captain Samuels, my C.O., Colonel Hart. And while he may not command the 352nd, it is one of the units he's responsible for."

Knowing the Army's fondness for saluting indoors, Quarry thought it would be the perfect gesture to save face for the James Bond comment.

"Sir," he said, coming to attention and saluting. Falagan didn't move an inch the entire time.

The colonel returned the salute with a slight smile.

"Staff Sergeant, bring a couple chairs over for us please. May I?" the colonel said, turning towards Quarry and dropping his eyes to the M-40.

Without hesitation, Quarry reached down and grabbed the stock of his rifle. In one smooth motion, Quarry transitioned it from an African carry and presented it to the colonel. "Loaded, one in the chamber, weapon on safe, sir," Quarry commented. The colonel accepted the rifle and tested it for balance.

"Nice weapon, Quarry. Some day you must tell me about the defense of Hill 224," the colonel said, returning the sniper rifle. The comment didn't surprise Quarry as he accepted the rifle back. Dole grinned. Falagan looked from one officer to the other.

"Be happy to, sir," Quarry said after a moment's pause.

"Mr. Smith and Jones ..." Stevens started to say.

"Still have the smell of dry cleaning on their clothes," Quarry interrupted. "How was the flight from Langley, boys?" The comment didn't break the smirk on their faces.

Chairs were brought and the three Marines sat.

"Captain Falagan," the colonel said, breaking the silent pause, "you'll be joining the 352nd Headquarters. You'll be working with the Civil Affairs representatives investigating Iraqi war crimes. Eventually, we hope to collect enough evidence to prosecute a few high-ranking Iraqi officials and generals. You and Captain Samuels are going to take the introductory tour of the city this afternoon and tomorrow."

"Begging your pardon, sir, my unit is going back to Jubayl as we speak." Hart looked over at Smith and Jones before looking Quarry in the eye and answering.

"There's still plenty of work to do here, Samuels. Should an opportunity arise, you might want to consider staying in country. You never know what you might end up doing. You'll see a small portion of what I'm talking about this afternoon. As for now, let's get Captain Falagan checked in, and we'll show you around a little bit." The colonel came from around the desk, and the Marines stood up to follow. Smith and Jones stood there with smug expressions etched in their faces. Quarry turned: "Hey Ding, Clark; you guys coming?" The two looked at each other and started towards the door.

The first stop was at the other end of the hall. Falagan checked in with the 352nd and met the C.O. of the unit. Colonel Hart told the lieutenant colonel he would get Falagan checked in at billeting and return him shortly. A short drive later, two Toyota Forerunners and the Marine Hummer pulled into valet parking of the Sheraton Hotel off of the 1st Ring Motorway. Even though the top seven floors where blackened from fires that had gutted the hotel's top half, the lobby and dining room were already completely refurbished. The colonel went to the main desk, said a few words, and returned with a key. "You're in 1028, Captain Falagan. Go drop your duffel bags off and join us in the dining room."

The dining room was exquisite. Quarry had only been in a five-star hotel once before. Now, he was a guest in their dining room, having one of the best meals of in his life, let alone the first hot one in weeks. Colonel Hart explained that they initially set up shop there in their offices, but when certain Kuwaiti officials, who were still running the country from Dhahran, Saudi Arabia, heard about it, they were quickly transferred to the Sheraton. Quarry looked around. If Kuwait was in ruins, you couldn't tell from where he was sitting. Though Dole had stayed with the Hummer when the officers went inside, Quarry didn't forget his little buddy, and a freshly boiled lobster was sent out to him.

Knowing Dole wouldn't leave Quarry's side, Hart vouched for the security of the hotel and placed an armed Kuwaiti guard on the Hummer. Dole and Quarry got in the first Forerunner with the colonel, while Falagan got in the second with Sharpe and Harper. The colonel didn't have to point out that every storefront was smashed, and few items were on display.

"The Iraqis stole everything," the colonel explained as he drove down the 1st Ring Motorway toward Arabian Gulf Street. "Every five-star hotel was looted and burned along the waterfront. The Emir's and Sief Palaces, and almost every government building, are in ruins. Every embassy was broken into and we can consider every code they were working with was compromised. Most electricity and water plants are non-operational. Those that work are under capacity and overtaxed. Fleeing soldiers stole every vehicle in the city and dropped their weapons where they got the cars. Emir Jaber Ahmed Sabah remains in Saudi Arabia. He declared martial law, and a few of us have been asked to hang around and help them."

"A few of us, sir? May I inquire as to whom that may be?" Quarry asked, looking at the silver crest on the colonel's black beret. The crest was a silver, eight-pointed star with a crown covering the topmost star. Within the star was a circle and the words "Kuwait Police" in English on the bottom and in Arabic around the top. In the center was the Kuwaiti flag.

"You may inquire, Captain," the colonel said, "but that doesn't mean I have to answer." The two smiled. The colonel showed Quarry and Dole what he had been talking about for a good portion of the rest of the day. Sure enough, any and all downtown businesses were wide open. A few of the foreign embassies' gates were open wide, the contents therein open for inspection. Kuwaiti soldiers now stood guard outside the gates, but the colonel walked past them without a challenge. Dead civilian bodies lined every street corner.

That night, Quarry and Dole stayed at the Sheraton. Quarry took a 15-minute hot shower. He would have taken a longer one if it weren't for the guilt he felt enjoying the few comforts the war-torn county provided.

They met at 0600 the next morning. The colonel suggested Captain Falagan eat lightly, as they were going to explore "possibly disturbing areas." Dole and Quarry wolfed down eggs over easy, bacon, ham, sausage, hash browns, toast, coffee, and fresh orange juice.

The first stop on the day's journey was the El Sharra Hotel, the Republican Guard Headquarters during the occupation. The first few floors were typical office areas. As they ascended to the fifth floor, the offices became more and more lavish. By the time they reached the penthouse, Quarry thought he was in a museum or an art gallery, not a commanding general's office.

Of particular interest was the first room in the basement.

"You have got to be kidding." The propaganda room contained a number of articles and artifacts still strung around the room: a poster of a strong-jawed soldier below a dove carrying an olive branch, pictures of Saddam Hussain waving to the crowd, leaflets showing the Iraqi and Kuwaiti people as one nation.

"Mind if I take a couple of these?" Quarry asked regarding stacks of posters.

"Be my guest," the colonel replied. Quarry picked up about a dozen posters that depicted a robust Iraqi soldier guarding the entrance to the Holy Mosque above a ring of united Arab flags, and a dove carrying an olive branch.

The rest of the "propaganda" floor wasn't quite as pleasant. Every room was equipped with chairs and tables. The interrogation chairs were easily discerned: they had barbed wire still wrapped around the arms, legs and back. While barbed wire was obviously the preferred method of holding a person in a chair, concertina wire was not uncommon either. Dark red stains smeared the floors and walls. Exposed copper wire was still plugged into wall outlets. One special chair was rigged with stirrups for female guests. As Quarry looked around, he realized Falagan was missing from the group.

The last place Colonel Hart took the Marines was the national hospital on Cairo Street at the 2nd Ring Motorway.

"You might want to put some of this under your nose," the colonel said, offering a wax that numbed the olfactory senses. After that, surgical masks were passed around. Falagan didn't make it inside the lobby before he had to turn around, run out the front lobby doors and puke. The further they went in, the worse it got. The colonel explained numerous video cameras remained on during the torture of thousands of helpless civilians. Filipino women seemed to be the victim of choice. Imported as laborers and house servants, hundreds were herded and brought here for unspeakable atrocities. Bodies still lay on tables where soldiers "operated" on fully awake and healthy people. Dozens of stripped or partially naked bodies had legs strapped to furniture, spread apart. A stack of small chunks of flesh lay on a table, stacked as if on display. Quarry couldn't figure out what he was looking at. The colonel opened the next door. Even through the mask and wax, the odor of death was overpowering. The colonel kept the door open long enough for Quarry and Dole to see the pile of dead women, each with human teeth marks around their breasts, neck and thighs. Their nipples had been bitten off.

The last room they went into was the showers. Here, no bodies remained but the floor moved as the flies gorged themselves in congealed blood. The colonel bent and removed a pen from his blouse. He stuck the pen more than half way into the mixture. When he removed his hand, the pen remained, sticking straight up in the air. The colonel turned to leave without saying anything else. Quarry and Dole were on his heels.

"There's a lot of work to be done here," he said as they stepped outside and threw the surgical mask into a nearby trashcan. "Don't forget what I said, Quarry. If you or any of your men can find a reason to stay in country, I'll know about it."

"Yes, sir." The two officers shook hands and the three exchanged salutes. Quarry and Dole said very little for the duration of the four-hour drive back to Mishab.

* * *

Quarry told Grier of their travels in Kuwait City and gave him the other silk-lined, red beret. He also returned Grier's camera. Many interesting pictures were waiting to be developed.

* * *

Tank Battalion was back in Jubayl by March 17th. Long days of maintenance, cleaning, and inspections awaited the tankers. The Scouts quickly fell into the daily routine of cleaning weapons, running, lifting weights, and playing volleyball. They watched films and played cards in the evenings. Many kept up with their Arabic language lessons.

By the end of March, the vast majority of 1st Marine Division had returned to Camp Pendleton, California. News of people lining the roadways waving flags and women showing their breasts to the Marines made it back to Camp 15. Using the first-in, first-out policy, as soon as planes refueled and turned around, MEF Headquarters and 2nd Marine Division started heading home. Eight Marines' Regimental Headquarters and selected personnel remained in Kuwait to show a military presence. 6th Marines headed home in early April. Around the camp, the rumor was that 2nd Tanks would follow 6th Marines, but due to the lack of maritime shipping, a contingency of tankers, maintenance, and Hummer drivers would have to remain behind to load the ships. After hearing the rumor and talking with Grier, Quarry approached Colonel Calhoune and asked to be in charge of those who stayed behind. With a difficult decision of determining who wouldn't go home made for him, the colonel simply agreed.

In the days that followed, numerous motor transport, tankers, maintenance, and TOW critters were identified as remain-behind personnel. Quarry became the officer in charge in what was known as the Redeployment Unit. An assistant supply officer took charge of the support platoon, and a 2nd lieutenant tanker came kicking and screaming as he took charge of the tank platoon. Until maritime shipping was available, there wasn't much to do except run, lift weights and continue lauguage training.

In mid-April, the first companies of the 2nd Tanks lined up at the Jubayl airport. Quarry got a cursory good-bye and good luck from the colonel, less from the other officers for volunteering to stay behind. He didn't waste any time saying good-bye to most of them. Quarry made his way in and around the Scouts, shaking each of their hands and thanking them personally.

"I sure wish you'd let me stay, skipper," Grier said, when Quarry came face to face with his platoon sergeant. Grier had placed his name on the "remain behind list," but as Quarry had to approve the list before it was submitted, somehow, Grier's name had disappeared.

"You have someone waiting for you at home. I still have Dole to take care of me and keep me out of trouble. Now get on the plane, you big lug."

Grier embraced his friend, then stepped back, and saluted his commanding officer.

"I'll see you in a few months, sir." Quarry returned the salute and walked from the staging area. Dole, Caine, Guy, Botsford and Tellado also said their farewells to the platoon before heading back to camp. From the other side of the fence, Quarry turned and took one final look upon a command he knew he wouldn't have upon returning to the States. He departed the area, before any of them saw his watering eyes.

* * *

With the departure of the Marine Forces Commander on 16 April, the remaining Marines in Saudi Arabia became known as Marine Forces Southwest Asia. Under the command of the former Deputy Commander of Central Command, a by-name roster of all Marines remaining in country was compiled and forwarded to the new commander's office.

It takes a lot of tonnage to move battalions of tanks. Days after day, ships came and went with little end in sight. One evening, while loading M-60 tanks, Quarry was told to report to the division logistics officer as soon as possible. When he reported to the G-4, he was told he'd been asked to escort a flatbed truck of food, water and port-a-potties, to a refugee relocation camp inside the Iraqi border. He was given a list of checkpoints, letters of passage, an official set of orders on 352nd Civil Affairs letterhead, and a sealed manila envelope addressed to him personally. When asked what equipment he needed, Quarry said he'd take his Marines, a driver and assistant driver for the flatbed, and two jeeps for his men. This was vastly less than the G-4 anticipated. Since he had more important things to worry about than one truckload of food and supplies, Quarry was dismissed and subsequently forgotten about.

"Well, skipper, what'd we get?" Dole asked.

Quarry opened the envelope and turned it upside down. Two black berets with silver insignia fell into his outstretched hand.

"We're warriors again," he said, handing Dole a Kuwait National Police beret, exactly his size.

Part III

Desert Calm: The Untold War

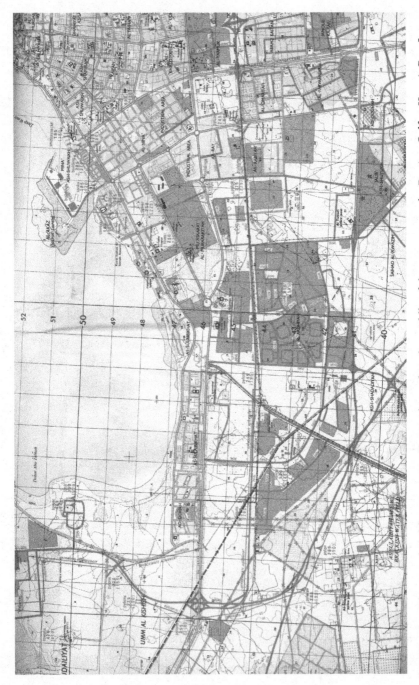

Kuwait City. The capital and largest city in Kuwait, located in the middle of the country on the Persian Gulf at Kuwait Bay. It was occupied by the Republican Guard during the invasion.

Twenty-Four

May 1991, Southwest Asia

With the Hummers cleaned, inspected, and in quarantine at the customs impound lot, Quarry arranged to use two Toyota 4Runners. Toyotas were the vehicle of choice as they were Japan's contribution to the war effort. Now that all U.S. military vehicles were returning to the States, it seemed everyone left in country was driving in sports utility vehicles.

The Scouts had their personal weapons. Quarry had kept a few sets of night vision goggles, one G.P.S. and a laser range-finder. Other than that, they were on their own as they rendezvoused with the flatbed outside the supply depot. The next stop was the bulk fuel farm near the Port of Jubayl gate. Fuel, in Saudi Arabia, was free to the U.S. military. Ammunition was the least of their concerns. Any ammunition not crated was required to be inspected before returning to the U.S. Ordnance inspectors allowed the Scouts to take all they wanted from the opened bins.

Quarry briefed the flatbed driver on their route. They would pick up several civilians at the 352nd in Kuwait City, before proceeding to the relocation camp inside the Iraq border. Quarry would take the lead, the flatbed would follow, and Caine's 4Runner would bring up the rear. As soon as they pulled out of Jubayl, Quarry and Dole put on their Kuwaiti National Police berets.

"You look pretty good as a spook."

"So do you, sir." The two settled down for the first part of their four-hour journey.

The border was vastly different from the last time they came through. Inspectors, Kuwaiti military and National Police were now stationed there. As the small convoy approached, they were waved to the far inspection lane. When the inspector got closer, he saw Dole's beret and waved them through without verification of credentials.

"Damn, now I know what it feels like to be an officer," Dole said, pulling out of the station.

"I'll bet it gets better," Quarry said.

After another hour, Dole was winding his way around deep inside Kuwait City. Eventually they saw what they were looking for, the white flag with a Red Crescent, the Arab equivalent of the Red Cross.

Even though they were an hour ahead of schedule, the administrators were expecting them and greeted them warmly. Lunch was provided for the enlisted Marines as Quarry was taken to meet the representatives of the 352nd.

Ten minutes later, Quarry was driven to the entrance of the Sheraton Hotel. As he made his way into the dining room, it wasn't difficult to find the table he sought. Colonel Hart was clad in his black ninja pajamas, as were Smith and Jones. With them were several high-ranking Kuwaiti military officers and a few businessmen in expensive suits. One officer wore the same black beret Quarry had been given. Colonel Hart rose as Quarry approached, "Where's your beret?" he asked after greeting Quarry cordially. Quarry reached into his right leg cargo pocket and extracted the black beret of the Kuwait National Police. "Even indoors, you should wear that anytime you're not at Camp 15."

"Yes, sir."

Quarry got a plate from the buffet. When he returned, Hart made introductions and pleasantries were exchanged all around, except Smith and Jones. Quarry finally couldn't resist the temptation: "Abbott, Costello, I noticed you're sitting obediently, hasn't the colonel taught you to speak yet?" There was a hail of laughter around the table.

"The operation is a simple one," the colonel stated after everyone finished lunch and started on dessert. "Transport the flatbed of food and water to a refugee camp inside the Iraqi border. You'll be taking a group of doctors with you and returning with a few international observers. While you're there, look around, talk to the people. We'll discuss your observations when you get back."

"No problem, sir."

"Captain Samuels," a Kuwaiti colonel asked, "What do you think the problem is, with Kuwaiti nationals being held in confinement at a refugee camp inside Iraq?"

Once again, Quarry was being tested. It was show time. He put down the bite of pie on his fork, picked up his napkin and wiped his mouth.

"Sir, the national infrastructure of Kuwait is in ruins. One particular portion of that is the national census. Of the six million people who were in Kuwait before the war started, only about twenty percent of them were, by definition, Kuwaiti nationals. You have, I believe, about a quarter of a million people who remained in this country during the war. The first problem is, with the infrastructure gone, even those nationals who remained in country can't be sorted from resident aliens. Secondly, how do you verify the nationality of those trying to return, now that the war is over? Lastly, for those who are in the camps, how do you separate those who claim to be nationals from those who aren't? This is especially difficult considering the nationals who fled the country for their lives didn't have a moment to secure their personal effects. Grabbing a birth certificate is not one of the first things that immediately comes to my mind when your family is in danger."

Quarry picked up the fork, took a bite, and waited for the reaction. There was an additional moment of silence before the colonel spoke.

"I agree. A most difficult task." The mood lightened considerably and small talk around the table continued. Quarry looked over to Colonel Hart who gave only the slightest nod.

They all met back at the international Red Crescent. Two doctors, real doctors this time, got in the 4Runner with Quarry and Dole. Another 4Runner with Falagan, two UN observers, and their driver pulled in after the flatbed. Caine brought up the rear. With only a P.R.C.-77 radio in each Scout vehicle, they headed out.

They didn't stop, but Dole slowed down significantly through the Mutlaa Pass. The doctors took pictures frantically as they drove by hundreds of destroyed vehicles and even more dead bodies. After going through the pass, the convoy headed northeast on the Basra Highway. As they got closer to the border, dozens of burning oil wells lined the horizon, another farewell gift from the fleeing Iraqis.

Ten clicks inside the Iraqi border, the refugee camp was clearly visible. The Civil Affairs 4Runner sped past and took the lead. After a minute of checking papers, the barbed-wire gate swung open and the vehicles entered. Most of the detainees had never seen a port-a-potty made of plywood and two-by-fours, and many mistook them for temporary lodging. Dozens of children stormed the flatbed when a tarp covering the bottled water was lifted. Without the disciplinary efforts of two young adolescents with sticks, the Marines would have lost control. Though the doctors and civil affairs representatives were more concerned about checking in with the local Red Crescent, the Scouts were too busy receiving hugs from the children to care about politics. With weapons locked inside the vehicles, the Marines did what they do second best: give hope and joy to needy children. After multiple games of tag, catch, and hide and seek, it was time to leave. Tellado summed it up the best: "This is what's it's all about."

"I wouldn't trade this moment for all the homecoming celebrations in the world," Bots added.

"You got that right," Quarry agreed as he received more hugs and kisses from the children.

When the convoy started to pull out, the children ran after the Marines, frantically waving good-bye. Well aware of the gate restrictions, the kids pulled up short of the open gate and flocked to the fences. Many had tears in their eyes. Quarry let the knot in his throat subside before asking, "What'd you get?"

"Iraqi military and National Police are making almost nightly runs into the refugee camps all up and down the border, kidnapping adult males and impressing them into service. They state they're picking out Iraqi deserters. Those picked up are treated pretty harsh, if they resist they get the shit beat out of them and are left as an example for the others. There's no pattern on how often they hit but they've hit that camp three times since the ceasefire," Bots informed his commander.

"I'd like to do something about that, sir," Tellado added.

"I think that's what Colonel Hart has in mind," Quarry said, as he thought about the children.

The debrief for the flatbed drivers was short and to the point. The drivers said they played with the kids and told of the need for more food and water. Colonel Hart thanked them and ensured them they would be receiving the Humanitarian Service Medal as an official thank-you for the help they provided. The debrief for the Scouts was very different. The Scouts entered closed rooms on the left side of the Civil Affairs complex and relayed as much as they recalled. Hart gave Quarry some additional instructions and paperwork. Quarry in turn tasked Caine with the safe return of the drivers and flatbed to Camp 15 but kept Bots and Tellado, who were given berets, and a room at the Sheraton. After warm sandwiches and hot showers, the four Scouts slept better and longer than they had in months.

Caine and Guy returned late afternoon the next day. After they got a taste of the royal treatment, they all changed into black ninja pajamas, and met in the lobby of the civil affairs building.

When Colonel Hart entered the room, the Scouts came to their feet. With him were a Kuwaiti colonel and a major.

"Seats," the colonel commanded. "This is Colonel Sagraa of the Kuwaiti Air Force, military commander of the Kuwaiti International Airport. He has a favor to ask."

"Thank you, colonel," the Kuwaiti colonel said in perfect English. Turning toward the Scouts, Sagraa continued. "With the permission of Captain Samuels, I would like to ask you to once again help my people. As you know, the Iraqis used the Kuwaiti International Airport as a base for one of their corps headquarters. They laid hundreds of land-mines around the buildings and airfield. Enough were removed that the airport is operational, but many more need to be removed so we can get on with normal operations. I ask you to help train my people, to supervise them, and to work alongside of them. I know this is asking a great deal, but I understand that you have experience in these matters."

Colonel Sagraa was looking at Quarry when he made his appeal. Quarry interpreted the request for what it was, a request. They actually had a choice. Quarry stood and addressed the colonel in Arabic, and then turned to the Scouts.

"Any Scout who doesn't want in, say so now. This is purely voluntary." There was a silent pause.

"You'll be working with Major Kammeel," Colonel Hart introduced the next officer. "Major Kammeel is the head of the explosive ordnance disposal unit at the airport."

Kammeel stated the majority of his command was killed in the defense of the airport. As such, there was no N.C.O. force to speak of. This is where the Scouts came in. They would first receive refresher training on the Italian-made Type 38 land-mine, the predominant mine laid around the airport. Next, they'd be assigned a squad of Kuwaiti soldiers.

"As members of the Kuwaiti National Police, you'll hold the equivalent military rank of sergeant with all the authority and privileges that go with the position," the major concluded.

After a moment of silence, Caine was the first to speak.

"When do we start, sir?"

Training started that morning. The Italian 38 is a particularly nasty little land-mine because it is so hard to detect. The casing is made entirely out of a polymer plastic and the only metal in the entire mine is the 20 grams of tin that contains the detonator. The rest of the 8kg mine is high explosive. After a thorough lecture, the Scouts went outside and practiced on inert mines.

After lunch, the Scouts went to work. Quarry and Sagraa devised a plan to expand the safe areas around the working areas and the entryways into the airport. A grid system was set up, with the roads and maintenance areas prioritized. After the areas were declared clear, a steamroller would proof for any deep-set mines.

That afternoon, the Scouts worked by themselves to practice their craft. The technique was simple: probe the ground with a wooden "knife" at a 45-degree angle until you hit something hard. After that, dig around to determine if it was a mine. If it was, the dirt was dug from around the mine and ever so gently brushed from around the top. After that, it was as simple as picking up the mine in two hands and holding it while a second Scout twisted the top off of the base, just like opening a can of strawberry preserves. Once the top was off, the detonator was plucked from the surrounding explosive. If the Scouts encountered any resistance during the unscrewing phase, the mine was gently walked over to a safe area where it would be blown up later. Simple as that, only an estimated 1,999 left to go.

The Scouts put in a full day honing their skills. After a few dozen 38s were pulled from around the administration building, the Scouts gained confidence, nerves settled down and technique improved. Kammeel was impressed by the professionalism and discipline of the Scouts. Quarry and Kammeel noticed the Scouts started showing signs of stress and lack of concentration within forty minutes after a break. Kammeel decided his men would work no more than twenty minutes at a time, a shorter duration so the Kuwaiti soldiers could stay focused without getting sloppy, or someone killed. Quarry and Kammeel figured they'd work in four teams, each led by a Scout. Two teams would work at any given time, 20 minutes on, 20 minutes off in a two-hour cycle. Extended breaks or daily prayers would fall in between cycles; after all, it wasn't like they were being paid by the hour.

The Scouts returned to the Sheraton that night in high spirits and sweat-soaked uniforms. They were assigned two to a room, though Caine and Quarry each had their own. In the closets of each room, the Scouts found their desert cammies cleaned and pressed and two new sets of black cammies at the foot of each of their beds. After showers, the Scouts met in the dining room and sat together.

"I could get used to this," Bots said, lifting his water glass.

"Here's to us," Caine said, raising his own glass in a toast.

"And those like us," Quarry added.

"Damn few left," they all choroused.

The next morning they arrived at the airport administration building prior to morning prayers. Dozens of Kuwaitis exited the building and faced the airport's minaret, where the muezzin called the Muslims to prayers. Quarry and the Scouts patiently waited inside for their Kuwaiti brothers. On their black uniforms, each Scout wore a leather tab with the rank of a Kuwaiti sergeant suspended from the pocket. Caine's indicated 1st sergeant and Quarry's, of course, indicated captain.

When prayers were over, a platoon of about thirty Kuwaiti soldiers marched to the front of the building. A corporal led the formation and reported it ready to Major Kammeel. Behind Kammeel, the Scouts were on line at parade rest. As Kammeel introduced the Scouts, Quarry brought them to attention. Kammeel introduced them all by name. Teams were assigned, and the new squads formed. Of the six squads, four were led by Scouts, the Kuwaiti corporal maintained one and a senior Kuwaiti private led one also. When not acting as platoon sergeant, Caine would supervise the last squad as well.

The new platoon marched over to the training building. Kammeel's Explosive Ordnance Disposal techs gave the same classes to the Kuwaiti soldiers the Scouts had received yesterday, but the pace was considerably slower and there were more breaks. The practical exercise was met with a general lack of enthusiasm, which did not go over well with the Scouts. Quarry decided an "attention gainer" was in order. A live 38 was planted in the ground and a burned-out jeep was rolled over it. The demonstration had the desired effect, and everyone gained an instant respect for the job.

After noon prayers, the platoon went out to the first grid, and the Scouts demonstrated the techniques the squads would use. Working as a single squad, the Scouts demonstrated the probing, digging, and disarming techniques on several live mines, which gained them the soldiers' undivided attention and full respect. The rest of the day was spent working in the multinational squads, slowly and methodically.

By the end of the day, new friendships were formed. By the end of the week, the squads had bonded. The Scouts and soldiers became inseparable. When Saturday rolled around, the Scouts were invited to the homes of many of the soldiers. Quarry and Kammeel were happy to see the squads getting along so well. The work was progressing smoothly and ahead of schedule.

Midway through the second week, Colonel Hart called the airport and asked Quarry to come over to the office.

"Colonel Sagraa is very impressed with your operation," Hart said as Quarry entered.

"It hardly my operation, sir," Quarry said, sitting down in a chair across from the desk on Colonel Hart's indication. "Kammeel and I came up with a plan jointly. The Scouts set the example for the Kuwaiti soldiers. In the presence of a little leadership, they're hard workers and good men."

"Exactly. You hit it right on the head, in the presence of leadership. Your leadership."

"Thank you, sir."

"Take a look at this," Hart said, handing a folder across the desk.

Quarry took the folder and opened it. Within was a copy of his officer qualification record, copies of his fitness reports, and copies of his personal award citations. Quarry, well aware of the contents of these pages, didn't bother looking deeper. He closed the folder and simply handed it back to Hart.

"Yes, sir," Quarry said not knowing if a question or a statement was being sought.

"You have a very good poker face, Quarry. You don't show surprise often." Again Quarry didn't know what direction the conversation was heading so he kept his face as blank as possible.

"Permission to speak freely, sir," Quarry asked after a second or two.

"By all means," the colonel said, leaning into his high-backed office chair.

"Stevens introduced you as his boss. Some would assume that since Stevens is Army Special Forces that you're Army Special Forces as well. An S.F. colonel would be a figurehead back at J.F.K. Special Operations Center at Bragg or down at CentCom in Tampa. He wouldn't be here because he still has the rest of the world to run operations in. S.F. units are very proud of their green berets. S.F. in country still falls under CentCom, that means desert cammies and a variation of the spear-tip patch on their left and right sleeves. You wear the black beret of the Kuwaiti National Police and black fatigues. If you were Delta, you'd have long hair and a beard and wear civilian or local clothes to blend in. You are as cleanly shaven and close-cropped as they come. That you have a copy of my personnel file doesn't surprise me. Men of your power only have to pick up a phone to receive stuff that's in the system; stuff outside the system, just takes a little longer. Sir, I know damn well you're not Army Special Forces and frankly, I don't give a shit who you are. This is still where the action is; it's where I want to be, and you're the ring master."

"You're a very perceptive young man, Quarry. So, as you say, if I'm not S.F., aren't you curious who I work for?"

"Curious? Yes. But if you wanted me to know, you'd tell me. But I don't need to know, so there's no point in asking." Hart finally broke a smile, stood up and nodded toward the map on the wall. Both men walked toward it.

"What's your assessment on the Iraqi raids on the refugee camps?"

"Hussein got his ass handed to him here, but that doesn't mean it's over. We took over 30,000 prisoners during the war, the equivalent of 21 divisions. Hussein still has interests with the Kurds, Iranians, and other people in the region. The raids on the refugee camps are his start to rebuilding his forces. It takes the loyalty of Republican Guards to subdue an area. It takes occupational troops to maintain an area."

Hart looked at Quarry a moment before turning towards the map.

"We think they're operating out of Basra," Hart said, pointing to the Iraqi city on the map. "If not, they are at least using it as a jump-off point. From there, they send out teams in trucks to the camps," he said, touching the map at half a dozen different unmarked locations. "The camps aren't defended. They go in, grab refugees, throw them in the back of trucks and return to Basra."

"There's no way to monitor all the trucking without stopping and inspecting every vehicle." Quarry thought out loud. "But there are obviously high-level Kuwaiti interests." Turning from the map to Hart, Quarry continued, "If not, why did the Kuwaiti colonel, the other day at lunch, ask me about the problem of the Kuwaiti nationals being held in detainment camps?" The comment made Hart turn from the map towards Quarry. He had hit a nerve. "Ah," Quarry said. "Confirmation."

Hart's response was firmer than normal: "Any other speculations, captain?"

The question and tone seemed out of place. Should Quarry pursue or back down?

"Do we have a missing royal nephew, or two, unaccounted for, sir?" Ever so slightly perceptibly, Hart's whole body stiffened. Rather than push the issue, Quarry gave Hart an out. "I can think of six Scouts who would like to help, sir."

The muscles by Hart's temples relaxed. A second more was all it took for him to continue.

"Have dinner with me tonight. A car will pick you up at the entrance to the hotel at 1900. What size jacket do you wear?"

"Medium long, sir."

"I mean, dinner jacket."

"Forty-six, long."

"See you tonight. Oh, and I'm sure I don't have to tell you, this conversation never took place."

"See you tonight, sir," Quarry said turning towards the door.

When Quarry got back to his room that evening, there was a black pin-striped suit, charcoal-gray shirt and dark tie laid out at the end on the bed. A pair of size ten, black dress shoes were on the floor.

"Sucks to be me," Quarry said, checking the material.

At 1900 exactly, a Lincoln Towncar pulled into the entrance of the hotel. The driver got out and noticed Quarry.

"*Naqeeb* Samuels?"

"*Aywa.*"

"*Min fadlak,*" he said, opening the door.

They traveled east. The ride ended in a neighborhood Quarry would never be invited to back in the States. As the gates opened, Quarry stretched his neck in an attempt to get a glimpse of the full scope of the mansion. When the car stopped, a valet opened the car door. Someone else opened the door to the main house, and a third staff member escorted Quarry to a reception room. As a former British colony, Kuwait was still very much influenced by the English culture. The mansion reflected it.

"*Naqeeb* Samuels," Quarry heard the man introduce him as he entered. There were several gentlemen in the room, two of whom Quarry immediately recognized from lunch a few days earlier: the Kuwaiti colonel, this time in full dress uniform, and one of the businessmen. The others he didn't recognize. Colonel Hart turned from where he was talking and came to greet him.

"Nice suit," Quarry thanked the colonel. The two made the rounds and Quarry was introduced to everyone. As they talked quietly, Colonel Hart gave Quarry a little background on each. As it turned out, Omar Rashid, the "businessman" from lunch and their current host, was the minister of oil production and foreign sales. He was also one of the royal cousins. The Kuwaiti colonel was the national security advisor.

"Lucky he didn't lose his head last August," Quarry whispered.

"He lost his wife and seven of his children during the occupation," Hart answered. Quarry immediately felt like dog shit.

The others in the room had similar titles and histories. Quarry smiled as he nodded and looked around.

"So what am I doing here, Colonel?" he said under his breath.

"I just thought you'd enjoy dinner out for a change." Quarry didn't believe that for a second, but for once, didn't say what he was thinking. At 1930 exactly, the same man who had introduced Quarry to the reception room, made another announcement: "Ladies and gentlemen. Please join Minister and Mistress Rashid for dinner." Quarry turned to see why men have been fighting in this region for centuries.

"That's the Minister's daughter," the colonel commented. Due to their colonial heritage and English influence, Kuwaiti women were not required to wear veils in the presence of strangers. "It's Omar's only surviving son who is missing," Hart said, immediately bringing Quarry back from his fantasy.

"You could have waited to tell me that after the mental image I was having," Quarry commented.

"That's exactly why I told you now," the colonel said, smirking. "Don't get any ideas, hot shot."

"Oh, I got ideas," Quarry said, missing the next announcement. "Boy do I have ideas," he added quietly as the distinguished guests started filing past him toward the dining room.

The evening was one out of a colonial period novel. The dining room table easily sat thirty, though tonight it was nowhere near filled to capacity. There were more plates and forks set in front of Quarry than he knew what to do with. Colonel Hart unfortunately was on the other side of the table and several seats down. Of greater misfortune, Mistress Rashid was at the head of the table on her father's left. Quarry was in the middle, having to make pleasantries. Only once, during who knows what course in the meal they were in, did Quarry make eye contact with Mistress Rashid. When their eyes met, she politely smiled and then looked away. *Like I'd have a chance*, Quarry thought to himself.

After dinner, the men retired to yet another room for cognac and cigars. It was the first time Rashid addressed Quarry personally.

"I hear from Colonel Hart, Captain Samuels, that you played quite an important role in the liberation of my country."

"The colonel greatly exaggerates the importance of maintaining surveillance on one of many Iraqi units in the middle of an open desert, sir. Hundreds of similar events took place all along the border of your country. My efforts were no greater than anyone else's."

"That is not how it was explained to me," Rashid said, gesturing towards the open door. "But regardless," a server approached with a small, crushed-velvet box on a silver platter, "I thank you, and my country thanks you." Rashid opened the box to reveal a 24-carat gold and precious gem lapel pin in the shape of crossed U.S. and Kuwaiti flags. "If there is anything you should ever need," Rashid said, pinning the gift on Quarry's suit, "now or in the future, please feel free to contact me personally."

"You are very kind, sir. Thank you."

* * *

Quarry and Hart didn't speak again for two days. Finally, after Hart called, Quarry met him in the civil affairs office.

"I was thinking about Mr. Rashid's son," Quarry said, opening the conversation as Hart walked in.

"His son?" Hart said with a smile.

"Well, maybe not as much as other members of his family, but yes, his son. Do we know for a fact he's not in one of the refugee camps, sir?"

"That was one of Mr. Jones and Mr. Smith's first priorities. They went through every camp personally. Since then, our observers continue to look for him. The doctors in the camps also have a picture of him and keep an eye out. I think it's safe to say that he was taken during the occupation." Quarry didn't say anything. Hart eventually continued. "I hear the removal of mines is almost complete?"

"The areas we're interested in, yes, sir," Quarry said, stepping over to a map of the airport. "All of the main operating areas are cleared and proofed. We still have to run the steamroller over the internal fields in the middle of the compound. While that is happening, the teams are checking outside the fence. After a preliminary look, we'll proof that as well."

"How soon do you expect to be finished?"

"One week, maybe ten days at the most, depending on how many hits the roller takes."

"Are you at a point that you can turn the remainder of the operation over to Major Kammeel?"

Quarry looked over at Hart with a smile: "Absolutely."

Hart thought for a moment before continuing.

"We still have the abduction problem. We have been asked to deter any further abductions from the refugee camps." Quarry didn't bother to ask where the request came from.

"What are the parameters, sir; time, rules of engagement, assets?"

"We can use any amount of force necessary, as long as it doesn't bring undue attention. We won't use military vehicles or anything that will leave a U.S. signature. We have observers in each camp but they're only observers. It will be your operation. You have your people and any assets within reason."

Quarry looked at the map for a long while before continuing.

"Suggestion, sir."

"Go ahead."

"If we think the Iraqis are coming out of Basra, there has to be a forward operating base they use before they head towards one of the camps. There must be some central point that takes them off the road and in the back door of the camps without being seen. This point has got to be easily recognizable as I doubt they use G.P.S."

"I'm following. Go on."

"We can go around the back side of the camps, pick up the footprints and backtrack until we find tire tracks. When we follow a couple sets of tire tracks back, we find the rally point. That's where we set up surveillance. Once we get a vector on where they're going, we intercept them before they get to a camp."

"But if we intercept them, all they'll do is put more firepower on the next convoy. Then you'll be out in the open, without extraction, indirect fire, air strikes, or other fire support."

Quarry thought for a moment longer.

"So we abduct the abductors. No witnesses, no ceasefire violations."

"I'm not following you on that one, Quarry."

"When we take 'em, we really take 'em, truck, bodies, everything. Make their operations officer think their patrols are deserting as well."

"O.K., I like it. What about the bodies?"

"A few more Iraqi bodies in the Mutlaa Pass won't raise any questions. Eventually, when the patrols don't return, their mastermind will come out to see what the problem is. We take out the brains."

"I like it. But you can't use military assets. They would be spotted too easily. Even your 4Runner would be vulnerable to interception."

"We'll go in at night," Quarry suggested. "Dig in hide positions. There's got to be somewhere we can set up observation from."

Colonel Hart was rubbing his chin between his thumb and index finger.

"I may have something that will work. I'll call you when I have your transportation ready."

"Aye, aye, sir."

* * *

On the evening of the third day after they talked, Quarry entered his room to find two sets of *thoobs*, *ghutars*, *'igaals* and sandals at the end and foot of his bed. One set was brand-new, the other was slightly better than rags; clean, but rags nonetheless. Quarry picked up and looked at the *ghutar* and *'igaal*. He measured the *thoob* by holding it up against him. It was only moments later that a knock came on the door.

"*Ta'aal*," Quarry called out for the guest to enter.

Dole walked in with similar clothing in his hands.

"I have the feeling we're going somewhere, sir," Dole said as he saw the matching items in Quarry's room.

After subtle inquiries, Quarry wasn't surprised to find only he and Dole had received the additional clothing. Neither was he surprised to see the message light blinking on his phone when he got out of the shower.

Quarry and Dole met Colonel Hart at the Civil Affairs building the next day. Also in the room were two Kuwaiti soldiers.

"This is Private Sura," Hart started the introductions. "Sura was a member of the Kuwait garrison prior to it being overrun last August. Since then, he has been a member of the Kuwaiti resistance. He's worked with Sergeant Stevens on numerous operations, members of the Navy Seals during their incursion into the bay, and even your own Force Reconnaissance prior to the retaking of the U.S. embassy. He's lived in and off the streets, coming and going in and out of the city as necessary since." Sura's uniform was worn, his skin looked like old, wrinkled leather, but Sura's eyes burned with an internal fire which penetrated the soul. Quarry offered his hand, but the private wouldn't take it. As a former Bedouin before turning soldier, Sura was more comfortable around sheep, goats and camels than cities and people. Now, far from his own nomadic family, Sura was as uncomfortable around officers as Quarry was around politicians.

"This is Lieutenant Magrail," the colonel continued. "Magrail was a medical intern at the national hospital before the war. He acted as a guide for Arab forces as they entered the city and helped flush out the remaining Iraqis. He will act as an interpreter."

"It is a pleasure to meet you, Captain," Magrail said in perfect English.

Quarry shook the lieutenant's hand.

"What got you into this line of work, Doc?"

Magrail took a moment and looked away before answering.

"I was working in the hospital the night it was overrun. I was forced to watch as atrocities were committed. One of the women tortured to death was my wife. My sister was gang-raped before being beaten to death."

Quarry felt his stomach turn over.

"Lieutenant Magrail, helping us will not bring your loved ones back."

"This I know, Captain Samuels. But as it says in the Holy Quran: To those against whom war is made, permission is given to fight, because they were wronged and verily, Allah is Most Powerful in their aid."

Quarry placed a hand on the doctor's shoulder.

"The Holy Quran also says: But forgive and overlook till Allah brings about his commands. You are a healer my friend. That is what Allah has commanded of you."

The two looked at each other for a long moment.

"Have not Allah's commands brought me to assist you? We will work together. And if I may be of service to you, then I have done Allah's will."

* * *

Quarry met Caine later that night. They jumped in a 4Runner and went for a drive to get away from any bugs crawling in the walls. Once parked next to the sea wall at the north end of the bay, Quarry and Caine took a walk down the streets of Kuwait City, doubling back on their own path a number of times. After the third lap, they quietly talked about the operation. Caine didn't like that he would take over the E.O.D. operation at the airport and answer the phone should Marine Forces Southwest Asia ever call.

"Should anything go wrong," Quarry finished, "get your ass out of this country as fast as possible."

"And tell MarForSWA what?" Caine asked.

"Tell 'em there was a mine. Tell them to contact the 352nd for additional details."

"Do I drop Colonel Hart's name?"

"Don't bother," Quarry said, exhaling, "it's probably not his real name anyway." The two talked for another two hours, making alternate operation plans before doubling back on their track one more time and returning to the car.

* * *

Quarry and Dole dressed in their desert cammies. They were picked up outside their hotel after breakfast and taken out of the city through the Mutlaa Pass. Instead of traveling north on the Basra Highway as Quarry anticipated, the driver of the first vehicle led them due west into the open desert. Dole sensed Quarry's uneasiness and tapped the outside pouch of his backpack where a G.P.S. was stored. Quarry looked over and ever so slightly shook his head. After an hour of driving, Quarry and Dole had no idea where they were or where they were going. Quarry didn't like it one bit, but reminded himself that Hart spoke highly of Sura, who was in the 4Runner ahead and leading this segment of the operation.

After another twenty minutes of traveling in silence, they saw a small camp on the horizon. This was too much for Quarry and Dole who drew their Berettas from the holsters. As they got closer, Quarry saw two men holding six camels. When the lead 4Runner pulled up and stopped, Sura got out quickly. The three men greeted and kissed each other.

"I guess it's O.K.," Quarry said putting his pistol back in his holster.

"I don't care how long I'm in this country," Dole said as he also secured his weapon, "I'll never get used to that."

Lieutenant Magrail listened to the three discuss their plans. Quarry picked up about thirty percent of the conversation but got lost too many times to follow.

"We are about a three-hour camel ride from the southern-most refugee camp." Magrail let Quarry know what the men were talking about.

"What does that equate to in distance?" Quarry asked.

"I don't know, Captain. In the open desert, distance is irrelevant. Travel is measured by how long it takes your camel herd to move from where you are to the next water hole."

Quarry looked over at Dole: "Makes sense."

"Yeah, right," Dole said under his breath.

"From here, we'll use camels to move around the desert to find the tire tracks. Once we do, we'll trace them back to their, what did you call it? Rally point? Is that satisfactory, Captain?"

"Yes it is. Thank you."

"At this point, we must get out of our uniforms and into our *thoobs*. There are bags for you and your soldier to put your weapons and equipment in."

"Of course," Quarry said.

Dole leaned over and whispered in Quarry's direction.

"A. If he thinks for a second he's in charge here, I cap 'em both. B. If he calls me soldier one more time, I cap just the lieutenant."

For the first time in five months, Quarry didn't know if Dole was being sarcastic or serious.

"Then I better go over and have a conversation with the young lieutenant," he said as Dole pulled the backpacks from the back of the 4Runner.

The soldiers changed into *thoobs*, *ghutars*, *'igaals* and sandals. Quarry and Dole simply pulled the *thoob* over their cammies. Boots were placed in camel skin bags, as were radios, rifles and supplies. Pistols were kept within easy reach under the first layer of blankets on the camel's back. It took another 15 minutes of instruction on how to make a camel do what you wanted it to do. Even then, there was a communication gap between camel and Scout. When all was ready, nonessential gear was placed back in the 4Runners and the drivers departed in the direction from which they came. Sura led his camel at a 40-degree angle to the overhead noon sun.

Camels take their own sweet time in the open desert. Quarry and Dole would have made better time on foot, but considering the amount of energy exerted and water consumed, it was easy to figure out why the camel was the primary means of travel in this environment. It took less than an hour to intercept the tire tracks that led southeast by northwest. On the horizon, they saw an outline of a refugee camp.

After two hours of riding a camel, Quarry couldn't remember when his butt ever hurt so bad. He looked at Dole, who was in much the same condition. Magrail looked a little uncomfortable but happy. Sura and his companions were in their element. Quarry resisted the temptation of pulling out the map and G.P.S. All it would show was that they were in the middle of the open desert.

Through the rest of the day, Quarry and Dole often dismounted and led their camels, much to the amusement of Sura and his friends. As night approached, they made camp.

"Should we take turns keeping watch?" Dole asked.

"The thought occurred to me," Quarry answered. "But Sura assures me that if anything moves in the night, the camels will alert us."

"You mean more than the amount of bellowing they let off all day?"

"Something like that," Quarry said, pulling a miniature satellite dish out of one of the many bags strung over the camel's back. Connecting a single wire from the dish to a hand-held transmitter completed the assembly. Dole shot an azimuth and Quarry sighted the dish in the direction and elevation Dole gave him.

"Wish I could take this home," Quarry said, initializing the system. Seconds later, Jones' voice was as clear as if he were standing next to him.

In the morning, after a humble breakfast and coffee, Sura knelt and looked at the ground.

"What's he doing, lieutenant?" Dole asked. Magrail asked Sura to show Dole how to navigate in the desert.

Sura started speaking.

"The winds in this region blow from south to north," Magrail interpreted. "That is what forms the ripples in the sand. The ripples gently slope in the direction of the wind. As the wind gradually deposits sand on the south side, it loses its power and stops depositing sand on the north side. That is why there is a smooth side and a steep side to sand dunes. One only has to look down and see the sharp drop-off side to determine which direction is north."

"Well I'll be damned," Dole said, looking around him. They followed the tire tracks for another day. Quarry's butt hurt so bad he cursed the day Hart came up with this plan. Finally, by the night of the second day of the camel ride from hell, Dole handed a set of binos over to Quarry.

"We're here, sir."

Quarry put the binos to his eyes. In front of him was a power line that ran north and south before taking an abrupt turn to the east.

"I'll bet a month's pay the turn in that power line is the rally point, sir."

"No bet there, Delta." Quarry forgot about the pain in his butt.

Twenty-Five

30 May 1991

The next night they set up a permanent camp, two clicks away from the closest tire tracks. Permanent meant setting up lean-tos. Sura explained they were on a convoy route and a half day's camel ride to the closest water.

"If we are a half day away from an oasis," Dole asked Magrail, "why not camp there?" Magrail explained that it was not a good idea to mix herds, unless they were for breeding. Therefore, camping away from the oasis was very common. If anyone approached, they were simply waiting for permission to enter the oasis of another tribe while their own herd caught up to them. Dole voiced his displeasure to Quarry under his breath.

They waited until morning to continue their work. Quarry and Magrail teamed up while Dole stayed at the camp with Sura. The first order of business was to find the exact location of the rally point. Quarry and Magrail mounted and continued another hour on camel back until they reached the power lines. When they reached the turn in the lines, tire tracks ran due north as far as the eye could see. At the same point, the tracks separated into six distinct directions. Each set was in various stages of aging but each had one distinguishable mark, a single set of old footprints going right in the middle.

"What do you make of that, Captain?" Magrail asked, looking down at the ground.

Quarry took a good look around before he pulled a set of binos from a pouch tied around his so-called saddle. After a detailed look around through the binos, Quarry dismounted.

"They followed this power line south from the Basra Highway," Quarry said, taking a map and compass out from under his *thoob*. He shot an azimuth and confirmed his suspicions. "After they got to this turn in the power line, someone shot an azimuth. That person then walked the azimuth as the truck followed behind. That way, the metal in the truck didn't affect the compass

235

and throw off the magnetic azimuth." He took a small hand-held radio out of yet another pack.

"Pound, this is Keeper."

Four clicks away, Dole put his eye to the spotting scope and raised his radio as he watched his commander.

"Keeper, this is Pound, over."

"Lane One, over."

"Roger." Quarry started walking down the middle of the first set of tracks. Magrail followed on his camel. The two continued to follow a path that led to the northernmost refugee camp.

After what Quarry gauged to be a click and a half, the encrypted radio squawked, "Keeper, this is Pound. Hold there, over." Quarry turned in what he considered to be the direction of their camp. Dole sighted the laser range-finder. On the receiving end, Quarry pointed the large lens of the binos in Dole's direction to give the laser something to reflect off o. "Got it, Keeper," Dole said, writing down the distance and azimuth from their camp to the furthest lane.

Quarry mounted his camel and turned southwest.

"More to your left," Dole transmitted over the radio. Quarry tapped the camel ever so slightly on the left side of the jaw with his riding crop until "steady" came over the radio. From the camp, Dole was making sure Quarry rode on a predetermined azimuth. In the future, the known distance on a fixed bearing would indicate which lane someone was on and therefore, which refugee camp they were going to.

After a 15-minute ride, Quarry came across a second set of tire tracks. He halted, pointed the binos towards Dole, and keyed the radio.

"This is Keeper, lane two, over."

"Got it," Dole reported. Quarry tapped the camel's butt with the crop and headed toward lane three.

* * *

It was still light when Quarry's watch read 2000.

"Catcher, this is Keeper, over."

"Keeper, this is Catcher. Good to hear from you, over." Caine's voice immediately came back on the other end of the radio.

"Same here," Quarry said, smiling. "The kennel is open for business, over."

"Roger. We are in the suburbs looking for strays. Oh, and Puss and Boots have joined us, over," Caine transmitted.

"The more the merrier. Keeper, out."

"Do you trust them, sir?" Dole asked regarding adding Smith and Jones to Caine's team.

"Not really," Quarry answered. "Caine's probably following orders. Nothing we can do about it from here."

"Do you trust Colonel Hart?" Dole asked.

Quarry had to think about it before answering: "Yes Dole, I do."

"That's good enough for me, sir."

* * *

It wasn't long after dark when the anticipated company arrived.

"*Ya naqeeb* Samuels," Sura said from a short distance away.

In the direction of the power lines, the outline of something moving could be made out with the naked eye.

"I see them."

"One Soviet-made, five-ton, U.L.4334 six-wheeled truck, canvas-covered and enclosed back. Moving from north to south," Dole reported from behind the 45-power spotter scope. It seemed to take hours, but it was only 30 minutes before Dole looked up from behind the tripod-mounted laser range-finder. "Lane three, sir."

Quarry keyed the radio. "Catcher, this is Keeper. You have a Dalmatian on the loose. I say again. You have a Dalmatian on the loose."

From inside the 4Runner, Caine keyed the net.

"Keeper, this is Catcher. I acknowledge Dalmatian, over."

"This is Keeper, confirmed, out."

It was still light enough that Caine wasn't about to move from his hide position yet. The two desert tan-painted 4Runners were currently parked behind a burning oil well. "They're moving toward the third camp," Caine said to his team. "Let's go through it one more time."

"We'll pull out of here when you give the word," Jones said. "We travel up the main highway ten clicks, pull off the highway, head due west until we pick up the third set of tire tracks. We follow them south until we're about a click behind the truck. By that time, the main body should be on foot and well away from the vehicle. I stay put and set up over-watch." Jones referred to his M-40 sniper rifle equipped with a fixed ten-powered infrared night vision scope.

"I'll head north when Jones reports he's leaving the M.S.R.," Smith continued. "I'll cross the hard ball when Jones calls 'set.' I'll come in due west until I'm two clicks out and perpendicular to the truck. I'll scan the truck and see if anybody remained behind and report. After that, I scan south until they return. I'll provide over-watch and only fire on order. If I do, it will be from south to north and only on targets carrying weapons." Smith was equipped with a 50-caliber sniper rifle, with silencer and a thermal imaging 40-power variable scope.

"Phase Three starts as soon as we dismount," Bots said. "Tellado and I follow the driver's side tire tracks as Sergeant Caine and Guy follow the passenger side tracks. We continue on foot until we approach the truck. Upon confirmation from Mr. Smith it's hot, we go in low and slow. First target is first threat. Sergeant Caine will determine if the snipers take out the threat. If not, we will neutralize any targets external to and on our side of the truck. If the target or targets are in the back, we stack on the tailgate and go as a team with Sergeant Caine as primary; I'll be the secondary shooter. If the driver and passenger are taking a nap inside the cab, we stack on the doors. Guy opens the passenger side door and Sergeant Caine neutralizes both targets. Tellado and I stay on the ground to prevent crossfire. If the targets are in both the back and the cab, Sergeant Caine and Guy neutralize the rear, shooting up and in, toward the south, Tellado and I neutralize the cab by shooting in and west. Upon consolidation, we place the evidence in the back.

"Phase Four starts as Sergeant Caine occupies the passenger side. I'll climb in the driver's side. Tellado and Guy take position in the back, tarp down. Upon return of the targets, we wait until they open up the back. Tellado and Guy neutralize the immediate threat. Sergeant Caine and I neutralize targets of opportunity per side. Upon confirmation of completion of the mission, we treat any refugees for wounds, and clean up the remaining evidence. Mr. Jones comes in for the extraction. We get the remaining refugees some food and water from the 4Runner and send them back to the camp. Sergeant Caine and I stay with the truck. Mr. Jones moves back to where he initially pulled in. I back up the truck the entire distance until we hit Mr. Jones' ingress point. I make a few runs back and forth until all signs of the 4Runner have been covered. I pull the truck out to cover Mr. Jones' tracks on the way out."

"Once all friendly vehicles are back on the hard ball," Smith continued, "I'll pull out. We meet back here for final consolidation and debriefing. Sergeant Caine will designate who takes the truck to the Mutlaa Pass. I'll escort them and make any additional supply runs as necessary to headquarters."

"Any questions?" Caine asked. There were none. "Weapons checks in three. Comm checks in five. Get to it ladies!"

Caine performed a functions check of his own mini A.R.-15 with night sights, laser designator, and brass catcher. He then checked the placement of his own extra magazines, portable radio and remaining equipment. The voice-activated throat collar felt strange but was a welcome addition to his communication gear. Finally, he placed the auditory canal speaker inside his ear and shook his head around violently to make sure enough slack led easily to his collar. A few touch-ups of the black cammie paint on his face and he was ready. He'd now go check his men.

Minutes later, Caine gave only a cursory check to Smith's and Jones' weapons. It was more of a show of acceptance for the Scouts than an inspection for Smith and Jones. Caine had placed his trust in these two after they came out and worked with the Scouts for a few days at the airport, and had no qualms of accepting Colonel Hart's offer of their services. The rest of the pre-combat checks were more in line with what the Scouts normally conducted.

Caine looked up into the star-filled sky. It wasn't going to get much darker than this.

"Saddle up monkeys!" The Scouts loaded into the second 4Runner without a word. Smith and Jones climbed into the driver seats. "Keeper, this is Catcher. Commencing Phase One."

It was 15 minutes later when the first report came in.

"Catcher, this is Big Eyes, cold. I say again, cold, over."

"This is Catcher, I acknowledge cold, out." There were no hostiles remaining in the truck.

The Scouts waited in the truck another hour until the next report came in.

"Catcher, this is Big Eyes. One nasty-ass big dog leading the pack. One on the east, one on the west, one in the back. Six pack of Chihuahuas in the middle, over."

It took an additonal hour for the guests to arrive at the party. Smith counted down the distance to Caine in 100-meter intervals. Caine gave final orders and went silent as Smith called distances in ten-meter intervals.

The Iraqi soldiers continued to move in a diamond formation even as they reached the truck. Tellado initiated the ambush when an Iraqi soldier pulled back the tarp. The Scouts dropped the flankers and Smith's 50-caliber essentially disintegrated the rear guard's chest. The entire encounter took less than four seconds.

The refugees acted in a variety of ways. Some stood in place, not realizing what happened. Some dropped to their knees and covered their heads. One threw his hands in the air and started running into the open desert. Others realized they were safe and tried to call the runner back. The Scouts continued to cover their targets with their weapons but were soon surrounded by the Kuwaiti detainees who hugged and kissed them. This was one safety point Caine and Quarry hadn't planned for. As soon as the Kuwaitis realized the Iraqi soldiers were dead, they left the Scouts and took out their frustrations on the bodies; another contingency plan to deal with on the next mission. When Caine finally regained control, he got a good look at the closest Iraqi soldier.

"Oh shit!"

"What's wrong, Sergeant Caine?" Guy came bounding over expecting trouble.

Caine used the end of his rifle to knock off and lift the black beret from the dead soldier's head. The gold embroidered emblem was that of a Republican Guard infantryman.

"Oh shit," Guy agreed.

* * *

"*Ya raa'id*," the Iraqi private said, waiting at the open door of the office.

"*Aywa, ya jundi.*" The Republican Guard major looked up from a stack of paperwork.

"The patrol has not returned yet, sir."

"I am going to morning prayers," the *raa'id* said, taking his time to get up from behind the desk. "Get them on the radio. Let me know when they expect to get back by the time I return."

"*Aywa.* It appears as if your legs are stiff this morning, *Raa'id.*"

"*Aywa*," Aziz said, grimacing. "The doctor said I must walk to stretch the scar tissue. They are particularly sore this morning."

* * *

"But everything went well last night," Magrail said, making a statement, though it was actuality a request for an explanation.

"Iraqi soldiers are one thing," Quarry said as an answer. "Republican Guards are quite another. When the patrol doesn't check in, things are going to get ugly at their headquarters. When the next patrol doesn't find their companions, they're going to know something is wrong. Being aware of a problem will make them prepare for a problem."

"You talked with Colonel Hart last night?"

"Yes, Magrail," Quarry answered. "We came up with several alternate plans. Two separate plans call for disabling the truck and then taking the soldiers out as they try and egress back through the desert on foot. Another alternative is to take out the driver and pick off the Guards from a safe distance using night vision. But we want to stay away from those options as we'd have to bring another truck up to pull the disabled one out. That would leave a larger signature than I'm willing to leave." Quarry paused for a moment. "Sura knows how to operate the radio. He's used one like it numerous times as a member of the resistance. All you have to do is get a distance, compare the azimuth set on the range-finder, and let us know which lane they're in."

Magrail looked nauseated, but then stood a little straighter and threw his shoulders back.

"I can do it, *ya naqeeb.*"

* * *

"Still no word from the patrol, *ya raa'id*," the private said as Aziz returned.

Aziz looked down and thought a moment before answering.

"Get me the personnel files and training records of every soldier who was on that patrol. Have the company sergeant major bring them to my office as soon as possible." Aziz walked slowly to his desk and sat down in the chair even slower. When he was approached in the hospital, he knew his life would change forever, not so much from the pus that still oozed out from the wounds in his legs, but from the assignment to the Republican Guards.

* * *

It was a short and happy reunion but they quickly got down to business. "What about setting up an ambush prior to the Guards reaching the camp? Hit them on their way in?" Jones asked.

"I agree they'll come back to Camp Three tonight," Quarry commented. "If for no other reason than to try and find out what happened to their first patrol. But how they come in, and where they dismount, if they dismount, are still variables. They have been using trucks up until now. Should we face a B.M.P. without antitank missiles, we'd be sitting ducks. That's a risk I'm not willing to take."

Jones nodded.

"Any other options we overlooked?" Quarry asked the entire group. There were none. "Any other contingency plans anyone wants to suggest?" Every Scout looked at the two spooks.

"No, sir," Jones said, looking surprised that all eyes were on them.

"None here, captain," Smith added.

"O.K. then," Quarry said, reverently picking up the M-40 Smith brought him. "Mount up for rehearsal of contingency plan one." With Quarry and Dole back, a new team was integrated into the Scouts' existing plans. Additionally, they'd rehearse several new alternative plans that Colonel Hart and Quarry had talked about. Lastly, Quarry needed a few rounds down range to zero his rifle, and there were only so many hours in a day.

* * *

"I knew every soldier on that patrol," the sergeant major said. "They were all veterans of the Great Patriotic Wars as well as the Liberation of Kuwait."

"Then let us not speak of them in the past, *ya raqeeb awwal*," Aziz said from behind a desk full of files. "That is why I asked you to come in. By their records, they are all fine soldiers in both loyalty, training and," Aziz paused, "in land navigation. Do you know of any reasons why they may have been delayed?"

"What other reasons would there be, *ya raa'id?*" the sergeant major asked with a hint of accusation.

"*Ya raqeeb awwal,*" Aziz said, looking down and shaking his head. "I am in charge of 21 infantry soldiers, whose job is to *recruit.*" Aziz put an inflection in his voice on the word "recruit." "This company should have over a hundred soldiers, a dozen officers and double the number of sergeants. The soldiers come to you for their recruiting assignments, yet I don't know where they go when they leave, and I do not greet new recruits when they arrive." The sergeant major started to protest but Aziz cut him off. "Do not take me for a fool simply because I did not come from your village, sergeant major!" Aziz raised his voice for the first time in months. "I also swore my loyalty oath! Now, do you know of any reason why our soldiers would be delayed!"

The sergeant major was silent before responding.

"*Laa, ya Raa'id.* I know of no other reason they would be delayed."

"Thank you, *ya raqeeb awwal.* We will find them."

* * *

The Scouts were hot, tired, and sweaty. Situation normal. They ran through every contingency plan, old and new, at least three times with immediate action drills thrown in.

"Is your boss always such a ball buster?" Jones said, catching his breath as he leaned up against the front quarter panel of his 4Runner.

"Nah," Caine said. "He's mellowed out a lot."

* * *

"All is ready, *ya raa'id,*" the sergeant said.

"Very good," Aziz replied, looking up from his desk. "May Allah smile upon you today."

* * *

"Add two clicks to the left and fire for confirmation," Dole transmitted from 500 meters away. Quarry sighted on the "X" Dole had marked on the M.R.E. case lid. Quarry made the adjustments, took a deep breath, a controlled exhalation, a natural momentary pause, a smooth easy trigger pull to the rear, and there was a hole in the center of the X. Dole, standing a mere four feet to the side, admired Quarry's handiwork. Two rounds later, a three-lobed cloverleaf appeared in what once was the middle of the X. "You're out of practice, skipper," Dole said over the radio, "but close enough for government work."

Quarry pulled the bolt to the rear and checked the chamber to make sure it was clear.

"The night vision device mounts directly over the existing scope," Jones said, taking out the I.R. sights from the container. Quarry looked at the second half of the system.

After he zeroed the night sights, Dole packed up the targets and drove back to the two snipers. Half way en route, a familiar but unexpected voice came over the radio.

"Catcher this is Keeper. I see a truck coming down the power line. What do you want me to do?" Magrail asked.

* * *

"There," the Guard sergeant said, pointing to the third set of tracks from the left. "Follow the tracks that lead down that lane." The driver looked in the direction the sergeant pointed and turned the truck in the direction of what he knew to be Camp Three.

* * *

Quarry looked at his watch: 1400. They were at their "base" inside the Kuwaiti border and southeast of some burning oil wells. Eventually, Magrail's voice gave the confirmation they waited for: "Catcher, this is Keeper. They are at Camp Three, over."

* * *

"Slow down," the sergeant ordered. Then speaking in a voice a few notes higher than before, the sergeant gave additional commands: "Stop. Driver, stop the truck!" Getting out of the truck, the sergeant walked the final few feet in the sand and knelt down. He looked at the most recent tracks, and then back at the tires on his vehicle. In the sand before him was a set of freshly made tracks turning 90 degrees from the direction of the camp. "Sons of dogs!" the sergeant said slapping the side of his leg. Storming back to the truck, he found the flap already opened.

"Hand me the radio!" he demanded. A private instantly complied with the order. The sergeant checked the frequency and then turned on the power. He keyed the handset but nothing happened. "Who checked this radio?" the sergeant screamed.

"I did," a humble voice came from the driver's seat.

The sergeant raced around the truck, yanked open the driver's side door and pulled the driver to the ground.

"Idiot! Did you change the batteries?"

"There were none available."

The sergeant kicked the soldier until he expended all the adrenaline. In his rage, the sergeant never went back to take a closer look at the tracks in the sand. If he had, he would have seen a second, smaller set of tracks intermingled throughout the weaving larger ones.

* * *

"Catcher, this is Keeper, they're just sitting there, over."

"This is Catcher," Caine replied. "Acknowledged, out," he said turning to look at Quarry.

Quarry gave a thumbs-up, indicating he heard as Caine put the radio back on the driver's seat.

"We wait until dark," Quarry continued. "Contingency Plan One with Smith on point unless Keeper comes back with a different update."

"I'm surprised they didn't come down the hardball," Guy said with inflection in his voice.

"By now, they believe the first patrol deserted," Bots answered, "or else they would have. Ain't that right, sir?"

"Hope so, Bots." Quarry said, looking around. "Maintain RedCon Four, but make sure someone always has eyes on the truck and ears on the radio. Everyone else, try and get some rest."

* * *

When the Iraqi private asked a question, the immediate answer was a back fist to the right cheek.

"As long as we are here, you camel herder," the sergeant screamed, "we will go into the camp." No one else asked any more questions, nor spoke louder than a whisper for the rest of the day.

* * *

It was an hour past dark.

"You're on, Mr. Smith," Quarry said.

"I'll be talking to you," he said as he got in the first 4Runner.

* * *

Smith didn't see any human thermal signatures, because there weren't any. The Iraqis had left the truck after dark. An hour and a half later, the truck had cooled in the evening air.

"Catcher, this is Big Eyes, cold. I say again, cold, over." Jones didn't wait for the order as he pulled out from where they waited.

Quarry led Dole on the driver's side; Caine and Guy stayed on the passenger side. Bots and Tellado followed the lead teams a few paces back.

"Catcher, this is Big Eyes. Kennel remains cold, your path is clear, over."

"Catcher, this is Little Eyes, concur, over." Quarry raised his hand palm up. The six shadows rose from the ground and finished moving to and around the truck. After a quick visual confirmation, the teams set in. Dole climbed in the driver's seat as Quarry rolled under the left front chassis and settled in by the tire. Caine took his position in the passenger's seat while Guy rolled under the truck from the right. Bots and Tellado climbed in the back.

The initial report came in less than an hour.

"Catcher this is Big Eyes. Large pack approaching from south. Lots of activity. Cannot pick out the Big Dogs."

The next report took about another hour.

"Catcher, this is Big Eyes. One leader well out in front. Another in front of the pack. One bringing up rear, over."

Jones waited for the initial report to end.

"Catcher, this is Little Eyes. Two flankers very close to pack. Working the pack hard. More than a dozen Chihuahuas, over."

The presence of additional soldiers didn't surprise Quarry. He'd expected more.

"This is Catcher. Ground teams neutralize the leader, Little Eyes neutralize west, Big Eyes south, I'll take east. Adjust to remaining target, acknowledge."

"Big Eyes, roger. Tracking. Inbound remaining 200 meters, out."

"Little Eyes, roger, tracking west, out."

Caine looked over to Dole. Dole nodded confirming his readiness.

"Cab, roger, standing by," Caine transmitted.

"Bed, roger, standing by," Bots said. Tellado took his mini 15 off safe.

Quarry looked over to Guy, who nodded. Quarry reached up to his throat collar and flipped a minute switch, placing the transmitter on voice activation. Cradling his rifle on his left forearm, Quarry settled the sights on the easternmost gun carrier.

"One fifty to leader," Smith reported. "He's 15 yards in front of the others." Smith waited until the first image passed the right-most vertical cross hair in his scope and then panned right. It took a few minutes for the leader to make his way into Smith's left field of view. "One hundred to leader, eighty-five to the pack," he said a minute later. "Seventy and eighty five." "Fifty and sixty now." "Forty, fifty." "Thirty, forty." "Twenty, thirty." "Fifteen and twenty, switching to rear target," Smith transmitted the last distances of the leader and the pack.

The Republican Guard sergeant angled toward the truck. "Passenger," Quarry whispered. Caine not only heard his commander but started to make out the footsteps in the sand as well. Yanking the passenger side door open was the last thing the sergeant ever did. Smith, Jones and Quarry fired almost simultaneously. Guy placed a short burst in the foremost leader of the pack before the flankers fell to the ground. Caine and Dole were out of the cab in a heartbeat, Bots and Tellado from the bed of the truck a second later. Quarry covered the pack while Guy rolled out from under the truck and smoothly transitioned into a kneeling firing position, also covering the pack.

"Clear," a chorus of status reports flew.

Over the radio, Smith and Jones checked in also.

"Clear west," Jones reported.

"Clear south," Smith confirmed.

Quarry tucked his rifle to his chest and rolled out from under the truck. The Scouts covered the pack while Caine and Guy inspected their targets.

"Consolidate," Quarry ordered.

The Kuwaiti detainees came up, greeted and praised the Scouts. In the camp, the word had got around about their guardian angels. Dole pushed one away to keep from getting kissed.

"O.K., O.K.," Dole said, keeping the man at arm's length, "You're welcome already."

Quarry looked around. Only five Iraqi soldiers. That wasn't a good sign. Quarry turned suddenly to the Kuwaitis who were trying to hug him and grabbed the nearest man by the *thoob*.

"*Bukra fi'l layl, sata'aaloo al askariyeen al-iraqiyeen, Bukra ana ata'aal. Laa khudhoo al-asliha! Laa ta'atoo lil musaa'ada! Hal tafhamoo?*" Tomorrow night, Iraqi soldiers come. Tomorrow, I come. Don't touch guns. Don't get in to help. Understand?

The bodies were collected and put in the truck. Jones drove up and picked up the Scouts. The Kuwaitis were fed and sent back to their camp. Vehicles were backed up and tracks were covered. Tellado, Bots and Jones took the truck to the Mutlaa Pass. The Scouts and Smith returned to their base.

Twenty-Six

31 May 1991

Aziz sat for a moment in silence, contemplating his new dilemma.

"Thank you," he said to the clerk. "Please inform the sergeant major and have him come see me at his convenience." Aziz turned to look out a window that revealed only a destroyed bridge spanning the Euphrates River.

* * *

"Begging the captain's pardon," Smith said looking at Quarry as if he were the village idiot, "but if I remove the silencer off my rifle, they'll know I'm on their flank."

"Why, Mr. Smith," Quarry looked at the man and responded in an equally sarcastic tone, "that's exactly what I'm counting on."

* * *

"I agree completely, *ya Raa'id*," the sergeant major said. "I will pass the orders personally."

* * *

The newest plan was a modification of an existing contingency op. After receiving the operations order, Quarry asked for any additional suggestions. All the Scouts, and this time even Jones, turned toward Smith.

"No suggestions, sir," Smith said, feeling a little self-conscious.

"Then let's rehearse."

* * *

Aziz conducted the pre-combat inspections himself. Radios were checked, weapons were test fired, and extra ammunition was broken out of boxes. All 14 Iraqi Guardsmen climbed into a single truck. They were not recruiting today. They were out to get the truth.

* * *

"Catcher, this is Keeper. One truck approaching the turn, over."

"They didn't waste any time," Caine commented.

"I'll wake everybody up," Dole said, climbing out of the 4Runner.

* * *

An hour after leaving the highway, Aziz's wounds opened. Blood and pus soaked through the top of his pants. Now in the open desert, the ride was even rougher than when they followed the power lines. The driver looked to the new major with admiration. The major sat there in pain, silently enduring the discomfort without comment. The driver considered saying something, but didn't.

* * *

"Catcher, this is Keeper. One fully loaded, KrAz-255 truck, Lane Three, flaps up."

Quarry looked at Caine.

"Want to bet Sura is three inches from his ear?" The Scouts smiled but immediately refocused on checking their equipment. Quarry loaded the fourth round in the internal magazine, pushed it down and placed a fifth directly in the chamber. He checked his own gear one more time before asking Caine to confirm his readiness. As Caine pulled and tugged on various items, the rest of the Scouts lined up for inspection.

* * *

The back of the truck contained the sergeant major and the remaining 12 soldiers of the platoon.

"Driver, pull over please," Aziz ordered. The driver saw what the major was looking at and pulled off to the side, not to disturb the tracks. As soon as the truck came to a halt, the soldiers deployed into a defensive perimeter. The sergeant major walked over, knelt, and looked at the tracks with an expert eye. Aziz was slow climbing out of the cab. The pain on his face was obvious; yet he walked over and inspected the ground alongside his S.N.C.O.

* * *

"At least ten," Magrail reported as Sura looked through a spotter scope. "Maybe more," he quickly added.

* * *

"Look here, *ya Raa'id*," the sergeant major said, using his hand to gauge the depth of the tracks. "This area has only been rolled over once, indicating the truck was in a turn and the back wheels did not follow in the same path as the front. Here," he said pointing to a similar set, "the turn is the same but the depth is not as great."

"A second, lighter truck?" Aziz asked.

"Yes, sir. Both sets turn east. Toward the Basra Highway. The tracks lead towards the Kuwaiti border. Should we follow the tracks, *ya Raa'id*?"

Aziz gave it a good deal of thought before answering.

"*Laa*, sergeant major. We would only find a road." Aziz paused as he considered his next option. "Let us continue as planned. It will be dark soon. We will go into the camp and ask if our patrols have been there in the last two nights."

"*Ya Raa'id*," the sergeant major said after looking at the major's blood-soaked trousers. "There is no need for you to go. No one here questions your loyalty. Stay here with the truck, sir."

Aziz knew that he would only slow them down.

"*Aywa*, sergeant major. I will stay here. Should you need it, I will bring the truck if you call on the radio."

* * *

"They're moving." It was dusk, the earliest a patrol ever headed for a camp.

Quarry put the radio down.

"We'll give it 20 more minutes, then we head out."

* * *

Aziz watched his platoon. They moved well together and it was plain they were a well-honed team. Aziz felt a little envious as he stood in front of the truck, watching them until they cleared the area. Only then did he reach out

249

and lean against the truck to help support his weight. Aziz used the front bumper to support himself, turned and sat down with his back against the tire. He pulled the radio next to him.

* * *

"Big Eyes, set." Smith reported, pulling into position and exiting his vehicle. Over a dozen clicks away, Jones pulled across the hard ball and followed the tracks west. Smith set up the rifle across the hood of the 4Runner and scanned the truck. Due to the twilight, the bed and cab were still fuzzy white in the thermal scope. Only the engine block glowed brightly. "Catcher, this is Big Eyes, cold. I say again, cold."

"This is Catcher, I acknowledge cold, out."

* * *

"We are here, *ya Raa'id*. Starting to check the camp."

"I hear you, sergeant major."

* * *

Quarry sensed, rather than saw Caine stop. As Caine lowered himself to the ground, the rest of the Scouts did also. Caine pointed to his ear. Quarry shook his head no.

"This is Catcher. Eyes report," Quarry whispered using the throat mic.

"This is Big Eyes, cold, over."

"Catcher, this is Little Eyes. Have you all in view. There is a bulge on the passenger side of the truck. It may be a flap or a blown tire, can't tell. No movement, over."

"This is Catcher, roger, out." Quarry brought his rifle up and scanned the truck. There was something on the west side. Quarry watched for several minutes, but whatever it was, it never moved. Quarry lowered the rifle and leaned over until he was almost touching Caine's ear. "Angle left on approach. Set middle back right, I'll go around the front." Caine looked over at his commander. He didn't like the order, but this was no time to argue. Quarry raised his hand palm up, then pointed forward. The Scouts rose and moved, very slowly.

The pace Quarry set was so slow, it made their legs burn. Each foot was raised, balance shifted, forward foot lowered toe-first, body weight transferred to the front foot, before the rear was lifted. It took over a half-hour to close the distance on the truck, but only the devil himself would have made less noise.

* * *

Aziz sat motionless, his leg throbbing. He knew in his heart he'd never command a tank unit again, let alone a T-72 Republican Guard Battalion. Aziz was not so naïve as to think he was actually in a recruiting battalion, but he also knew that he was in a special unit outside the normal combat arms. He would join the Ba'ath Party, make a new career for himself, and prepare for the next war. He was a veteran of the Great Patriotic War with Iran and now involved in the Liberation of Kuwait. He could be an instructor at the armor school or branch out as a staff officer. With any luck, he might be selected to attend the Military University of the Ministry of Defense of the Russian Federation in Moscow. Allah was truly merciful.

* * *

Caine approached the middle back of the truck. Quarry continued down the driver's side. Caine placed his rifle against his chest and moved like a sloth until he peered around the passenger side. It took less than a heartbeat to analyze the threat, a person. Caine eased back into the shadow of the tailgate and turned his head while keeping his body perfectly still. Two quick nods in the direction of the passenger side spoke volumes to the Scouts. Dole saw Caine's message and nodded in response. Too close now for verbal communications, Dole continued to follow Quarry with the vital information.

Quarry paused when he reached the front driver side. As a sniper always checks with his scout before making a change in direction, Quarry looked back to Dole. Dole signed "P" in American Sign Language and tilted his head toward the passenger side. A gun shot, or any loud noise now, would jeopardize the operation. A radio transmission from the Iraqi would be even worse. Quarry momentarily looked at his rifle and then, ever so slowly, passed it back to Dole. Dole took the weapon as Quarry reached for and removed his K-bar from the scabbard.

Quarry transferred the knife to his left hand and placed a single finger on the truck's front bumper. Any shift of his enemy's body would be transmitted through the truck. Quarry opened his mouth and took a few silent deep breaths.

Quarry lost all sense of time. Foot up, transfer weight. Foot down, transfer balance. Set forward foot, shift body weight. Each step seemed an eternity. With no sense of movement coming through the bumper, Quarry finally reached the front passenger side of the truck. Without turning the corner, Quarry calculated the height of the tire and figured where a man would be sitting if he were leaning up against it. Quarry visualized his plan and then rehearsed it in his head. The single finger on the bumper turned into two, three, and then four. He lowered himself into a crouch to use the tension in his body like a spring.

251

It must have been a good plan. Quarry's body acted while his brain analyzed events in slow motion.

The side of the target's neck seemed to be the size of a barn door. Quarry watched as the tip of the knife entered his field of view and continued towards the carotid artery. The knife loomed larger and larger compared to the victim's neck. The tip started to disappear into flesh as the body before him started to react. A drop of blood appeared at the point of entry as the victim's head started rotating in Quarry's direction. When a third of the knife had disappeared, the Iraqi's neck seemed to collapse upon itself. When the tip of the knife struck something firm, Quarry used the resistance as a fulcrum and rotated the knife forward towards the throat. The left carotid artery was severed as the knife continued toward the trachea. The enemy was dead, but his brain didn't realize it yet. The body started to slump in the direction of least resistance as muscles went limp. The change in resistance pulled Quarry off balance.

Quarry recoiled, back into a fighting position. He sensed movement to his front and started to react. He shifted his center of gravity to his back leg and brought his right hand up to gauge the distance to the new threat.

"Skipper!" Caine's voice entered the recesses of Quarry's brain, "Ease down." Quarry looked from his target to his squad leader. Caine's right hand held his rifle at arm's length and his left hand was palm forward, facing Quarry. "Ease down," Caine said in a calm voice. "Clear."

Quarry's world returned to normal.

"Police up the evidence," he said, taking a bandana from a cargo pocket.

"Jesus Christ!" Bots gasped, turning the corner of the truck and seeing the partially decapitated body. Caine shot Botsford a glance that stopped Botsford in his tracks. Quarry didn't look down or back as he walked a short way into the desert. His body shook as it burned off excess adrenaline.

Quarry tried to wipe the blood from his hands. There was no need to reflect on or justify his actions. There was still a mission to conduct and preparations to be made. Caine met him a few paces away from the others.

"That was a righteous takedown. Anything less would have endangered the mission and us."

Quarry unconsciously reached up and placed a blood-soaked hand on Caine's shoulder. His hand still shook.

"Thank you, my friend." Quarry stood there for a second or two as his command looked on in silence. He took his hand back and turned to the Scouts. "L-shaped ambush. Caine and Guy west, me and Dole in the center, Bots and Tellado east. Fifty meters out from the truck, continue to improve fighting positions until Smith reports contact. Move!"

"Sir?" Dole said, gaining Quarry's attention. Dole had Quarry's rifle slung over his shoulder and a number of objects in his hand. "We searched the body for intelligence. Typical stuff except these." Dole showed them two maps.

Quarry, Dole and Caine walked to the front of the truck where Dole unfolded the first map.

Quarry took off his equipment harness and blood-soaked blouse as Caine held the map against the truck. The map was a 1:50,000 tactical military map that showed the route from Basra to the six camps, with sufficient details to keep any driver from getting lost. Quarry excused himself and threw his blouse in the back of the truck. On his return, Dole had the second map, a locally produced city map of Basra. This one traced a route from the Basra Highway back to an isolated building on the north-west side of city. Quarry broke the silence.

"I believe Dole found their headquarters. What else?" he asked as Caine folded the map inside the first. Dole handed him a beret. Quarry looked at the gold-embroidered crest. The eagle's wings dropped down until they touched the upward frond of a laurel wreath with a tank in the center. The beret belonged to a Republican Guard armor officer.

"I think we took out the brains of the operation," Quarry said more to himself than to the others.

"*Ya raa'id* Aziz, *ya raa'id* Aziz." The Scouts flinched at the sound of the transmission. Quarry walked over to the radio which was still at the base of the tire. He picked up the handset and keyed it.

"*Ya raa'id* Aziz, we are on our way back. We have over a dozen deserters and some very interesting news." Quarry heard the pause in the transmission and keyed the net for a few seconds without talking. "We can't hear you, *Ya raa'id*, but we should be there within ninety minutes," the sergeant major's voice said over the net. Quarry keyed the net for one long period and then two shorter periods.

Fifteen minutes later, Quarry stood 100 meters out, and centered on the truck.

"Marked," Smith said over the radio.

"Marked," Jones, Caine, and Bots all echoed. Quarry took a final look around. At this distance, it looked as if there was nothing but open desert. The Scouts had dusted the front of their fighting positions with a fresh sand to blend in with their surroundings. Quarry shuffled his feet on the way back to the truck. After a final check, he rolled under the truck with Dole.

It seemed like hours before Smith picked up the thermal signatures and started calling out distances. At 150 meters, silhouettes were visible against the moonlit sky. Quarry settled his left arm in a slight depression in the sand and cradled his rifle. A few squirms in the sand and he was ready.

"One thirty," Smith transmitted. Quarry started taking a few deep controlled breaths. "One twenty." Quarry closed his eyes. "One ten." Quarry opened his eyes and checked his natural point of aim; the cross hairs were still on target.

There was no call at 100 meters. From off in the distance, to the east, a single shot sounded something just short of an explosion, as 50-caliber bullets do.

None of the Scouts saw the rear-most Iraqi fall among the Kuwaitis. For that matter, neither did any of the other Iraqis. The shot had its desired effect. The Iraqi soldiers turned in the direction of the sound. Quarry fired, and the first of the easternmost flankers fell. A moment later, a second flanker fell to his second shot as another rear guard dropped further to the south. The Iraqi infantrymen deployed a dozen meters to the east and fell to the ground, returning fire. The Scouts now had clear fields of fire. Quarry acquired the next flanker and silenced his A.K.-47. A loud shot to the east neutralized another Iraqi further down the line. The remaining Iraqis oriented their fire in the direction of the muzzle blast and laid down impressive counter-fire. They didn't realize their target was almost untouchable due to the distance.

It takes only a few seconds to expend 30 rounds from a fully automatic A.K.-47. When a soldier rolled on his side to retrieve a magazine from an ammo pouch, the movement caught Quarry's attention. As the Iraqi rolled back into the prone position, he never loaded the magazine into the rifle.

The Iraqi sergeant major continued to yell orders, but his words were drowned out. Raising his head a few inches too high, it flopped back to the earth. A hundred meters away, Quarry reloaded another five rounds.

Then there was silence.

The Scouts heard the orders commanding the remaining Iraqis to move. Three dropped as the Scouts distinguished friend from foe. The two surviving soldiers dropped to the ground among the Kuwaitis. For over ten minutes, like grazing sheep, the pack moved this way and that as individuals shuffled for position. Then, something happened in the midst of the pack, and the two Iraqi soldiers appeared at the far west side. Standing and sprinting for their lives, they only made it 20 meters when short bursts of 5.56 dropped them as well. Once again, all was silent.

Moments later, chatter came from among the Kuwaitis, and chatter became cries of jubilation. Individuals got off the ground and danced.

"Caine, Bots, this is Six. Segregate and search by twos." Like ghosts rising up out of the graveyard, four black-clad figures appeared near the refugees. The initial reaction among the Kuwaitis was surprise, but soon they realized they were among their liberators. It took longer for the ground teams to call "clear" than Quarry cared for.

Jones brought the truck while Smith continued to scan from his position. Bodies were placed in the back. The Scouts treated numerous refugees for lacerations caused by horrific beatings. All in all, they were in fair health and good spirits.

While the site was sanitized, Quarry called Hart on the radio and gave him a status report. "Dispose of the truck, and bring me what you have," Hart ordered.

Quarry acknowledged and looked around. The same man he talked to the night before was again among the detainees of this evening.

"We do good?" asked the man through a swollen face and closed left eye.

Quarry grabbed the man by the back of the neck and touched his forehead to his.

"Yes, my friend. You did good." A hail of cheers rose up among the Kuwaitis.

The Scouts returned to the 4Runner. Bots seemed to be the expert on Soviet trucks and Quarry got in the truck's passenger seat. They followed the same procedure of backing up and turning at the same location. Just because they had a good hunt didn't mean it was time to get sloppy.

Smith followed the truck to the Mutlaa Pass. Once there, Bots drove a fair distance into the thick of the remaining destroyed vehicles before pulling into a spot he and Smith had found nights before. Smith produced a five-gallon can of gasoline and poured it among the cargo.

"You want to keep that?" Smith said, pointing to Quarry's black blouse.

"By no means," Quarry said, slightly disgusted. Smith shrugged his shoulders and gave the blouse its own dousing. Smith went to his vehicle and came back with two thermite grenades. He tossed one to Bots and each went to opposite fuel tanks.

"Ready?" Smith called across the truck.

"Ready." Bots yelled back.

"Pull 'em." The two didn't run, but moved with purpose away from the truck. As the grenades created an ever-increasing amount of heat, the diesel in the tanks caught fire. Seconds later, the gasoline in the back caught. There wouldn't be much left by morning.

* * *

The ride back passed quickly. Smith drove the 6th Ring in excess of 120km per hour. Quarry was thinking that he didn't want to go out like General Patton. Less than a half-hour later, they pulled into their headquarters.

The sentry on the outer gate looked into the vehicle for confirmation. The sight of the three was one thing. Quarry's blackened face, and pale white arms ending in blood-stained hands, was quite another.

Hart was waiting behind his desk as usual. Quarry's appearance took him off guard. If circumstances were different, he would have probably made some kind of comment, but for now, he was more interested in what Quarry had to offer.

"How'd you come about this?" Hart asked in his official business voice as he looked at the local map. Quarry gave him a quick rundown and a chronological sequence of events. Hart listened without interruption.

Hart also examined the beret and the large tactical map Quarry brought. Quarry finished the preliminary debrief.

"Follow me," Hart said as he started walking for the door. As they entered a hallway, in part of the building Quarry hadn't been in before, Hart called out to no one in particular, "Someone get Captain Samuels a new blouse, water, and a towel." As they made their way in and around the building, Hart asked over his shoulder, "What did happen to your blouse, Quarry?"

"It got a little messy, sir," Quarry said to the man's back as they rounded another corner.

In front of them was a chain-linked fence that sectioned off the corridor.

"He's with me," the colonel told the two armed sentries on the other side. A padlock was removed and the concertina wire-wrapped gate opened.

"Sir," a voice came from behind them. A corporal came running up and gave Quarry a new black blouse, baby wipes and a couple of towels.

"Thank you," Quarry said, turning, putting on the blouse and following Hart all in one motion.

Beyond another set of doors, and another set of sentries, was a situation room. With maps on three of the four walls and a bank of radios on the fourth, there must have been over a dozen soldiers, airmen and spooks monitoring events happening all around the world. Hart walked over to one of the many desks and picked up what could be described as a phone. Looking over to one of the first stations, Hart caught the eye of an Army Special Forces Sergeant First Class and simply held Quarry's local map out at arm's length. The sergeant immediately got up, retrieved the map, and took it over to what Quarry guessed was a fax machine.

"Put it through," Hart said with a tone of urgency. Quarry's head turned back to where Hart was on the radio-telephone. A rustle of movement snapped Quarry's head back in the opposite direction. The map came out the other side of the machine and was now being handed off to an Air Force technical sergeant who took it over to one of the many walls and compared it to other sites on yet another map. Quarry watched the flurry of activity as he wiped some of the black cammie paint from his face.

"Sir, this is Hart," the colonel said into the R.T. Quarry's head snapped back. *Hart is calling someone "sir"? Now isn't that interesting.*

"Sending it now," Hart said. "Yes sir," moments later. "Yes sir, I do think it's legitimate. Will do, sir." Hart looked back to Quarry. "Bring your team in. I want a full debrief by every member ASAP."

"Aye, aye, sir." Quarry turned to leave the room.

* * *

The spooks started with Quarry in one room, Smith in another. Quarry was pretty sure he was one of the good guys, but this was an interrogation, not a debrief. After being asked questions, cross-referenced and double-checked, Quarry felt like he'd been put through a wringer. When he was released, he walked out of the room and flopped on a couch. Bots was escorted into the room Quarry exited.

"Have fun," Quarry called sarcastically as the door closed behind Bots.

* * *

"Skipper?" Caine asked from a safe distance. Quarry shot up from the couch where he'd fallen asleep. "What's going on?"

Quarry looked over at his squad leader and then at his watch: "Debrief time."

The same nerd who'd run Quarry ragged, stepped out of the room.

"You," he said, looking at Caine, "In here." Quarry sprang and crossed the distance in less than a second, grabbing the pencil-necked spook by the collar, and pulled him close. The Scouts automatically moved in behind him.

"Hey, sparky!" Quarry said in no uncertain tone. "Lighten the fuck up!"

Fear registered in the analyst's eyes and blood drained from his face. Quarry's bloodstained hands were inches from the man's nose. When he spoke next, the tone in his voice was vastly different.

"Corporal. Please come in here for debriefing."

"Guess Bots spilled the beans about your cutlery skills," Caine said, tapping the knife that hung inverted on Quarry's H-harness. Caine looked back and caught the spook's eyes and grinned. "Yea though I walk through the valley of the shadow of death …" Caine recited as he entered the room and the door closed behind him.

The Scouts were separated until debriefs were completed. The sun had long since risen, and they were provided breakfast.

"Captain Samuels." Once again, Quarry shot up out of a dead sleep. Colonel Hart stood over him looking a little ragged; he had been up all night. "Come with me. You may bring two of your men. The rest will be taken back to the hotel."

"Caine, Dole, with me. Guy, take charge."

"Damn," Tellado let out. "Always a bridesmaid!"

* * *

"*Aqiid*?" the sergeant said in the doorway of the colonel's office.

"*Iiwa*," he said without looking up from the paperwork on his desk.

"*Raa'id* Aziz is not at his desk this morning."

"It is of no consequence," the colonel said, sounding annoyed by the interruption.

"Neither is the sergeant major," the sergeant said. That made the colonel look up.

"Go down to the motor pool. Find the senior soldier from the recruitment platoon and find out where they are."

"*Iiwa, Aqeed.*"

* * *

The three Scouts moved through another set of corridors and checkpoints, similar to those of the situation room. This room wasn't as packed or as active as yesterday's, but it was busy nonetheless. On the far end wall, there was a T.V. set. Hart looked at his watch: 0852 local time.

"I made a few phone calls last night," Hart said, addressing Quarry. "They made a few others."

"They, sir?"

"D.O.D., State, N.S.A., Pentagon. That sort of thing. Ah, here it is," Hart said, looking at the television screen as it started to show a picture. The Scouts' heads turned; for that matter, everyone in the room stopped working and watched the TV screen. The picture improved in clarity and definition each second. It appeared as if they were flying and the view was from behind a spotting scope with a set of cross hairs in the middle. The scenery was open desert. There were no landmarks, but it appeared the ground was going by awfully fast.

"Sir," Caine whispered, "are we watching cruise missile telemetry?"

"Very good, young man," Hart commented, "now watch." The counter in the lower right hand corner clicked 0857. The Saudi/Kuwait berm came into view and then quickly disappeared. The counter passed 0858, and the number of buildings and towns started to increase. At 0901 an entire city filled the screen. By 0902 a single building lay in the middle of the cross-hairs. As the seconds ticked by, it became larger, and larger and larger ....

* * *

"What do you want now?"

"*Aqeed,*" the sergeant said from the doorway. "*Ana laa ....*"

* * *

The TV screen went blank. A hail of cheers went up around the room and many of the soldiers and airmen slapped Quarry and the Scouts on the back.

"Captain, have your men wait outside." Quarry simply looked over at Caine and Dole, who turned to leave. The crowd that gathered around them hindered their progress. The colonel walked over and poured two cups of coffee. Hart came back and handed one to Quarry. "So your blouse got a little messy, huh?"

Quarry's back straightened.

"I'm not proud of what I did. At the time it seemed like the best option for the completion of the mission and the safety of my men."

Hart looked at Quarry quizzically.

"Captain," he said calmly, "I'm not criticizing your actions." Quarry raised his eyes and looked directly at Hart. "You did a splendid job. After hearing the different debriefs, I doubt anyone could have done it better. We'll use an unclassified version of your debriefs as narratives for any level of awards you want for your Scouts, and I'll see they get them. They can't be higher than the Silver Star, that's what I'm recommending for you. Congratulations and thank you," Hart said, stepping closer and putting out his hand. Quarry shifted his coffee cup and shook the man's hand.

* * *

From the hotel, the Scouts were taken to the open shopping malls of downtown Kuwait and later to the Soft Rock Cafe for the rest of the evening. Quarry, dressed in his suit, was picked up in a limo and taken to Minister Rashid's house for dinner. None of the events of the last few days were openly spoken of, but there was no doubt the dinner was in his honor. What made matters worse; Mistress Rashid was nowhere to be seen. *What a shitty night this turned out to be,* Quarry thought.

Quarry set reveille for 1000. They checked out of their rooms and packed the 4Runners, then drove to the Civil Affairs office, where they turned in their equipment.

"Sure would like to hold on to some of this stuff," Caine said as he checked in his communications collar.

"You never know," Quarry said, passing his through the equipment cage as well.

A half-hour later, the Scouts stood on line in front of the 4Runners. As Quarry followed Colonel Hart out of the building, Caine called the Scouts to attention. Colonel Hart put them at ease and made a little speech, after which he trooped the line and personally thanked every Scout for a job well done.

"By the way," the colonel added, "As you drive back to Camp 15 today, I thought you might like to know, your division is marching down the streets of New York City in a ticker tape parade."

"Ain't that fucking great?" Tellado said as he climbed in the back seat of the second 4Runner.

Colonel Hart drew Quarry's attention.

"Ya know, son," the colonel said under his breath, "should you ever put in a request to transfer into the intelligence community, I'll know about it."

Quarry looked into the colonel's eyes and paused. After a moment, he took one step back, came to attention and saluted.

"Permission to carry out the plan of the day, sir."

"Permission granted. Dismissed, Captain."

"Aye, aye, sir." Quarry cut his salute, walked around, and got into his side of the lead 4Runner.

* * *

Upon returning to Camp 15, Quarry learned the vast majority of the MEF's equipment was loaded and shipped. The few hundred or so remaining vehicles would finish being loaded by the Fleet Service Support Group. Logistics personnel would load the few remaining tanks upon the Maritime Propositioned Shipping when the shipping became available. All remaining 2nd Marines Division personnel had a flight date of June 13th.

On June 11th, Quarry was summoned to the office of the Commanding General, MarForSWA. There, he was handed a sealed manila envelope. Quarry retrieved a set of 4Runner keys, a map and a bridge pass for the causeway that lead from Saudi Arabia to Bahrain, the island nation that lay a few miles east of Dhahran. A hand-written note told him to be in the dining room of the Holiday Inn at 1800. Quarry looked at the orders, turned them over, found the back blank and turned the orders over again.

"This is it?" he asked the Marine.

"Sir, you know more about this than I do."

* * *

Quarry and Dole arrived in Bahrain after noon. They parked the 4Runner in the Holiday Inn parking lot and walked around the downtown area, shopping. Both Quarry and Dole were in civilian attire they pulled out of sea bags long ago placed in storage. Dole wore jeans and a collared shirt. Quarry wore gray pants and a black button-down shirt. Both Marines wore the black beret of the Kuwait National Police.

At 1750, Quarry walked into the dining room of the Holiday Inn. Around the room there were numerous people of various nationalities. Finally, Quarry's eye fell on a man who was obviously an American. As he walked over, the gentleman in the suit stood up.

"Captain Samuels?"

"Yes, sir."

"I'm Captain Elson, United States Navy, Judge Advocate General's office. Please have a seat."

"Yes, sir," Quarry said as he squirmed his way into the booth.

"I'm the head of the American war crime tribunal investigating Iraqi atrocities during the war. I received the preliminary report on the events that occurred in and around the city of Kuwait. But yesterday, there was a hand-written message on my desk when I arrived at work. The note said I should talk to you here, tonight."

"Yes, sir?" Quarry said to fill the momentary pause the captain made, not knowing where to go next.

"Captain Samuels. My office was locked. No one has access to the keys, and the officer of the day swears no one entered the building after normal working hours, let alone my office." Quarry simply smirked and grinned. The captain continued when Quarry didn't say anything. "I believe I have something for you." The Navy captain slid a manila envelope across the table. It had been sealed, but the seal had been broken then taped shut again. Quarry took the envelope and opened it. Inside there was a black beret with a gold emblem on it. On a single piece of paper, there was a hand-written note: "I don't know if you want this, but I suggest you keep it. You'll never know how much good you did. That's the nature of our work. Tell Elson whatever he wants to know."

Quarry reached out and took the beret. His eyes watered and his voice cracked when he said, "What would you like to know, sir?"

* * *

The Commanding General, Marines Forces Southwest Asia, personally shook the hand of every Marine boarding the plane. Sixteen hours later, they landed at Cherry Point, North Carolina.

* * *

There were no cheering crowds lining the way back to Camp Lejeune; no one waved banners of congratulations. On 15 June at 3:00 p.m. eastern daylight savings time, a bus stopped in the parking lot of Headquarters, 2nd Tank Battalion. The chaplain was the only member of the battalion staff to meet them. He had sodas and candy bars. As Quarry stepped off the bus, Grier stepped up and saluted his commander. Just like that, it was all over.

Glossary

A.A.V.	Assault Amphibian Vehicle or reference to the Assault Amphibian Battalion
ANGLICO	Artillery and Naval Gun Liaison Company; Marines assigned to other units to support them with fire support
A.O.	Area of Operations, the boundaries within which a unit conducts missions
ASAP	As soon as possible
Battalion	Approximately 600–800 men, made up of at least three companies
B.B.C.	British radio network
Bent	Indication a vehicle is not operational
Brigade	Approximately 2,400 men, made up of three battalions
B.M.P.	Soviet-made infantry fighting vehicle with a 73mm smooth bore cannon and 7.62mm machine gun; holds up to seven infantrymen
B.P.	Battle Position; in ground operations, a defensive location oriented on an enemy avenue of approach
B.T.R.	A lightly armored, eight-wheeled personnel carrier, armed only with a 7.62mm machine gun
Cammies	Camouflaged utilities uniform
C.E.O.I.	An alphanumeric code book with radio call signs and frequencies

Charlie Mike	Continuing mission
C.O.	Commanding Officer. Officer in charge of a unit, regardless of size. In radio transmissions, the call sign is "Six"
COF	Conduct of Fire net, used to call for artillery support
C.P.	Command Post; a leader's established location or position
C.W.O.	Chief Warrant Officer, an officer by warrant, not commission. A rank above enlisted, N.C.O.s and S.N.C.O.s but below commissioned officers.
DASC	Direct Air Support Center, the unit that controls close air support
FAC	Forward Air Controller
FastFAC	A winged pilot sitting in the back of an aircraft controlling close air support for other aircraft
FROGs	Free Rockets Over Ground, usually 122mm
Gunner	The less formal term for a chief warrant officer, based on a historic reference to the time when Marines manned cannons or provided sniper support on colonial period ships
Hatch	Doors on ships are called hatches, thus to Marines, all doors are hatches
Hummer/ HMMMV/Humvee	High Mobility Multi-purpose Wheeled Vehicle
I.T.	Interrogator Translator
LAV	Any reference to the Light Armored Infantry Battalion or the actual eight-wheeled 25mm chain-gunned vehicle. Crewed by three Marines, carries 6 Infantry Marines. Later to be renamed Light Armored Reconnaissance Battalion.
L.P.	Listening Post. Similar to an observation post but line of sight might be obscured
M-16A1 rifle	5.56mm, 550 meters maximum effective range

MEF	Marine Expeditionary Force. A fighting force of two or more divisions, service support and aviation wings
M.O.S.	Military Occupational Specialty, the military job performed, such as tanker, infantryman, engineer, etc.
M.R.E.	Meal Ready to Eat; a bag of dehydrated food
M.R.L.S	An Army multiple rocket launcher system
M.S.R.	Main service route, the most likely used road
Natural point of aim	The shooting position where the body is so comfortable that if you close your eyes, take a few breaths and then open your eyes again, you pick up the same sight picture as when you first looked
N.B.C.	Nuclear, biological, chemical
N.C.O.	Non-commissioned officer; enlisted rank of E-4 Corporal or E-5 Sergeant
N.V.G.s	Night-vision goggles
Oorah	The battle cry of the Marines, similar to Hooah of the Army and Hooyah of the Navy
O.P.	Observation Post; a position from which military observations are made, or fire directed and adjusted from. Sometime called O.P./L.P. (see Listening Post)
Op	Slang for operation, task or mission
Oscar Mike	On the Move
P.R.C.	A tactical radio, either high frequency or very high frequency
RedCon	Ready Condition: 1 = all personnel ready for combat; 2 = 75%; 3 = 50%, 4 = 25%
REMF	Rear Echelon Mother F....
S-1	Administration officer in a battalion or general's staff
S-2	Intelligence officer
S-3	Operations officer

S-4	Logistics officer
SANG	Saudi Arabia National Guard
SAW	Squad Automatic Weapon, a light machine gun
S.F.C.	Sergeant First Class
Skipper	The casual term for a captain in a command billet
S.N.C.O.	Staff N.C.O.; enlisted rank of E-6 Staff Sergeant, E-7 Gunnery Sergeant (Gunny), E-8 Master Sergeant (sometimes called Top) or 1st Sergeant (always call 1st Sergeant, never "Top"), E-9 Sergeant Major
SRIG	Surveillance, Reconnaissance and Intelligence Group
T.A.C.P.	Tactical Air Control Party; qualified to call in close air support
TOW	Tube-launched, Optically tracked, Wire-guided anti-tank missile system
Wadi	Arabic for dry riverbed
Weapons statuses	Hold = Don't fire unless fired upon
	Weapons Tight = Fire upon positive identification of the enemy
	Weapons Free = Fire at will
Wilco	Will comply
X.O.	Executive Officer, number two in a battalion or company, call sign "Five"
Z.S.U	A self-propelled Russian-made anti-aircraft gun system

Arabic Ranks

Aqeeb	colonel
Muqaddam	lieutenant colonel
Raa'id	Major
Naqeeb	captain
Mulaazim	lieutenant
Raqeeb Awwal	1st sergeant, the highest-ranking enlisted man in a company